SECRET WAR

By

Albert Schwartz
Captain, U.S. Navy, Retired

SECRET WAR

This is a work of fiction. All characters and events portrayed in this book are fictional except for those clearly part of the historical record. Any resemblance to real people or incidents is purely coincidental with one exception. LCDR Ron Rinaldi is based on my Engineer on USS Will Rogers (SSBN 659)(Gold), an excellent officer.

ISBN: 978-1503079038

Revision 1.31

Dedication

This book is dedicated to the men, and now, women serving in the Submarine Force. Even in times of peace, the dangers are real. The sea is unforgiving of the smallest mistakes.

There have been many stories featuring nuclear submarines. A number have been interesting and exciting, but to those that have served in submarines, they were not very realistic. This is my effort to give my readers an honest feel of submarine operations in the nuclear age. I commanded USS Haddock, though not at the time depicted in this tale.

. I have tried to be as accurate as possible. I found and fixed a number of errors in the editing process. I'm sure there must be some I've overlooked.

I'd like to thank my wife Lin for her support. She was my first reader and I could not have done this without her.

I also thank Marty and Cathy McDonough, my Executive Officer on Haddock and his wife, for their review of my work and their suggestions and editing assistance. Marty went on to command USS Tunny (SSN 682).

The character of Haddock's Engineer Officer, LCDR Ron Rinaldi, is drawn from the Engineer of USS Will Rogers (SSBN 659) Gold when I served on her. An excellent officer, he died in a house fire in Idaho, probably brought on by extreme exhaustion and chain smoking cigarettes. Don't smoke. The Navy lost a good officer and I lost a friend. In my novel I hope he can live on in fictional form.

Charts are adapted from NOAA digital chart products. Diagrams of equipment and layout are from the USS Haddock Piping TAB. RPCP and EPCP diagrams and all tactical graphics are by the author. Soviet submarine schematics are adapted from Wikimedia Commons files, original author, Mike1979Russia.

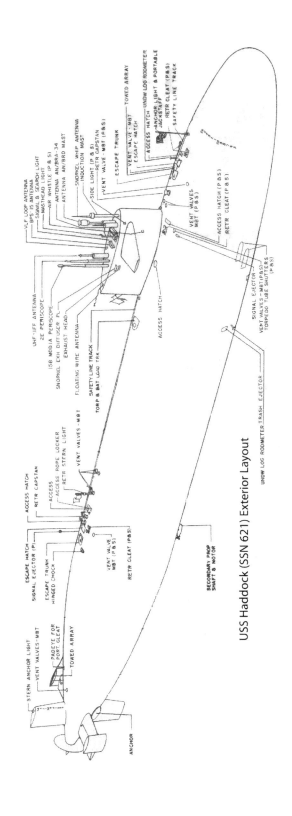

USS Haddock (SSN 621) Exterior Layout

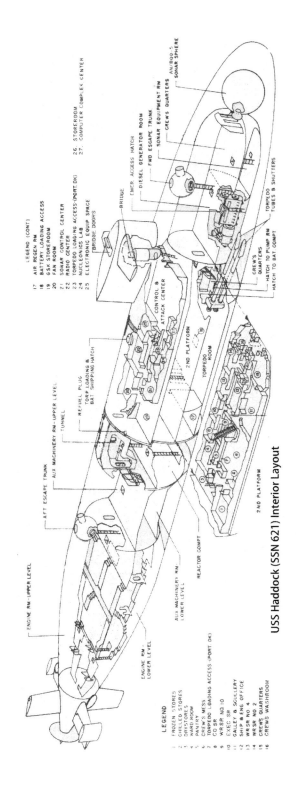

USS Haddock (SSN 621) Interior Layout

***

According to official U.S. Navy sources
events on the following pages did not happen.

***

Chapter 1 - Arrival

Submarine Base, San Diego, California
Saturday, August 10, 1991
0905

"Welcome to Haddock, Mr. Ryan," said the khaki uniformed chief petty officer. "I'm Master Chief McHenry, Chief of the Boat. Rogers, bring Mr. Ryan's bag to the XO's stateroom," he directed to a young man following him in dungarees and life jacket.

"I'm happy to be here, Master Chief McHenry. It looks like a nice day to start our trip."

"Call me, COB, everyone does. Wait on the pier a minute. We're just finishing loading some fresh provisions."

Haddock, tied up in the middle of a long pier, bow toward the shore, was a mass of last minute activity. About half the crewmen on the deck had lifejackets on. A group near the stern was swinging a boom from the pier holding several large cables away from the ship. A chain of crewmen was passing boxes from the pier over to the deck and down the open hatch behind the sail structure that stuck up above the deck level.

"Let me give you a quick topside tour while we're waiting. Almost 90% of the hull is below the waterline. The hull extends about twenty feet beyond the waterline at the bow. That's where our sonar is. The brass circles are the vents to the forward ballast tanks. We'll open the vents to let the air out when we submerge. The large circle on the hull is the forward escape trunk. It's shut now. Then we have the sail structure that contains the Bridge we use for surface operation and the masts. The ones raised now are the two periscopes and a radio mast. The small wing is the fairwater or sail plane. It's locked now and we use it to hold lookouts as we get underway. Aft of the sail is the torpedo-loading hatch. That's the main personnel access. There are more vents for ballast tanks around the machinery spaces. Then there is the Engine Room hatch. We're just closing it after removing shore electricity. There's another ballast tank at the stern and then you can see the top half of the rudder."

"It doesn't look very big."

"I guess it's not, but much bigger than the World War II submarines. I toured one at the museum in Hawaii. It looks like we're done loading and the brow is clear. Follow me."

I followed the chief across the brow that bridged the space between the pier and the submarine. It was wide enough for one person to walk easily with railings on each side. He stopped in the middle, faced the flag and saluted, then saluted toward the deck. A sailor, the only one in a white uniform, returned his salute.

"This is Mr. Ryan," the chief said to the sailor in white.

"Welcome aboard, sir. Can I see your ID?" I handed him my Maryland driver's license. "Thank you," he said, handing it back.

The chief led me to the hatch a few feet behind, aft, of our position.

"It's best to go down facing the stern. I'll handle your briefcase so you have both hands free. Make certain your foot is on the step before shifting your weight. The ladder narrows after the first couple steps."

I handed over my case, watched the chief descend and followed his actions. At the bottom there was a corridor that seemed dark compared to the bright sunlight above. The sides were covered in a light wood-grain Formica. There was white vinyl tile on the floor and pipes ran along the top of the space. A massive hatch was hinged open to the top of the passage behind the ladder. A sailor was inserting screws in a section of the floor just ahead of the ladder.

"The decks here and below are removable to load torpedoes. The Torpedo Room is two decks down. For stores, we just remove one section to pass items to the deck below where we have the Galley and Mess. Our first stop is the XO's stateroom, where you'll be staying, and we'll get you checked in."

He led me to a staircase that went down one level and left to another short corridor, stopping by a door. A sailor in dungarees was standing nearby.

"This is the XO's stateroom, your home for the next couple of weeks."

"Welcome aboard, Mr. Ryan," said the officer in the room, standing up and offering his hand. "I'm Lieutenant Commander (LCDR) Johnson, the XO.

2

"You'll have the upper bunk. I have a drawer for your stuff and some locker space. Just toss everything on the bunk and we'll get you checked in and up to the Bridge for underway."

"Glad to be here. I'm looking forward to the trip."

"Have a seat," he said indicating the second chair in the small space in front of a fold-down desk. "Doc, you're up." The sailor standing outside stepped into the door. "This is Hospital Corpsman First Class (HM1(SS)) James. He'll issue you your TLD."

"Mr. Ryan, would you fill out this form?" He placed a five by seven card on the desk. This is your thermo-luminescent dosimeter or TLD. It will record how much radiation you receive on your stay on Haddock."

"It will probably be zero to 2 millirem, a small fraction of what normal background radiation exposure would be for the period," explained the XO.

"What do I put down for previous occupational exposure?" I asked about a question on the form.

"It's a standard form. You would have worn a dosimeter before and know it if you had any exposure. Put down zero," Doc explained. "You're also not pregnant in my medical opinion," he added, referring to another question.

Taking the form he handed me a small black cylinder with an integrated belt loop.

"Wear this on your belt on the buckle side so you don't lose it if you open your belt" He pointed out the TLD on his own belt.

"What happens if I lose it?"

"We have methods to estimate your dose," explained the XO. "But doing that too much reflects poorly on our radiation control procedures."

Another sailor in dungarees appeared in the door. "Can we send the sailing list ashore now?"

"Yes," said the XO. "What about the quality assurance letter?"

"The engineers delivered that earlier," he explained and left.

"We're done for now," announced the XO. "The COB will take you to Control. You can observe the underway from the Bridge. The Captain is there now."

"OK, that sounds good."

"We can get you sneakers for traction on the deck," offered the COB. "What's your size?"

"I'm wearing Topsiders. Are they satisfactory?"

"Perfect, the Captain wears those too. Follow me."

I followed back the way we came. The chief pointed out the CO's stateroom, officers' wardroom, and the officers' head, that is, washroom, as we went. At the top of the stairway we turned left toward the bow and entered the submarine's control center that was abuzz with activity.

I was led to the front, passing consoles with computer screens and a railed-off area holding two periscopes. There was a ladder going up. On one side was a table with a chart of San Diego harbor and on the other a pair of seats in front of an array of dials. My guide grabbed something composed of several orange straps.

"This is your safety harness," he said, helping me into it and making adjustments until it fit securely. "It's required for everyone on the Bridge outside the cockpit. It wouldn't be good to fall off. This is your safety line," clipping a rope to a ring in the center of my chest. It was attached to a ring on my back and hung to the floor. "Hand the end up before you enter the Bridge and they will attach you to the ship before you go up."

To a sailor in one of the seats wearing a headset, he said, "Request permission for Mr. Ryan to go to the Bridge." After a few seconds permission was granted.

"Up you go, Mr. Ryan. Just make sure of your steps and hold onto something all the way."

"Thanks, COB."

I looked up. The passage was dimly lit with a bright circle of daylight a couple dozen feet above. The first ladder stopped just below a circular hatch set in the ceiling. Another ladder started just above that. I climbed and stood on the hatch that was at the bottom now of a long tube with pipes and wires along the wall. I climbed to the upper hatch.

"Come on up, Mr. Ryan," said a voice from above. I handed up the end of my safety line and climbed into the light.

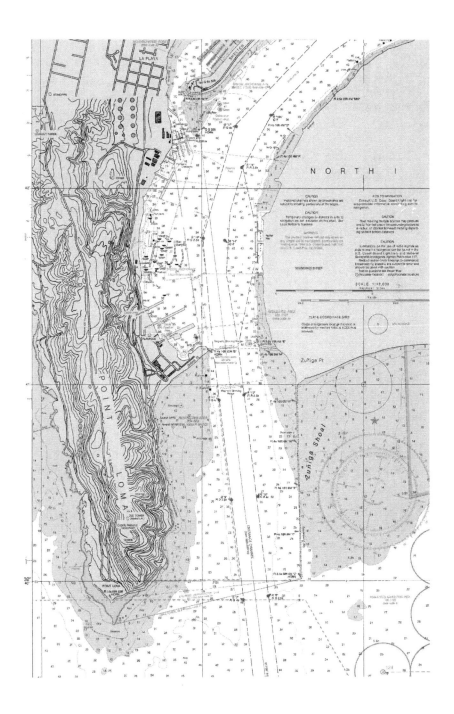

5

Chapter 2 - Underway
Submarine Base, San Diego, California
Saturday, August 10, 1991
0935

The Bridge already had two people in it and three was very cozy. I'd guess the area was not much more than a good-sized bathtub and part of that was taken by equipment, including the hatch for the opening I'd just climbed through, a massive disk of metal.

"Welcome to Haddock," said a voice from above, an officer standing on top of the ship inside a railed area. The tops of the periscopes and another raised device formed the backdrop. "I'm Commander (CDR) White, the Captain and a big fan of your novels. The Officer of the Deck is Lieutenant (LT) Nguyen and Lieutenant Junior Grade (LTJG) Reed will be doing the underway as the Conning Officer. They'll need some room, so you're up here with me; best view on the ship."

I went up. There were some cutouts in the rear frame of the Bridge for footholds. The rails encompassing the top were not completely rigid but were firm enough to offer support.

It was indeed a good view. The Captain and the two officers in the Bridge were wearing khaki uniforms with blue Haddock ball caps. The Captain's had decoration on the bill that identified him as a senior officer. He wore a harness attached to the ship's structure. He looked about forty, give or take, and was an inch or two above average height with a normal build; not an athlete but in shape for his age. He looked about constantly, taking in the activity on the Bridge, deck and pier.

There were two sailors on each of the wings that jutted out of the sail, also in harnesses, with blue dungarees uniforms and the blue ball caps. The sailors' ball caps had silver dolphins instead of the gold for the officers. One on each side had black binoculars on straps about their necks. The other sailor was wearing a phone headset.

I could see sailors on the deck ahead and behind the sail structure I was on. All wore orange life jackets and those near the bow also had safety harnesses like I wore that were fastened to a track set into the deck. Most wore blue dungarees but there were two chief petty officers in khaki. The watch that checked me on was still at his post near the brow in his white uniform.

"Continue with the checklist," urged Nguyen.

Nguyen, a Vietnamese, was quite short, just over five feet. He had taken a seat on the top of the rim of the open hatch once I'd left. This gave him a perch to see activity on the deck.

"OK. Maneuvering, rig out the outboard, test, shift to remote," said Reed. It was repeated by one of the sailors with a headset.

"The outboard is a retractable propulsion unit that is located under the hull about halfway to the stern," explained the Captain. "We have one shaft and this is the emergency backup. It gives us about two knots. For today, we'll use it to push the stern away from the pier.

"I saw in the message authorizing your ride that you were given access to engineering spaces. That's pretty unusual for civilian guests. By the way, nice shoes."

"Thanks. I have fans in the Pentagon too."

"Outboard, lowered, tested and shifted to remote," said a sailor.

"Very well. Helm, test the outboard in remote."

A sailor repeated it back to Reed and passed it through his headset.

"The tug is inbound Mr. Reed," announced a sailor on the right wing.

"Make it up in a Chinese power moor," Nguyen suggested to Reed.

"Mr. Nguyen," the Captain said in a stern voice.

"Sorry, sir. A reverse power moor. There's no one here to be offended."

"Not the point. You know better and standards don't change when we have guests."

"Deck, tie the tug up in a reverse power moor," ordered Reed and the sailor relayed.

"Helm reports the outboard is tested in remote."

"Very well. Helm, train the outboard to zero-nine-zero."

"That will direct the thrust to push the stern away from the pier," explained the Captain. "The bow is zero-zero-zero, then around the circle with zero-nine-zero as the starboard, right, beam, one-eight-zero for the stern, two-seven-zero for the port beam and around to the bow again. The outboard can push in any direction. Straight ahead and exactly port or starboard are the directions most used."

"It hangs below the ship?"

"Yes, when lowered we like to have about 10 feet below the keel."

"Captain, the XO reports the mail run is back. Request permission to remove the brow."

"Yes, remove the brow."

"Remove the brow, aye. Deck, remove the brow."

"Deck acknowledges and reports the tug is made up."

"As you can see, the tug is tied so its bow is pointing to our stern. This lets the tug thrust forward to back us out of our berth. That's best for letting the tug control our direction as we move backward. Submarines are really unpredictable when backing. Even with rudder and the outboard it can be difficult to hold a steady course. We'll just kick the stern out and leave the rest to the tug."

Sailors assisting our departure on the pier raised the steps on the brow by adjusting chains that connected them to the brow's railings. They must have been weighted because, when lifted, they counterbalanced the long ramp to the submarine's deck. It was rolled on its two pier-side wheels away from Haddock. A sailor tossed the wooden pallet that had protected the sub's deck onto the end as it retreated.

"The brow is removed, Captain. Request to test the shaft on the EPM."

"Test the shaft on the EPM."

"Test the shaft on the EPM, aye. Maneuvering, test the shaft on the EPM."

Reed relayed this order through a microphone that was connected to a box in front of him. The speaker sounded an acknowledgement of the order. I noted that the sailor with the headset also repeated the order.

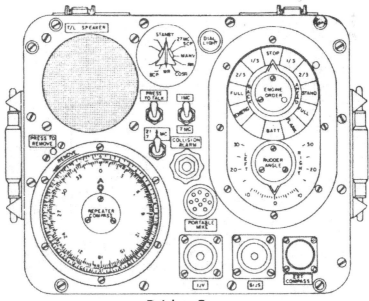

Bridge Box

A few seconds later the ship surged, restrained by the lines, astern then ahead.

"Bridge, Maneuvering, the shaft has been tested on the EPM."

"Bridge, aye. Shift propulsion to the main engines. Captain, request permission to test the shaft on the main engines."

"Shift propulsion to the main engines, Maneuvering aye."

"Test the shaft on the main engines."

"Test the shaft on the main engines, aye."

"Bridge, Maneuvering, propulsion shifted to main engines."

"Bridge, aye. Maneuvering, test the shaft on the main engines."

They acknowledged but the surge was much less this time.

"Bridge, Maneuvering, tested the shaft on the main engines."

"Maneuvering, Bridge, answer all bells, answer all stop."

"Maneuvering, answering all stop."

"Radio, Bridge, request permission to get underway."

"Bridge, Radio, request permission to get underway, aye."

"On deck, single two and four." This was shouted over the side and acknowledged by personnel on deck. They went to work on the lines, one just before the Bridge and one all the way aft, reducing them from three strands to one and hauling the excess aboard the submarine.

"Bridge, Radio, we have permission to get underway."

"Bridge, aye. Captain it's oh-nine-fifty. Request to get underway."

"Since we're a day late a few minutes early won't hurt. Mr. Reed, get us underway."

"Get us underway, aye. On deck, take in one and three." The lines by the bow and just behind the sail were cast off the pier and hauled onboard.

"Lines one and three are on deck," reported the sailor on the headset.

"Slack four," was shouted aft and "hold two," shouted forward. The in the microphone, "Helm, start the outboard."

"Start the outboard, Helm aye. Outboard is on."

The ship's stern started shifting away from the pier. The sailors handling line four fed more rope to keep it slack. The bow, held by the remaining line, pivoted on the float that separated the hull from the pier. In a minute the stern was pointed well clear of the submarine tied up behind us.

"Take in four." To the man on the tug's bridge, just a few feet away from us the way it was tied up, "Take us out." The tug answered with a short toot of its whistle.

As we began to move, "Take in two," was the order. As the line was cast into the water from the pier, Reed shouted, "On deck, watch your ears."

He bent down and pulled a lever. A loud horn sounded and sounded and sounded. Finally there was, again, silence. As the horn sounded, Mr. Nguyen raised a small American flag on the short pole attached to the left railing.

The flag on the aft deck was hauled down and sailors then started dismantling the pole.

"Colors shifted," Nguyen announced. He asked to Reed, "Why didn't we sound three short blasts from our whistle?"

"Stop the outboard," Reed said into the mike and got an acknowledgement back over the speaker. "Our engines are stopped. We'd do that if our engines were going astern, but the tug is pushing us out, going ahead."

"Good, Mr. Reed," agreed the Captain. "The tugs we have here are twin engine, twin props and twin rudders. This is much easier."

The tug was pushing us backward in the space between our pier and the next one over. As we cleared the end it turned us so we were pointed toward the harbor exit. On the submarine's deck the crew was securing the lines in bins under the deck.

"On deck, cast off the tug," shouted Reed while Nguyen gave the tug a thumbs-up signal that was answered with a short toot.

The tug backed well clear once its lines were free.

"Helm, all ahead two-thirds."

"All ahead two-thirds, Helm aye. Maneuvering, answers ahead two-thirds," came from the box and the indicator moved to two-thirds.

"Helm, come left, steer one-six-zero."

"Come left, steer one-six-zero, Helm aye."

The water started to churn behind the submarine as we started to move forward and slowly turn to the left.

"Helm, all ahead one-third. Helm, train the outboard zero-zero-zero."

"All ahead one-third, Helm aye. Answers one-third. Train the outboard zero-zero-zero, Helm aye."

"Look astern, Mr. Ryan," said the Captain while turning to face that way. "Do you see the two signs with the vertical line down their center?"

"Yes."

"They form the range that defines the harbor entrance course. The lower of the two is closest to us. When it aligns with the upper sign we are at the center of the channel. The exit course is one-seven-three. Since the lower sign is right of the upper, we have to steer left of one-seven-three to get over to center."

"I see." The two signs were starting to get closer.

"Bridge, Helm, outboard is trained zero-zero-zero."

"Bridge aye. Helm, steer one-six-five. Maneuvering, rig in and secure the outboard." Acknowledgements came back over the speaker.

"As we close, we'll ease onto the course. Mr. Reed, would you keep our speed to one-third until we pass Ballast Point."

"Stay at one-third, aye-aye sir."

"Hand me the phone." He squatted down to get the handset from the console. "Talker, ask the XO to get on the line."

After a few seconds, he continued. "XO, your wife and a few others are out on Ballast Point. Personnel not on watch can go on deck to wave goodbye. Make sure they have lifejackets and stay near the hatch… Yes, arrange reliefs as needed."

He handed the phone back and stood up.

"Bridge, Maneuvering, outboard is secured."

"Helm, steer one-seven-zero."

"Steer one-seven zero, Helm aye," came over the speaker.

"The forward deck is clear," reported Nguyen.

"Steering one-seven-zero."

"Bridge aye," said Reed into the mike.

"We keep our speed down to four knots, one-third, with personnel forward to keep water from the areas they stand and work. We'd normally speed up to two-thirds now, but not today."

Most of the crew that had handled lines was now off the deck when the first crewmen came up. There was still one man working further aft pounding on the hull with a big mallet.

"What is that man doing, hitting the hull?"

"He has a rubber mallet," explained the Captain. "We have to make certain that the cleats and locker doors won't rattle with water flowing over them. That would make a distinctive noise and be incredibly easy to track on sonar. A few minutes now, getting everything secure, saves a lot of trouble later."

"Helm, steer one-seven-three."

"Steer one-seven-three, Helm aye."

I noticed the signs behind us had almost aligned.

"Steering one-seven-three."

We now had a half-dozen crew by the hatch waving to their wives. The Captain and bridge crew joined in the waving. A couple minutes and we passed beyond the group.

"Mr. Reed, you can increase speed now."

"Yes, sir. Helm, all ahead two-thirds."

"All ahead two-thirds, Helm aye. Answers ahead two-thirds."

The indicator on the box shifted to two-thirds.

There were many pleasure boats on the water. It was a very nice summer weekend.

"Does the civilian traffic cause you any problems?"

"Not usually," explained the Captain. "Small boats are required to give way to vessels that need to navigate in the channel. Most do so instinctively to get out of the path of a large vessel. Of course, we don't want to hit anyone even if we are in the right. The paperwork is a bitch."

"Control reports that the deck is rigged for dive and requests permission to rig the vents for dive," stated the phone-talker. The

Captain looked aft and I followed. The deck was empty of people and the hatch was shut.

"Very well," acknowledged Nguyen. "Rig vents for dive." The phone talker repeated and passed it on his headset.

"Let's go to standard, Mr. Reed," the Captain urged.

"Helm, all ahead standard."

"All ahead standard, Helm aye. Answers ahead standard."

"What's rig for dive," I asked the CO.

"We have two conditions, rigged for surface and rigged for dive. Entering port we'd rig for surface and before we submerge we rig for dive. We check each compartment to make sure we haven't left a path for water to enter and the systems we'd need submerged are properly aligned. A sailor does the initial check and an officer double-checks independently. Both men sign for the rig in Control.

"The main ballast tank vents are a special case. In port they are physically locked shut with a standard padlock and the hydraulic operation is bypassed. The duty officer controls the key. Covers with rubber gaskets are bolted over the openings in the deck. The covers are removed just prior to stationing the watches for getting underway and we rig them for dive about now. They will be unlocked and set for hydraulic operation by an auxiliaryman and an officer will check. They'll be operated from Control when we dive."

"It sounds like you really don't want them to open in port."

"Yes, though I heard of a sub in Charleston that submerged a few feet to rest on the bottom when a hurricane broke most of their lines to the pier. That was good thinking and they must have planned ahead for that possibility."

"Bridge, NAV," sounded from the bridge box. "We hold you on track. Three minutes to next turn, right to two-one-five when buoy five is abeam to starboard."

"I'm sorry we're a day late getting underway. I hope it wasn't too much an inconvenience. We developed a packing leak on #2 scope; not bad, but they only get worse. It's best to fix it and that took an extra day."

"It was no trouble. I'm happy to get the opportunity. I have a laptop and always have some writing I can do."

14

"Good. You should get an idea of our routine. Long transits like this are great for training, but there's not much excitement. We can go a few days without a sonar contact unless we are near the shipping lanes."

"Bridge, NAV, standby to turn right to two-one-five... Mark the turn."

"Helm, right fifteen degrees rudder, steady two-one-five."

"Right fifteen degrees rudder, steady two-one-five, Helm aye. My rudder is right fifteen."

There was a rudder indicator on the box that Reed checked before looking at the stern where you could see the exposed portion of the rudder angled to starboard. A minute later we were reported on our new course.

"So, Captain, what are your duties here on the Bridge?"

"Well, the Captain is responsible for everything on his ship, whether he's present or not. When we enter or leave port we are operating near shoal water and near many other vessels. The only way to meet my responsibilities is to be up here where I can see the situation. Under normal circumstances I just give permissions and watch. If we have a casualty, say a line broke or the tug lost power, things could get interesting. I don't like interesting. If I give an order directly to the helm, I've taken the conn, the direction of course, speed and depth."

"Did you ever have to take charge like that?"

"Once on our last deployment to the Western Pacific. We were getting underway from Buckner Bay on Okinawa. They have a very long pier and no tugs, just Mike boats. Those are like landing craft you see hitting the beach in old war movies. They have no padding to allow them to push against our hull so we can just toss them a line and have them pull on it. We'd used the boat and our outboard to pull well off the pier and were backing out when the stern started to turn toward the pier. The rudder and outboard had no effect. I had to step in and order ahead full to kill our motion astern before we hit. I left it on a bit too long and needed back emergency to kill our headway before we hit the shallow water off the pier."

"What then?"

"We were dead in the water but clear of the obstacles. We brought back the Mike boat to pull our bow around and used the outboard to keep the stern off the pier and then twist until the bow faced the open sea. From there we just went straight out. That was a bit of excitement I didn't need."

While I talked with the Captain we steadied on our new course and the Navigator relayed information on our next course change.

"Bridge, NAV, standby to turn right to two seven zero… Mark the turn."

"Helm, right fifteen degrees rudder, steady two-seven-zero."

Helm acknowledged and shortly announced steady on course.

"Mr. Nguyen, secure the maneuvering watch. I'm going below. We should be at the dive point by the time you get the Bridge rigged." Facing me, he started to climb down. "Mr. Ryan, you can enjoy the fresh air for a few more minutes."

"Control, Bridge, secure the maneuvering watch."

Over the speaker came the announcement, "Secure the maneuvering watch. Set the underway watch, section 3."

The phone talkers on the planes were first to depart, disconnecting their headsets, climbing in to the cockpit one at a time and requesting permission to go below.

"I need to get to Maneuvering," stated Mr. Reed.

"OK. Two-seven-zero, ahead standard, I relieve you of the conn," replied Nguyen.

"I stand relieved; laying below."

"Quartermaster, Mr. Nguyen has the deck and the conn," was the next remark into the microphone and acknowledged.

One of the lookouts then climbed in to the Bridge cockpit and lay below. Then Control requested permission for the relieving lookout to lay to the Bridge and a petty officer soon appeared. He discussed the few contacts, all behind us now, with the remaining lookout and relieved him. The former lookout went below.

"Mr. Ryan, you'll need to get down in the cockpit. We need to dismantle that area to prepare for diving."

I climbed down into the cockpit. There was a flow of cool air coming up through the open hole that occupied the center of the tiny space. Nguyen was still sitting on the rim of the raised hatch.

Control requested to send a man up to unrig the Bridge and a sailor came up the hatch wearing a harness. He climbed to where I'd

16

been standing and started to dismantle the structure and hand the pieces to the lookout. It was pinned together or screwed, hand tight, into the ship's structure and came apart in less than five minutes.

I took the time to find out a bit more about LT Nguyen. "Nguyen is a Vietnamese name. What brings you to serve on a U.S. submarine?"

"Yes, I was born in South Vietnam in 1966. So I was born in Vietnam and educated in Moscow and now I'm on an American nuclear submarine."

"How is that possible?"

"Navy ROTC, University of Idaho, Moscow, Idaho.

"My father was an electrical engineer who was employed by the American Army and Embassy at various times on projects. We lived in Saigon until the North invaded. We fled on a fishing boat my uncle owned five days before the city fell. We had the whole family on there, about forty people, but the boat was in good shape and had plenty of fuel, water and food. We made it to the Philippines in three days.

"We spent nine months at a camp in the Philippines. My father had contacts with former personnel at the Embassy, so we got resettled fairly quickly to Boise, Idaho. That was quite a change from Vietnam."

"Did you have trouble adjusting to life here?"

"Father taught us English back in Vietnam and we all practiced hard at camp in Philippines. We had some resettlement assistance when we arrived, but I guess you could say we were poor. Still, poor in America was an easier life than we had in Vietnam and I'm not talking about the war that never really intruded into the areas we lived until the end.

"My parents found jobs working in a dry cleaner. After a couple years they started their own place and now have six locations around Boise. My brother and I helped out after school and weekends. So, now, we're doing well."

"How about you personally? Has being Asian been a problem? You're also a bit short. Is that a problem?"

"Yes, I'm five-two. That causes a few problems, but not with people. Operating a nuclear submarine is a demanding job. If you know your stuff, you'll get respect. It's a small crew. Everyone knows who knows their stuff and who is just getting by."

"Mr. Nguyen is one of the good guys," interjected the lookout, currently passing pieces down the hatch.

"Thanks, Petty Officer Wheeler."

"Bridge, Control, greater than four miles from land."

"Bridge aye. Maneuvering, Bridge, rig emergency cooling for at sea."

"Rig emergency cooling for at sea, Maneuvering aye."
"What is that about?"

"In port, if we were to lose all AC electrical power the emergency cooling system activates automatically in about two minutes to cool the reactor. At sea it is set to require manual initiation because we don't want it activating accidentally. We switch modes at the 4 mile from land point."

"Bridge, Control, this is LT Gonzales. We're almost at the dive point. I'm ready to relieve you," blared the box.

Nguyen picked up the mike. "I'm ready to be relieved. We're on two-seven-zero, ahead standard, surface ventilating with numbers one and two scopes and the IFF/UHF mast up. All the contacts are astern and not of concern. I've ordered XC rigged for at sea."

"I relieve you of the deck and the conn."

"I stand relieved."

"Bridge, rig the Bridge for dive and lay below."

"Rig the Bridge and lay below, aye. Control, secure power to the bridge box."

"Secure power to the bridge box, Control, aye." The box went dead.

"I'll take the box below," said the man in the hatch who had been securing pieces.

Nguyen lifted the compass repeater from its mount and secured it in a hole in the box, then pulled the box off its bracket, revealing the large plug that had been pushed into its back. He handed it down.

A large cap with an O-ring seal went over the plug. The mount for the compass went into a bag. A plastic cable tie was removed from the bag and used to secure the whistle handle.

"Lookout, laying below." Wheeler grabbed the bag and went down the hatch.

Thunk.

"What was that?"

"That was the head valve. It's at the top of the snorkel mast, air operated, with an electric sensor to shut it automatically if it goes below water. The mast isn't raised but we had it open to draw in outside air while we were on the surface. We shifted to the recirculate mode to prepare for diving. Now there's no airflow up the hatch. The hydraulically operated main induction valve was also shut.

"You need to go below now Mr. Ryan. I have to secure the cockpit and shut the hatch."

"OK."

I carefully found the ladder steps and descended into the dimly lit tube. The bright circle of daylight got smaller and smaller. It went out as the cockpit opening was covered over. As I passed the lower hatch I heard the solid thud of the upper hatch being closed.

Chapter 3 – Diving

Off San Diego, California – 32° 30.0' N 117° 50.4' W
Saturday, August 10, 1991
1130

The control room was a lot quieter now than it was preparing for getting underway. The harbor chart on the table by the hatch was gone and the table covered with a fitted piece of simulated brown leather. Wheeler came over and helped me remove the safety harness that he stowed in a locker near the ladder.

Nguyen came down, shutting the lower hatch and turning a wheel in its center to secure it. "Last man down, hatch secured," he announced. "Bridge is rigged for dive."

"LT Gonzales, the ship is rigged for dive," said the chief petty officer sitting just in front of the raised area where the periscopes were located. "Petty Officer Wheeler, inform Mr. Gordon and the Captain."

"Aye aye, Chief." He headed off.

"Mr. Ryan, I'm Chief Lloyd, the Diving Officer of the Watch (DOOW). Would you like to take the fairwater planes for the dive?"

"What do I do?"

"Just take Seaman Miller's place in the chair next to you. He'll show you what to do and keep you out of trouble."

"Lowering #1 scope, shifting to #2," announced LT Gonzales, twisting an orange ring around the periscope barrel above his head. The scope descended into a well in the floor.

"#1 scope, indicates down," said a petty officer seated in front of a panel filled with lights and switches.

"That's Torpedoman First Class (TM1(SS)) Sheldon, the Chief of the Watch (COW)," explained Chief Lloyd. "He operates the Ballast Control Panel, BCP, and supervises the enlisted watch in section 3. As you see, a good petty officer first class can qualify for the job."

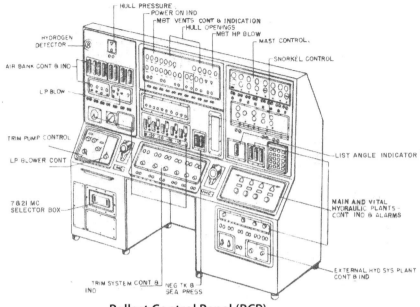

HYDROGEN
DETECTOR

HULL PRESSURE
POWER ON IND
MBT VENTS CONT & INDICATION
HULL OPENINGS
MBT HP BLOW
MAST CONTROL.

SNORKEL CONTROL

AIR BANK CONT & IND

LP BLOW

TRIM PUMP CONTROL

LP BLOWER CONT

LIST ANGLE INDICATOR

7&21 MC
SELECTOR BOX

MAIN AND VITAL
HYDRAULIC PLANTS
CONT IND & ALARMS

EXTERNAL HYD SYS PLANT
CONT & IND

TRIM SYSTEM CONT &
IND

NEG TK &
SEA PRESS

Ballast Control Panel (BCP)

Miller unbuckled his seat belt and got out of the seat. I sat
down and buckled in. It was just like the belt on an airplane. In front
of me was a post on which a control wheel was mounted. I tried but
the wheel couldn't turn. "The wheel is to control the rudder. It's
pinned. The rudder is controlled from the outboard station right now.
Don't do it, but if you pull the wheel toward you the planes rise, and
if you push it, dive. There are two modes of operation, emergency
and normal. In emergency the stick controls the hydraulics directly.
Pull or push and the planes move until the stick is back in neutral.
That's the mode we're in now. In normal the position of the stick
positions the planes electrically with a servo system. On the panel
ahead of you there is a position indicator for your planes. Then there
is a compass repeater, and in the center, digital and analog depth
gauges."

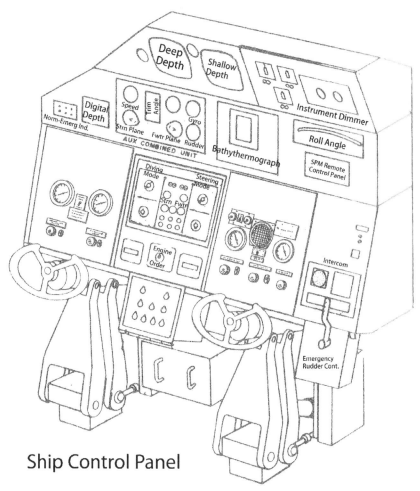

Ship Control Panel

"I see," I said examining all the indicators.

"Mr. Gonzales, request to test the planes in emergency and normal," said Chief Lloyd.

"Dive, test the planes in emergency and normal. Helm, all ahead one-third." Gonzales said while continuing to sweep around on the periscope.

"Helm, all ahead one-third aye." The sailor sitting left of me answered and turned a knob on the console between us. The indicator shifted to match the new position. "Maneuvering answers ahead one-third."

"Test the planes in emergency and normal, aye sir," the chief responded. "Mr. Ryan that is the engine order telegraph. It's controlled by the helmsman. That's whichever seat is controlling our course with the rudder. OK. Test planes in emergency."

Both sailors responded, Miller for me. He urged me to pull the stick and push forward. I did and saw the indicator move in response. I returned the planes to the zero position.

"Fairwater planes tested sat in emergency," reported Miller and the stern planes reported the same.

"Shift both planes to normal and test."

The helmsman flipped a switch and pressed a button on the console between us to shift the stern planes and then did a second switch and button for mine. Now moving, pulling or pushing, changed the angle with the position determined by how far off center the stick was held. It was more responsive than in emergency mode. I returned the stick to center and the planes returned to the zero position.

"Planes tested satisfactorily, Mr. Gonzales."

Petty Officer Wheeler had returned during our testing along with an officer.

"We're ready to dive, Mr. Gordon," reported the chief. "Mr. Ryan, LT Gordon is the Damage Control Assistant and Ship's Diving Officer." Gordon was a big man, mid twenties, six-two or so and a bit husky.

"Nice to meet you Mr. Ryan. I've read your books. I run the training for ship control and make sure we have our buoyancy and balance right before our initial dive. I also run the Auxiliary Division. We take care of most of the non-nuclear mechanical systems."

"Where do we stand, Mr. Gonzales?"

The CO had entered Control. He had changed from khaki to a blue one-piece coverall.

"We're in our area and can dive any time, Captain."

"Very well, submerge the ship."

"Submerge the ship, aye sir. Chief of the Watch, on the 1MC, Dive, Dive."

"On the 1MC Dive, Dive, aye sir." The petty officer at the BCP answered, picking up a microphone. "Dive, Dive." He shifted a lever. The diving alarm sounded, twice, through the speakers, two blasts of an electronic klaxon. "Dive, Dive." He then flipped two switches on his panel. A row of indicators shifted from lines to circles. "All vents indicate open.

"Maneuvering answers ahead two-thirds," reported the helmsman, pushing his planes to dive. I went to do the same but Miller stopped me, saying they were still above water.

"Venting forward. Venting aft," reported Gonzales, looking forward and aft through the scope.

"Sounding, one-hundred-forty fathoms," came a report from somewhere to my left.

There really wasn't much change. The depth gauge crept from twenty-six to twenty-seven, twenty-eight, twenty-nine then thirty.

"Deck is awash."

When we reached forty in, what seemed like, a couple minutes, Miller told me to shift to full dive. You could see the effect as the depth gauge began to roll over faster and the submarine took a small downward tilt.

"Passing fifty feet," report Chief Lloyd.

"Scope is under. Lowering the scope."

"Sixty-eight feet," reported the chief. "Shut the vents."

"Scope indicates down. Vents indicate shut," added the COW a few seconds later.

"Passing one-hundred feet."

"We go to one-fifty if no depth is ordered on the dive," added Miller. "Keep the planes on dive until we are about twenty feet away."

As we passed one-thirty I started to ease off the planes' angle. I saw the other sailor had pulled his control toward him. The angle of the ship started to come off.

"One-hundred-fifty feet."

The depth was still dropping slowly. I had pulled my stick back to put the full upward angle on my planes. The depth stopped increasing at 155 and we had a small upward tilt. Miller pointed out the angle indicator on the display. It read a one-and-a-half degree upward angle. The depth ticked up above one-fifty and I shifted to dive on my planes. The depth increased again.

"Mr. Ryan," said Lloyd, "you need to anticipate the motion with the planes. It takes several seconds for your actions to have an effect on the boat. Find the angle that holds the depth steady and adjust around that."

I found that about fifteen degrees up seemed to work.

"We're a bit heavy," observed the chief. "Pump auxiliaries to sea."

After acknowledging the order and a few switch manipulations the COW counted off each thousand pounds.

"Helm, ahead one-third," ordered the chief and it was rung up. The speed began to drop from our eight knots.

"Shift your suction to after trim."

"Shift suction to after trim, aye," acknowledged the COW. "Suction shifted, six-thousand pumped from auxiliaries."

By another three thousand pounds I only needed about five degrees to hold depth.

"Secure pumping to sea. Cycle the vents." That was accomplished by opening the forward vents, then the aft vents, for a few seconds each. "Pump 1000 from after trim to forward trim."

When that was completed Chief Lloyd reported, "Mr. Gonzales, 150 feet, trim satisfactory."

"Captain," interjected LT Gordon. "My guys would like to grease the packing gland on #2 scope and cycle it before we go deep. We're ready to go."

"Very well. Mr. Gonzales, grease #2 scope, then proceed on track." After being acknowledged he continued. "You did well on the dive, Mr. Ryan. If Seaman Miller can take over we can continue your orientation."

Chapter 4 - Tour
Off San Diego, California – 32° 30.0' N 117° 54.8' W
Saturday, August 10, 1991
1200

"Mr. Ryan, I'd like you to meet our Engineer Officer, Lieutenant Commander (LCDR) Ron Rinaldi. Everyone usually addresses him as ENG. He'll show you around Haddock."

We exchanged greetings. Rinaldi was about thirty, average height and quite thin. He wore wire-frame glasses. He was still in his khaki uniform. He looked at me, not as a fan, but like he was trying to see what type of problem I might be. His expression showed intensity and focus.

"ENG, Mr. Ryan is cleared for secret and is authorized for propulsion plant access," continued the Captain. "Give him the Three Hour Tour." The Captain turned and left.

"Three hours?"

"No, lunch is at thirteen-hundred. I'll have you back for that. It was just a reference to an old TV show, before my time."

"Oh." Not before my time, now that he mentioned it.

"Let's begin right here in Control. This is the uppermost of three levels in the Operations Compartment. The bridge hatch is forward and the opposite direction is aft. Facing forward, right is starboard and left is port. Closer to the hull is outboard and toward the center is inboard. Walls are called bulkheads." He pointed up. "That's the overhead." He pointed down. "This is the deck.

"The panel in front of where you sat is called the Ship Control Panel. We have two people on the planes and a messenger in each watch section. They rotate positions. Where the Chief of the Watch sits is the Ballast Control Panel. It moves water around and into or out of the sub to balance us, forward and aft, and control buoyancy. It has indicators or controls for masts, hydraulics, vents, and hull openings. Having all our hull openings shut, a good thing when submerged, is called a straight-board. The shut indication is a straight line and open is a circle.

"Starboard and outboard of us is the fire control system where we can direct and launch our torpedoes and Harpoon cruise missiles. We don't carry the Tomahawk missiles that were used in

26

the Gulf War. That's why we stayed home, doing training for deploying battle groups. You'll see it in action when we exercise at battle stations next week. Petty Officer (FTG2(SS)) Boyle is the Fire Control Technician of the Watch (FTOW) and is running a three-sixty plot of contacts. He or the OOD could use the fire control system to track any that appear to be of concern.

"Inboard is the periscope stand. #1 periscope is purely optical with a visually small head that is hard to spot. If we want a close look at something, we'd use that. It's called the attack scope. #2 has antennas to receive radio and radar signals. It's good to know if there is radar active that could detect you and it might alert us to the presence of a ship or plane we couldn't yet see. It looks like we're ready to cycle the scope."

There were pipes and cables running along the hull above our heads. The sailors had connected the grease gun to an air manifold and a small fitting in that mix. The device was thumping slowly as the air operated a piston pumping grease. LT Gonzales reached for the orange ring above his head and twisted it right. The scope barrel moved up through an opening in the hull. The last few feet had the eyepiece, handles and thick cylinder almost as wide as the opening it rose from. As soon as the scope was up he twisted the ring to the left and the periscope dropped smoothly into the deck.

"The barrel contains electronics that connect the antennas to the ship's systems. It's resistant to water but still it's bad to have salt water dripping on it day after day."

"Dive, make your depth two-four-five feet. Helm, ahead standard."

"Sounding, one-seven-three fathoms," came the voice from the left just after Dive and Helm acknowledged.

"Moving aft we have the radar. We never use it because it is unique to submarines. If we turn it on we assume a Soviet satellite will detect it and they'll get at least an approximate location. We have a commercial Furuno that we can mount on the Bridge, if needed, for surface navigation. Everybody uses them so it doesn't mark us as a sub.

"At the aft end of Control we have our inertial navigator, called SINS. The ones on missile subs are good within feet over several days. Ours isn't nearly that good. We need a navigational fix every day, more often if we can."

"Do you have GPS?"

"We don't have the modification to use it submerged. Haddock is too close to decommissioning to justify the expense. We did buy a portable commercial unit we can use on the surface.

"Next is the panel that lets us analyze the radar signals that we pick up. We can get a good idea of what type of radar we're seeing and how well it might be in detecting us. Electronics Technician Third Class Wong is the ET of the Watch (ETOW) in this section.

"Petty Officer Wong, this is our rider, Mr. Ryan. How are your sub quals coming?"

"Welcome aboard, sir. I should be done before Japan, Mr. Rinaldi."

"Continuing to port we have the NAVSAT receiver that is our primary method to fix our position at sea. We also have LORAN-C and OMEGA but they're not nearly as accurate. Port side of the periscope stand is the Quartermaster of the Watch (QMOW), Petty Officer (QM3(SS)) Flores. He's running a dead-reckoning track and plotting SINS on the local chart containing our approved track. Because we are near some shallow water, Senior Chief (QMCS(SS)) Spillman is supervising the ship's navigation. He or the Navigator, LCDR Cooper, will be supervising until we clear the shallow spots.

"We're taking depth soundings continuously now. The fathometer is almost undetectable unless you're right under it. The Navigator sets a Red Sounding and a Yellow Sounding. Yellow means we are not where we think we are and have to operate cautiously until we determine our position. Red indicates we are in danger of hitting the bottom and have to slow, go shallow or reverse course to avoid grounding."

"Have you every had such an emergency?"

"Not in my career. I hope never in future too. Anyway, time to move on; head aft.

"Just aft of Control on starboard are the Nucleonics Laboratory and Sonar. Nucleonics is where we analyze water from the reactor plant. We'll skip it for now."

We passed Nucleonics and he opened the door to Sonar. We entered a space dimly light in blue light. There were three computer consoles with operators seated at them and an array of other equipment and two sailors standing.

"Sonarman First Class (STS1(SS)) Johnson is the Sonar Supervisor in this section. Petty Officer Johnson, would you explain to Mr. Ryan a bit about your operation."

Johnson was a black man, about thirty, six foot and in shape. All the watches in Sonar were wearing the blue dungarees uniform.

"Sure, sir. We have three consoles, each with two screens that can be configured in various ways. The two on the ends are doing passive search and the one in the center is for analyzing any contacts. Sound intensity is displayed visually as a darker color on the screen. We look three-hundred-sixty degrees continuously but the area behind us is blocked by our own noise. Bearing is across and time in the past is down. That line you see here is a contact. On the analysis screen we can see a four-bladed screw turning at 85 RPM. It's probably a small merchant. We are sending bearings about every five minutes to fire control so they can plot them."

"Thanks Petty Officer Johnson, we need to move on."

We went back to the passageway.

"Aft are the steps leading to the watertight door to the Reactor Compartment. The Torpedo Loading Hatch is in the overhead. Since we're submerged, the upper and lower hatches are secured and the ladder has been stowed to open up the passageway.

"We'll head forward. Starboard is the Nucleonics Laboratory. On the port side is Radio. That's above your clearance. Take the steps to the second level."

We went down.

"To our right is the Galley where all our meals are prepared. To port is the passage to officer country and off the passage is the Ship's Office and the Engineering Logroom. As we head forward we have crew quarters on starboard and the crew's washroom, or head in Navy parlance, on port. The ladder down goes to additional crew berthing, used for first-class petty officers.

"That brings us to the watertight door to the Bow Compartment. The door is normally latched open except for emergencies. The levers above the door shut the ventilation ducts.

Shutting both and the door isolates the compartment. The bulkhead is rated to 700 feet. The ocean is deeper than that here.

"Mr. Ryan"

"Wait, ENG. I'll be here for a couple weeks; Tom is fine."

"Tom, sure. To go through the door, grab the handrail above the door and duck your head through while stepping a leg through. Watch."

He demonstrated. It was easier to do than explain.

The compartment was lit with a few dim reddish lights. There were bunks, three high on the right and a bulkhead with a door to the left. Most of the bunks had curtains pulled shut and had sleeping sailors.

"This is the primary crew berthing area and is always rigged for night except for field day, battle stations or ship emergencies."

"What's a field day?"

"That's when the entire crew is up cleaning the ship. Normally we hold it Saturday afternoon when we're underway, but not today.

"To port is the Chiefs' Quarters. They have berthing, a head and a small sitting area with a four-person table and a coffee mess. Above here is the forward signal ejector. We can launch torpedo countermeasures or smokes and flares from it. There's another in the Engine Room.

"Also in the overhead is the operator for the #3 main ballast tank vents."

"I heard them order the vents rigged for dive when I was on the Bridge."

"Yes, this vent is rigged for dive. This is the lock. It's unlocked. The holes for the padlock don't line up in the unlocked position and the lock is stowed around a bit of piping. The orange valve operator is for the hydraulic bypass. It would be open, aligned with the pipe, rigged for surface. Now it is perpendicular to the pipe, indicating it is shut and allowing hydraulic operation. The hand-wheel on the bottom of the vent operator can be used to control it manually."

"How do you know what to do to rig for dive?"

"Each compartment has a list of things to check. It's in a holder located in every space."

He went to the bulkhead by the watertight door and opened a metal plate mounted there, labeled in red, "Compartment Bills." There were several plates hinged inside, each holding a laminated sheet of paper.

"This is the rig for dive checklist for Bow Compartment," indicating a sheet with numerous lines that had a double rows of checkmarks in grease pencil down the sides.

"We also have bills for fire, flooding, battle stations and other situations. In an emergency the senior man takes charge in each compartment and has another man a phone set. A phone is stowed in this box," indicating a small metal box mounted below the bill holder.

"What's in the big box next to it?"

"This is an oxygen breathing apparatus or OBA for short. It's used for fighting fires. We have six mounted in various locations about the ship. Next to it is stowage for the canisters that generate the oxygen by a chemical process."

He opened the box. Inside was a black object that had a full-face mask connected to it by flexible hoses. The canisters beside the box were green and about the size of a hardback novel. There were six in the stowage bracket.

"Let's continue our tour. The hatch in the deck leads to the Diesel Generator Room."

He opened the hatch. White lighting flooded the room. Looking down you could see the gray bulk of the diesel filling the center of the space surrounded by gray metal walkways. We didn't go down.

"The diesel is our long term backup if we had a reactor problem. We have a battery that can supply us for a few hours, but normally, it just takes the load until we can start the diesel. We can operate the diesel at periscope depth drawing air in through the snorkel mast. The other way of moving air uses a low-pressure blower that is also located down there.

Moving forward there were bunks on both sides of the passageway. We came to a point where the passage split into port and starboard aisles, both lined with bunks. At the split was a ladder going up.

"Above us is the Forward Escape Trunk. Theoretically you could use it to reach the surface if we are disabled in two hundred feet of water or less. We have trained with SEALS using it to lock in and out while we're submerged at periscope depth.

"Heading forward we have the access hatch to the Sonar Sphere. It is a watertight space, but the hatch is kept shut underway. This hatch drops down to the Sonar Equipment Room."

It was a white-lit space filled with electronic equipment racks. Again we did not go down. We retraced our steps through the Bow Compartment. He pointed out the operators for the main ballast tank vents. The forward three ballast tanks surrounded the Bow Compartment.

Crossing back to the Operations Compartment we continued straight aft passing through the Crew's Mess, filled with rows of tables. Sailors were setting up for lunch. There was storage for frozen and refrigerated food and dry stores. We took a ladder down to the Torpedo Room.

We were at the back of the room. It was filled with green cylindrical shapes that were the weapons, stored on two levels on three platforms that were split by two aisles running to the front of the space. On the lower level, adjacent to the aisles, were rows of bunks. Torpedoes were outboard of the bunks. The room was lit brightly but gray blankets were draped over the sides of the upper platform to darken the berthing area. We headed forward.

"This is a Mark Forty-eight (MK-48) torpedo," indicating a green-colored weapon stowed on an upper spot next to the aisle. "All the way outboard is an encapsulated Harpoon missile. We are carrying two of those and the others are torpedoes." The Harpoon was just a plain green cylinder.

"We have twelve racks here for berthing. We don't have bunks for everyone so a few of the crew need to hot bunk. The Torpedo Room bunks are not shared as a bit of compensation for the less desirable location."

At the front of the room it was easy to spot the torpedo tubes, two port and two starboard, stacked at levels that matched the height of the stowed weapons. Each was angled to the side. A maze of piping surrounded each tube. In the center was a control panel with a sailor seated facing back toward us instead of the panel.

32

"These are the torpedo tubes. In older submarines the Torpedo Room was in the bow. It was moved back to dedicate the bow to the sonar. The tubes are pointed ten degrees outboard but fire control adjusts the course automatically. The panel is the Weapons Launch Console that controls the torpedo tubes. The weapon is expelled by water pressure. You can open the outer door, unlock the breech door or flood the tube from here. The firing of the tube is normally done from Control but it can be done locally.

"Petty Officer (TM3(SS)) Stokes, this is Tom Ryan, who'll be with us to Japan. What do we have loaded?"

"Hello, sir. We have torpedoes in one, two and four and the test set connected to three."

"The ship's battery is just below us. The access hatch is in the crew's berthing just forward. It has one hundred and twenty-six cells, each about as tall as we. The energy stored in the battery is more than that in a torpedo warhead. You'll have a chance to go down later if you want. You'll need to remove all metal from your body first. We enter the well before each time we do a battery charge, several entries a week."

He led me aft again, stopping by the front of a torpedo to remove a blue plastic protective cover to reveal the flat, dinner-plate-sized black tip that was the sonar seeker. We went through the door to a space filled with mechanical equipment.

"This is the Air Regeneration Room. We have two air compressors used to recharge our air banks. There are five banks located in the ballast tanks. One through four are normally full at forty-five hundred PSI and off-line, in reserve for emergencies. Number five is on service, and as we use air, the pressure in the boat will rise. Running an air charge pumps the air back to storage.

"To port we have a catalytic burner that converts carbon monoxide to carbon dioxide and hydrogen to water. Just aft is a scrubber for carbon dioxide. It has a chemical that absorbs the gas when cool. We then heat the chemical to release the CO_2 then dispose of the gas in the ocean and cool the chemical down to absorb more gas. We have a second unit aft but normally only run one. These are both running. Be careful, some parts are hot.

"We store about twenty-one days' oxygen in two banks of cylinders in the forward and aft ballast tanks. We can produce several weeks more by a chemical process using oxygen candles. Here we have one candle furnace. The chemical reaction generates a lot of heat. There is another in the Auxiliary Machinery Space aft. For the transit we'll have plenty of chance to ventilate with fresh air so we shouldn't need them."

The candle furnace was a cylinder, about two-thirds the size of the standard oil drum. The outer surface was an open weave of heavy-duty stainless steel bars. Rinaldi opened a locker containing green cylinders, the candles that would fit inside.

"How long can you stay submerged?"

"With the reactor operating, we are essentially unlimited if we can ventilate. We have the banked oxygen and hundreds of oxygen candles. It takes about one candle per hour to support the crew's needs and that's about how long each burns. That would be good for several weeks with no need for outside air. We are carrying about seventy days food right now and could load about ninety. To do that we'd convert the chilled stores to more frozen and we'd probably be walking on boxes of cans for a bit until we eat our way down to the deck."

"What was the longest you've been under the ocean?"

"Seventy days on my first sub, Michigan, a Trident missile submarine. They have much more space and storage and an oxygen generator to supply the crew by breaking down water into oxygen and hydrogen."

While we talked we walked back to the upper level and headed aft toward the shut watertight door leading to the reactor plant. On the way he pointed out the system that monitored the submarine's atmosphere. There were digital displays for pressure, oxygen level, carbon dioxide, carbon monoxide, hydrogen and two of the types of Freon used in ship's systems. You could monitor the air in any compartment.

By the aft door to port was the ventilation fan room. The door had an airtight seal. The ventilation system could be configured to take suction on any space and push that through the diesel or low-pressure blower to an exhaust at the back of the sail. Fresh air from the snorkel is drawn in to replace the bad air and the bad stuff, smoke, gases or radioactive particles, isn't mixed with the air in the rest of the submarine.

34

There were a few steps leading up to a small platform before the door. He demonstrated how to seal the door by turning the operating bar in the center. When not sealed a lever released the latch that held it shut. There was another latch that went over the door's frame to hold it in the open position. There were two levers, one above each side of the door, to shut off the ventilation lines that went to and from the aft compartments. We went through and he reached back to shut the door.

"We're in the Reactor Compartment now. This is our personnel access from forward to aft, called the Tunnel. It is shielded from most radiation, but it is one of the highest radiation areas onboard. It's rated for three hours per day occupancy but we direct all hands to minimize the time spent in the higher radiation areas. That's not a problem for normal duties, and don't worry, you'll get way less than a dental x-ray dose on this trip."

On the starboard side was an access to the rest of the compartment. The door was secured by three metal strong-backs with the dogs immobilized by wire ties. The access is never opened with the reactor operating. He lifted the cover of a window set in the deck. Below the window was a mirror that could be adjusted to view the brightly lit compartment below. He showed me the reactor vessel. It was topped with twelve cylinders that were the mechanisms to operate the rods controlling the nuclear reaction.

There were three steps down to the next watertight door. The steps were flanked to port by copper piping that was part of a cooling system for reactor plant components and to starboard by piping made from some type of stainless alloy that I hadn't seen elsewhere yet. It would be a distinctive mark of reactor plant piping.

We went through to the next compartment aft, the Auxiliary Machinery Space. There was another platform and some more steps down to the main passageway. Large diameter pipes in the overhead by each side of the door were the steam lines. There were valves with wide, light-tan-colored, solid disks that could be operated by somebody standing on the platform. They were the main steam stop valves and they could be shut remotely by hydraulics.

"Is it always so cold in here?" The compartment was the coolest spot on the submarine so far.

"Yes. By the way, do you mind if I smoke? Engineering is an area where it is allowed."

"Go ahead. It's not a problem for me. I never got the habit. What are the rules?"

"Thanks, Tom." He pulled out a pack, lit up and obviously enjoyed the first puff. "Ex-smokers are the worst. The CO never smoked so he only follows Navy policy. There's no smoking in berthing compartments or in the Crew's Mess or Wardroom during meals or training. Smoking is forbidden during battle stations or ship emergencies. I can smoke in my stateroom if my roommates are not there. Since I write the officer watch bill I put them on the same section when possible so I always have some time. There's usually someone that objects to smoking in Control, Sonar or Maneuvering so that leaves Sonar Equipment, Diesel, Air Regeneration and Engineering as smoking refuges. The Chiefs' Quarters, except berthing, is also smoking friendly, but I can't use that.

"Some submarines have banned smoking in engineering spaces. That actually works well for us because all the smokers on the tender want to work here.

"Let's continue. I have to get you back for lunch in fifteen minutes. We have reactor plant instrumentation and rod control in the cabinets right aft of the steps."

There were aisles leading left and right off the main passage with cabinets on both sides.

"Next are the main electrical switchboards. We have port and starboard electrical busses and the switchboards are port and starboard of the passageway. The aisles on the outboard side of the switchboards have access to the lower level where we have pumps to feed water back to the steam generators in the Reactor Compartment. There are also reactor support systems to charge and discharge water and operate some primary loop isolation valves.

"Let's continue to the Engine Room. The watertight door is open because that is the ventilation air return. There is only one valve, a supply line through the bulkhead. This is a seven hundred foot bulkhead because we have an escape trunk built into the hatch just above the door."

Just on the other side of the door was the ladder leading to the hatch. The lower hatch was shut.

"On the starboard side is Maneuvering, the control center for Engineering. You should request permission to enter Maneuvering. Mr. Ryan requests permission to enter Maneuvering."

"Mr. Ryan, enter Maneuvering," came the reply from inside.

Rinaldi unhooked the metal chain across the entrance and I went in. He followed. Inside were three consoles. The inboard station had two large chromed wheels on the aft end and an array of gauges with a petty officer standing behind it. The next two panels had seats for their operators and an array of switches, lights and dials. On the far end was seated LTJG Reed. Two cases of thick books were beside him. One book was open on the desk just outboard from his stool.

"Mr. Ryan, welcome to Maneuvering."

"You all can call me Tom. I'm just a guest, not an officer."

"Yes, sir. I'll give you the quick brief. Nearest the entrance is the Steam Plant Control Panel (SPCP) manned by Petty Officer (EM2) Tanner, the Throttleman. The wheels control the forward and astern throttles. He can monitor various parameters in the steam system. You see the Engine Order Telegraph on the sloping panel. Ahead standard is the ordered bell and we are doing one hundred twenty turns.

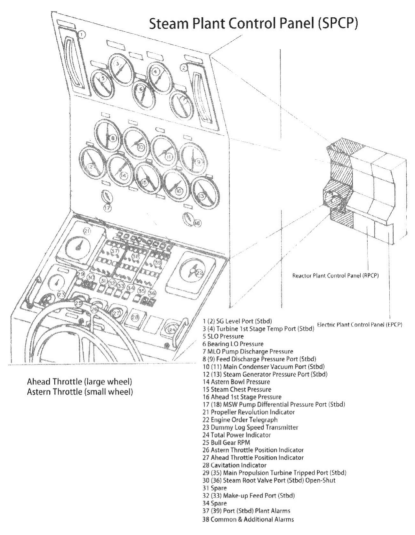

Steam Plant Control Panel (SPCP)

Reactor Plant Control Panel (RPCP)

Electric Plant Control Panel (EPCP)

Ahead Throttle (large wheel)
Astern Throttle (small wheel)

1 (2) SG Level Port (Stbd)
3 (4) Turbine 1st Stage Temp Port (Stbd)
5 SLO Pressure
6 Bearing LO Pressure
7 MLO Pump Discharge Pressure
8 (9) Feed Discharge Pressure Port (Stbd)
10 (11) Main Condenser Vacuum Port (Stbd)
12 (13) Steam Generator Pressure Port (Stbd)
14 Astern Bowl Pressure
15 Steam Chest Pressure
16 Ahead 1st Stage Pressure
17 (18) MSW Pump Differential Pressure Port (Stbd)
21 Propeller Revolution Indicator
22 Engine Order Telegraph
23 Dummy Log Speed Transmitter
24 Total Power Indicator
25 Bull Gear RPM
26 Astern Throttle Position Indicator
27 Ahead Throttle Position Indicator
28 Cavitation Indicator
29 (35) Main Propulsion Turbine Tripped Port (Stbd)
30 (36) Steam Root Valve Port (Stbd) Open-Shut
31 Spare
32 (33) Make-up Feed Port (Stbd)
34 Spare
37 (39) Port (Stbd) Plant Alarms
38 Common & Additional Alarms

Next is the Reactor Plant Control Panel (RPCP) manned by Petty Officer (ET1(SS)) Smith, the Reactor Operator or RO." He pronounced each letter, 'R' 'O'. "He can monitor primary system parameters and there is a big array of alarms, none of which are activated. The center is for shimming the control rods in or out. Then there are controls for main coolant pumps and loop isolation valves.

"In front of me is the Electric Plant Control Panel (EPCP) manned by Petty Officer (EM2(SS)) Allen, the Electrical Operator or EO. We are in our normal underway lineup, called a full-power lineup. Both the turbine generators are powering the port and

starboard electrical busses and the battery is on-line to pick up if
needed in emergency.

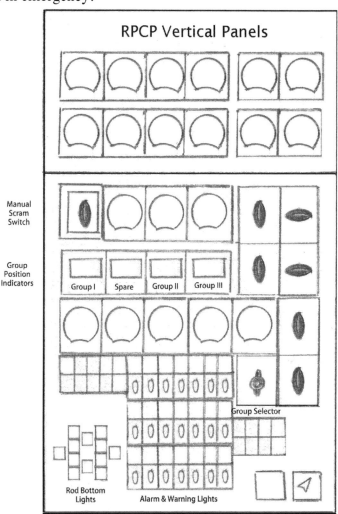

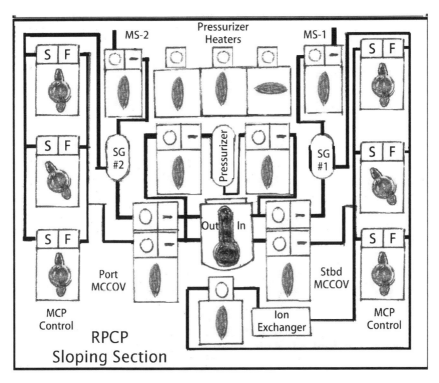

RPCP
Sloping Section

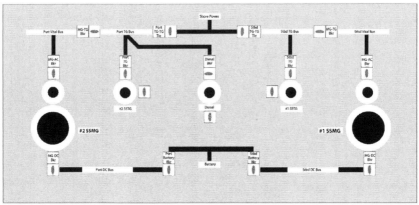

Electric Plant Control Panel - Mimic Bus
(Shown in Normal Full Power Lineup)

"Let's see…what else? Behind you are monitors for temperature and salinity. Putting salty water into the steam generators can lead to tubes cracking. One more, above me are emergency controls to secure seawater piping in the Engine Room or Auxiliary Machinery Space in the event of piping failure and flooding. We can stop it from here in seconds. Of course, then we have to deal with the fact that we lost cooling water for part of the plant."

"I guess that's a lot to take in."

"You'll have a chance to see us in action when we do casualty drills," added Rinaldi. "Thanks, Mr. Reed."

We left and continued aft past the two turbine generators and the main propulsion turbines. There was a panel between the main turbines similar to the SPCP, including the two throttle control wheels. Continuing aft to the reduction gear and shaft. The Emergency Propulsion Motor was built right on the shaft aft of a clutch that could disconnect the reduction gear.

Dropping down a ladder into the lower level we visited bays devoted to lubricating oil. Then, going forward were the condensers and big pumps for seawater. The forward bay had air conditioning plants, seawater piping and a steam distilling plant. The watch indicated that the water was being sent forward to be stored for drinking or washing. We climbed back to the upper level.

"It's surprisingly quiet for all the mechanical devices," I observed.

"We are talking precision machinery, but it's even quieter than you suspect. All the noise and vibration is isolated from the hull. See, up here is a speaker box for the announcing system. It's mounted to the bracket with rubber isolation dampers. Everything is like that.

"We better head forward. I only have a few minutes to get you to lunch. It's bad form to be late."

Chapter 5 - Lunch

Off San Diego, California – 32° 25.7' N 118° 12.8' W
Saturday, August 10, 1991
1300

A single table offset toward the port wall dominated the Wardroom. This allowed passage through the other side of the room and space for storage and a shelf. An 'L' shaped bench with a brown imitation leather cushion provided seating on the forward and far sides with four chairs on the opposite long side and a single chair on the other. A row of cabinets was mounted against the overhead above the long side of the bench and extending the length of the outboard wall. There was a phone box and course, speed and depth indicators inset into the bulkhead aft of the bench.

The walls were clad in a light-color, wood-grain, Formica that was used extensively in the forward compartments. The ceiling was white and held several fluorescent light fixtures that made the room quite bright. An off-white vinyl tile covered the floor.

When the Engineer and I entered a number of the ship's officers were already standing. Most had changed to the blue coverall. I saw the XO on the far side with four others waiting to slip into seats along the bench.

"This is the Captain's seat," Rinaldi said, indicating the single chair. "As our guest, you'll be here," indicating the chair to the right. The Engineer stood behind the next chair.

The table was set with a white tablecloth, place settings for twelve, five on the port side and two on the forward end. There were white cloth napkins in metal napkin rings. Mine had gold dolphins, the submarine officer symbol, and 'GUEST' engraved on it.

At 1300, nearly on the button, the Captain entered, went to his place and sat down. Everyone else took seats.

The Captain started with introductions. "This is Thomas Ryan, who'll be our guest for this trip. I guess most of you have read one or more of his books or seen a movie based on them. He's been cleared for secret and has full plant access, so let's give him a good feel for submarine life. You've met some of my officers, but we'll go around the table for quick introductions."

"Lieutenant Commander George Johnson, Executive Officer and your roommate for the trip."

"Lieutenant Commander Ron Rinaldi, Engineer Officer."

"Lieutenant Commander Henry Cooper, Navigator." Cooper was a strongly built black man over six feet tall.

"Lieutenant Dave Cohen, Sonar Officer." He was mid twenties with an average build and glasses on a thin face, more like a graduate student than a military officer.

"Lieutenant Tony Nguyen, Main Propulsion Assistant."

"Lieutenant Anthony Gordon, Damage Control Assistant. I'm Big Tony in case there's confusion." I doubted there would be any problem telling them apart.

"Lieutenant Junior Grade Tom Jackson, Reactor Controls Assistant." Jackson was another black officer but of normal height and build.

"Lieutenant Junior Grade Kevin McCarthy, Chemistry and Radiological Controls Assistant."

"Lieutenant Junior Grade Jeff Ohanian, Communicator and Forward 'E''T' Division Officer." The letters of the division's name were pronounced individually. He was seated at one of the two spots on the end opposite the Captain.

"Lieutenant Junior Grade Bruce Banner, Supply Officer."

"You don't want to make him mad," added Jackson while Banner groaned.

"I'm honored to be with you for this voyage. Please call me Tom."

A petty officer entered carrying a serving plate stacked with fried chicken. He offered it to me and I took a piece. It was then offered to the Captain and then taken by the XO who passed the plate around the table.

"Petty Officer Glenn (MS3(SS)) is the Wardroom 'M''S'," explained the Supply Officer. "He'll take your breakfast order and bring your food. Breakfast is zero-seven-hundred (0700) to zero-eight-thirty (0830). The other meals are family-style with lunch at eleven-hundred (1100) or thirteen-hundred (1300), depending on whether we're running four or six hour watches during the day. Dinner is at nineteen-hundred (1900)."

"The Chop will be giving you a bill for your meals while onboard," XO added. Bowls of mashed potatoes and peas were passed around.

"Chop?"

"That's short for pork chop," Banner explained. "It's my name. In port I charge officers for the meals they really eat and I get credit for meals I serve to the crew. At sea I charge for every meal whether you eat it or not and get credit for the entire crew for every meal. There's also a modest extra meal allowance for submarines. Since nobody eats every meal we can build up a surplus in the messing account that can be used for special meals."

"I think we eat very well; probably too well, considering the lack of exercise opportunities," said the Captain.

"If the rest of the meals are like this, I would agree. To change the subject, what do you think of the depiction of submarines in books and movies?"

"Well, about a year ago we had an Air Force colonel aboard for a few days of submarine familiarization to assist him in his duties in Pacific Command operations. We were discussing your book, the one with the world war theme. He told me that the aviation sequences were all screwed up but he loved the submarine stuff. Maybe you'll get enough insight this trip to give us the first realistic nuclear submarine novel."

"What did you think of the movie 'Hunt for Red October'?"

"I saw it last summer and we have the videotape onboard. I liked it. The biggest problems were that the Red October didn't need to go anywhere to launch its missiles. The missiles could reach targets in most of the Northern Hemisphere from its base. The other issues were that the submarines had too good a picture of what the other submarines were doing. One on one is hard, multiple submarines and torpedoes are almost impossible. You focus on the highest threat and ignore everything else.

"The movie and the movie company were very popular in the Submarine Force. They donated a number of items from the movie to the Dolphin Scholarship Fund. I bid on a directors chair from the movie. It was supposed to be for Klaus Maria Brandauer. He was signed for the Russian CO role Sean Connery took. Another CO outbid me."

"What is the Dolphin Scholarship Fund?"

"They provide college scholarships to children of submariners, officer and enlisted. It is our only submarine specific charity."

"Captain, may I be excused? I have the next watch," LT Nguyen requested.

"Me too," added McCarthy as the Captain nodded his consent.

As the sailor collected the plates I changed the subject. "Captain, I noticed you wore the Vietnam Service ribbon. Were you on submarines then?"

"Yes, technically I'm a Vietnam veteran from my first submarine tour. Every Pacific submarine would try to get scheduled for a few days in the war zone, usually providing anti-submarine training to the destroyers. I guess it was a good break from the gun line for them. For us it meant the monthly pay for enlisted sailors and the first $500 for officers was tax-free. If we could straddle the end of a month that could be two months break for a day's work. Any sailor that reenlisted in the war zone got the entire reenlistment bonus tax-free too."

"I guess submarines weren't much use in that war."

"There was one operation, though my submarine wasn't tasked for it. The North Vietnamese would run guns to the South using fishing boats as cover. In a rational war we should stop and inspect them, but this was Vietnam. We couldn't take action until the boat entered South Vietnamese territorial waters, and they wouldn't do that if they thought they were being watched. So, a sub was tasked to watch them covertly and everybody else stayed clear. When they made their run the sub called in an airstrike. There's a variant of that still in use today against the narcotics traffic from South America with the Coast Guard and DEA substituting for the airstrike."

Dishes of vanilla ice cream were served for dessert.

"Does it bother you that we lost that war?"

"Not in the way it does the Nguyen family and the millions in and out of South Vietnam. I look at it as one battle in the Cold War with the Soviet Union. We won that war."

"The Soviet Union still exists."

"Yes, but their economy has collapsed. The threat of war in Europe is over. Germany is unified; Poland, Hungary and Czechoslovakia are free. Even if they wanted a war, the Gulf War showed the Red Army would not stand a chance. Sometimes I even think the Walker spy ring may have inadvertently done us a service. By showing the Soviets how badly their submarines were outclassed, they must have caused some doubt about the outcome of any war. It bought time. If you take a long view, with the Berlin Airlift, Korea, Vietnam, the Cuban Missile Crisis and countless other proxy battles along the way, I think we did pretty well. Communism could function, after a fashion, in a nineteenth century industrial economy, but collapsed because it couldn't keep pace with the late twentieth century information technology revolution.

"I think we're due for a Cold War victory medal for everyone who held the line."

"It's an interesting take, but maybe it's best not to gloat when your adversary still has thousands of nuclear weapons."

"Perhaps. XO, we need a good cleanup after the deployment preparations. We normally leave Sunday free but we can't wait for next Saturday."

"Yes, sir. We can shift to our five-section rotation tomorrow and run field day from 1300 to 1800. Do you want to run a zone inspection afterward, as normal?"

"Yes, I'll take Machinery Lower Level."

"Captain, Mr. Ohanian has taken his EOOW" (pronounced 'E' 'OW' as in how) "qualification exam but needs a second scram to be ready for his board. Can we kick off the field day with a quick drill?"

"OK, ENG. We'll run it at 1230 and start the cleanup right after. It will be a good wake-up call. XO announce the drill in the Plan of the Day, so we can get as many trainees involved as possible. ENG, we will hold Mr. Ohanian's board after dinner Sunday. Are you ready for your board, Mr. Ohanian?"

"Yes, Captain."

"NAV, when will we be in an area where we can do the deep dive?"

"We'll be turning west about 1430. By 1500 we should be clear."

46

"Good. We'll be doing angles after the dive. Chop, you've got an hour and a half to get the galley and mess secure."

"No problem. We'll be ready."

"Gentlemen." The Captain stood up and left the Wardroom.

"Mr. Ryan," said the XO. "Come and we'll get you settled."

I followed the XO to his, our, stateroom as the other officers went on their way. The door to the CO's stateroom was open. It was identical in size to the others but had only one bunk. The CO was not there.

At the room, my stuff was still on the upper bunk with some additions, two sets of blue coveralls and a nametag with 'Thomas Ryan' and the ship's seal.

"We have a couple submarine coveralls for you. We figured you're a large. We can change them if they don't fit."

"Large should be fine."

"You'll have this drawer." He pulled out the top drawer of three on the side near the bunks. It was empty, awaiting my stuff. "You can use the desk next to the bunks. If you have hanging clothes, they can go in here." He opened a tall locker near the door. "We have a wash sink here." He pulled down a stainless sink that folded up into the forward wall.

"XO, here's the mail," said a petty officer at the door. "There was one, CO's eyes only, that I gave directly to the Captain."

"Mr. Ryan, This is Petty Officer (YN1(SS)) Mason, our leading yeoman."

"Welcome aboard, Mr. Ryan."

"Nice to meet you, Petty Officer Mason, but everybody, Tom is fine."

"If you need any supplies, just contact me or any of the yeoman. We can do any printing or copying you might need."

"Thanks." He left.

"XO, what's CO's eyes only? Did we get secret orders?"

"We'd never get operational orders in the mail. It's usually some personnel issue that's marked like that for privacy to keep the yeomen from opening it. The Captain will let me know what it is if we have to take some action.

"Do you have a laptop in your briefcase?"

"Yes, I have a Toshiba 1200XE, running Windows 3. It has a 20-megabyte hard drive and a really good, lighted, screen with full VGA resolution. I use it for writing. It has a floppy drive that I use to backup my drafts."

"Sounds nice. We have word processing for the ship's office, but we are pen and paper prior to that. We generally have a very smooth ride, but to keep it safe be sure to put it in the drawer when you're not using it."

"The Captain told the Supply Officer to secure the Galley. What's coming up?"

"You'll see."

Chapter 6 – Deep Dive

Off San Diego, California – 32° 04.6' N 119° 35.9' W
Saturday, August 10, 1991
1500

"Rig ship for deep submergence," blared the announcing system.

I put my laptop in the drawer and walked up to Control. The submarine deck was angled noticeably so walking forward was going slightly downhill, though it was still easy to move around.

"Passing five hundred feet, heading to seven hundred feet," came a report from the Diving Officer of the Watch as I entered the space. I saw it was Senior Chief Spillman. LT Nguyen was on the periscope stand and I saw the Captain over on the left, port, side checking the chart with the Quartermaster.

"Maneuvering, Conn, make turns for twelve knots," Nguyen said into a microphone mounted above the starboard side of the periscope stand.

"Make turns for twelve knots, Maneuvering aye. Making turns for twelve knots," came back immediately over a speaker.

The speed indicated on the display in front of the planesmen dropped slowly from its initial reading of fifteen.

"Passing six hundred feet."

The Chief of the Watch, a petty officer first class, still in dungarees, was getting reports from a sailor who had donned a phone headset. "Mr. Nguyen, the ship is rigged for deep submergence. The evaporator is secured."

"Very well, Chief. Captain, the ship is rigged for deep submergence."

"Thank you, Mr. Nguyen," said the Captain stepping onto the periscope stand.

The Captain picked up a microphone. "This is the Captain," came through speakers. "We are starting our deep dive. Afterward we'll run angles and dangles. You have a few minutes to double check that everything is secure."

The deck leveled off, followed by the report, "At seven hundred feet."

"Very well. All stations check for leaks." This was relayed over the phone network.

A petty officer shined a flashlight up to where the #2 scope penetrated the hull. He shined the light over by #1 and then looked at other areas. "No leaks," he reported.

"The scope packing is why we're doing this evolution. We can't test it to full submergence pressure in port. We blast 100 psi air up from inside the hull and look for bubbles in soapy water spread on the seal in the sail. That test gets us a waiver until we complete the deep dive."

"All stations report no leaks at 700 feet," came the report.

"Very well. Dive, make your depth 900 feet," ordered Nguyen. He acknowledged and the deck tilted slightly as depth began to increase.

"Haddock is a submarine in the Permit or 594 Class. A class is named for the first submarine in the class. It was originally the Thresher or 593 Class, but Thresher was lost in 1963 doing a deep dive like we're doing now."

"Thanks for sharing that little fact."

The crew in Control didn't seem particularly nervous about what was happening so I resolved not to show any apprehension myself.

"Thresher was at her maximum operating depth as part of testing after a shipyard overhaul. There was an escort vessel on the surface that she was in contact with by an acoustic telephone. They reported having minor difficulties and were never seen again until the wreck was discovered on the seafloor.

"The best guess on what happened was a failure of seawater piping in Auxiliary Machinery followed by a loss of propulsion from a reactor shutdown. The shutdown was either caused by the flooding or initiated by the crew. They were unable to blow their ballast tanks to get buoyancy to reach the surface because moisture in the high-pressure air froze to ice and plugged the lines. We think they made it to 200 feet before sinking to a depth that crushed the hull.

"Thresher, as first ship in a new class, was subjected to shock testing just before her overhaul. They set off explosive charges near her hull to cause up to 0.6 of her design shock rating. There are films from the test. I've seen the video version. It's impressive to see the equipment and piping react to the shock. Officially, the shock test had nothing to do with the loss. However, we haven't shock tested a submarine since."

"At 900 feet."

"All stations check for leaks."

"The loss of Thresher resulted in many changes. The biggest was the SUBSAFE certification program. Every repair we do on critical systems is documented and tested. We changed designs as well. We can isolate seawater piping in the propulsion plant in seconds using hydraulically operated valves controlled right from Maneuvering. An emergency blow system was added to push air into our ballast tanks twenty times faster than the normal system that Thresher relied upon. Dehumidifiers were added to remove moisture from the stored air. You've seen the videos of submarines leaping out of the water, that's what happens when we test our emergency blow system from deep depth, and we do test it, every year."

"No leaks reported at 900 feet."

"Dive, make your depth 1,100 feet."

"What would you do if we had flooding like Thresher did?"

"Mr. Nguyen, could you answer that?"

"Yes, sir. At this depth, I'd order an immediate emergency blow. The controls are just above the Ballast Control Panel. Chief of the Watch could you point out the emergency blow actuators for Mr. Ryan." He pointed out a couple valves just above his station. "The Diving Officer would get about a twenty degree up angle and we'd use our speed and propulsion to reach the surface. As we get shallower the lower sea pressure allows air in the ballast tanks to expand and we get even more buoyancy."

"Even if we lost the reactor," continued the Captain, "we could answer a standard bell for about five minutes to help us drive to the surface. Our speed now, twelve knots, is a compromise. The faster we are going the better we are for recovery from flooding, but that puts us at greater risk if we have a planes failure. At flank speed, a stern planes failure on full dive might result in a three to four hundred foot depth excursion, which is dangerous if we're already near our maximum depth."

"At 1,100 feet."

"All stations check for leaks."

"How deep could we go before hull failure?"

"The design spec is 50% below our test depth, but there is probably some conservative engineering assumptions built into that calculation so we might get a few hundred feet extra. It won't help us here. We have about 2,000 feet of water below us and that's way too much.

"There have been submarines that have, inadvertently, exceeded their maximum depth. One reason was a stuck digital depth gauge. That's why we have it covered for deep submergence."

I hadn't noticed before, but it was covered. I glanced up at the mechanical gauge. It read 1,100.

"We have a sailor on the phones back at a sea pressure gauge in the Engine Room. He reports pressure that is compared to the depth gauge as an independent backup. It's about 44 psi each 100 feet of depth. That's around 490 pounds on each square inch of our hull here at 1,100 feet. It actually results in a small decrease in the hull diameter from compression as we go deeper. The pressure hull is inches thick high tensile steel, welded, every few feet, to frames that are like massive 'I' beams formed into circular hoops. You can look at the frames easiest in the Engine Room where they are on the inside of the hull. In the Bow Compartment and Auxiliary Machinery, the frames are outside and form part of the structure of the ballast tanks."

"All stations have reported. Engineering reports 10 drops per minute leak from the mechanical seal of #2 main seawater pump and about half a cup per minute from the shaft seal."

"Very well. Dive, make your depth 1,300 feet."

"The crew seems alert but not concerned or nervous."

"We rarely operate this deep for extended periods. We don't expect a problem, but we have personnel on the phones at every level of every compartment reporting conditions. The shaft seal is designed to have some small leakage and the pump seal drip, while not normal, is too small to be of concern."

"At 1,300 feet."

"All stations check for leaks."

A couple minutes later came the report, "Engineering has 15 drops per minute from #2 main seawater pump and three-quarters cup from shaft seal. Other stations report no leaks."

"Dive, make your depth 700 feet. Use twenty up angle." Dive acknowledged. The deck took a significant slant.

"Mr. Nguyen, I'll take the conn," said the Captain.

"Yes, Captain. Quartermaster, Captain has the conn."

"Dive, make your depth 200 feet, twenty up. Helm, all ahead full."

They acknowledged and speed started to increase as the Diving Officer called out each 100 feet change. At 1,000 feet "Secure from Deep Submergence" was announced. The planesman's first action was to uncover the digital depth gauge. The digits spun rapidly as depth decreased.

At 250 feet the Diving Officer ordered, "Full dive both planes." Both control sticks were shoved fully forward. The angle started to come off but not quickly enough. "Passing 200 feet. 190. 180. 170." Finally the ascent stopped. "Take charge of your planes. Five degree down bubble. Conn, 160 feet returning to 200 feet."

"Dive, make your depth 700 feet. Use a twenty degree down bubble."

The deck tilted again as I held the rail surrounding the periscope stand. The Captain and Nguyen had hold of the two periscopes. Others had hold of whatever equipment was handy with the Diving Officer bracing himself against the chair back of the stern planesman.

This time full rise was ordered about 100 feet short of the ordered depth and the ship pulled nearly level a dozen feet short of the ordered depth and eased right on to 700 feet.

The next order was 200 feet at twenty-five up. There was a bang from somewhere on the level below Control. The crew controlling depth was getting better as we didn't overshoot this time.

800 feet at twenty-five down was next. 200 feet at thirty up was followed by 800 feet at thirty down. There was another bang as something slipped loose.

"Helm, all ahead flank," ordered the Captain. Helm acknowledged and turned the telegraph.

The lights dimmed momentarily. "What was that?"

"The main coolant pumps are shifted to fast speed when we order flank," explained Nguyen. "It's a big load dropped onto the turbine generators."

The speed started to come up from the twenty knots we were doing at full speed until we indicated just over twenty-five knots.

"Left full rudder," ordered the Captain.

"Left full rudder, Helm aye. My rudder is left full."

"Passing two-six-zero," reported the helmsman, who had his control wheel turned fully left.

"Belay your headings," said the Captain.

The submarine's deck tilted steeply to port and took a down angle. The planes were pulled to rise as depth began to increase. 820, 830, 840 feet passed before depth stabilized. The ship control was helped by speed dropping in the turn.

The Captain ordered steady on course two-zero-zero and allowed the speed to build back to over twenty-four knots as we regained the 800 foot depth.

"Helm, right full rudder, steady three-three-zero."

"Right full rudder, steady three-three-zero, Helm aye. My rudder is right full."

The ship heeled toward starboard side and angled down again, but less than before as the planes were used promptly to counter the effect of the rudder. We took only a twenty-foot excursion before stabilizing.

"That was good, Senior Chief. Well done to your ship control team."

"Thank you, Captain."

"Helm, left five degrees rudder, steady two-seven-zero. Dive, make your depth five hundred feet. Mr. Nguyen, will you take the conn."

"Yes, sir. Ahead flank, coming to five hundred feet, coming left to two-seven-zero. I relieve you of the conn."

"I stand relieved."

"Quartermaster, this is Mr. Nguyen. I have the deck and the conn."

"Captain, this is the clearance message for the scope packing. It's ready for your release," said the Navigator, stepping up to the periscope stand.

"OK, NAV." The Captain signed the paper on the clipboard. "When do you want to transmit?"

"There's a Transit pass at 1650. We can catch that, transmit our outgoing and clear the midnight Zulu broadcast."

"That sounds good, NAV. Mr. Nguyen, I want you to be at periscope depth by 1640. Catch the NAVSAT, transmit our outgoing, clear the 1700 local broadcast and ventilate the ship for half an hour."

"Aye, sir. Periscope depth by 1640, NAVSAT, transmit, clear broadcast and ventilate."

"I'll be in my stateroom."

The Captain left Control, followed by LCDR Cooper, who stopped to check the chart and talk with the Quartermaster before heading to Radio.

Chapter 7 – Periscope Depth

Off San Diego, California – 32° 04.1' N 119° 47.3' W
Saturday, August 10, 1991
1600

"It's 1600. Time to get ready," stated Mr. Nguyen. "Petty Officer (FTG1(SS)) Quinn, rig the periscope. Helm, all ahead two-thirds. Dive, make your depth 150 feet."

As Helm and Dive acknowledged the orders, Quinn pulled out an object from behind the fire control consoles. It was a ring, about six inches high and a foot wide, split in two sections, which clamped about the fairing that surrounded the hole in the deck where the #2 periscope dropped.

"What is this, Petty Officer Quinn?"

"Mr. Ryan, Mr. Nguyen is too short. We can stop the scope at his eye height but it would be too low to make the connections for the antennas and electronics. We designed this to fix the problem. The other officers step back a little and can still use the scope with this in place."

"Thanks. You can call me Tom."

"Mr. Ryan, excuse me sir," Nguyen interrupted, "but in Control we are a bit more formal. In messing or berthing areas or on individual watches it's more casual when no evolutions are in progress. The ring works really well. Before we made it I was standing on the fairing, only a couple inches wide."

"At 150 feet."

"Sonar, Conn, report all contacts," Nguyen said out loud.

"Conn, Sonar, we hold one contact, Sierra-8, bearing one-seven-five. Sending it to fire control."

"We have an open mike to allow Sonar to listen to Control," Nguyen explained. "It means I can talk with them when I'm on the scope or working a contact solution."

"Mr. Nguyen, we held Sierra-8 for about forty minutes," reported Quinn. "Initial bearing was two-zero-eight." He indicated a paper plot hung over one of the fire control consoles. "We're getting the data in fire control now."

Dots were being displayed on the cathode ray tube of the display with text along the sides and bottom. Quinn adjusted some knobs and the dots formed a vertical line down the screen with new dots appearing at the top every few seconds.

"This is our contact, Mr. Ryan," said Nguyen, indicating a CRT display on the vertical panel that formed the aft end of the periscope stand. It looked like the displays I'd seen in Sonar. The contact was a darker line, angled a bit to the left.

"Sonar, Conn, do you have a classification on Sierra-8?"

"Conn, Sierra-8 is classified as a merchant, doing 120 turns on a single four."

"Conn, aye. We'll be clearing baffles to port."

"Clearing baffles to port, Sonar, aye."

"Helm, left twenty degrees rudder, steady one-five-zero."

"Left twenty degrees rudder, steady one-five-zero, Helm, aye. My rudder is left twenty."

As the ship turned the dots on the display began to diverge from vertical. Quinn fiddled with the knobs.

"Passing one-six-zero to steady on one-five-zero."

"Try a speed of 12 to 15 knots. That should be good for a merchant," suggested Nguyen.

"Steady one-five-zero."

"Sonar, Conn, we've cleared our baffles, report all contacts."

"Conn, Sonar, hold just one contact, Sierra-8, bearing one-seven-three."

"Conn, aye."

"I have a decent solution on Sierra-8," stated Quinn. "Course zero-one-five, speed twelve, range 28,000 yards. The display dots were stacked vertically again, except for a bit of a bow where we changed course.

"Helm, right twenty degrees rudder, steady two-seven-zero." Helm acknowledged and Nguyen informed Sonar.

When steady he asked for another report on contacts and adjusted the solution on Sierra-8 a bit to 27,000 yards and course 018°. Then he ordered speed one-third. Nguyen picked up a phone and turned the crank a couple turns.

"Captain, Conn, I'm at 150 feet, course two-seven-zero, ahead one-third. I've cleared baffles and hold one contact, Sierra-8, bearing one-six-nine. I've a good solution and it's outside twenty-thousand yards and won't be a problem. Request permission to go to periscope depth and conduct the ordered evolutions."

"Zero-one-eight." A slight pause then, "Go to periscope depth, aye, sir." He hung the phone in its cradle.

"Dive, make your depth 58 feet. Raising #2 scope." Nguyen twisted an orange ring that surrounded the scope well above head height.

"58 feet, Dive, aye. Eight up. Full rise on the fairwater planes. Line up to flood auxiliary trim from sea."

The silvery barrel of the scope rose into the hull above Control. The eyepiece assembly and below it a thicker gray cylinder rose from the deck. It stopped. Nguyen flipped down two handles and rotated an eyepiece and began turning the scope barrel in circles.

"#2 scope and fairing indicate up," reported the Chief of the Watch. A couple lights on his panel had changed.

"Passing 100 feet...90...80. Zero bubble. Take charge of the fairwater planes. Flood auxiliary 3000. 70 feet."

"Breaking," announced Nguyen, who started to spin the scope around rapidly, one full turn, then a second as the Diving Officer reported 68 feet and the Chief of the Watch counted out the total flooded in thousand pound increments.

"No close contacts," reported Nguyen. "Conducting air search."

"At 58 feet," reported Dive. "Flood another thousand."

"No air contacts. Conducting high power search." He conducted a couple circles with the periscope, taking a bit under a minute for each. "Fire Control, what's the bearing for Sierra-8?"

"One-six-six," reported Quinn.

Nguyen looked down and adjusted the scope, to look port and a bit aft. "I don't see it," he said after searching around that direction.

"I still have it at 26,000 yards," stated Quinn.

"Conn, Radio, in synch on the broadcast," came over the speaker. Quinn grabbed a mike and acknowledged. Nguyen was busy on the scope.

"Dive, 56 feet, prepare to ventilate. Quinn, please take the scope."

58

These were acknowledged and the Chief of the Watch passed "Prepare to ventilate" over the announcing system.

"Captain, Conn, at periscope depth and hold no visual contacts," said Nguyen over the phone.

"Request permission to raise the snorkel mast," asked the Chief of the Watch.

It was given and he flipped a switch on his panel. "Snorkel mast indicates up. Request permission to test the head valve." That was also granted and he did some operations at his panel while Quinn called out 'Open' and 'Shut' while looking forward through the periscope. When the valve shut there was a loud 'clunk' coming from above Control.

"Head valve tested satisfactorily."

"Ship is prepared to ventilate," reported the Diving Officer.

"Commence ventilating."

That was acknowledged and then passed over the announcing system. The COW announced opening the outboard induction and ventilation exhaust valves, using switches on his panel. Two indicators turned from straight lines to circles. Another switch started the low-pressure blower.

"Ship is ventilating, sir. Time 1648. Request permission to start an air charge."

"Very well, Dive. Start an air charge, two compressors."

"Start a two compressor air charge, Dive aye."

"Conn, Radio, we're set up to transmit when you are ready."

"Very well, Radio. We'll transmit after we copy the NAVSAT."

"Locked on to the satellite," reported the Quartermaster.

"I'll take the scope, Petty Officer Quinn."

Nguyen replaced Quinn searching with the periscope. There was a clunk.

"Head valve shut," reported the COW.

"58 feet going up now," reported DOOW. There was another sound. "56 feet."

"Head valve open."

"Mr. Ryan, would you like to look through the periscope?"

"Of course. Thanks. What just happened with the head valve?"

"The head valve is on the top of the snorkel mast. It has a sensor that shuts it if it gets wet to keep water from entering the boat."

"What if it failed?"

"We'd take water down the induction mast until we shut the outboard induction valve from the Ballast Control Panel or the inboard induction manually.

"Here's how the scope operates. You can pick the eye you want to use and flip the eyepiece to partially cover the other eye." He demonstrated. "The right handle controls elevation to look up or down with a twist of the handle. Also on the right are buttons that engage a power-assist for turning the scope. Push with your thumb to go right and push the button on the other side with your index finger to turn left. The left handle controls magnification. Twist toward you for high power and away for low. The knob above the handles on the right controls focus."

He stepped back to let me try. Looking through I saw the ocean. There were small swells stretching to the horizon. It was a sunny day.

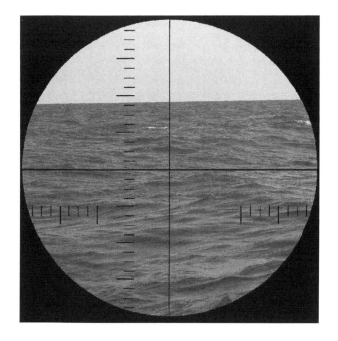

The view through the periscope was circular like the view through binoculars, but with crossed lines dividing the image into quadrants. There were marks all along the vertical line and partly below the horizontal. I tried the controls, adjusting the position of the horizon and changing the magnification.

"What is the purpose of the markings?"

"The vertical line marks the center. Put that over the target and press the red button on the right handle and you send the bearing to fire control. The divisions help you estimate the range of the target. As a rule of thumb, a ship with a 100-foot-high mast at 8000 yards is one division in high power. The high power image is the same as you see through our binoculars."

I was turning around and saw a mast. "Is that our snorkel mask?"

"Yes, You're looking forward. The red object sticking up is a mechanical indicator that the head valve is open. It retracts so it's not visible when the valve shuts. The wire is the snorkel whip antenna."

"We're bringing air in. Where does the air go?"

"The air is brought in with fans and distributed around the ship from the fan room. The low-pressure blower takes air from the ship and pumps it overboard. We could direct the air to our ballast tanks if we were surfacing, but now, it's going to the exhaust where it is diffused into the water at the aft end of our sail."

"I'll take the scope now."

"Satellite onboard, plotting the fix now," came from the Quartermaster.

"Petty Officer Quinn check if Radio is ready to transmit."

"Radio, Conn, are you ready to transmit?"

"Conn, Radio, we're getting the downlink broadcast now. We'll call you back when we're ready."

"We need to search continuously with the periscope. Coming up you look underwater for shapes or shadows. As the scope breaks you do a couple quick circles in low power looking for any contacts. If you see anything it's probably close and you might have to take immediate action to avoid a collision."

"Wouldn't you hear something close on the sonar?"

"Not necessarily. Sound in water is tricky. Anyway, if there is something close, I'd order 'Emergency Deep' and lower the scope. Dive would flood auxiliaries, put dive on the planes and go back to 150 feet. Helm rings up a Standard bell. We limit our angle to three degrees to avoid kicking the stern up into danger."

"Have you had to use that often?"

"I haven't seen it used for real, but we practice it."

"Conn, Radio, ready to transmit. Request you raise the BRA-34."

"Chief of the Watch, raise the BRA-34."

"Raise the BRA-34, aye. BRA-34 coming up. BRA-34 indicates up."

"Petty Officer Quinn, order Radio to transmit."

"Radio, transmit, aye. Radio, Conn, transmit."

"Transmit, Radio aye."

I spotted the Navigator over by the Quartermaster and moved over to see. He was examining a nautical chart.

"Mr. Cooper, what are you doing?"

"You can call me NAV. We just got a fix from the NAVSAT. I'm double checking the plotting of the fix and directing the Quartermaster to use it to reset our 'D''R'."

"What's a 'D''R'?"

"That's short for our position by dead reckoning. This is the chart we're using. The line drawn on it is our proposed track. It was directed in our movement order. We're allowed to be 50 nautical miles ahead or 100 behind and within 10 miles to either side. The track times are marked. Our previous fix was just before we dived. We advance that based on our course, speed and the time. This is done by hand. Here is the plot where we cleared baffles. We project our DR into the future four hours to see if it points to any trouble.

"As a check on the hand DR we plot or position from SINS, that's ship's internal navigation system. This is the SINS position. There's about two miles divergence and our fix is a bit closer to SINS than the hand DR. We'll reset our DR to the new fix and ease back to the center of our corridor."

"Conn, Radio, transmitted the outgoing and received satellite response. Clear on the zero Zulu broadcast. Finished with the BRA-34."

That was acknowledged and the mast lowered.

"We are on a twelve hour broadcast. Each message is repeated on six broadcasts that start on the even Zulu hour. The satellite system dumps all the messages every fifteen minutes and we copy the broadcast on VLF too. We normally copy a broadcast every eight hours but anyone sending something to us has to assume it could take twelve hours for us to receive and act on it."

"How often do we transmit?"

"As little as possible. We assume that any transmission will be intercepted, and at least, an approximate position obtained. We're still not far from San Diego, so our position isn't unusual. We might transmit again a day before arriving in Yokosuka to give the base a heads up on any critical parts or repairs we might need. That's not important as the Soviet spy satellites will see us in port there the next day."

"Dive, secure ventilating, pressurize ship," Nguyen ordered. It was 1718.

"Secure ventilating, pressurize ship, aye."

It was passed then on the announcing system.

The Chief of the Watch called out pressure as I felt my ears pop. "Point one...point two...point three. Head valve shut, outboard induction shut, straight board. Lowering the snorkel mast."

"Recirculate," Nguyen ordered and it was acknowledged and passed on the announcing system.

"We'll be heading deep to resume our transit. We generally try to stay toward the front of our moving box."

"What happens if we go outside it?"

"Nothing good. If we have a casualty that prevents us keeping up with our track, we'd have to send a message to report it. That's why it pays to stay ahead. It gives us time to resolve any problems. Going out by mistake reflects badly on the ship, not to mention my performance as Navigator. There could be another submarine assigned those waters and that risks a collision."

"If nothing happens who would know?"

"We'd have to report it. Trying to cover it up raises all sort of integrity issues and that's much worse than an error in navigation."

"Ship is recirculating," Dive reported.

"Very well. Make your depth 400 feet. Helm, all ahead two-thirds."

"Two-thirds, aye. Answers two-thirds."

"400 feet, aye. Five down."

"Scope is under, lowering the scope." Nguyen flipped the handles and eyepiece to vertical and twisted the orange ring, causing the scope to descend through the deck.

"68 feet."

"Scope indicates down."

"Passing 100 feet going to 400."

"456 fathoms beneath the keel," reported the Quartermaster.

Nguyen went to the phone and turned the crank. "Captain, Conn, completed evolutions at periscope depth. Going to 400 feet and full speed to resume our transit... Go to flank, aye, sir."

"Passing 200 feet headed to 400."

"Helm, all ahead standard. Dive, make your depth 500 feet."

"All ahead standard, Helm aye. Answers all ahead standard."

"500 feet, Dive aye."

"432 fathoms."

"We use soundings as a check on our navigation," explained the Navigator. "In this section we have set 200 fathoms as our Yellow Sounding. If we get that it means we're not where we think we are. There is no water that shallow along this part of the track. Yellow is caution. We need to fix our position. If we see 100 fathoms it's a Red Sounding, meaning danger, slow, go shallow, reverse course to avoid hitting the bottom. At high speed we might not have much time to react."

"Passing 300 feet, heading for 500.

"Does that ever happen?"

"Unfortunately, too often, sometimes causing major damage. Haddock hit the bottom off San Diego back in 1987. There was no damage, but it was not good for the career of anybody involved."

"Passing 400 feet, heading to 500."

"I've got to go. You'll want to be sure to make dinner. Saturdays underway are always pizza night."

"Thanks."

"At 500 feet."

"Very well, Dive. Helm, all ahead flank."

"All ahead flank, Helm aye. Answers all ahead flank."

"Why did the lights not dim this time?"

"The main coolant pumps were already in high speed. Once we shift up, I'd have to order Maneuvering to downshift them."

"Shifting to high speed mode," reported the Diving Officer. "Shift stern planes to emergency."

I moved to the forward end of the periscope stand just behind the Diving Officer's seat, a padded circular disk, mounted to the railing framing the raised area.

"I've been watching your ship control party. I'm quite impressed with the teamwork displayed."

"Thanks sir. I'm Senior Chief Spillman, the Leading Quartermaster and Assistant Navigator. The Chief of the Watch is Petty Officer O'Leary, the leading first auxiliaryman. On the outboard station and stern planes is Seaman (SN) McCain, on the sail planes and Helm, Quartermaster Seaman (QMSN) Porter and the messenger is Seaman Apprentice (SA) Rogers."

"I'm honored to be aboard with you. What is high speed mode?"

"Let's see," said Spillman. "At low speed, like at periscope depth, we use both planes. The stern planes for control of angle and the sail planes are for depth. At intermediate speeds, say 12 to 18 knots, we set the sail planes at zero and control depth with the stern planes only. At high speed we shift the stern planes to emergency, set to a neutral angle, about half a degree dive right now. That reduces the risk of a planes failure to rise or dive, which is a serious emergency at high speed. At high speeds a small motion of the sail planes is enough to control our depth.

"A bit more dive on the stern planes." The planesman pushed his stick forward and then back to neutral. The indicator moved a fraction of a degree. "Good. Shift helm outboard." The sail planesman flipped a switch and locked his wheel while the stern planesman unlocked his and tested his control with tiny rudder movements.

"It doesn't take much to affect the ship at this speed."

"That's true. We normally use the rule of one hundred divided by our speed to limit the maximum planes angle for normal maneuvers, so four degrees for our current speed.

"Would you like to try a turn on the planes?"

"Thanks, but not at this speed. How do you train for casualties?"

"When we're in port for our quarterly maintenance periods, we try to get each ship control party an afternoon at the diving trainer. We can simulate almost every casualty with full motion on a hydraulic platform."

"Thanks senior chief; you too, Mr. Nguyen. I have some notes to write. One last question, Mr. Nguyen, why did you pressurize the air before going deep?"

"We were running an air charge while we ventilated to top up the service air bank. When we finished our ventilation time we still had a few hundred pounds of pressure to go. The air compressors would reduce the pressure of the air we breathe like being at high altitude, so we add a bit, and when we finish the air charge, pressure will be about normal. We just keep the fans drawing air in from outside after we secure the blower and we can add a few tenths of a psi."

"Won't the pressure increase again as we use air from storage?"

"Yes, but you won't notice the change normally. It does change the partial pressure of oxygen in the air. We keep it between 140 and 160 millimeters of mercury. Too low is dangerous and too high raises the fire danger. The Auxiliary Electrician Forward monitors everything hourly and I review it. We're at 158 on oxygen and about 0.4 percent on carbon dioxide. We're running a CO_2 scrubber and a $CO-H_2$ burner to keep things in our normal bands. As long as we can ventilate a couple of times a day we won't need to bleed any oxygen or burn candles."

"There's a lot to keep track of," I remarked.

Nguyen laughed.

Chapter 8 – Sunday

Eastern Pacific – 32° 14.7' N 123° 58.2' W
Sunday, August 11, 1991
0915

I'd slept through breakfast. There was no sense of motion while the submarine was submerged.

As I returned from a shower in the officers' head, the XO was working at the inboard desk.

"Good morning. If you're hungry you can find bread and a toaster in the Wardroom Pantry, but you'll have to wait until 1000. The Catholics have the Wardroom for the weekly lay-leader worship service. The Protestants are holding a service in the Crew's Mess. You're welcome to join them if you want. With the name Ryan, I'd assume Catholic."

"Yes, Catholic, but I'll pass."

"A word on some ship procedures. We take Navy showers to save on water usage. Turn the water on to wet your body. Then turn it off while you soap your skin. Then back on to rinse off."

"Don't we make enough water?"

"We can make 8000 gallons a day with the evaporator, but we will be doing drills and can't run it full time. We need about 1000 gallons a day for propulsion plan uses and about twice that for the crew if we're careful.

"The next item is really important. When you use the toilet your waste goes to sanitary tank #2. When it gets full we get rid of the tank's contents by pressurizing the tank and blowing it into the ocean. Normally we do that when we're at periscope depth on the overnight watches. When we're doing that the auxiliaryman will first post a sign on each stall securing it until the tank is blown and vented to normal pressure. It takes about half an hour to forty-five minutes.

"If you forget about the sign and open the valve to drain your stuff, the tank's contents will blow back in your face. Besides being filthy and mightily embarrassed, you will be the one to clean up the head."

"Does this happen often?"

"I've seen it a few times in my career on submarines. Nobody does it twice."

"What if I really need to use the facilities?"

"Some go with the intention of not flushing until the system is returned to service. That group includes all those that forgot and flushed anyway. The better choice is the urinal in the Engine Room. It's on a different sanitary tank."

"Since we're on wastes, what happens to the waste from the showers and galley?"

"The shower water and wash water from the galley drain to #1 sanitary. Since it's liquid, we can pump it overboard and never need to secure service. The solid waste is compacted, weighted and dumped to the bottom of the ocean via the trash disposal unit or TDU. It's like a vertical torpedo tube located in the Scullery. We generally shoot trash on the overnight watch too, and for all overboard disposals, only when we're far out to sea and in deep water."

"It seems even simple things are hard on a submarine." I had gotten dressed in my coveralls. "I think I'll walk around."

"Sure. We've shifted to our five-watch rotation so lunch is at 1100. Dinner is at 1900 like yesterday and midrats at 0100, if you stay up late. We run three, four-hour watches during the day because it fits our training plan."

"I'll see you for lunch then."

The Captain's stateroom door was open. He was sitting at his desk reading a paperback.

"Good morning, Captain."

"Morning, Tom. Did you have a good night?"

"Yes, thank you. What are you reading?"

"Not one of yours. 'Mutation' by Robin Cook. I have with me about fifty; science fiction, mystery, techno-thrillers and assorted nonfiction on history and science. I find I have lots of time for reading on the long transits when we're deployed."

"I'm going to look around. See you at lunch."

I took the steps to the upper level. I decided to stop in Control. LT Gonzales was on watch. He spotted me as I entered.

"Good morning, Mr. Ryan."

"Good morning. What do you have going on?"

"It's a quiet watch. We're at flank speed trying to get further ahead of PIM. The last watch was at periscope depth for the 1400 Z broadcast and we'll just run fast."

Chief Lloyd was DOOW again with TM1(SS) Sheldon as COW. There were different planesmen from the initial dive but I recognized Petty Officer McKay and Seaman James from the Maneuvering Watch. They were in high-speed mode and I saw we indicated 25.5 knots.

I went to the chart where QM1(SS) Lamar was on watch. The chart showed only ocean with our intended track marked and our estimated position. I asked Lamar about it. He explained that the track is plotted on a small-scale chart containing a good chunk of the Pacific Ocean and then transferred to individual charts holding the most detailed information for each piece of the transit. Each chart was updated with the latest corrections and checked by Senior Chief Spillman and the Navigator before being approved by the Captain. I saw his signature in the corner dated 8/8/91.

Looking at the chart I noted that the ocean here was over 2,000 fathoms, 12,000 feet. The chart had a note of Yellow Sounding, 1500 fathoms, and Red Sounding, 1,000 fathoms, but I saw nothing indicated anywhere above 1,800 fathoms.

On the way out I saw the contact plot. We'd no contacts for several hours, so I decided to skip Sonar and headed aft. There was a sailor recoding information on a clipboard. I introduced myself. The sailor was IC1(SS) Keller, the Auxiliary Electrician Forward or AEF. He was reading the atmosphere analyzer where a number of parameters were displayed on several digital readouts. He could check samples from various locations throughout the submarine but it was normally selected to the main fan room to get an overall reading.

I saw air pressure read 752 torr. We had just completed an air charge about an hour ago, he explained. Oxygen was 154 torr, with CO_2 at 6 torr. Hydrogen was zero percent, with CO and the two types of Freon they used, R-12 and R-114, at small parts per million and well within specification.

"It's not what I expected. I guess I thought it might smell a bit, maybe stale or like a locker room with so many people in a small space, but it smells normal."

"It should smell good. All the air goes through activated charcoal filters. We just changed them two weeks ago, both the fan room and the sanitary tank vents. Excuse me, sir, I have to continue my rounds."

As Keller went forward I continued aft and opened the door to the Tunnel. There was a sailor with a couple instruments in the space. It was MM3 Shafter, the Engineering Laboratory Technician (ELT), conducting a radiation survey while the propulsion plant was at 100% power. He had an instrument that looked like a black cylinder about a foot in diameter that detected neutrons and a gray box with a couple of silver tubes attached by a cord that was a standard Geiger counter for measuring beta and gamma radiation. The Geiger counter was indicating about 20 millirem per hour. He assured me that was normal, but when he suggested I continue aft, I didn't hesitate.

The Auxiliary Machinery Space was as cool as I remembered from the tour. I saw LCDR Rinaldi seated at a workbench at the aft end. He was smoking a cigarette with the remnants of a few others visible in a metal ashtray on the bench. He was working with a couple large loose-leaf binders with a senior chief seated beside him.

"Good morning Engineer. What are you doing?"

"Tom, morning. This is Senior Chief Electricians Mate (EMCS(SS)) Jay, the leading chief of the Engineering Department. We're going over the drills for this afternoon and next week. We have records of the drills we've run on each watch section and how well they did."

"What is the procedure?"

"We do three sections of drills, Monday to Friday, unless we are assigned an operation that precludes them. We can often do drills that won't impact propulsion or require us to make noise even when we have operational tasks. Being a mechanical rabbit for a P-3 isn't very demanding. They don't mind if we make noise and let them find us. Then we can practice breaking contact.

"Anyway, a long transit like this is perfect. On the morning watch, eight to twelve, we run drills that don't sound a ship's alarm or need off-watch personnel to assist. For the next watches we run the big drills, fires, flooding, steam ruptures and reactor casualties. I have a cadre drill team headed by Senior Chief and a few others that are off the watch rotation. The morning drills are done with the cadre and the big drills might have a dozen or more to conduct and critique the drill. We draw the extras from the oncoming watch because we use the off-going watch to assist the personnel on watch as needed."

"I'll be interested in seeing it in action."

"We'll be briefing today's reactor scram in the Wardroom at 1230."

"What about drills outside engineering?"

"The CO definitely emphasizes engineering drills, but most exercise the whole ship too. Every Tuesday and Thursday we hold battle stations on the first afternoon session and add a casualty drill initiated forward."

"I see. If I can switch topics, what is that I see hanging above all the watertight doors?"

"That's actually not a change in topic. They're smoke curtains, made out of Nomex nylon. All nuclear ships have a major safety inspection about every fifteen months. It's called an Operational Reactor Safeguards Examination, or ORSE, conducted by a board of officers attached to CINCPACFLT's staff. As the Captain tells it, when he was a junior officer the drills were more simple and straightforward. As crews got better the drills got tougher.

"One addition was to mark down a crew if they didn't simulate the reduced visibility that results from the heavy smoke from a fire. Almost everyone now uses a translucent shower cap that's snapped over the visor of the breathing masks everyone dons. You can only discern shapes. We'll let you try it on our next fire drill.

"Then they started to require us to simulate bigger fires that required two fire hoses to combat. That required that we open the Engine Room door to run a hose from the AMS. When we did that, it let the simulated smoke spread. Crews adopted smoke curtains over an open watertight door to contain the smoke while still allowing running a hose.

"The board countered by requiring us to simulate ruptured hoses and stuck shut fire nozzles. Crews then staged extra lengths of hose and nozzles. We even added a 'Y' gate on our fire connection in the Engine Room so we could use two hoses without opening the door. They now require three hoses on some drills.

"The Captain was involved in a recent innovation when he was XO. When there's a fire we secure ventilation fans in the space to avoid fanning the flames. They were normally kept off until the sub was ready to evacuate the smoke using the diesel or blower. He remembered that the NAVSEA, that's the Naval Sea Systems Command, manual on submarine damage control said that our electrostatic precipitators and our cooling coils were effective in removing smoke. It was 90% for precipitators and 50% for the cooling coils. When you did the calculation for any compartment it turned out that half the smoke is removed every three minutes just by restarting the fans once the fire is put out.

"The Board was surprised, since they'd not seen that before, but the calculation was solid and based on official sources, so they had to accept it. After a few minutes you could restore normal vision and that greatly helps. You still need the breathing masks since we must ventilate to restore oxygen and remove CO_2 and carbon monoxide.

"Is this just training for the exam or does it apply in the real world?"

"You never know what the real world will throw at you. I hope my engineers will see enough situations in training to react properly if they need to."

"I hope you never need to find out."

Chapter 9 – Reactor Scram

Eastern Pacific – 33° 40.0' N 125° 51.5' W
Sunday, August 11, 1991
1230

There were three sailors besides the ENG and Senior Chief Jay in the Wardroom when I entered and took a seat on the bench at the forward end of the table. The Captain entered and everyone started to stand up.

"Seats, please." He took his place at the end of the table. "ENG, get started."

"The drill today is a reactor scram. It has been preannounced so there's no need to rig for drills. We have trainees as EOOW, Electrical Operator, Reactor Operator and Throttleman."

"Also Engine Room Supervisor and Machinery Lower Level," added Jay.

"I'm monitoring in Maneuvering. Senior Chief is monitoring the Engine Room Upper Level actions. Petty Officer Howard is in Machinery Lower Level. Petty Officer Smith will initiate the drill on my signal with the manual scram switch in AMS and then return it to normal. Smith and I get radios. We let the scram continue until all loads are assumed on the battery and the turbine generators are secured mechanically. Then Petty Officer Smith will confess that he initiated the scram for training and we'll perform a Fast Recovery Startup."

"What speed do you want initially?" asked the Captain.

"Standard with main coolant pumps in fast speed."

"Good. I'll do that while you're getting staged."

"Tom, this is your drill monitor hat." The ENG passed me a red ball cap with 'Drill Monitor' embroidered on the front. "You can observe the action from the outside of the chain across the Maneuvering door. Try not to block the entrance or the passageway."

"Thanks."

"Does anyone have questions or concerns? No. OK. Get on station. Captain, I'll call you when we are ready to initiate."

"Very well. I'll be in Control."

The meeting broke and I headed aft, putting on my cap. Maneuvering was crowded with eight people. At the panels the trainees were seated with the normal watch standing beside, and at the throttles, the trainee was answering the standard bell, 120 turns, with the regular watch behind him. LTJG McCarthy was in the EOOW seat in the far corner with Ohanian standing just beside.

The Engineer entered and took station all the way aft between the EPCP and RPCP. He placed a short call via the phone system and keyed the radio headset.

A siren sounded and lights illuminated on the vertical panel of the RPCP.

"Reactor scram," announced the trainee operator. He flipped a switch by the flashing red light and the siren stopped and the light became steady. "Shifting main coolant pumps to slow speed. Reactor out of power range, restoring startup rate scram protection." He worked his panel.

The throttles were spun shut and the engine order telegraph was switched to 'All Stop' as the announcing system blared, "Reactor Scram." The second indicator on the telegraph shifted to stop as well.

Ohanian was on the intercom. "Conn, Maneuvering, reactor scram."

"Conn, aye," came the reply followed on the speakers by, "Reactor scram. Reactor scram. Rig ship for reduced electrical power. Casualty Assistance Team lay aft, section 1."

Fans slowed or were secured and the Engine Room became very quiet.

"Going to Low Pressure Cutout," came from the Reactor Operator and Ohanian acknowledged. "Securing main coolant pumps one and two."

"Maneuvering, Conn, prepare to shift propulsion to the EPM."

Ohanian acknowledged and brought up a mike. "Prepare to shift propulsion to the EPM," sounded from the speakers.

Additional sailors were arriving from forward. Two entered Maneuvering and donned phone headsets.

"Ready to shift propulsion to the EPM," came from one of the phone talkers.

"Conn, Maneuvering, ready to shift propulsion to the EPM," went out over the intercom.

"Shift propulsion to the EPM," came back and was passed out by phone.

"Clutch indicates disengaged," Throttleman trainee reported.

"Machinery Upper Level reports the cause of the scram is unknown," came by phone followed shortly by "Answering bells on the EPM."

Ohanian reported, "Shifted propulsion to the EPM."

The acknowledgement was one-third rung on the engine order telegraph and relayed to the EPM via phone. The shaft speed indicator ticked up to around twenty turns.

"I'm able to assume all load on the battery," stated the Electrical Operator trainee.

"Assume the load on the battery," ordered Ohanian.

The Electrical Operator flipped some switches on his panel and said, "Loads assumed on the battery. Both turbine generators secured electrically."

"Engine Room Upper Level, secure both turbine generators mechanically." This was passed via the phones.

"Machinery Lower Level reports commenced charging with two charging pumps," came from the phones, followed shortly by, "Engine Room Supervisor reports both turbine generators secured mechanically."

I saw Rinaldi speak through his radio set.

"Energizing source range," reported the Reactor Operator, turning a switch. "Source range reading normally."

"Machinery Upper Level reports the cause of the scram was for training, initiated by Petty Officer Smith," came from the phone talker.

"Machinery Upper Level, reset and shut group one scram breakers," ordered Ohanian. He passed on the announcing system, "Commencing a fast recovery startup.

"Conn, Maneuvering, cause of the scram was training. Commencing a fast recovery startup."

The red light flashed on the RPCP vertical panel. When the RO flipped its switch it winked out.

"Machinery Upper Level reports group one scram breakers reset and shut."

"Reactor Operator, latch group one and commence a fast recovery startup."

"Latch group one and commence a fast recovery startup, aye. Latching group one."

He pulled a switch on the vertical panel while twisting a control in the center of the slopping section. He released the switch and reversed his twist.

Six lights went off on the RPCP. "Group one rod bottom lights are clear. Continuing the startup."

Everyone was watching the RPCP but nothing much was happening. The counter moved, tracking the motion of the control rods. The watches were focused mostly on one dial, reading about zero. The reading started to creep up, to one-half, then one.

"Reactor is critical." Said the RO.

Ohanian repeated it on the announcing system. It came over the announcing system again from Control.

The dial moved quicker now, two, three, four, five. He stopped moving rods out. The power indicators began to move up quickly.

"De-energizing source range nuclear instruments."

"Machinery Lower Level, secure charging. Line up to discharge purified coolant overboard," ordered Ohanian. "Conn, Maneuvering, request permission to discharge purified coolant overboard."

The qualified RO watch whispered something to the trainee, who started moving rods inward. The dial dropped quickly from five to one.

"Reactor is adding heat, commencing warm-up. Going to startup rate scram cutout."

The Reactor Operator was now using his control switch between out and neutral as a phone talker was plotting time and temperature on a chart stuck to the back of a clipboard.

"Engine Room Upper Level, restart both turbine generators mechanically." This was passed by phone.

"Maneuvering, Conn, you have permission to discharge purified coolant overboard."

"Engine Room Supervisor reports both turbine generators are on the governor."

"Electrical Operator, start the turbine generators electrically and shift to a normal full power electrical lineup."

He repeated the order and started to work his panel. Soon, "Normal full power lineup."

"Reactor Operator, start main coolant pumps one and two in slow speed. Engine Room Upper Level warm up the main engines. Conn, Maneuvering, reactor plant is self-sustaining. Warming up the main engines.

"Main coolant pumps are two slow, two slow."

"Secure from reduced electrical power," came from the speakers.

"Machinery Lower Level, commence discharging at 55 inches pressurizer level."

"Machinery Lower Level reports commenced discharging." The phone talker turned to a panel on the rear wall and pressed a switch. "Monitoring ion exchanger inlet, temperature, 110° and stable."

"Engine Room Supervisor reports the main engines are warmed up and control transferred to Maneuvering."

"Conn, Maneuvering, ready to shift propulsion to the main engines."

The telegraph rang 'All Stop' and the intercom said, **"Maneuvering, shift propulsion to the main engines."**

"Shift propulsion to the main engines, Maneuvering, aye." The order then passed on the announcing system.

"Clutch indicates engaged."

"Temperature is in the green band." The Reactor Operator was looking at one of the gauges on the vertical panel that was marked in green over part of its range. "Returning low pressure cutout to 'Normal'."

"Engine Room Supervisor reports propulsion shifted to the main engines."

"Conn, Maneuvering, propulsion shifted to the main engines. Ready to answer all bells."

The telegraph rang two-thirds and the Throttleman turned the large wheel to admit steam to the main engines. The submarine took a small downward angle.

"EPM. Secure the EPM."

"The EPM is secured," came back quickly.

"Machinery Lower Level reports secured discharging."

"Pressurizer level looks good," reported the Reactor Operator.

"Good. Machinery Lower Level, secure the discharge line up. Commence post discharge checks."

The telegraph rang full and throttles were slowly opened as turns increased.

Rinaldi took the mike. "Secure from reactor scram drill. Monitors assemble in the Wardroom for critique," came from the speakers. "Well done, everyone. Mr. Ohanian, get ready for your board this evening."

"All hands commence field day," sounded from the speakers.

Chapter 10 – Field Day

Eastern Pacific – 33° 48.2' N 126° 03.1' W
Sunday, August 11, 1991
1330

The crew was busy. Most of the effort seemed to be opening up access panels and cleaning inside or above and behind the mounted equipment. Rags, brushes and several shop vacuum cleaners were in use. Sailors were working outboard of equipment and in the overhead. There was a bit of a lull as watches were relieved before 1600.

I entered the Bow Compartment. The lights were bright and white, unlike on my tour. The hatch to the diesel space was open and a couple of sailors were working below. Some of the deck plates that formed the walkway around the diesel were raised up with one man cleaning below the deck level.

"Tom, join me in the Chiefs' Quarters."

It was the COB. He opened the door. There was a small table set in a nook with bench seats for two, fore and aft. He motioned me to take a seat.

"Coffee?"

"Thanks, COB. One cream, no sugar."

He poured a cup for me from a coffee maker set on a shelf and placed it on the table with a small packet of artificial creamer and a wood stirring stick. He got a cup himself, black, and sat down facing me.

"How is your trip so far?"

"Interesting. I've typed up several pages of notes. It's not as small inside as I'd imagined. I don't feel claustrophobic, though, after a couple weeks, that might change."

"You should walk through a Trident someday. They're huge."

Chief Lloyd entered. "Good afternoon, sir."

"Chief Lloyd just got off from Diving Officer of the Watch. We're running a four section rotation for that and Chief of the Watch. The others are in three section."

"What will you be doing now?"

"I'll see how my guys are doing. Field day is about a deep cleaning. 'A' Division has Diesel and Air Regen. I dropped into Diesel on the way and it's under control. COB, do you know who's inspecting?"

"The XO has the Bow Compartment today and Mr. Gonzales has OPS Lower Level."

"And COB, what will you be doing?"

"I walk around and observe. I'm looking to see that the men have good direction from their chiefs or LPOs."

"What if there's a problem?"

"It does happen sometimes. We prefer to deal with it in here and not get the officers involved."

"Thanks for the coffee. I think I'll wander about some too."

The crew seemed hard at work all over. After looking through the rest of the Bow and Operations Compartments, I headed back to the Wardroom. LCDR Cooper was there, reading documents on a metal clipboard while a petty officer stood behind him.

"NAV, what are you reading?"

"Messages. We cleared the 2000 Zulu broadcast when we went to periscope depth during the drill. This is just routine administrative stuff, but we got sports news and scores. I'm an Atlanta fan. I think the Braves have a good chance to take the NL West this season."

He initialed a couple pages and handed the board back to the sailor and picked up a book.

"This is Radioman Second (RM2(SS)) Leonard, the Radioman of the Watch this section. There's no action in Radio when we're deep."

"I wasn't able to visit Radio in my tour."

"We can do it if it's OK with NAV. I'll put the crypto in the safe. We're doing cleanup now. Come by after field day; we'll still be deep."

"Sounds like you got your tour. Very well, Petty Officer Leonard."

"What's the book?"

"Sailing Directions. I'm brushing up on Tokyo Bay."

"Is navigation difficult?"

"With satellites and an inertial navigator, it's really simple, except when we're entering or leaving port or operating near shallow water. On this transit, there's no hazard until we approach Japan. We still carry a sextant and the books needed to shoot a celestial fix. I even did it a couple times.

"The Sailing Directions help to identify visual landmarks we can use to fix our position and what we can expect on radar if visibility is poor. We'll have the portable GPS programmed with the waypoints on the track but you never depend solely on a single piece of equipment.

"So, NAV, do you like the Navy life?"

"I'm on my second tour on submarines, so it's certain I liked it. I'm Academy and I had a chance to go back as a company officer for my shore tour. I'm working on my command quals and hope to be a submarine CO someday."

"Are there any things you don't like?"

"I married right after graduation. My wife, Alicia, and I have two sons, Henry, Jr. and Mike, seven and five. The separation on a six-month deployment is hard. My first submarine was a Trident, Georgia, out of Bangor, Washington. We were only gone a bit over two months at a time and I was home a lot when the other crew had the boat."

"What's next for you then?"

"I'll be with Haddock until we enter the shipyard for inactivation next year. The Operations Department is the first to go once there are no more operations. It's mostly just engineers then, though, we remain 'In Commission' with a CO until the nuclear fuel is removed."

LTJG Jackson, the other black officer, walked in with a stack of papers and took a seat as Cooper continued.

"I should do a shore assignment before an XO tour. The Captain thinks I should do a split department head tour and transfer after deployment for a couple years as Engineer on another sub. That would mean no shore tour. I don't really think I need it though."

"Of course you don't, at least, not for promotion," Jackson broke in. "I'd do it if I don't get Engineer for my department head tour."

"Don't mind Jackson. He's just against anything that looks like affirmative action."

"You bet I am. I worked hard to get where I am and I'll work hard to earn my way from here."

The Captain walked in to refill his coffee cup, but kept silent.

"But you can't say that policies haven't helped you on the way."

"That's the point. Every achievement is suspect or tainted. General Powell gets to be Chairman JCS, and some say, it's just because he's black. Are people pushing these policies really our friends? Look what else they offer, welfare laws that destroy families. You and I are probably here because we had a mother and father at home, but fewer every year are getting that advantage. And don't forget abortion on demand. Proportionately more black babies are aborted each and every year. In court that sort of disparate impact would be proof of racism. There's a reason Margaret Sanger, the founder of Planned Parenthood, was greeted favorably when she spoke before the Klan."

"Our people fought hard for equality. You benefit from their success."

"The fight made us stronger. It's easier to recognize enemies when they come at you with cattle prods than when they're offering you free stuff."

"Captain, what are your views on this?"

"Tom, I've heard this argument before and learned not to get in the middle. Stop by my stateroom later and I'll offer my thoughts." He left with his fresh coffee.

"I've got to check the nav picture," Cooper said abruptly and got up and left.

"Do you two always argue?"

"No. It was mainly for your benefit." Jackson smiled. "I wanted you to see there's another viewpoint, admittedly, a minority opinion. I don't mind being a minority when I'm right. I've had a lifetime of practice."

"It sounds like you're a Republican."

"Yes, I am. Dr. King was too."

"King's party preference is not a settled issue."

"King wouldn't join the party of Bull Conner, George Wallace and Lester Maddox. My family also has a history with Democrats. My grandfather tells of hard times when he was young and his dad lost his job when President Woodrow Wilson segregated the federal civil service."

"Wilson did what?"

"Yes, they don't mention that when you learn history in school. My great grandfather ran an auditing division in the Treasury Department, 10 whites and 2 negroes beside himself. He was told he was being demoted because negroes were no longer permitted to have authority over whites. They didn't use the word negro, of course. He was fired a couple months later.

"What happened then?"

"Several months of hard times with occasional accounting jobs. A friend on the former White House staff put in a good word and ex-President Taft hired him to a financial management position at the American Bar Association. When Taft became Chief Justice in 1921 he brought him over to a similar position with the court. He also helped my grandfather get into Yale law. My dad is a lawyer too and so is an older brother. I always had a preference for science."

"Your family has a lot of history."

"I guess so. We can trace back to the early Nineteenth Century. I'm sure it goes back a couple hundred years further in America but records for slaves are not easy to find. My father's side goes back to slaves of Hiram Jackson, a tobacco plantation owner in Virginia. With no living children and a wife that preceded him, he freed his dozen slaves upon his death in 1832 and divided the land among them. They all took his name out of respect. He was a good man in the context of his time and place."

"What happened after gaining freedom?"

"He married my many greats grandmother, also one of Jackson's newly-freed slaves. They sold their land and moved North. He worked as a laborer on the new railroads being constructed in New Jersey and later on the Pennsylvania Railroad where he headed crews laying new track. In the Civil War he scouted and marked routes for the railroads that supported and followed the Union armies."

"That's very interesting. You should write your own family's version of 'Roots.' What are the papers you're working on?"

"These are the checks of the primary plant instrument panel we performed last night. The checks were fine but we review everything to make sure the documentation is flawless."

"What about field day?"

"RC Division has Machinery Upper Level. I stopped by to see how my guys were doing. Chief Allen has them well organized. I'm inspecting Engine Room Upper Level after we secure the cleanup."

"I'll let you get to your paperwork then."

I left the Wardroom. The CO's stateroom is just forward. The door was open with the Captain sitting with his coffee on his desk. There was a framed photo of a young girl. I knocked on the panel beside the door.

"Come in Tom." He shifted to sit on the bed. "Take a seat."

"Thanks. Is the photo your daughter?"

"Yes, Nancy. She's ten. I'm divorced from her mother."

"That's too bad. Do you want to tell me why?"

"It was a while ago, when I had a shore tour in D.C. She got a job with good career potential and wanted to stay. I could have gotten out. There are plenty of jobs for experienced officers. I just didn't care for them. I like the Navy. Every day is different. The split was as friendly as it gets. I've seen some really nasty divorces. The hard part of our deployment schedule is that I'll miss Christmas with my daughter."

"Navy life can be tough on families, I guess."

"Yes, some things are beyond my control, but I try my best to make Haddock family friendly."

"How?"

"In port, I try to leave every day by 1630 and make the XO leave too. If I stick around, the XO stays, and the department heads don't want to leave before the XO, so the junior officers stay too. We spend half our time at sea or away from homeport. When we're in, the crew should get time to be home. You'd be surprised, when they know they can get off, the work gets done in time.

"Has the XO told you about his situation?"

"No."

"It's not a secret. All the officers and the COB know, so I'm not giving away any private information. His wife, Emily, has breast cancer. She had a mastectomy last month, but will need chemotherapy. He has twin daughters, now eight. I arranged a job on the Submarine Group FIVE staff for him. He'll be relieved as XO when we get to Japan but we haven't gotten the name of the replacement yet."

"How does that impact his career?"

"I'm sure that's the last thought in his mind now, but he should get his own submarine in a couple years. That should be enough time for his wife to recover. The prognosis is very good.

"Emily runs the wives' organization since I'm not married. We don't know the new XO's situation, and even if married, his wife hasn't met the others. Emily wants to stay active, but that will depend on her health. The COB's wife will help out, but it may fall to Alicia Cooper to lead."

"Why is it so important?"

"When we're around San Diego, any problems with family services, medical, dental, pay, ID cards, and the like, are brought to us by the sailor. When we're away the wives need to know where to get help and we bring the problems to Squadron THREE for assistance. They're ready to assist but it helps to have someone to keep their feet to the fire. The last thing we want is a crewman worrying about the welfare of his family back home. At least we had a few weeks to prepare for it and bring Alicia up to speed."

"That's a good point to bring up your views on affirmative action."

"Affirmative action, that we are looking extra hard to advance qualified minorities, is Navy policy. As a CO, I support all Navy policies."

"What does that mean in practice? Do you give a boost to minorities on evaluations?"

"Evaluations are tricky. This is a small ship. Everyone has a good idea of where people rank. If you rank someone where they don't deserve the system would lose respect and integrity."

"Well, let's say you had a majority and minority that were about equal, would you give the minority the higher rank?"

"In that case, probably just the opposite. You need to understand that I want to identify those sailors that are ready and able to assume higher rank and get as many of them advanced as possible. We get them into the supervisory watch stations and give them extra assignments that we can boast about on their evaluations. Even something like running a Combined Federal Campaign charity drive can be a plus for a selection board. For a white Petty Officer First Class being ranked first can be a huge plus on the chief's selection board but being second won't hurt a minority. The net result is we'd get both advanced and that's best for the Navy, and us."

"What about officers?"

"That's even tougher. Let's take our lieutenant commanders. If I don't rank the XO first, his career is over. So, I need to decide if the XO has the stuff to be a CO. He does. If I had an XO that I felt wouldn't make a CO, I'd go to the squadron commander and arrange an early relief. There's no point on wasting a valuable XO billet on someone that won't be moving on.

"Next are the department heads. The Engineer will almost always be ahead of the others unless it's his first evaluation and the NAV has been around and will leave before the next cycle. It's a cheap way to boost his selection prospects without hurting the new Engineer. When José, the Weapons Officer, makes LCDR things get a bit more complicated, though, as a lieutenant and a department head, I have to be sure to rank him above the other lieutenants to keep his career on track.

"Is that why you recommended Cooper serve as an Engineer?"

"No. I think he'll make the cut for selection to command. It's just that he'd be a better CO when the time comes if he has served as an Engineer. You have to act as Engineer for a couple weeks as part of the command quals, but that's not the same as being it. I've served under COs that didn't know enough about the plant. They had the theory. Naval Reactors, makes sure of that. But they didn't have the experience. It led to problems."

"Naval Reactors?"

"That's the office in D.C. that runs the nuclear propulsion program; Admiral Rickover's old office. It's Admiral DeMars now.

Every nuclear officer is interviewed there before being accepted for training. My interview was with Rickover, but DeMars has made it much less intimidating. Officers go back to D.C. to take the engineer's exam. Everyone must pass it to become a department head but only the top performers get to be Engineers. Then all prospective commanding officers go back for three-months training before command. There's an exam and you have to do better than the engineer candidates. Some don't hack it, so goodbye command."

"So, does Cooper need the experience to pass that hurdle?"

"No, he's smart. He passed his engineer's exam and can pass that. It's about being a better CO when it's his turn. You only get to serve as CO for a few years then someone else gets a turn. One of my jobs is to train my XO and department heads to replace me."

"I'm confused. Where do you stand on affirmative action? Do you support it?"

"I already said it's Navy policy and I support it. If we want qualified minorities to choose the Navy and submarines we need to show that they will be given the opportunity to succeed. That said, there is a downside. Let me use another affirmative action program that I benefited from as an example."

"You?"

"Yes, the Navy needs nuclear trained officers to fill billets on the nuclear ships. When I was coming up the submarine force was expanding, new attack subs and missile subs, each with two full crews. The civilian nuclear industry was happy to take anyone tired of the long hours or deployments. We were short of officers to fill the billets. What that meant is any officer, not terminally incompetent, achieved promotion and advancement. Some officers reached command, XO or department head, that shouldn't. I served under a CO like that. He was backed by a weak XO and a poor Engineer. It was...bad."

"You said you benefited."

"Yes, my Engineer tour was not the best. I knew the plant inside out, but my training program... Let's just say I wasn't good at running drills. It helped that selection for XO wasn't tight. So affirmative action might be necessary, but it can result in people being advanced to positions they're not able to fill. I'm just trying to help ensure they're prepared."

"Do you feel you were?"

"I spent my XO tour figuring out where I went wrong as Engineer and finding solutions. Part was simply finding and applying best practices already in use. Then I modified the drill guides. We use a large number of monitors to initiate and run the drills so the Engineer is just a safety observer. The final piece was our five-watch rotation. It was mentioned in my training before taking over as CO. I like it because I can train each section every day. The crew seems to like it too. We used to shift to straight six-hour watches on weekends, but the preference was to stay in five-watch rotation. We only shift now when we won't be drilling for many days.

"I do run a lot of drills. As Engineer I needed to fight to get drill time. Ron doesn't have that problem. He's a much better Engineer than I was."

"Secure field day."

"You'll excuse me. It's time for my zone inspection." He pulled a flashlight and mirror out of the desk.

Chapter 11 – Qualification Board
Eastern Pacific – 34° 51.1' N 127° 40.8' W
Sunday, August 11, 1991
2045

We were in the Wardroom. LTJG Ohanian was seated at the forward end of the table in the Supply Officer's normal space. The XO and Engineer took seats flanking the Captain's seat. I took a seat on a chair next to Ohanian.

The Captain entered, saying, "Seats," before anyone could react and took his place.

"It's a good day outside. Seas are calm, about a sea-state one."

"Prepare to ventilate," came over the speakers.

"Mr. Ohanian, this board is to examine your knowledge for qualification as Engineering Officer of the Watch. Do you mind if Mr. Ryan observes? It's your board, and if you'd feel more comfortable, we will exclude him."

"I'm fine, Captain."

"Good. I'll start."

"Captain, these are Mr. Ohanian's qualification card and exam."

"3.62, a good score on your exam. Have you reviewed the questions you missed?"

"Yes, sir, with the Engineer."

"Give the immediate actions for Engine Room flooding."

Rinaldi was writing the question down on a sheet of paper.

"Answer a standard bell. Shut emergency closure levers, right above my chair, for Engine Room ASW and port and starboard MSW. Switch off MSW pumps using the emergency control next to the levers. Shift main coolant pumps to slow speed as soon as reactor power drops below 50%. Oh, and report it to Control if they hadn't already gotten the initial report and collision alarm."

"Commence ventilating."

"You get low vacuum alarms, port and starboard. What then?"

"Continue to answer the standard bell. Have the Electrical Operator open the MG-TG breakers to protect the vital buses in case the root valves trip and we lose the turbine generators. Has the flooding been reported stopped?"

"Yes, flooding has stopped. Flooding was from starboard main sea water."

"I'd reopen port MSW valves and restart the port MSW pump in slow. I'd go to permissive open on the Engine Room ASW and announce that and order ASW restored for air conditioning and the port condenser. Report the flooding stopped and location to Control.

"We're going to lose the starboard TG when the starboard root valve trips on overpressure, about 5 psi. Go to a half power lineup on the port TG. We're also in single main engine operation. Can we draw any vacuum on the starboard condenser?"

"We'll see. The vacuum in the port condenser initially improves and then begins to fall quickly."

"On the 2MC I'd say, 'Dropping vacuum on port condenser. Engine Room Upper Level check steam reset to the port air ejector condenser.' Does that fix it?"

"Yes. XO, your turn."

"What if the flooding caused a reactor scram?"

"Take the actions for a scram except answer the standard bell instead of stop."

"How long could you answer the bell?"

"About 5 minutes before steam pressure gets too low. But it's only 3 to 4 minutes before we get below the 400 degree limit on a fast recovery startup."

"What do you do if you reach 400 degrees?"

"Continue to answer the bell if that's ordered for flooding recovery. Hopefully we've isolated the flooding before that. We have to insert all rods at 400 degrees by full scram or selecting shutdown."

"What is the basis of the 400 degree and one hour limits?"

"As the plant cools down, the cooler, denser water adds reactivity. Also, time after shutdown can add reactivity as neutron poisons in the core decay. So, it's possible, under some circumstances, for the reactor to regain criticality with the scram group rods fully inserted if the limits are exceeded. That can't be allowed."

"ENG, your turn."

"Yes, OK. What is the purpose of step 13 of the pre-critical checks?"

"It tests the interlocks between the main coolant pumps, main coolant cutout valves and the scram group position."

"Why do we have them?"

"Restoring flow from a cool, idle or isolated, loop with the reactor critical would result in a severe power excursion, so the interlocks prevent that."

"How do you restore from an isolated loop?"

"If the loop is isolated by the main coolant cutout valves, you can start a pump in the loop in fast speed. The energy of the pump pushing the water against the friction in the pipes will heat up the loop. We have to get it within 32 degrees of the other loop. When you're within limits setup for a reactor scram. We can get to periscope depth, even snorkel, rig for reduced electrical and shift propulsion ahead of time.

"Get permission and insert a normal group scram from the RPCP scram switch. Secure the main coolant pump in the isolated loop, open the main coolant cutout valves, restart a main coolant pump in the idle loop and secure one in the operating loop so you're in a normal one slow, one slow configuration. Then bypass and open the main steam stop on the formerly isolated loop. Then conduct a normal fast recovery startup."

"Oh, and restore feed to the previously idled steam generator."

"When can you do a short-form pre-critical check?"

"You can do it to extend the validity of a long-form check. The long-form must be completed within 24 hours of the startup and the short-form within 8 hours. Also if the shutdown from power operations were within 24 hours and the nuclear instruments were continuously energized and exhibited normal shutdown characteristics, you only need do a short-form within 8 hours of the startup."

"What are normal shutdown characteristics?"

"Overlap between the power range and intermediate range nuclear instruments. They show overlap now because we are at a low bell. Observe a negative startup rate during shutdown that should be about negative one-third decade per minute by the bottom of the intermediate range or top of the source range. Observe overlap between the intermediate range and source range. That means you have to remember to energize the source range instruments before you drop below the intermediate range."

"**Secure ventilating, recirculate,**" was announced.

"Why do we have an on-off switch on the source range?"

"The high neutron flux at power would burn out the detector. We energize or de-energize it when we are about one decade into the intermediate range."

"What is the only all uppercase warning in the Reactor Plant Manuals?"

"THE BATTLESHORT SWITCH REMOVES ALL AUTOMATIC SCRAM PROTECTION. IT SHOULD NOT BE USED EXCEPT IN AN EXTREME TACTICAL SITUATION AT THE DIRECTION OF THE COMMANDING OFFICER.

"Captain, what's an extreme tactical situation?"

"It's not my board but I'll give you what I think. It's a situation where the life of the ship or the success of some really critical mission depends on avoiding a loss of power or propulsion at all cost, even if we risk reactor core damage. I guess I'll know it when I see it. COs have been fired for deciding wrong. None resulted in damage though."

SA Rogers knocked and entered the Wardroom. "Captain, the Officer of the Deck sends his respects and reports that we have completed evolutions at periscope depth and are proceeding to 500 feet to resume transit." The Captain acknowledged and he left.

"Your turn again. How does the battleshort switch do its function?"

"It applies rod control DC power directly to the under-voltage coils of the scram breakers."

"What reactor protection remains active?"

"Automatic cutbacks and the manual group or full scram switches."

"OK, switching topics. Why do I prohibit work or testing in port between 2000 and the duty section turnover next day?"

"Personnel are less alert and more prone to mistakes in the late night and early morning. Both Three Mile Island and Chernobyl happened on the mid watch. We also want the duty section personnel to get enough rest to stand alert watched in the overnight hours."

"That includes you and your Engineering Duty Chief too. What should you do if you see something that's a problem or you don't understand?"

"For a problem or question call the appropriate Division Officer and the Engineer, and the Ship's Duty Officer. He should call you if it is an equipment casualty or impacts planned operations."

"I think we heard enough. You passed. You've got the twenty to oh-two watch every day starting as soon as you bring me the watch qual book from Maneuvering."

"Thank you sir." Ohanian left.

The others applied some signatures to the qualification paperwork and then the XO left.

"ENG, who do you want with sections one, two and three? I want to move Reed to JOOD to finish his quals. He can also help you out as a drill team member."

"We'll do Gordon, section one, Jackson, two and McCarthy, three, with Ohanian taking their places when the section has his watch."

"Good."

The Engineer left. Ohanian returned and the Captain entered his name in the book and signed it. He left again to take the watch.

"We already knew he had the knowledge to qualify. The board is really more about putting the candidate in a pressure situation and seeing how he responds. I like to qualify watches as quickly as they can stand it safely. The real training starts once they're qualified. We'll give Ohanian a few weeks of routine watches to get his bearings. We do battery charges, instrumentation checks and simple training evolutions on his watch."

"What sort of training?"

"Stopping the shaft, shifting propulsion, shifting the electric plant around, simple stuff where we don't need monitors. Once he's ready we'll shift him to the morning watch for the easier drills and in a couple months he'll be ready for the big stuff."

LT Gonzales came in and left the door open.

"If the board is over, we'd like to play a videotape. Are you interested Captain?"

"What are you showing?"

"Die Hard 2, with Bruce Willis. It came in last month."

"I'll pass. I saw it last summer. A bit of business first. Who's next up for Sonar Supervisor?"

"That would be Petty Officer Renner. He should be ready by the time we reach Yokosuka. We have four qualified. Is there a reason for the question?"

"Johnson is up for selection to chief. If he makes it, we can expect him to be transferred quickly."

"I'll pass it on to Mr. Cohen and Senior Chief Harvey. We should be able to speed the process a bit."

"That should be good." He got up and left.

"Tom, will you be joining us for the movie? There'll be popcorn."

Returning to my stateroom after the movie, I saw XO still up and working reviewing some papers.

"The Captain told me about Emily. I hope everything works out and she's well soon."

"Thanks. We're hopeful. My mother is staying with her while I'm away. Her first round of chemo left her weak for several days. Emily lost her mother to breast cancer when she was fifteen. We had been doing yearly mammograms and frequent self-exams given her family history and think we got it early. Still, the memory of her mother's death is very vivid."

"You must be eager to get home."

"Yes, my relief will meet us in Japan. I should be back with Emily in 3 weeks. She is scheduled for more chemo on September 10th. Everybody has been very supportive. I'm trying to get everything organized for a smooth and quick turnover."

"I'll say a prayer for her."

"Again thanks. We've said more than a few ourselves. It helps."

Chapter 12 – Training Day 1
Eastern Pacific – 36° 34.7' N 130° 10.4' W
Monday, August 12, 1991
0830

"Tom," Rinaldi said from the door to the XO's stateroom. I'd been typing some notes into my laptop. "We're going to run some drills this morning, answering various bells, loss of shaft lube oil, loss of turbine generator and a power-flow cutback. Grab your monitor hat if you want to observe."

I closed the screen, grabbed my hat and headed out. The XO was in the Ship's Office discussing something with YN1(SS) Mason. I told him where I was headed and went up the stairs. The Captain was coming out of Sonar.

"Morning, Tom."

"Good morning, Captain. Will you be heading aft to observe the drills?"

"No. I'll be in Control. I never go aft for drills. I'd see all the mistakes and want to offer suggestions. That's one reason I was so bad running them. Intellectually I know mistakes are part of the process but it's better for my blood pressure to hear about them in the critique. I find I have a very good idea of how the drill went by the flow of actions and reports and I can monitor the ship control response from personnel in Control. That can also be important to handling an engineering casualty."

"I see."

"I have the sequence of bells for the OOD," indicating a card he was carrying. "We'll be starting in a few minutes."

He headed forward and I aft. The Tunnel was empty. I passed into the Auxiliary Machinery Space and decided to see the lower level. I spotted a hatch outboard of the panels containing the main electric plant breakers on the starboard side. The deck plate was hinged and latched open with the opening guarded by chains extending across the walkway.

I descended the vertical ladder. The deck in the lower level was metal instead of the vinyl tiles used in the upper level and most of the forward spaces. A walkway extended down the port and starboard sides with equipment outboard and in the center. There was another ladder between levels opposite mine on the port side. I spotted the watch at the aft end of the compartment and headed back there.

"I'm Tom Ryan. Are you on watch here?"

"Yes, sir. Keith Johnson. Machinist Mate second and an 'E' 'L' 'T'."

"ELT?"

"Engineering Laboratory Technician. We do primary and secondary sampling and chemical analysis and the radiation surveys. As the Machinery Lower Level watch I can sample the steam generators at the station just forward from here."

"**Back emergency**," sounded over the speakers. The lights dimmed momentarily as main coolant pumps shifted.

"Excuse me." He turned a switch on the panel in front and I heard a piece of equipment start up behind me. He then hustled up the port side walkway and turned another switch. Returning to the panel he picked up the phone and turned the crank. "Machinery Lower Level started #1 feed pump, shifted forward ASW to fast speed."

"**All stop.**"

"We were in our slow, quiet, mode, good up to a full bell. When back emergency or flank is ordered we automatically shift to high-speed mode. I started a second feed pump and turned forward ASW to fast to handle the extra cooling load from the main coolant pumps. Do you want a quick tour?"

"Sure. Thanks."

"**Ahead flank.**"

"We're rigged already. We'll stay like this until Maneuvering orders a change. The four feed pumps are behind us. We can monitor the output pressure on the panel in front and the water level in the steam generators. The amount of water we feed the steam generators is controlled automatically by a system the ETs maintain. It's in the upper level but it controls these two valves here." He pointed aft and above to two valves with vented covers and a large wheel. "The hand-wheels allow us to control feed manually, if needed. There's a manual-electric mode we normally use, if not in full auto, controlled by switches on the panel here. The programmed level is higher as we operate at higher power."

He walked along the starboard side.

"The big gray machines are motor-generator sets. #1 is here and #2 over on the port side. They convert AC to DC or DC to AC. Forward of the ladder are the forward ASW pumps. The cross walkway has an oxygen candle furnace and aft is the secondary sampling station. We analyze the steam generators for chlorides, pH, phosphate and total dissolved solids. Chlorine in the steam generator can lead to stress corrosion cracking of the tubes."

"How often to you check?"

"Every eight hours. We alternate port and starboard, so we run a sample every four hours. We also sample for chlorides, both generators, if we get a salinity alarm on the condensate system."

"So having an ELT on watch here is convenient."

"Yes. Continuing on the port side, forward we have the coolant discharge station to remove water from the reactor plant. At sea, beyond 12 miles, we can discharge to the ocean. Inside that or in port we have a tank, in the ballast tank below here, to collect the water. The cylinders in the center have water to operate reactor plant valves. Then on the starboard side, we have the system to charge water into the reactor plant. Heading aft again we have air cylinders to pressurize the valve operating system when needed and #2 CO_2 scrubber. We normally run the one in Air Regen when we're running drills."

"Loss of shaft lube oil. Stopping and locking the shaft."

"Got to go." He went back to his station and picked up the phone handset.

The ship took a modest upward angle as it headed shallower. A couple minutes later the phone box screeched.

"Machinery Lower Level. Lower the outboard, test and shift to remote, aye."

He went down the port passage, stopping at a panel just forward of his station. He moved a lever and pressed a button. A device in the central space began to descend.

"That's the outboard. It's raised and lowered hydraulically. The motor and propeller is in the ballast tank below the hull. A green "Gear Extended' light illuminated on the panel. He did a couple other operations and went back to the phone.

"Outboard, lowered, tested, shifted to remote."

Shortly I heard it turn on.

"Secure from loss of shaft lube oil drill."

"Thanks for the tour, Petty Officer Johnson."

He was on the phone and as I headed up the ladder I heard him acknowledge the order to secure the outboard. I went to the Engine Room and took station outside Maneuvering. Rinaldi was standing just inboard of McCarthy, the EOOW, while EM2(SS) Nichols stood behind the Electrical Operator.

We were at ahead one-third. Word that the outboard was secured came up and was passed to Conn by intercom. Standard came over the engine order telegraph as the ship angled to go deeper. The Throttleman slowly turned the large chromed wheel counterclockwise and shaft turns began to increase.

As we leveled off the Engineer spoke into his radio mike. I saw Senior Chief Jay a few feet aft of me in the upper level passageway acknowledge on his radio. He pushed on something on the port turbine generator.

"Loss of port TG bus," announced the Electrical Operator. "TG breaker and MG-TG breaker indicate open." He flipped a couple switches on the left side of his panel.

"Lost #1 and #6 main coolant pumps. #2 and #5 running in fast speed," added the Reactor Operator.

"Loss of port turbine generator," McCarthy passed over the engineering speakers. "Conn, Maneuvering, loss of port turbine generator, shifting to a half-power lineup, limited to a full bell.

"Reactor Operator, shift to two-slow, two-slow. Electrical Operator, shift to half-power lineup on the starboard TG." Over the announcing system he passed, "Engine Room Upper Level, shift main sea water to slow speed."

The Maneuvering watches acknowledged and became busy with their panels. Aft of me one operator was between the main engines while another with Chief Dawson the Engineering Watch Supervisor (EWS) were at the port turbine generator. Dawson came forward.

"Main coolant pumps 1, 2, 5 and 6 are running in slow speed."

"Electric plant is in a half-power lineup, starboard."

"Very well. Conn, Maneuvering, electric plant is in a half-power lineup, starboard."

"Request to enter Maneuvering," asked Dawson.

"Enter."

"The port turbine generator was tripped mechanically for training. Restarting it now."

"Very well, Chief." He left and headed aft.

The phone box by the EOOW sounded. The Electrical Operator picked up the phone handset from the cradle between the Reactor Operator and himself. "The port turbine generator is up and on the governor," he reported.

"Very well. Shift the electric plant to a normal full power lineup."

He acknowledged and started to manipulate his panel. The generator was started electrically and checked for output before paralleling with the bus. He split the connection between the two turbine generators and paralleled the port turbine generator with the port motor generator. Finally he did a few tweaks on the panel and reported his task complete.

"Conn, Maneuvering, electric plant in a normal full power lineup. Ready to answer all bells."

Rinaldi took a mike. "Secure from loss of turbine generator drill." He looked toward me. "Mr. Ryan, enter Maneuvering." I unhooked the chain, entered and secured it behind me. "You'll get a better view of the next drill from here. Stand between the Throttleman and Reactor Operator."

Rinaldi spoke in his radio.

"Power-flow cutback," reported the Reactor Operator. A siren sounded. It stopped when a switch was thrown under a red light on the vertical panel of the RPCP.

The Throttleman spun the throttles shut and rang up all stop.

"Go to cutback override," ordered McCarthy.

"Cutback override, aye."

The Reactor Operator got up from his seat and reached to the vertical panel to twist a switch. It took some effort to turn and he needed to hold his left hand on it to keep it turned.

"Power-flow cutback. Conn, Maneuvering, power-flow cutback. Investigating."

"In cutback override. Flow is normal for two-slow, pumps indicate running, main coolant cutout valves indicate open. Power is with limits. No indication of cause. Out of the green band low, going to 'Low Pressure Cutout.'"

"Recover from the cutback."

"Recover, aye." He turned his head to the Throttleman. "Could you hold the override switch?"

The Throttleman took over holding the switch in the override position freeing him to use both hands. He turned a switch on the vertical panel. This one stayed.

"Recovering group two rods." He twisted the control in the center of the slopping panel counterclockwise for several seconds. He released it and twisted the first switch one position. "Recovering group three rods." Again he twisted the central control for several seconds. He returned the switch on the vertical panel to its original position. "Pulling group one, adding heat, warming up." He was going intermittently on the central control. A counter on the vertical panel, labeled 'Group I', was moving a few tenths each time. "In the green band again, going to 'Normal' on low pressure cutout switch."

The red light on the RPCP cleared.

"Machinery Upper Level reports the cutback was initiated for training and the cutback condition has been cleared," the Electrical Operator reported from his phone.

"You can release the switch now." The Throttleman did. It sprang back to 'Normal' from 'Override' and there were no alarms.

"Conn, Maneuvering, recovered from the cutback. It was for training. Ready to answer all bells."

Conn acknowledged and ahead full was rung up as the submarine angled to go deeper.

"Secure from drills," Rinaldi announced. "Monitors assemble in the Wardroom for a critique." He put away the mike. "Will you be coming, Mr. Ryan?"

"Go ahead, ENG. I'm going to look around and then head to Control."

He left.

"You were on watch when I came in for my tour, Petty Officers Tanner, Smith and Allen. You're a good team."

"Thank you, sir," said Smith. "That's one of the goals of the drills."

"Mr. McCarthy, I'll be going now. I'm sure I'll see you in action some more."

"Have a good day, sir."

I left and walked forward. I entered Sonar.

"Good morning sir," Petty Officer Johnson, the black Sonar Supervisor greeted me.

"Do you have any contacts today?"

"We're holding one, Sierra-23, a merchant doing 120 turns on a single five-bladed screw. He now bears 043° and is past CPA and opening. This is his track here." He pointed to a dark line running down one screen. "Petty Officer Stanley, call it up on the analysis screen."

The sailor on the middle console of the three pushed some buttons and the display changed.

"You see four lines and a darker fifth line. That's the key to a five-bladed screw. The darker line shows 120 times a minute to show how fast it turns. These lines are from a diesel engine. You can tell the number of cylinders and how fast it's turning. While most of our work is visual, we can still listen to the contacts. Listen here."

He handed me a headset. I could hear the beat of the contact's screw, one, two, three, four, Five, one, two, three, four, Five. There was a distinct emphasis every fifth beat.

"Yes, I hear the screw beat."

"Small vessels, like fishing trawlers, heavy merchants or warships have different sound qualities. You can hear rain on the surface of the ocean or the splash a sonobuoy makes. A modern nuclear submarine sounds a lot like a rainsquall, just an increase in noise with very few distinctive features. It's easy to miss."

"I see. By the way, the Captain mentioned you were up for Chief Petty Officer."

"Yes, we should get the results of the selection board in a few weeks."

"I hope you're successful. I'll head on to Control."

LT Nguyen had the watch as OOD with QMCS(SS) Spillman as DOOW. Haddock was at 400 feet running at a full bell, about 20 knots. The plot showed the history of the sonar contact I'd seen. I was discussing the drills from the perspective of ship control with the watch standers when the phone screeched. Nguyen took it.

"OOD. Yes, Captain. I'll check.

"Chief of the Watch, ask the AEF to come to Control. The CO thinks we have a ventilation lineup problem."

"Yes, sir." He used his phone box to call a few stations. "He's on the way, Mr. Nguyen."

A minute later a petty officer enters, carrying his log on a clipboard.

"Sir?"

"Petty Officer Frye, the Captain feels we have a problem with our ventilation lineup."

"I checked it after the drills. Everything is normal. I'll check it again."

He left, returning about ten minutes later.

"Mr. Nguyen, fan #2 had tripped. I restarted it and it appears to be running normally. I didn't see anything else."

"Good." He picked up the phone. "Captain, OOD, we found fan #2 tripped and reset it. The lineup is normal now. Yes, sir." He replaced the handset in its cradle.

I left Control and headed to the XO's stateroom. It was nearly 1100 and lunch. The CO was in his room reading a book. I knocked on the wall.

"Captain, how did you know the ventilation lineup was bad?"

"Well, Tom, what do you hear?"

I listened carefully but everything was quiet. Even at 20 knots there was no vibration or rocking.

"Nothing."

"You're not really listening. Can you hear the whisper of air flowing out the vents in my room and the passageway?"

"Yes, but it's really soft."

"True, but if you didn't hear even that, that means the lineup is wrong. You need to use all your senses to look for problems."

"All the senses? I get sight and you just demonstrated hearing. How do you use touch, smell and taste?"

"Easy. When I walk through the ship I often put my hand on electrical panels. If there's a fault or high resistance connection, it will feel hot. Some panels run warm normally so you need to know

102

what is normal and what is abnormal. You can smell electrical insulation when it gets too hot. If caught early you can avoid a fire. If I can smell rotted food in the Scullery it's not clean enough. If you get up around midnight, you can smell bread baking. That's MS2(SS) Michael, our night baker. He's good. Try the bread at lunch today. He also bakes hot dog and hamburger buns; Wednesday lunch is burger day every week. In the Engine Room if you see an unknown leak you can use taste to determine if it's fresh or salt water. I don't try that in the forward end of the Machinery Space, where a leak might be radioactive."

"Fair enough."

"The key is to engage your brain. Too many people look but don't see.

"Time for lunch. Go in. I'll be right behind you."

1430

The drill briefing for the next watch had just finished. Before the brief Rinaldi had the morning's section in the Crew's Mess to review the morning drills and yesterday's scram drill. The next drill would be a steam leak that would be difficult to isolate. I decided to observe from Control.

LT Cohen, the Sonar Officer, was OOD and LTJG Banner, the Supply Officer, had DOOW. The CO was already in Control, reviewing the chart by the quartermaster. He finished there and sat down on the bench in front of fire control. I sat down beside him.

Haddock was still at 400 feet, doing 20 knots.

The phone box screeched. The OOD picked it up, talked and handed it to the Captain. He gave his permission to start and handed the phone back.

A long minute passed.

"Conn, steam leak in Auxiliary Machinery," came over the speaker.

"Maneuvering rings up all stop," announced the Helmsman.

"Steam leak, Auxiliary Machinery," came over all speakers as Cohen spoke into a mike. "Chief, sound the Power Plant Casualty Alarm. Dive, 150 feet, 10 up."

The COW was already getting up from his seat and reached above the BCP to throw a switch. A jump tone, repeating between a lower frequency and a higher frequency, sounded for several seconds, as the deck took an up angle.

"Steam leak, Auxiliary Machinery," Cohen repeated. "Rig ship for reduced electrical power."

Fans stopped. "Lost port and starboard non-vital buses," reported the COW.

"Conn, the steam leak is from the starboard side, upstream of the steam stop. Going to single loop. Machinery Space is filled with steam."

Cohen passed, "Auxiliary Machinery is filled with steam," then over the intercom, "Maneuvering, prepare to shift propulsion to the EPM." Maneuvering acknowledged.

"Mr. Cohen, would you select 2MC monitor," the CO requested.

Cohen flipped a switch on the intercom box. Meanwhile the Messenger had donned a phone headset.

"Conn, ready to shift propulsion to the EPM."

"Maneuvering, shift propulsion to the EPM."

"At 150 feet."

We were still indicating 8 knots even though we had been without propulsion for a few minutes.

"Helm, right ten degrees rudder, steady zero-seven-zero."

"Right ten, aye. My rudder is right ten, steady zero-seven-zero, aye."

"Conn, answering bells on the EPM."

"Helm, all ahead two-thirds."

"All ahead two-thirds, aye. Maneuvering answers ahead two-thirds."

"Conn, Maneuvering, we sent the ERS into Machinery in a steam suit to locate and isolate the leak. Carrying all loads on the battery. Operating single loop on the port loop."

"Sonar, Conn, clearing baffles to starboard. Report all contacts. Dive, prepare to snorkel."

"Prepare to snorkel, Dive aye. Chief of the Watch, prepare to snorkel."

"Prepare to snorkel," passed over the announcing system from the COW.

"Sonar, aye. Hold no contacts."

Our speed had dropped to about four knots. Dive had the COW pump a few thousands pounds to sea.

"Conn, Maneuvering, the leak was from pressure relief piping and has been isolated. Steam is clearing from the Machinery Room. Damage control personnel can lay aft."

"The steam leak is isolated. Damage control party lay aft."

"Passing zero-six-zero to zero-seven-zero."

"Engineering Watch Supervisor, bypass the port steam stop and open when equalized."

"That was over the 2MC we're monitoring," observed the Captain.

"I'm confused about the various communication circuits."

"The basics are easy. The 1MC is the general announcing circuit. We have speakers all over the ship. Alarms are sounded through that system. The OOD, EOOW and Chief of the Watch have mikes."

"Steady zero-seven-zero," announced Helm."

"The 2MC is the engineering announcing system, for the propulsion plant and diesel. 7MC is for ship control orders with stations at Conn, Helm, Maneuvering, EPM and Bridge."

"Sonar, Conn, report all contacts."

"MS-2 indicates open. Engineering Watch Supervisor, startup the Engine Room."

"With everything already warm, restoring normal power will only be a few minutes."

"Conn, sonar has no contacts."

"Captain, sonar holds no contacts. Request permission to go to periscope depth and snorkel when ready."

"It looks like we're recovering. Hold at 150 for a few minutes and turn back to base course."

"Aye, sir. Helm, left 10 degrees rudder. Steady three-one-zero."

"Left 10 degrees rudder. My rudder is left 10. Steady three-one-zero."

"Mr. Cohen, recommend three-zero-seven to return to the center of our track," said the Quartermaster.

"Helm, steady three-zero-seven."

"Steady three-zero-seven, Helm aye."

"Continuing," continued the CO. "The 21MC is selectable to various stations, SCP, BCP, Bridge, my stateroom and the Wardroom. The 27MC is what we use to call Radio or Sonar from Conn or the Bridge. There's an open mike above the periscope stand that allows Sonar to know what's going on in Control. Usually the OOD just asks Sonar a question out loud and they answer with the 27MC.

"The main phone circuit is the JA. We man that in Battle Stations, Maneuvering Watches and all emergencies, as we are now. Next is the 2JV that is for Engineering. They are manning that now for the drill, while Maneuvering talks to us on the JA. You've seen the phone boxes where you can select the station and turn the crank to ring it up."

"Conn, Maneuvering, in a normal full power lineup. Warming up the main engines."

"Conn, aye. Chief of the Watch, secure from reduced electrical, secure the diesel, recirculate."

That was acknowledged and passed on the 1MC. Fans came back on.

"Captain, what is your role in the drills?"

"Why I make it happen. We run very many more drills that I was allowed to run when I was an engineer. I like running single loop drills so the EOOWs and the watch sections get comfortable doing it and recovering. Take the plant to its knees and recover often enough and it becomes routine."

"Passing three-one-seven to three-zero-seven."

"I monitor from Control. From the sequence of reports and time, the drill went well. Ship control was good too. I didn't need to say a word until the decision to abort going to periscope depth and that's my call in any event."

"Conn, Maneuvering, ready to shift propulsion to the main engines."

"Helm, all stop. Maneuvering, shift propulsion to the main engines."

"All stop, Helm aye. Maneuvering answers all stop. Steady three-zero-seven."

"Shift propulsion to the main engines, Maneuvering aye."

Shortly, "Answering bells on the main engines. Limited to a full bell by single loop."

"Conn, aye. Helm, all ahead two-thirds. Dive, make your depth 250 feet."

"All ahead two-thirds, Helm aye. Maneuvering answers ahead two-thirds."

"250 feet, Dive aye. Five down."

"Mr. Cohen, secure from Power Plant Casualty. Let's run standard until we recover the loop on the next watch."

"Aye, Captain. Chief of the Watch, secure from Power Plant Casualty." It was passed on the 1MC.

"Mr. Ryan, the critique will be in the Wardroom in a few minutes." The Captain left Control.

1615

I was in Maneuvering for the recovery, standing between the Throttleman and RO. It was crowded. There were JA and 2JV phone talkers besides the normal watches, drill monitors for the RPCP and EPCP, the ENG and I.

It would not be normal; a problem was to be initiated during the recovery. Haddock was at periscope depth, rigged for reduced electrical power and ready to snorkel, but not yet actually snorkeling. Propulsion had already been shifted to the EPM. Personnel from the last watch were assisting the current watches throughout the plant. LTJG Jackson was the EOOW.

"RO are you ready to make the recovery? I hold us within limits."

"Yes, sir," replied ET1(SS) Seabright. "I agree we're within limits."

The RPCP had shut lights, straight lines, on the starboard loop valves and open lights, circles, on the port loop. Main coolant pumps 2 and 4 were in slow speed and #3 was in fast. The starboard main steam stop valve also indicated shut. On the vertical section, three rod-bottom lights were illuminated. That was normal. There was an alarm for low flow in the starboard loop.

"Shift #3 main coolant pump to slow speed."

"Shift #3 main coolant pump to slow speed, aye." He moved the switch to the left and pulled. The 'F' light went out and the 'S' light came on. "#3 main coolant pump is running in slow speed."

"Very well. Conn, Maneuvering, ready to recover the starboard loop. Request permission to scram the reactor and recover the loop."

"Maneuvering, Conn, scram the reactor and recover the loop."

"Scram the reactor and recover the loop, aye." On the 2MC, "Commencing loop recovery."

"Reactor Operator, insert a group scram."

"Insert a group scram, aye." He opened the cover of the scram switch on the vertical panel and turned it one spot, then back to normal. Six more rod-bottom lights illuminated and a siren sounded. He cut out the alarm. "Reactor scram. Going to low-pressure cutout. Restoring startup rate scram protection." He turned a couple switches.

"Reactor scram," Jackson passed on the 2MC. "Conn, Maneuvering, reactor scram. RO, secure #3 main coolant pump."

"Secure #3 main coolant pump, aye." He turned the switch to the left. The 'S' light went dark. "#3 secured."

"Reactor scram," came over the speakers from Control.

"Unloading the turbine generators," reported the Electrical Operator.

"Charging station, commence charging." This was relayed by the phone talker.

"Charging station has commenced charging."

"Loop equalized," reported the RO.

"Secure charging. RO, open starboard main coolant cutout valves."

"Open starboard main coolant cutout valves, aye."

"Charging secured."

"Opening. Starboard main coolant cutout valves indicate open." The circle indicators were lit.

"Start #3 main coolant pump, secure #2."

"Start #3, secure #2, aye." He shifted the controls. "Main coolant pumps running one-slow, one-slow." The low flow alarm cleared.

"Engineering Watch Supervisor, bypass and open MS-1," went over the 2MC.

"EWS acknowledges," reported the phone talker.

"Indications of bypassing," reported the Throttleman.

"MS-1 indicated intermediate. MS-1 indicates open," reported Seabright.

"Machinery Lower Level, restore feed to the starboard steam generator." This went by phone.

"EWS reports MS-1 open, bypass positioned to vent upstream. Machinery Lower Level reports feed restored."

"Conn, Maneuvering, loop recovered, commencing fast recovery startup."

"Conn aye."

"Machinery Upper Level, reset and shut group one scram breakers."

It was acknowledged. The scram alarm cleared.

"Machinery Upper Level reports group one scram breakers are shut."

"RO, commence a fast recovery startup."

"Commence a fast recovery startup, aye. Latching group one."

Seabright pulled a switch on the vertical panel while moving the rod control inward. He released the switch and shifted to move rods out. After about 15 seconds six rod-bottom lights for the scram group winked out. Then a monitor stuck a tag over one light that looked like a lit light.

Seabright stopped rod motion. "Rod-bottom light for rod one-two (I-2) did not clear. Stopped rod motion."

"Insert a group scram." On the 2MC, "Rod one-two rod-bottom light did not clear. Inserting group scram." On the 7MC, "Conn, a rod-bottom light did not clear. Reinserted a scram, troubleshooting. Recommend snorkeling."

"Conn aye."

The scram alarm and the six rod-bottom lights were back on. The monitor pulled his tag once the real light lit.

"Energizing source range." Seabright flipped a switch and four meters became active.

Over the 1MC came, "Commence snorkeling."

"Machinery Upper Level reports they saw no outward motion of rod one-two. Chief Allen is troubleshooting the problem."

"Machinery Lower Level reports commenced charging."

"I'm ready to assume all loads on the battery and secure the turbine generators."

"Assume loads on the battery."

"Assume loads aye. Load is on the battery. Two hours of capacity at this rate. Turbine generators secured electrically."

"Engine Room Supervisor, secure the turbine generators mechanically."

"ERS acknowledges," came via phone. "Diesel reports the diesel is ready to assume light loads."

"Electrical Operator, start the diesel electrically and bring it on the port bus."

The EO replied and worked his panel. Soon. "The diesel is carrying light load."

"Chief Allen reports finding a bad fuse for rod one-two. Replacing it now."

It was soon done and the sequence for recovery resumed. This time the rod-bottom lights all extinguished as expected. The report came that the diesel was warmed up and it was fully loaded, almost, but not quite, eliminating discharge from the battery.

From here on everything went, mostly, like the previous scram drill I'd observed. Control came through with permission to discharge coolant without being asked. When turbine generators were online, the diesel was unloaded and ordered cooled down. When cool, snorkeling was secured and ship pressurized. By then propulsion was back on the main engines.

Chapter 13 – Training Day 2
Eastern Pacific – 40° 45.3' N 139° 19.6' W
Tuesday, August 13, 1991
1300

Rinaldi had just finished a review of drill performance with the off-going section in the Crew's Mess. It included the drills we'd run this morning and the loop recovery this section had done yesterday afternoon, as well as key points learned from drills on other sections. I thought most of the problems were minor.

"Man battle stations," came over the speakers followed by an alarm, a repeating, sharp, tone that continued for 15 seconds. This was the general alarm. "Man battle stations." Everyone headed briskly to where they needed to be.

"Follow me," urged Rinaldi and I did.

We headed to Control. It was already crowded. The contact plot over fire control had been shifted to the forward side of the consoles and a petty officer was plotting data on it. Rinaldi sat down at the forward console and put on a phone headset. Petty Officer Boyle was at the second console. LT Gonzales, the Weapons Officer, sat next to him. The XO came in and stood behind Rinaldi. He also donned phones.

"Mr. Ryan, get on the periscope stand," the XO directed. "It gets crowded in here."

I did. The Navigator was OOD. The CO came in and Cooper filled him in. We were at 400 feet, ahead two-thirds, on course two-nine-eight. There was a possible submarine contact bearing 317° with a small left bearing drift.

"I relieve you of the conn."

"I stand relieved. The Captain has the conn, Navigator has the deck."

"Helm, all ahead standard. Maneuvering make turns for 10 knots."

"All ahead standard, Helm aye. Maneuvering answers ahead standard."

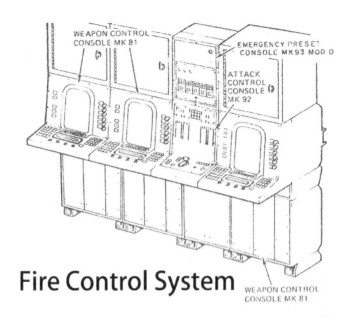

Fire Control System

WEAPON CONTROL
CONSOLE MK 81

"Maneuvering acknowledges make turns for ten knots," came from the phone taker.

"WEPS, make tube #3 ready in all respects." I remembered that was the tube connected to the test set from my tour. "NAV, load water slugs in forward and aft signal ejectors."

Both acknowledged and relayed the orders through the phone circuits. Rinaldi had the dots displayed on his screen roughly in a vertical line. LTJG McCarthy was at the third screen but did not seem to be working on the problem. I asked him and he explained his console was feeding the target to Sonar based on parameters specified by LT Cohen. LTJG Jackson and LTJG Banner were at the plot table. ET1(SS) Smith, an RO, was laying down bearing lines while Banner tried various courses and speeds looking for a combination that fit.

"Captain, battle stations are manned," reported the COW, Chief Lloyd. The COB had DOOW.

"Tube three ready in all respects," WEPS reported.

"We have a curve," Jackson said.

"Captain, we're ready to maneuver," XO said. "Last bearing to the target, 314°. Recommend coming right."

"Helm, right twenty degrees rudder, steady zero-two-zero."

""Right twenty degrees rudder, steady zero-two-zero, Helm aye. My rudder is right twenty."

"Captain, water slugs loaded in both signal ejectors."

A water slug was when a device was shot when flooded but without a signal or weapon loaded. Torpedo tube #3 was in that condition for this exercise.

"Crossed bearings on last leg, 3,200 yards," said Jackson. Don't know if it's a minimum or maximum range."

"We should have a higher bearing rate on this leg. When we get a solution on this leg I intend to shoot tube #3 at the target."

"Passing zero-one-zero to zero-two-zero."

"We're looking at about one-seven-five, 10 knots and 4,500 yards," XO said.

"Captain, recommend 400 feet, plus four, high to medium, long ping interval, Doppler in on our unit. We have 1,800 yards laminar distance with those settings."

"OK WEPS. We may need to shift to short ping interval and dial down laminar distance if range gets much shorter."

"Steady zero-two-zero."

"Get a curve," said XO.

"Crossed bearings, 2,400 yards, a minimum range.

"I have a fair solution," ENG said. "Course 170°, speed 11, range 4,000."

"WEPS, shift the unit to short-range settings."

"WEPS aye. Short ping interval, high to low and 1,000 yards laminar distance set. Enable run, 1,200 yards."

"Have a curve," said Jackson.

"Possible target maneuver," said ENG. "My solution is falling apart."

"Concur maneuver," said Banner from the plot.

"We'll stay on this course until we have a bearing rate after he's steady, then maneuver ourselves. Intend to shoot on next leg."

"Ekelund range, 4,400 yards, before his maneuver. Anchoring the plot there," said Jackson.

"I believe he turned away," said Banner. "It fits best. Crossed bearings, 3,200 yards, believed to be minimum range."

"Have a curve," said Jackson.

"We're ready to maneuver," said XO. "Recommend left. Target bears 263°, drawing left."

"Helm, left twenty degrees rudder, steady two-seven-zero."

"Left twenty degrees rudder, steady two-seven-zero, Helm aye. My rudder is left twenty."

"I'm looking at course 220°, speed 11, range 3800 yards," ENG reported.

"Range is opening now," WEPS added. "We may be able to shift to normal settings soon."

"I don't want to let it open too far. Intend to shoot early on the next leg."

"Passing two-eight zero to two-seven zero."

"Crossed bearings now 3,800 yards. Still believed to be minimum range."

"Steady two-seven-zero."

"Get a curve."

"I have a good solution, course two-two-five, speed 11, range 4,500 yards."

"Captain, request to shift to normal tactics on the unit."

"Shift to normal, WEPS. Use shallow trajectory to conserve fuel. We're in a stern chase."

"Have a curve. Ekelund range 4,800 yards. Crossed bearings 4,000 yards."

"Firing point procedures, tube #3, target one," announced the CO.

"Ship ready," Dive reported immediately.

"How's your solution for range?" XO asked ENG.

"It's not very sensitive to range variation."

"Plot, what's your latest crossed bearing?" Captain asked.

"4100 yards," reported Banner.

"Add a thousand to that and go," directed the Captain.

ENG did and looked at his dots. It seemed OK but not perfect.

"Solution ready," said XO.

"Weapon ready," WEPS said. "Enable run, 2,200 yards. Normal tactics set."

"Match sonar bearings and shoot."

"Bearing matched," ENG reported.

"Shooting tube three," WEPS announced. He took the handle on the third console, the one with no display screen, and turned it left. "Standby." He threw it full to the right. There was a rumble from below the deck. "Tube #3 fired. Torpedo course 230°."

Boyle passed a paper to plot. They drew a line on the chart and used a template to draw a couple more.

"Shot looks good from plot," announced Jackson.

"Torpedo in the water, bearing two-three-three," came over the Conn speakers.

"Ahead flank, cavitate." the Captain ordered. "Right fifteen degrees rudder, three-four-zero. Dive, 1,000 feet, twenty down. Launch both signal ejectors."

Everyone acknowledged. The lights dimmed as pumps were shifted. The deck angled and speed began to increase.

"Aft signal ejector away."

"Torpedo bears 231°," reported XO.

"Forward signal ejector away."

"Passing 600 feet."

"Secure the signal ejectors. WEPS secure tube three."

"Passing 700 feet."

"Torpedo bears 227°, drawing left."

"Torpedo will pass astern. We should be clear," stated Jackson from the plot.

"Passing 800 feet."

"OK. Secure from torpedo evasion. Secure from battle stations. Bring the plots to the Wardroom."

"Secure from battle stations; underway watch section 3," COW passed.

"Dive, 500 feet. Helm, left five degrees rudder, steady two-nine-five."

"860 feet, coming up to 500. Ten up."

"Rudder is left five, passing three-two-eight, starting to move left to two-nine-five."

"Tube #3 secured."

"NAV, take the conn. I'm at flank, coming left to two-nine-five and up to 500 feet. Waiting on reports that the signal ejectors are rigged for dive."

"Flank, coming to two-nine-five and 500 feet. I relieve you of the conn."

"I stand relieved."

"Quartermaster, Navigator has the deck and the conn."

"NAV get us on track. Full speed is good enough. We're well ahead of PIM. You can downshift pumps when you're ready."

"Yes, sir. We'll need a broadcast in a few hours."

"ENG has that covered."

He spent a couple minutes checking the chart with the quartermaster and then left for the Wardroom. I followed.

In the Wardroom the contact plot had been spread out and LT Cohen had drawn in the target's true course, speed and range. It looked only slightly different from our estimate. Our course was off 5 degrees, one knot in speed, and our range was short by 600 yards. The actual target was still in the area of detection for the torpedo.

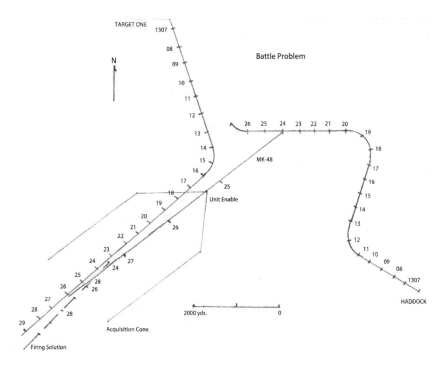

"Captain, how did you know you had a perfect shot?"

"I don't want perfect. I want good enough. If you try for perfection you take too much time and the target gets too close. This one got too close and we maneuvered for a stern shot. Ideally I'd like to shoot outside of six thousand yards so we can evade any counterattack. If we get inside 3,000 there's a good chance we both get sunk. I'd never evade a torpedo shot down the bearing to our unit.

"The stern shot is easily the safest. The other sub will never hear it coming until it goes active and won't have a good bearing. It's hard to evade. You can try to run it out of fuel, but if you can get the Mk-48 to acquire the target, it has a good enough rate of closure to make the chase very short. The Mk-48 ADCAP is better still, but we don't carry that."

"You seem quite confident."

"In battle stations, I'm in complete control. I think I have a good sense of the situation, converting the bearings, which is all we normally get, into a picture of what's happening in three dimensions. But in training, there's nothing at stake."

"What do you mean?"

"I'm naturally risk adverse. You need to be, running a nuclear submarine. If you take a chance with a 99% success rate once each week, in a year, you're likely to lose. In battle you need to take risks with much longer chances."

"Do you think you're up to it?"

"Who can know until you face it? I used to think my first CO was a tactical genius. He would be very aggressive in positioning his submarine. As I got more experienced I realized that he didn't understand the risks he was running. Maybe a bit of ignorance helps. It worked for General Custer for fifteen years. If I take a risk, I'll, at least, know it."

Chapter 14 – Training Day 3
Northern Pacific – 42° 47.5' N 146° 15.2' W
Wednesday, August 14, 1991
1100

The Captain entered and we all sat down to lunch. The table was set with a white tablecloth as usual for meals. Plates of lettuce, onion and sliced tomatoes were set out, along with a tray of just-baked buns. Bottles of ketchup, mustard and mayonnaise completed the preparation for burgers. They were passed around to get ready for the meat.

Petty Officer Glenn entered from the pantry, carrying a tray with burgers; half had melted cheese. I'd been expecting preformed patties, but these were hand-made.

"We don't use the hockey pucks," Banner stated, possibly seeing my surprise. "We can buy higher quality ground, lean, beef for less cost. The taste is worth it. We have a few cases of the standard stuff in the depths of the freezer. Hopefully we never eat our way down to it. Be sure to enjoy the lettuce and tomatoes. They'll be gone by next week."

I tried my cheeseburger. "It does taste good."

"Tom, tell everyone your impressions so far," requested the XO.

"I've entered many pages of notes in my laptop. Haddock is an incredibly complex piece of technology. It's hard to believe that it is almost 24 years old. You keep it in good shape."

"We try," said the ENG.

"Haddock has been updated during shipyard overhauls over her lifetime," added the CO. "The last, completed in early 1987 brought her up to an early 80's technology level."

"Your crew seems to be able to get the most out of what you have."

"That's what we train for."

"To me the runs of piping are a maze and panels filled with dials and switches almost incomprehensible. Everyone, officers and enlisted, seem to be studying something all the time. The newer ones are tracing systems, working on qualification in submarines to earn

118

their dolphin insignia, or learning what they need to stand their first watches. Others are working on more advanced qualifications. All that is in addition to the ship's training and routine administrative paperwork. No one has much free time."

"We like to keep everyone busy at sea," confirmed the CO. "You might have noticed that we don't have much space for recreational activities. There's the nightly movie and games, mostly card games. We regulate gambling to limit the amount a sailor can lose on the deployment."

"I noted that the average crewman is very smart and hard working. It seems quite a few had some college before joining up."

"That's true," XO confirmed. "The nucs and many of the forward ratings, Sonar, ET, FTG, require high scores on the aptitude tests and everyone is a volunteer, knowing the requirements for submarines are tougher than Navy normal."

"Many of our petty officers could have been sitting here, even in my seat, if circumstances in their lives had been a bit different," added the CO. "They're screened in initial training, looking for candidates for NROTC or the Academy and we're on the lookout too for late bloomers. We've managed to get a nominee selected the last two years."

"Not everybody can be an officer."

"We're a democracy," the CO stated. "We believe everybody could be an officer. There are no limits of class or background. Not everyone wants the responsibility. We get to make decisions, but have to accept responsibility for them. Decisions made by anyone at this table could cost lives or millions of dollars; maybe not lives in the Chop's case. It's what we signed up for. However, it's wrong to imagine that being an officer makes you better than the men you lead. It's not American.

"It's an interesting perspective. I've been impressed with the training drills. The fire drill in the Engine Room after Battle Stations was interesting. I did notice that you haven't given me any instruction in the use of the breathing masks."

"You shouldn't need them," stated the Captain. "We'd evacuate you from the compartment or put you in one if that's not possible."

"I'll have someone familiarize you with them after the next drill set," ENG offered.

"This is not a cruise ship," the CO said. "We don't do lifeboat drills. In fact we only have two, small, inflatable, rafts stuffed into the escape trunks; room for a dozen, maybe, women and children first. We stopped training submariners to escape from a bottomed submarine more than ten years ago. We have the gear and it's still possible. I think the COB and I are the only ones that got to try it in training when we were young."

"So, then what's the plan?"

"That should be clear from our training. We need to save our ship. Have you heard of the Soviet submarine, Komsomolets?"

"Was that the one that sank in 1989?"

"Exactly. They had a fire in the ninth compartment, the one furthest aft. Soviet subs tend to have more watertight compartments than ours. From what I've read this compartment comprised what we'd have in shaft alley. You know that we'd fight the fire. They evacuated the compartment and sealed the door, expecting the fire to exhaust the oxygen and burn out.

"The heat from the fire ruptured high pressure air lines which fed the fire. It also weakened seawater piping that started flooding the compartment. The fire shorted electrical cables and that caused a fire in the fifth compartment where the main switchboards were.

"The submarine surfaced. The fire may have damaged the stuffing tubes that run cables between compartments, or they were poorly maintained, because water flooded the eighth compartment. Their CO didn't recognize the danger they were in. The problem is called longitudinal stability."

"What's that?"

"Mr. Gonzales, will you explain it for him."

"Yes, sir. Longitudinal stability, in this case instability, is where the increasing angle caused by the flooding aft results in air spilling from the ballast tanks. This increases the angle and results in more air spillage, more angle, more air lost and the submarine sinks."

"Which is exactly what happened. They had personnel on deck and hatches open. The men found themselves in freezing water. The submarine sank and flooded through the open hatches. A few made it to an escape capsule built into the sail, released it and popped to the surface. However, when they opened the hatch, the seas flooded in, sinking it and only one made it out."

"How would you handle that?"

"The XO is normally the man-in-charge at the scene of a casualty. Lay out the options."

"Well...First we'd try to dewater using the drain pump, trim pump or both. That is, if we couldn't stop or isolate the source of the flooding. Second we can try to pressurize the compartment with air. About 12 to 15 psi should be enough to stop water coming in and even force it back out. That assumes we're on the surface. Anybody in the compartment would be trapped, but we might be able to lock people in or out by way of the escape trunks. The valve hand-wheels you see above each watertight door are for pressurizing compartments. Lastly, we could pump water from aft to forward, even counter-flooding as an extreme measure, to reduce the angle. Counter-flooding eats into our buoyancy but might buy some time."

"That's a good summary. My guess is they didn't even realize the danger they were in. They thought, we're on the surface, we're safe and help is on the way. The sea punishes the foolish and ignorant."

There was a knock on the forward door and SA Rogers entered, carrying a green book.

"I have a casualty report for Mr. Jackson, Engineer, XO and Captain." He opened the book and handed it to Jackson.

"We have a ground on rod control DC on inverter 'A'." He initialed the book with the attached pen. "I'm on watch next. I'll check it out. May I be excused?"

The book was passed to Engineer, XO and CO. Gonzales, due to be OOD, also left.

"It's not prudent to do drills involving cutbacks or scrams while there's a rod control issue. Does that impact your plans, ENG?"

"I had Engine Room flooding and a chloride drill that would have put us in single loop but I can shift to one that's less severe. I'll let you know what we want to do about the ground. If you'll excuse me, I'll get on it." The Captain nodded and he left.

"Is that a serious problem?"

"It's not immediately serious. We have ungrounded electrical systems, so, a single ground, will not result in current flow. A ground on the rod control system is quite rare."

"What will you do about it?"

"The first step is to localize it. I expect ENG to come back and ask to transfer the six rods on the inverter to the spare inverter. That will tell us if the ground is in the inverter or the circuitry leading to a rod drive mechanism, and if so, which one."

1300

That proved to be an accurate prediction. It was decided to do the rod transfer after securing from the next drills. We were ready to begin the first drill. I was in the Control Room. Haddock was at 400 feet, ahead full with main coolant pumps in fast speed.

An alarm sounded, like a screech, repeatedly rising and falling in pitch, the collision alarm. "Flooding in the Engine Room," came over speakers in Control followed by the collision alarm once more.

LT Gonzales grabbed the 1MC mike. "Flooding in the Engine Room." Then to the COW, "Sound the collision alarm." The alarm that sounded initially, sounded again. "Flooding in the Engine Room."

"Maneuvering rings up standard," reported Helm.
"Helm, answer all ahead standard. Dive, 150 feet, 10 up." They acknowledged and we angled up.

"Conn, Maneuvering, activated emergency closure, main coolant pumps running in slow speed."

"Flooding has stopped," came over the speaker.

"There's a collision alarm in Engine Room Lower Level, Machinery Lower Level, Torpedo Room, Diesel and some other spots. The phone by the alarm can function to make reports to Conn and Maneuvering like a 7MC," explained the Captain.

"Lost the port and starboard non-vital buses," reported Petty Officer Sheldon, the COW.

Gonzales passed "Rig ship for reduced electrical power," over the 1MC.

"Maneuvering rang up all stop," said Helm.

"Helm, all stop."

122

"Port and starboard non-vital buses reenergized."

"Passing 200 feet to 150 feet. Still have 9 knots and no effect on trim."

"Conn, Maneuvering, flooding was from air conditioning ASW, the inlet to #1 R-114 plant. The source is isolated. Restoring main seawater and unaffected ASW. Both root valves have tripped."

"We'll hold at 150 feet, Dive. We should get the main engines back in a few minutes."

It was only a couple minutes before we heard, "Conn, Maneuvering, main engine propulsion restored, limited to a standard bell. We're in one-slow, one-slow while we bring on the turbine generators."

"Helm, all ahead two-thirds."

"All ahead two-thirds, Helm aye. Maneuvering answers ahead two-thirds."

"Conn, Maneuvering, electric plant in a normal full power lineup. Ready to answer all bells. We are troubleshooting a ground on the starboard non-vital bus."

"Secure from reduced electrical power. Secure from rig for collision," passed Gonzales on the 1MC.

"Maneuvering requests to pump Engine Room bilges," piped up SN Hamm on the phones beside the BCP.

"Maneuvering, pump bilges to waste oil," directed Chief Lloyd, the Diving Officer.

"Captain, when would you use the emergency blow capability?"

"We never use it for drills, just periodic testing. In a real casualty we'd use it immediately if we were deep, say below 700 feet, if we lost propulsion, if we saw an effect on trim or if emergency closures failed to stop the flooding within 30 seconds."

"Conn, Maneuvering, the ground was on #1 R-114 plant. Secure from flooding drill."

LT Gonzales passed, "Secure from flooding drill," on the 1MC.

"WEPS, we'd like to be 400 feet, full speed to start the next drill."

"Why are those conditions needed?"

"Different initial conditions might require different immediate actions. We try to vary the conditions so the sections are familiar with all situations and the drills don't become stereotyped. For this drill Maneuvering should request a low bell and shallow depth. In the previous drill, flooding, starting at full with main coolant pumps in fast, required Maneuvering to drop the bell and downshift the pumps. That's different from their actions if the bell were low to begin."

The conditions were set. The CO took a phone call and granted permission to begin.

"Conn, Maneuvering, high salinity port condensate. Request minimum bell. Request Casualty Assistance Team."

"Conn aye. Helm, all ahead one-third." He picked up the 1MC mike. "High salinity port condensate. Engineering Casualty Assistance Team lay aft; section 1 provide."

"All ahead one-third, Helm aye. Maneuvering answers ahead one-third."

"Dive, make your depth 150 feet."

"150 feet, aye. Ten up."

"What is the Casualty Assistance Team?"

"We use personnel from the off-going watch to assist the current watches in combating the casualty. The stations vary depending on the casualty. Some become phone talkers. In this casualty we have personnel in Engine Room Lower Level testing water for the chlorides and ELTs in Machinery Lower Level analyzing the steam generators, mixing chemicals and getting set for steam generator blowdowns. For casualties where we sound an alarm, we use damage control parties to do the same function, but that's just a different name for, essentially, the same people."

"Conn, Maneuvering, chlorides in port condensate. Shutting down port side. Shifting to half power lineup, starboard, and single main engine operation. Limited to a full bell, but still request minimum bell."

"That's the hard part and the timing looks good. The next step is to get results from the steam generators and start blowdowns. We're almost at 150 feet so the ship is ready. Mr. Gonzales, Maneuvering has my permission to blowdown steam generators as needed."

124

"Yes, Captain."

"What does the blowdown do?"

"Here the idea it to reduce the amount of chloride compounds in the steam generators. Chlorides can lead to corrosion and cracking of the tubes, so we want to keep it within limits and fix it as quickly as possible if it gets high. A single blowdown drops the level by a factor of 0.7. It does the same for phosphates and pH, so we add chemicals to keep those parameters in specification."

"Conn, Maneuvering, chlorides greater than point five. Request to blowdown steam generators as needed."

"Maneuvering, Conn, blowdown steam generators as needed."

"Blowdown steam generators as needed, Maneuvering aye. Commencing blowdowns."

"That's just under nine minutes to the first blowdown. We consider under ten to be good. Mr. Jackson probably already started raising steam generator level before he called Control. We'll do a blowdown on the other steam generator and three more on this one. The only really critical point is to make sure we're adding water back into the secondary plant as fast as we're blowing it overboard. I don't expect a problem though."

It did go smoothly.

1600

"Captain, I've been properly relieved as Engineering Officer of the Watch by Mr. McCarthy. Except for the rod control ground, conditions normal aft. We did the rod transfer and the ground is on rod I-5."

In the Wardroom, besides me, were CO, XO, ENG and LTJG Jackson.

"Very well, Mr. Jackson. ENG, what do you want to do next?"

"Rod transfer showed the ground is from the rod transfer switch to the control rod drive mechanism. We need to pull the rod fuses. If, with the fuses out, we still have the ground, it means the ground is between the rod transfer switch and the fuses, essentially in the bottom of inverter 'A'. If not it's in the cable or the mechanism."

"When do you want to do it?"

"It requires a group scram. Is that a problem?"

"I said no scram for training, but this is troubleshooting, so no problem. However, once we need to scram for troubleshooting, there's nothing preventing us from getting maximum training value out of it. We'll use it for watch qualification, like we did for Mr. Ohanian's."

"We can be ready in half an hour. We'll do a small primary leak at the sample sink with a contaminated man for the second drill. It will give Mr. Jackson and Chief Allen a chance to consider the next steps based on the results."

"OK, we'll do that. XO, let's get Mr. Ohanian up as Dive under instruction."

"Yes, sir. I'll check with the COB to see who needs it as Chief of the Watch."

LT Gonzales came in to report his relief as OOD as the meeting broke up.

2100

In the Wardroom again, the table, cleared from the evening meal, had a brown cover matching the upholstery on the chairs and benches. I was with the XO, ENG, LTJG Banner, LTJG Jackson and ETC(SS) Allen.

The Captain entered. "Seats." He took his spot at the aft end of the table. "It's your meeting ENG."

"As you know, the ground is between the switch and the fuses. We'd like to try to replace the rod transfer switch. We have a spare in supply."

"Is that the spare you're holding, Chop?"

"Yes, sir." He passed it down to the CO, who looks it over.

"It seems very robust. I don't see how it could cause a ground. There's a lot of wires to remove and replace."

"Yes," said Jackson. "We think two to three hours to replace the switch and two hours to retest it. We'll need to do rod testing for rod I-5. Then we do a short form precrit and a normal startup, another hour and a half."

"There's still a possibility it could be the fuse holders. How do you handle that?"

126

"We can write the repair procedure to remove the wires to the fuse holders first and recheck for grounds," ENG explained. "If the ground clears, we just replace the fuse holder. We have a spare. Just doing the fuse holder would save about an hour, but we still need to do rod testing."

"We can do it. Plan on tomorrow after lunch. I'd want to see the repair procedure. Do we need anything other than a regular short form because of the work on the rods?"

"No," stated ENG. "The precrit is done with all fuses removed. The rods aren't involved. The interlocks are based on inverter limit switches and we're not affecting that area."

"OK." He turned to the phone and cranked it. "Mr. Nguyen, go flank. We need to get 45 miles ahead of PIM."

"Captain," said Chief Allen, "we can save some time by labeling all the wires before we scram. I've looked at it, and if we have your permission to work on energized gear, we should be able to do it and save half an hour."

"I'm thinking you've opened it up. Did you set up an electrical safety area?"

"Yes. I gave permission," said ENG. "We were only looking, not working."

"A fine point, but acceptable. I would have authorized it, had you asked. Do you still have the area set up?"

"Yes, Captain," said the chief.

"I'll come back and take a look. I'd like to see what we're getting into."

"Give us five minutes, Captain," said ENG.

Everyone except the CO and I filed out. I went aft with him five minutes later. Inverter 'A' was in Machinery Upper Level on the starboard side on the first cross aisle aft of the steps leading to the Tunnel. Rubber mats had been placed on the deck and shielding the panels on the aft end of the aisle. The lower panel of the inverter, used for ventilation, had been removed and set aside. This allowed a view of the interior, just below where the fuse holders and rod transfer switches were mounted.

The Captain removed his belt and took a couple pens from his upper pocket. He checked the other pockets.

"Do you have a safe flashlight?"

Chief Allen handed him one, already on, that had the metal switch taped over. The CO got down on his back on the mat and scooted over until he could see inside. He brought the light to the opening and moved it to see various spots.

"It's very many wires, but you could get at most of them. I think there will be a few you can't label until we pull the next panel off after shutdown. Interesting…Will you hand me a coffee stirrer; unused, of course."

The watch, ET2 Dixon, went aft and returned with the wooden stick. Chief Allen handed it to the Captain. He used it to touch something inside.

"Could you check the ground reading now?"

"Ground clear," said Dixon.

"Try again."

"It's back."

"Again."

"Gone."

"Chief, see this brown wire. It was resting against the cabinet frame. I've moved it clear. Vibration must have rubbed it against the metal and worn a cut in the insulation. A bit of electrical tape and we should be good until we can replace the wire in port."

"Yes, sir."

"You have my permission to do that energized with normal safety precautions."

The CO got up and retrieved his pens and belt. While he put it back on, Allen, Dixon and Jackson took turns looking.

"ENG, it looks like we're back to a normal drill schedule tomorrow." He walked forward and I followed.

"Captain, how did you find that?"

"I'd seen it before, so I was prepared to see it again. I'm no smarter than anyone else. I just have more experience. Though I don't mind if they think I'm smarter."

Chapter 15 – Training Day 4
Northern Pacific – 44° 08.3' N 153° 24.7' W
Thursday, August 15, 1991
1230

I was in the Crew's Mess where section 3 sat at the tables awaiting a critique of the morning drill and those from the 16 to 20 watch yesterday. LTJG McCarthy and the Engineer entered by the door from the Pantry. Rinaldi took a spot in the forward end between two rows of tables while Jackson took a seat next to the aisle opposite MMC(SS) Dawson, the EWS.

"We'll start with morning drills," said the ENG. "First was a series of bells. In the shift to flank the fast speed indicator for #5 main coolant pump was disabled. Petty Officer Allen correctly was calling out the starting surges on the turbine generators. Petty Officer Smith saw the lack of running indication but reported normal flow and told Mr. McCarthy he was continuing with the pump shift. That's the way it should be. Petty Officer Lynn went right to the fuse on the breaker and spotted the burnt fuse indicator. Any questions?

"OK. Next was loss of main lube oil. Petty Officer Tanner stopped the shaft from flank in 27 seconds. Petty Officer Powers spotted the high differential pressure on the strainer and requested permission to shift the strainer. While permission to shift strainers is required for routine cleaning, in a loss of lube oil casualty, if you spotted what looks like a strainer problem, report the problem and shift strainers on your own initiative. Prompt restoration of flow could minimize damage. Question? Chief."

"Yes, sir. We'd want to observe the situation for some time with propulsion on the EPM. In normal operations we never get a clogged strainer, so finding out what's going on is important."

"A good point, Chief. Next was high temperature ion exchanger inlet. Smith immediately shut CP-3. Remember, if we get this alarm while we are discharging, the first step is to stop discharging before shutting CP-3. We don't want to depressurize a section of primary piping, and potentially, allow back-flow of seawater that could introduce chlorides into the primary loop. Questions?

"Yesterday afternoon we did an Engine Room flooding and a high chloride drill. This section did a reactor scram to troubleshoot the inverter 'A' ground. There were trainees on most spots. They did well. You've probably all heard that the ground problem was fixed. Your second drill was a small leak at the primary sample sink with personnel contamination.

"The flooding drill went very smoothly. We started at full speed with main coolant pumps in fast. That required dropping the bell to standard and downshifting the pumps. The emergency closure stopped the flooding but we kept the source unknown until the main steam root valves tripped on condenser overpressure. That gives you the most to restore but this section did well in restoring main engine propulsion. That is key to keeping us operating and avoiding a need for an emergency blow.

"The second drill was chlorides in port condensate with high steam generator chlorides. There are a couple of key points I want to reiterate. The first key to doing well on the drill is to find the affected condensate header and quickly secure it by shutting down its condensate pump. You want to draw turbidities and backup samples on both headers quickly, but have care handling the test tubes and samples. Nothing screws the drill up more than fingering the wrong side as the problem and a misplaced finger or a drop of sweat can give you a false positive. Petty Officer Powers?"

"Yes, sir. What should we do if only one sample is positive?"

"Draw two more ASAP. Remember you can call a positive result immediately, but you need to wait two minutes to be sure it's negative. In the drill yesterday, you got it right and secured the port condensate header and reported that to Maneuvering. They moved to shut down steam into the port condenser to stop wasting water. The second key is to identify the level of contamination in the steam generators and get the corrective blowdowns started. We simulated a level that could be fixed by blowdowns for this drill.

"Now the key to doing the blowdowns properly is having enough water in the secondary plant. Here Mr. Jackson ordered makeup feed bypassed early, but surge tank levels got too high before the initial blowdowns were ordered, so bypassing was secured. We waited too long to restart bypassing when blowdowns started. This resulted in losing a couple minutes when we started the rapid blowdowns, and it might have been more significant, had we continued the series. Petty Officer Owen?"

"I'm the surge tank watch when we're Casualty Assistance Team on this drill. I'm on the phones. Could I just recommend restarting bypassing when I see tank levels dropping?"

"Yes, an excellent idea. I'll bring that up with the other sections when I review this drill. Maneuvering can get distracted but the surge tank levels are your only responsibility in this.

"On the leak at the sample sink, priority one is to stop the leak, even if it causes you to get contaminated. Set boundaries for potential contamination of surfaces and decking. Set them conservatively. The next priority is getting any contaminated personnel evacuated and decontaminated. You took 10 minutes to move the contaminated man. That's good but there was a delay at the monitoring station forward of the Tunnel. Once you see there is contamination, don't try and analyze it, just send him to the decontamination shower.

"What about cleaning up the contamination?" Petty Officer Hughes, the Machinery Upper Level watch in this section, asked.

"Once we have the spill or leak stopped, boundaries established and verified and the affected personnel evacuated to decon, we can deal with that in a deliberate manner with personnel suited in proper clothing. Realistically, it's going to take some time.

"Any other questions or comments? That's all for now then."

1500

I entered the Wardroom after the afternoon drill session that included battle stations and a fire in the galley drill. I got to wear an EAB with all the other personnel in Control, including the CO, as we went to periscope depth to ventilate and remove the simulated smoke. With no sonar contacts, it was considered an excellent time to practice ship control in severe conditions. LT Gordon walked in carrying a couple books.

"Good afternoon Tony. Do you mind if I ask you a few questions?"

"What type of questions?"

"How do you like your job? What are your plans? I'm trying to get an idea of what motivates the officers and crew."

"It's not a career for me. I'm planning on getting out when my commitment is up in June '93."

"Why?"

"My wife, Barbara, is pregnant, due in early November."

"Congratulations."

"Thanks. I might not be there for her. The Captain said he'd try to get me home. We're scheduled to be in Guam for an upkeep period, but that could change. I just want to be with my family and see my children grow up."

"Why did you join and choose submarines in the first place?"

"You mean, besides the full college scholarship? I was Navy ROTC at the University of Missouri. If you could handle the calculus and science requirements and the extra commitment, going nuclear increased your selection chances. I thought I'd like submarines better than being on a huge aircraft carrier. I think I might work harder on a sub, but we have very good people."

"How about patriotism?"

"I'm glad I live in the USA and proud of my country. I'm doing my part to defend it. Communism is an abstract concept to me. I guess I don't have Nguyen's perspective on the issue. I've nothing against Russians or Chinese. As long as they do nothing against us, I'd say, live and let live."

"What are your plans for after the Navy?"

"Nothing firm yet; it's too early to start interviewing. There's always civilian nuclear work, but nuclear submarine officers are in high demand in other fields. Smart hard working people are always needed."

2030

After dinner I was back in the propulsion plant talking to the watches. Petty Officer Seabright, the Reactor Operator from the previous section, was working in Machinery Space Upper Level. He had a phone headset on and was writing on a clipboard.

"What are you working on, Petty Officer Seabright?"

"I'm doing weekly checks on the reactor protection system, Tom. I'm Kevin, by the way."

"Kevin, how do like serving on Haddock?"

132

"It's OK, I guess. It's my only submarine. I have friends on some of the other submarines in San Diego and we're better than most."

The CO came up from the lower level.

"Tom, Petty Officer Seabright."

"Good evening Captain. What are you doing this evening?"

"Just walking around. I usually visit every space on board, every day. I look around and talk with those on watch."

"And check whether they're awake?"

"I doubt it. Petty Officer Lynn called every watch station as soon as he spotted me aft. Isn't that right?" Lynn, standing a few feet aft nodded, confirming what was supposed to be unmentioned. "I don't sneak around my own ship."

"What's in your hand?"

"A 3x5 card I use to write down any problems I find. I haven't seen anything major. My next stop is Engine Room Lower Level. Want to come along?"

"Thanks."

We dropped down the access between the switchboard outside Maneuvering and the LiBr air conditioning unit.

"We have our air conditioning units here, the LiBr and two R-114 plants. We're in cold water now so just the LiBr is sufficient. Petty Officer Powers, can I see your logs."

"Yes, sir." He handed him the clipboard.

"Any problems?"

"No, sir."

"How are you doing on your upper level card?"

"I'm almost done. I'll get my interview with the chief tomorrow."

"Very good. I see you're well ahead on your submarine quals too." He initialed the log sheet and handed it back. "We'll be walking around."

We did. He had a bright flashlight, not government issue that was shined into dark places behind and above some of the equipment. The evaporator and a couple seawater pumps were in the space with the air conditioning units. The next bay aft had the much larger main seawater pumps and four condensate pumps. He climbed outboard of each condenser and made a note on his card before continuing aft.

The next bay had the main lube oil pumps. The passage split to port and starboard walkways as the bottom of the reduction gear occupied the central space. There were auxiliary seawater pumps on the starboard side. The fourth bay had shaft lube oil and a passage from port to starboard behind the reduction gear. We climbed the ladder on the port side, opening a hatch in the upper level deck and shutting it behind.

We walked forward, stopping to chat with Chief Dawson and the watch. He stepped into Maneuvering where LTJG Ohanian had the watch. We were at full speed gaining distance after the day's drills. He handed his 3x5 card to Ohanian and asked him about the results of the protection system testing. It was satisfactory. I suspect he would already have been informed if that were not the case.

We left and continued forward. At the Wardroom we both got ourselves fresh coffee. The CO went to his stateroom, sat and picked up a green book on his desk, marked with a stamp saying Confidential. The door was left open.

"Do you have time for more discussion?"

"Sure, I have plenty of time."

He shifted to the bed, taking the book. I took the seat. He opened the outboard desk and put the book and coffee mug on them.

"I noticed that. I'd expected you would be giving more direction."

"The less I do the better I like it. I expect my officers to handle their watches and run their departments and divisions with minimal direction. I set policy, coordinate and monitor how things are going. There are different styles for being a CO. I try to use the coach style. I call the plays but depend on my team to execute them and train them to do so.

"The natural inclination is to give orders and demand approval for everything. As CO you know you have experience and you have confidence in yourself. That mode fails when someone on watch is confronted with a situation that requires immediate action and they are trained to clear everything with the CO first. It's also not satisfying to work for such a CO. You feel, correctly, that you're not trusted."

"People will make mistakes."

134

"Yes, myself included. We try to learn from our mistakes, even better, from other persons' mistakes. I try to show support when someone screws up. Then we work to see it never happens again. Excuse me."

He cranked the phone box.

"Chief of the Watch, could you send your messenger down for the night orders?"

"What's that about?"

"This is my night order book. NAV drafts them with input from ENG and WEPS. I might add something before I sign them. This tells the watches what to do overnight. We'll get the 0300 broadcast, that's 1000 Z, and ventilate, shoot trash and blow sanitary #2. There's an 0307 satellite pass too. The reactor protection and alarm system checks are listed but those are already done. I asked each section to shift to a half power electrical lineup and back to a full power lineup and to practice stopping the shaft from a full bell."

There was a knock on the bulkhead and SN Hamm appeared in the open doorway.

"Captain?"

The CO handed him the book and he left.

"Who reads it?"

"The OOD, Dive, Chief of the Watch, Sonar Supervisor, Quartermaster, Radioman, FTOW, TMOW, ETOW, AEF, Auxiliaryman, EOOW and EWS, plus the XO. They use it to plan for the scheduled events."

"When you became CO did you make many changes?"

"Yes, several. When you assume command is the ideal time to make changes. The crew expects that each CO will be somewhat different. The crew wants their CO to succeed. It's their success too. You want to continue things that are working and improve the areas that are weak.

"I told you I emphasized engineering training and that was my major change. I also rewrote the CO's Standing Orders. They are a set of policies that the watches, particularly the OOD and Ship's Duty Officer, should follow. The standard version is filled with boilerplate and cover your ass statements. They are useless. If the OOD violates my standing orders and gets us into trouble, I'm still responsible. I tossed all that out and made my policies in simple, clear statements, that would be easy to follow."

"I can see you're proud of them. Can I read them?"

"There's a copy in Control. I guess I am proud of that. Simple, clear and easy to follow is my basic command philosophy. I'm happy with it so far."

Chapter 16 – Change in Plans

Northern Pacific – 45° 11.2' N 162° 54.5' W
Friday, August 16, 1991
1500

Haddock was at periscope depth, emergency ventilating the Engine Room to wrap up a loss of main lube with a lube oil fire drill. The drill had gone well, even with a simulated fire hose rupture and a simulated failed battery on the thermal imager used to spot the sources of heat in the simulated heavy smoke. I had gone to Control as we prepared to emergency ventilate.

The difference between emergency ventilating and normal ventilating is that the bad air is drawn right from the affected space to the low-pressure blower or diesel and doesn't impact the other compartments. However, for the Engine Room, the flow path requires the bad air to flow through the watertight door into the Auxiliary Machinery Space before entering the ventilation ducts. This means that personnel in the AMS must don breathing masks before emergency ventilating starts. The watertight door and the ventilation supply damper are opened on the announcement to commence.

We had started ventilating five minutes ago. Word was just passed to secure from the drill and general emergency, but continue emergency ventilating. The plan was to copy the 2200 Z broadcast and catch a 1512 Transit pass before resuming our track.

"Conn, Radio, copied the 2200 Zulu ZBO. We have two op-immediate messages on the broadcast."

"What's op-immediate?" I asked LT Cohen, the OOD. The CO had left when we started ventilating.

"Wait one." He got on the phone and passed the news to the CO and NAV. Both were in the Wardroom.

"We have four message priorities. Flash is highest for something that needs urgent action right now. It should go out inside 10 minutes. Immediate is usually used for operational or time sensitive intelligence and goes off within an hour. Op-immediate means it impacts our operations. Priority is next and we usually use that for material support requirements. Routine is used mostly for administrative traffic."

"What does it mean?"

"We'll know soon enough. The messages are probably printing out right now. The highest priority goes at the top of the broadcast. They'd even break the stream if a new flash or immediate message gets released. I'm sure NAV is in Radio right now, getting his first look."

1530

Haddock had secured ventilating and was heading deep again. In the Wardroom was the Captain, XO, ENG and NAV. NAV was explaining the requirements of the new messages.

"The first message shifts us to a new broadcast. The new broadcast was effective 1600 Z and messages will be duplicated on both broadcasts until 0400 Z on the 17th. We are directed to copy the 0600 or 0800 broadcast. The second message revises our track. The new track takes us to the Bering Sea through the Amukta Pass through the Aleutians. We've plotted the new track on a chart of the Northern Pacific and are working on the detailed track now."

"When do we reach Amukta Pass?"

"Sometime on the 18th, Sunday. The new track intersects our current track in 125 miles. It's active now through to 1200 Z on the 19th. We have 50 miles on each side of the track, so we could make a turn in 6 to 8 hours depending on how much distance we cover."

"What do you want to do about the drills for next watch?" ENG asked.

"Run them as scheduled. We'll be able to catch the new broadcast when we go to periscope depth during the scram. We'll keep our schedule for now."

"What does all this mean?" I asked.

"Directing us to copy a certain broadcast means they have a long message and don't want to repeat it. It's probably our operation order for what they want us to do in the Bering Sea. The diversion also means we'll be a few days late reaching Japan. Will that be a problem?"

"No. My publisher has arranged some events for me but the dates are flexible. I need to call them on arrival. I was told that planned dates and even our destination might change."

"Good. ENG, you're on deck with your drill team. NAV, I'll look over the new track once it's ready.

1900

Everyone had just taken seats for Friday dinner. Fried chicken was on the menu, but first up was salad. This was the last of the fresh lettuce according to the Chop.

"You already know we're being diverted to the Bering Sea," the Captain began. "We'll copy our op-order in four hours, but we got some intel on the last broadcast that gives a clue to what's up. It appears that three Soviet subs are missing from Petropavlovsk, a Delta I, a Victor III and an Akula. The Russians have been staying close to home the last few years, but a triple deployment would still be unusual at any time."

"They must think they are not just on a week's training," ENG stated. "Why send us to the Bering?"

"They are estimated to be out of the local training areas, but the message didn't share the reason for that assessment. I don't think there is anything special pointing to the Bering Sea other than Pet-er being on the western edge of it. There were two other units indicated on the intel message, Louisville, and CTU 14.1.1; that's probably someone already deployed to Westpac."

"They'll probably be assigned search areas too," XO said.

"Well, we should know in four hours. Plan on a briefing tomorrow during field day. WEPS, you and Dave work up a search plan and briefing on the Soviet subs. Use historical environmental data. We'll update that when we get on station. We'll need weapons settings too. NAV will be briefing the op-order and the transit through Amukta Pass. Everyone should reread and initial my Patrol Orders."

"Yes, sir. I'll be ready," WEPS assured.

"Tom, that brings us to you. The operation will likely be classified top secret. The fact that US subs look for Soviet subs is a secret everyone knows, but we still control how successful or unsuccessful we are. You're only cleared for secret. Most of the crew is only cleared to that level. Just officers, less the Chop, radiomen and a few key others have top secret. We handle that by getting everyone to sign a security statement. If you have no problem with that we'll keep you fully involved."

"Don't they know I'm onboard?"

"I'm sure somebody at COMSUBPAC knows, but it's not like they had a choice of attack subs near the Bering Sea. That issue was left for me to deal with, and I am."

"OK, I'm in."

Chapter 17 – Briefing

Northern Pacific – 48° 54.0' N 168° 10.8' W
Saturday, August 17, 1991
1300

We were back in the Wardroom for an operations briefing. LT Gordon relieved NAV as OOD and LTJG Ohanian took over for LTJG Jackson as EOOW. Besides the officers, also attending were the COB, QMCS(SS) Spillman, RMC(SS) Moore, STSC(SS) Harvey, STS1(SS) Johnson and STS2(SS) Gardner. The chiefs and petty officers, except for the COB, were standing. The Captain came in and took his seat.

"As you have already heard, we've been tasked to search for three Soviet submarines that have been missing from their base in Petropavlovsk for, now, 5 or 6 days. We got our operational orders in last night and NAV will brief us on them. Mr. Cohen will brief on our quarry and the search plan. Our search area is the Bering Sea, east of 180. NAV, you can start."

"Our targets for this operation are the Delta I, Victor III and Akula that are missing from Petropavlovsk. We are tasked to locate and track one, or more, of these submarines. If we find one we are tasked to track it for 24 hours then pull off at least 20 miles and report contact. After reporting we are to try to reestablish contact and maintain trail until the operation is terminated or 2359 Z August 31st. As the Captain said we have the Bering Sea, east of 180. If we are in trail and it appears the Soviet submarine will cross west of 180 in the next 24 hours, we should pull clear 20 miles and transmit. In any event we are not to cross west of 180 without authorization."

"Another submarine is assigned a search area west of 180," added the Captain. "There is also a large search area northwest of Hawaii."

"We will compile a patrol report for this operation. All materials will be marked top secret. Collect the sonar, fire control, mast exposure logs and plots at the end of each watch."

"If we are in contact, we will wait on collecting the plot until we need to change paper and reset the plot," XO said. "NAV is responsible for assembling the final report and data package. We've already started on the required appendices."

"We will begin the patrol report when we clear Amukta Pass and deploy the towed array," NAV continued. "Sonar will reset their contact numbers back to Sierra-1. A target will be assigned a master contact number once it is identified.

"That brings me to the transit of Amukta Pass. At 1300 we were about 215 miles from where we will go to periscope depth for a final fix. We should be there at 0300 ship time and there is a 0322 pass. The plan is to get the 1000 Z broadcast and ventilate before the transit. Amukta Pass is about 30 miles wide, and mostly, deep water. There are pinnacles that rise, some as high as 65 fathoms. We should not see any water worse than 85 fathoms. For the transit, we'll be at 200 feet and Yellow Sounding is 50 fathoms and Red sounding is 35 fathoms. Either Senior Chief Spillman or I will be supervising the navigation picture during the transit."

"We don't know what to expect on fishing activity," the CO said. "The majority of our contacts in the Bering are likely to be fishing. We don't want to pass close behind a trawler. I don't want to break its nets or risk them fouling on our submarine.

"Do you have anything more NAV?"

"I'm done, Captain."

"Before we get Mr. Cohen's brief on the targets, I want to discuss where we'll be searching and why I decided to go that way. The Walker Spy Ring told the Soviets they were vulnerable. They know about SOSUS and that slow and shallow are the best ways to avoid it. Our drills and high speed have probably given the SOSUS operators some good training, but they're on our side.

"Since we can't cover the entire Bering, I plan to search in shallow water. We will go north from Amukta Pass and intersect the 100 fathom curve. There is a broad flat shelf of shallow water that is generally a little deeper than 60 fathoms. We'll operate at 180 feet with the towed array at short stay. We'll head west paralleling the 100 fathom curve a few miles inside it. There are some pinnacles we'll need to look out for and we'll give them a wide berth. Yellow will be 25 fathoms and Red, 20. That's not much warning but search speed will be two-thirds, 7.5 knots."

"I've seen the numbers," said LT Gonzales. "We have a real possibility of long range detection of the Delta, and possibly, the Victor III in deep water. Why give up on that opportunity?"

"The Russians know that too," said ENG. "They won't give us the chance."

"Exactly, ENG. That's why we're looking shallow. I'm also betting they won't get too far from deep water, because they wouldn't want to be trapped in shallow water in case they are detected. I think P-3s out of Adak will be flying on these guys too and I'll give them the deep water; it's where their sonobuoys are most effective anyway.

"Mr. Cohen, you're on."

"Thank you Captain. We are looking for a Delta I, a Victor III and an Akula. Here is a representation of them.

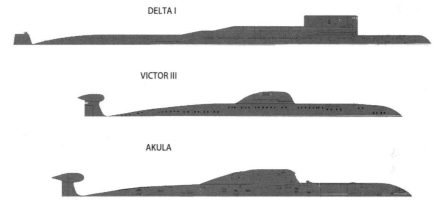

DELTA I

VICTOR III

AKULA

"The pods on the Victor III and Akula are believed to house a towed sonar array, similar to ours, but not as capable. They also house the latest 'Shark Gill' sonar system with a 2.4 kHz active component. The Delta I carries 12 missiles with multiple nuclear warheads and a range sufficient to strike targets anywhere in the Northern Hemisphere from any spot in the Bering or even pier side in Petropavlovsk.

"The Delta and Victor have similar propulsion plants, like we and the pre-Ohio Class SSBN, both have S5W nuclear plants. The Delta does have two of them though. The Victor runs a single 5-bladed screw and the Delta has two. The Victor has two small screws mounted on the stern planes that may serve them like our SPM for emergency propulsion. The Akula has a new type of propulsion plant and a quieter 7-bladed screw, similar to ours. That makes it a much tougher opponent.

"The following sonar detection estimates are based on historical environmental data. We'll shoot a bathythermograph buoy after we exit Amukta Pass and again when we enter the shallows. We'll update that daily and environmental noise on each watch. That said, the Bering Sea is a quiet environment except for geologic noise from active volcanoes along the Aleutian Islands."

"A comment on that," XO broke in. "You have to be careful that, in using the towed array, you don't have a noisy volcano on the opposite side of your contact. You need to choose your courses to put them in different beams."

"Sonar will tell you if there is a problem," said Petty Officer Johnson. "But it's best to avoid it."

"Yes, thank you. Now back to our detection ranges. For the Delta we estimate detection ranges from 6,000 to 10,000 yards. That's assuming he's at slow speed, around 5 knots, and we're at our 7.5 knot search speed. Counter-detection of us by him should be about 3,000 to 4,000 yards. For the Victor, it's 4,000 to 8,000 yards to detect and 4,000 to 5,000 to counter-detect. The Akula is a problem. At slow speed it's as quiet as we are and might have almost as good sonar. The estimate is 2,000 to 5,000 for detection and counter-detection. It might come down to who has the best sonarmen."

"I like our chances then," said the Captain and I could see the sonarmen took it as the intended praise. "Thank you, Mr. Cohen.

"We're about done, but first, a few final items. Chief Moore, we'll be deploying the floating wire antenna once through the pass. On our search speed and depth we should be able to copy the broadcast almost continuously.

"The patrol report is in Zulu time but I've decided not to shift our clocks. We'll stay on San Diego time until a couple days before Japan, whenever that is.

"We won't be running drills, so we'll go to a straight 6-hour watch rotation, starting with 08-14 tomorrow. ENG, since there won't be drills I'd like the nucs to take the written exams we prepared based on what the ORSE has been asking lately."

"Yes, sir. It's ready to go. Is Monday OK?"

"Fine. Finally the watch bill. XO and ENG are port and starboard as CDO. NAV, WEPS and LT Cohen are OOD. LT Gordon, LT Nguyen and LTJG Jackson are JOOD. Since you all have your OOD quals, you can swap off as OOD when we're searching, with the CDO's permission. COB, you and the Chop will be JOOW, responsible for the narrative log and collecting the other logs after the watch. Mr. Ryan, we can use a third JOOW to fill out the third section watch. It's yours if you want it. You'll get no better experience than that."

"I'm in. But I'm a civilian, can I do that?"

"You're breathing and you know how to write. You're qualified. This work will have a smaller readership than your last effort."

"Captain," said LT Gonzales. "You wanted four 48s loaded. We need to exercise tubes. We did tube #3 at battle stations, but I need to withdraw the torpedoes from the others and shoot a water slug."

"I see. Load tube #3 after field day. We can do the other tubes, one at a time, starting 1100 tomorrow. Will that work?"

"Yes, sir."

Chapter 18 – The Game

Northern Pacific – 50° 35.3' N 169° 55.6' W
Saturday, August 17, 1991
2100

After the pizza dinner I was back in the XO's stateroom typing some notes into my laptop. The XO was at the inboard desk reviewing enlisted evaluations. There was a knock on the bulkhead. The CO was at the door.

"Tom are you interested in a game this evening?"

"What game?"

"Ukkers. It's originally British, I believe, but it's played by Canadians and Australians too. I once had a match against some Aussie submariners when I was on a sub visiting Perth. The rules are simple. There are two teams of two. You can be my partner. XO are you in?"

"I'll try it."

"I'll play too," XO said. "I'll see if NAV is available."

"Great, I'll meet you in the Wardroom."

The CO left and the XO went to find a partner. I headed to the Wardroom. I was the first there. I got myself some coffee. The CO came in carrying a rectangular wooden box, a couple inches thick, and a can of Pepsi. He put the box in front of his seat and went into the Pantry to get a glass with some ice. While he was gone the XO and NAV came in.

"Take the second chair," The XO suggested to me.

He took the first chair and the NAV was on the end of the bench outboard. The CO returned and took his customary spot. He poured some soda into the glass and opened the box, revealing a game board.

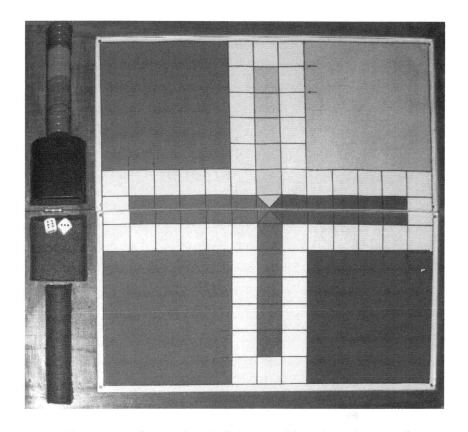

There were four colored disks matching the colors on the board, a dice cup and two standard, six-sided, dice. He handed me some laminated cards.

"These are the rules. Rule #1 is most important."

I read. It seemed simple.

The CO took a red and green piece and put his hands behind his back. He presented two fists to the XO. He chose the right hand that was opened to reveal the red piece. The board was turned so red faced the XO. I was blue, the CO, green, and the NAV, orange.

We arranged our pieces on the large squares. The others lined theirs up before the exit square and I copied them.

"This is Harbor Stations. You need a SIX to come out," CO explained.

The XO rolled. There wasn't a SIX. He passed the cup to the CO, again no SIX. NAV also failed to roll SIX. My roll was a SIX and THREE.

"Move a piece to the white square. That's your SIX, then count three spaces clockwise," CO explained. "You get another role because you rolled a SIX."

I rolled again, FOUR and THREE. I advanced my piece seven spots. I passed the dice cup to the XO. He rolled a SIX and FIVE and brought out a red piece. Next was a SIX and ONE. He brought out a second piece. Next was FIVE and TWO. He moved his second piece five and the first two.

The Captain again failed to roll SIX. NAV rolled SIX and TWO and brought out an orange piece. His next roll was TWO and TWO. He advanced his piece four spaces.

I rolled SIX and FOUR.

"Tom, bring out a piece but take the four on the first piece. You'll be in position to kill red on your next roll."

I did as the Captain suggested. My next roll was FOUR and ONE. I sent both red pieces back to Home Harbor.

The XO failed to roll SIX. The CO rolled double SIX. He moved two green pieces to the exit square. The next roll was SIX and ONE. He brought out a third piece and advanced it one space. Next roll was THREE and ONE. He advanced the single piece four spaces, leaving the Tit in place.

The NAV rolled FOUR and THREE. His orange piece moved a space ahead on my exit square piece but since neither four nor three would land on me he failed to kill me.

I rolled FOUR and FIVE and took nine spaces with my first piece, advancing it beyond CO's Tit.

The XO rolled SIX and TWO and brought out a piece. Next was THREE and TWO. The CO rolled FIVE and THREE and took them with his single piece. NAV had a SIX and TWO. He brought out a piece and moved his lead piece two spots. Next was FIVE and ONE. He moved his lead piece six.

I rolled SIX and FOUR and brought out my third piece. Next was FOUR and TWO. I killed an orange piece. The XO rolled a double THREE but could only advance four before being blocked by CO's Tit. The CO rolled SIX and FOUR and brought out his last piece and moved his lead piece four. He now had a stack of three, an Impregger, on the exit square. Next role advanced that piece nine spaces.

148

"I'm getting the feel of the game. Do you want me to try to get my pieces home while you block?"

"Yes, we'll try that."

The NAV rolled a SIX and brought out a piece, but on that roll and the next he failed to roll a TWO to kill my piece. He took the spaces with his forward piece that was closing on CO's Impregger.

A SIX and TWO brought out my last piece. Next was a total of eight that put my lead piece in the blue entrance squares. I would need a roll of four to get home.

The XO rolled double SIX and brought out two pieces. Next was seven and he took that with one of the new pieces because the other piece was blocked. I could see the requirement for the maximum forward move could have interesting consequences.

"Captain, do you think we have a real chance to find those submarines?"

"Realistically, the chance is small. It's a big ocean and we have no idea where they are. The odds favor the bays north of Petropavlovsk. They've run exercises where they've used surface ships patrolling the entrance to form protected bastions for the missile submarine. It's not as good a tactic as they think."

The NAV brought out a piece but was forced to break the Tit on his next roll. I got my piece home and started another forward.

"How would you handle that situation?"

"I'd observe the surface units for some time to get their patrol routine and try to sneak in behind one into the bastion. Then we'd look for the missile submarine and take it out. On the way out I'd try to get a couple destroyers."

"Why not attack the destroyers on the way in?"

"That would alert the missile submarine to its danger. You also need to be concerned that there might be an attack submarine there too."

"It sounds like you're taking some big risks for someone who likes to avoid them."

"It's what would be required if that were our mission. Some risks are unavoidable. You can try to minimize them with a good choice of tactics."

"Isn't choosing to search in shallow water a risk for our

current operation?"

The NAV had pushed a Tit up behind my Tit. He was forced to move his forward piece to the spot behind the CO's Tit that already had three red pieces forming a Glom that was vulnerable to a kill. I bypassed it. It could no longer block. The CO killed it with his first piece, bypassing the entrance. All four red and two orange were back in Home Harbor while we had all our pieces in action.

"Yes, it is but the bottom there is fairly flat. There are only a few pinnacles we'll need to be careful with. If I guessed right and they are doing a shallow water transit, we have a real chance of finding them. It's still less than 50% though. It's a big ocean even in the shallow spots."

"I think we'll be OK on navigation," NAV added. "With the floating wire we should be able to receive Loran C or Omega and update our position. They're not as precise as the satellite system but it is good enough."

"There's always a chance for an unmarked seamount. They've been found before. We'll be searching at two-thirds and our slow speed should give us time to react if the bottom doesn't rise too quickly."

I rolled double FIVE and was able to advance my Tit. That forced NAV on his next turn to break his Tit behind mine. I got my second piece home and the CO did a kill on one of NAV's pieces before passing my Tit.

"Take your next roll on only one piece," the CO suggested. "Try to race that home."

I did get it home and the CO brought home his piece on the Victory Lap. He was then forced to break his Impregger as I tried to finish my final piece. It was killed by NAV so I was back in Home Harbor. As the CO tried to bring his second piece home he was forced to break his Tit to avoid backing. His lagging piece was then killed.

Now it was our turn to be helpless when the XO built a Tit and then an Impregger, blocking our way while the NAV brought his pieces home. The three pieces left to the CO and I formed a helpless Glom on the space behind the Impregger. The XO did two Victory Laps while the NAV got three pieces home.

"I see they roped you into the game, Tom," ENG said on the

way to get fresh coffee.

"Yes, it's interesting. What do you think about our new orders?"

"I'm usually focused on engineering. The chance to think tactically is always a welcome diversion. If we can get contact, the opportunity to shadow a Soviet submarine would be great experience. I've only done it in training and exercises."

The ENG watched for a few minutes then left with his coffee. The NAV was down to one piece and the XO was about to bring his first home after passing the spot twice. It was then he was forced to downgrade his Impregger to a Tit to avoid backing. We were no longer completely helpless. It took three turns for the CO and myself to get the roll we needed.

"Snake eyes," I announced, seeing double ONES.

"You can't kill from a mixed Tit," NAV stated.

"He can move the one space," said the CO.

I did and XO's Tit became a useless Glom.

On his turn the XO tried racing forward one piece. The CO killed it on his turn. It was a race between the NAV and I to get our last piece home and role SIX while our partners worked their last pieces, two for each now. The NAV got home two moves before me but I rolled SIX a turn sooner that he. That and the XO having one piece killed back to Home Harbor when he lost his Tit was the difference.

"A good game, Tom," CO said. "We start our transit of Amukta Pass on the 02 to 08 watch. I'm going to get some sleep before then."

Sleep sounded good to everyone.

Chapter 19 – Amukta Pass
Northern Pacific – 51° 58.4' N 171° 00.7' W
Sunday, August 18, 1991
0300

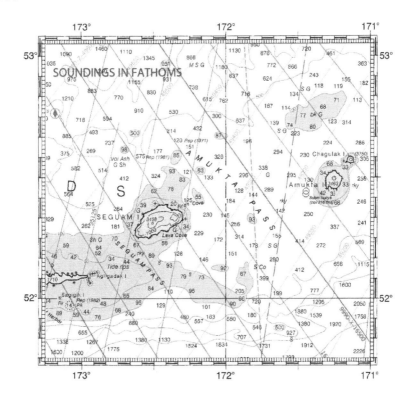

Amukta Pass

    I was up in Control. It was dark. It was night outside and Control was rigged for black. The lights were out and the only illumination was from the faint glow of indicator lights and gauges. The passage aft of Control had a few red fluorescent bulbs glowing in the overhead. The periscope stand had an opaque curtain drawn around it to exclude even the feeble glow from outside.

    Haddock was at periscope depth, ventilating, copying the broadcast and waiting for a navigational satellite pass. We were a

152

few miles southeast of Amukta Pass, our gateway to the Bering Sea. LT Cohen was OOD and the Chop was on Dive.

I'd had a chance to look outside. It was as black outside as in Control. The moon had already set. You could barely distinguish the boundary between sky and ocean. Amukta Island was 25 miles away but unseen. We had contact on sonar with a trawler to our northeast, but it was over the horizon. Yet LT Cohen and Petty Officer Quinn maintained a constant scope watch over the empty sea and sky.

At the navigation station, the Navigator and QMCS(SS) Spillman were talking softly. QM2(SS) Holt was working on the chart. The fathometer was running continuously tracing the contour of the bottom on a chart. It still showed over 1500 fathoms beneath us.

"Good morning, Mr. Ryan," said Spillman. "Are you interested in our navigational plans?"

"Our base course is three-three-zero through the center of the deep water," NAV said. "We might adjust that a degree or two based on the fix. When we cross the 500 fathom curve outbound we'll turn north. There are a few shallower spots in the pass, but none are of concern with our 200 foot depth. We'd need to be right near the islands to see dangerous water."

"Copying the satellite," announced ET2(SS) Law from the aft port corner.

"Petty Office Law will be fathometer watch during the transit and Senior Chief will supervise the navigation picture. I have the next watch as OOD."

"What about when we're searching? We plan to operate in much shallower water."

"Yes, and that might go on for days. We will use the ET as the fathometer watch, continuously manned in addition to the Quartermaster. The CDO will supervise navigation as part of his duties and the Senior Chief and I will be checking frequently when we're off watch. We also have charts based on hydrographic surveys covering the first couple days of our search. They're much more detailed and we should be able to get bottom contour fixes."

"How do you do that?"

"If you look at this chart you see the 1500 fathom curve, the 1000 fathom curve and the 500 fathom curve. We'd mark when we cross the 1500 fathom curve. Since we're at 10 fathoms at periscope depth, we're looking for a 1490 fathom reading. We put a square of tracing paper over the chart, mark our position and the time and trace the curve of few miles on each side of our track. We then do the same for the other curves. Finally we move the 1500 and 1000 fathom curves along the track based on our course, speed and time, so the three curves superimpose. Where they intersect is our fix. If the fathom curves have good shapes you'll get only one intersection. The survey charts have curves plotted every 10 fathoms."

"Fix is onboard." Law handed a paper to Holt, who plotted it on the chart.

The Navigator double-checked the latitude and longitude with dividers. It was about a mile west of our plotted track.

"Mr. Cohen, we have a good fix and are clear on the1000 Z broadcast. We're ready to transit the pass. Recommend course three-three-one."

"Yes, NAV. Helm, steer three-three-one. Chief of the Watch, secure ventilating, pressurize ship."

"Steer three-three-one, Helm aye. Steering three-three-one."

"Secure ventilating, pressurize ship, Chief of the Watch aye."

"Secure ventilating, pressurize ship," came over the 1MC passed by RMC(SS) Moore.

"Blower secured, outboard exhaust indicates shut," reported Chief Moore after manipulating a couple switches on the BCP. "Pressure point-one...point-two...point-three...point-four. Head valve shut, outboard induction shut. Secured pressurizing."

"Secure pressurizing, recirculate," was announced.

"Lowering the snorkel mast." Another switch was thrown. Some seconds later, the indicator changed. "Snorkel mast indicates down."

IC2(SS) Baker entered Control from aft. "Chief of the Watch, recirculating."

"Mr. Cohen, ship is recirculating."

"Very well. Dive, make your depth 200 feet. Helm, all ahead two-thirds."

"200 feet Dive aye. Three down." The planesman on the inboard station, fairwater planes, went to full dive.

154

"All ahead two-thirds, Helm aye. Maneuvering answers ahead two-thirds."

The Helm/stern planes had dive on, but so far, the angle was slight but noticeable.

"Scope is under. Lowering #2 scope."

"67 feet."

"#2 scope and fairing indicate down."

Cohen and Quinn were pushing the curtains surrounding the periscope stand back and securing them with sashes.

"Passing 100 feet to 200 feet."

"Rig Control for white," ordered Cohen.

It wasn't acknowledged but the white lights came on. The bright light was a shock for eyes used to the previous dark.

"Take charge of your planes. Zero bubble," Banner said in a low voice. "At 200 feet," was announced louder.

"Helm, all-ahead standard. Maneuvering make turns for 10 knots."

Helm acknowledged and turned the engine order telegraph. The COW acknowledged the turns and passed that over the phones.

Cohen was cranking the phone when the Captain walked down the starboard passageway.

"I'm here, Mr. Cohen."

"Yes, Captain. We've completed operations at periscope depth and I've commenced transit of Amukta Pass."

"Very well."

He crossed the periscope stand to the navigation station where he looked at the chart and had a few minute's discussion with the Navigator and senior chief. He headed toward me.

"Mr. Ryan, I think things will be quiet for the rest of the night. I'd recommend getting as much rest as you can. If we're fortunate enough to get contact, we'll be quite busy."

"What will you be doing?"

"I'll read and check back on navigation a couple times as we transit. I don't expect a problem but it never hurts to see that things are running smoothly."

While talking, we headed down to the middle level and the officer staterooms.

"Would you like a Pepsi? My treat."

"Sure, thanks."

"I'll grab a couple cans and meet you in the Wardroom. Get a couple glasses of ice."

He entered his room while I opened the door to the Wardroom. It was deserted. The glasses were in a locker on the starboard side. I grabbed two and passed through the Pantry to the Crew's Mess.

It was also empty except for Petty Officer Beam who was making a coffee run for Sonar. He was filling four cups on his tray and collecting some sugar and creamer packets. I greeted him and filled my glasses from the bin of the ice machine. The CO was sitting in his chair when I returned to the Wardroom. I took the chair to his right and set down my glasses. He pushed me a can and we poured our sodas.

"Captain, what is your goal for your Navy career?" I asked.

"This is my goal." He spread his arms. "Command of a ship at sea. It should be the goal of any officer of the line. I have it, and if I'm lucky, I'll get to do it for a couple more years on a Trident sub.

"I was told that should be my goal by my first commanding officer. Unfortunately, he was using his command tour to get noticed for admiral, but I decided, he was right."

"Isn't making admiral a worthy goal once you've made it to command?"

"Sure, it is. It's just that, as CO, I don't want to put my own interests ahead of what's best for my ship and crew. I've seen that. I'll settle for a good command tour and let the rest happen, or not. Besides, I've talked to a number of admirals, some quite senior. They all admit that their best times in the Navy were when they were in command of their own ship, or squadron for the aviators. That's where I'm at now. I'd best enjoy it while I can."

"Is there any part you don't enjoy?"

He took a long sip from his glass and topped it back up from the can.

"I guess, holding Captain's Mast. That's how we enforce discipline when more conventional methods have failed. We hold it here in the Wardroom. A green felt cloth covers the table. I sit right here with the subject's service record and details of the offense in front of me. The formal parts are read off a script. It's not a court.

We look for the facts and determine what punishment, if any, is deserved. It's usually straightforward.

"The XO, department head, division officer, leading petty officer and COB, stand in the passage behind you. The COB calls the accused in. He is directed to salute and uncover, that is, remove his hat. We go over the offense, hear any witnesses, get a statement from the sailor if he wishes and his chain of command talks about his performance.

"I tell my officers not to run down their men at mast. A simple 'no comment' or 'nothing to add' will be understood as a negative without the need to get into details.

"Then I pass judgment and announce the penalty, usually with a lecture. Some CO's manage a good display of anger. I don't do anger well. My tone is more one of disappointment."

"What type of things do you deal with?"

"Drug and alcohol offenses are the most common. Drugs are easy. We take the man to mast, give him the maximum and kick him out of the Navy. Alcohol is harder since it's legal, used responsibly. The sailor gets a chance to redeem himself but it's still a career killer for a chief or an officer. If the COB, XO or I had an alcohol incident we'd be fired within a day, and rightly so. That's why I stick to soda at any function where I'm driving."

"How many of these do you see?"

"Drug offenses are less than one a year now. Everyone, including me, knows they are subject to random urine tests. Alcohol comes up once or twice a year. We don't take a civilian DUI to mast like we would if it were on base but it counts as an incident and we have the sailor evaluated for possible alcoholism. Navy has excellent treatment programs, but the first step requires the individual to acknowledge their problem. I always ask our new men about their drinking habits when we do a welcome aboard interview. It's amazing how many drink regularly and have been since high school. I try to get everyone through the Alcohol Awareness training on base."

"Is alcohol so readily available?"

"At San Diego County bases you can get alcohol at 18. They don't want personnel driving down to Tijuana to drink. I don't think it's a good trade."

"What else do you handle?"

"We only do a few masts each year, maybe less than one a quarter. Occasionally we get an unauthorized absence, missing movement or dereliction of duty. We don't punish honest mistakes, but if someone says they did a check or test, and didn't; that's pretty serious. We rely on many men checking vital equipment for our safety. If we can't trust someone, they can't serve in submarines."

"Do you ever do a court-martial?"

"I've never seen one in my career in submarines. I did have one case where I was considering it, but it didn't pan out."

"What was that?"

"We had a sailor who was accused of sexual abuse of his infant daughter by his wife and her parents. They were going through a divorce. Photos that were described as sexually suggestive were produced as evidence. I didn't see the photos as much more than parents always take of a new baby, yet the charge was very serious. I turned the photos over to NIS and asked them to investigate and had XO check with the squadron JAG on how we'd organize a special court-martial. We had to report the accusation to the Bureau of Personnel and have our sailor evaluated by a Navy psychiatrist and a child sex abuse counselor. That last step didn't go well as the counselor took the sailor's denials as proof of his guilt."

"What was the result?"

"NIS reported that the incriminating photos were actually taken by our sailor's wife's parents. When confronted, they admitted making the charge to influence the divorce proceedings. With that report we, of course, dropped the charges and reported the NIS findings to BUPERS. They came back and directed our sailor to take a course of sexual abuse prevention counseling. He refused and we backed him, writing back that this was unnecessary as NIS had cleared him of wrongdoing. BUPERS came back and ordered us to discharge our sailor."

"What did you do?"

"We were ordered to discharge him by BUPERS and we were obligated to obey that order. However, a sailor is entitled to contest a discharge in a Discharge Review Board that we appoint. NAV was the senior member. He was also entitled to JAG representation at the board and we arranged that for him. We made a

158

complete record of the facts and had the NIS agent testify about his investigation. I testified about his excellent performance. In short, the board recommended retention. We greased the report through squadron, group and COMSUBPAC. BUPERS, faced with a formal report of the facts and a unanimous endorsement from our chain of command, caved."

"You sound pleased."

"You bet. It's always nice to make the system work and I really loved the chance to go to bat for one of my men so dramatically. A crew notices."

"If you'll excuse me, I'm going to check the picture in Control."

"Sure, I'll get some rest. I have the 08 watch this morning. I think I'll skip breakfast."

"No need to go hungry. I can smell that Petty Officer Michael is baking sticky buns tonight; just grab one and a coffee before watch."

He left the Wardroom, dropping his can and glass in the Pantry. I sniffed the air and smelled the sweet aroma of the freshly-baked treats before heading to my own bunk.

Chapter 20 – Patrol Routine

Bering Sea – 52° 36.2' N 171° 54.4' W
Sunday, August 18, 1991
0800

I was again in Control. It was the first watch with the patrol watch-bill. XO was Command Duty Officer, CDO, with authority to give permissions normally retained by the CO, like going to periscope depth. LT Gonzales was OOD and LT Gordon, JOOD. MMC(SS) Lloyd had DOOW with TM1(SS) Sheldon as COW. The rest was basically the normal section 3 watches, and though we were first watch on patrol, we were designated section 3.

FTG2(SS) Boyle handed me a blank pad of lined white paper. How to start? 'Call me Ishmael.' That story has a downbeat ending. 'It was the best of times. It was the worst of times.' That's not much better.

"First entry: 1500Z Commenced operations in accordance with CINCPACFLT 180550Z AUG 91," directed the XO. He must have seen my hesitation. "For routine search we only need to write down significant events. The trawler we hold to the west, now Sierra-1, doesn't need to go in. If we need to change course to avoid it, then we could mention it."

"What if we see one of the submarines?"

"Then write down everything, periodic solutions from fire control or plots, what Sonar is reporting, what we do. You can never get too much. We'll smooth things up after watch when we reconstruct the interaction."

"Do you have any other guidelines?"

"Any entry that is not a fact, say an opinion or an explanation of why we are doing something, is tagged as a 'CO's Comment.' Here is your first one. On course 331°, speed 10 knots, depth 200 feet, completing transit of Amukta Pass."

"I saw the chart. When do we exit the pass?"

"We'll be in deep water by 1000 ship's time. That's when we turn north and deploy the array and wire."

"Chief of the Watch, rig ship for patrol quiet. Start burning candles, forward," ordered Gonzales.

"Rig ship for patrol quiet. Start burning candles forward,

160

aye."

"Rig ship for patrol quiet" came over the 1MC.

"I'm going to rig," announced IC3(SS) Frye.

The recirculation fans got quiet.

"We shift recirculation fans to slow speed, latch open the watertight doors to the Tunnel and shift the propulsion plant to the quietest mode that still allows full power when needed," XO explained. "You can log that, 1505Z Shifted to patrol quiet."

We settled into our watch routine.

At 1614Z I logged sunrise; that's 0914 ship's time and undoubtedly earlier in the local time zone. At 1000 Haddock turned north. I logged the turn at 1700Z. The XO entered a CO's Comment, explaining we intended to search the waters inside the 100-fathom curve.

After the turn we streamed the towed array sonar, using 1,000 feet as the length of the tow. It can stream over double that length but the array is negatively buoyant and would be towed below the ship's depth. That's a concern in shallow water. The array is housed in a tube running down Haddock's port side hull and bending out to the outer edge of the port stern plan. The tow cable reel is in the Bow Compartment.

We also streamed the floating wire antenna. The reel for that is in the access trunk to the Bridge. We opened the lower hatch and RM3 James went up to operate the mechanism. You could hear the sound in Control as the wire was deployed. In the end, at 200 feet, we were copying our broadcast. James secured the reel, climbed down and we shut the hatch.

We slowed for a few minutes to shoot a bathythermograph buoy from the aft signal ejector. The buoy floats to the surface and then sinks, sending data to Haddock by a wire. We got a good trace. It was used to determine settings for the Mk-48 torpedoes.

Gonzales explained that the problem was that the water near the surface was warmer than the deeper water. That bent sound waves downward and made detecting a submarine near periscope depth harder. I pointed out that we were holding contacts on the surface, like Sierra-2, currently to the Southeast. It turned out that was not the same. We can get sound reflected off the bottom or, if the water was deep enough, the sound can be bent back up by the increased pressure at great depths. That effect leads to convergence zones and long range detections as the sound bends back to our depths, 20 miles, give or take, from the source. Preventing that type of long-range detection is one reason we thought our targets might be in shallow water.

Our optimum weapon setting turned out to be running the torpedo at 1000 feet with a +10 pitch angle to direct its active sonar toward the surface. Running that deep uses more fuel and shortens its range, and of course, we won't have that much water where we're going.

Our best shallow options were 200 feet with a +4 pitch or 300 feet with +6. Using a short ping interval would limit interference from returns off the ocean bottom. The maximum detection range would be 2800 yards in that mode but calculations show 1800 yards is what we might expect.

These were compiled onto a tactics sheet with recommended options and sent to the CO for approval along with the full series of printouts showing the expected acoustic performance. They were returned with an approval signature and entered into fire control by Boyle.

Now, at 1100, LT Gonzales gave permission to exercise tubes #1, #2 and #4. Tube #3 had been loaded yesterday with a Mk-48. SKC(SS) Aquino relieved TM1(SS) Sheldon as COW so he could supervise. While the COB is a master chief torpedoman, he does not involve himself in divisional affairs. He works for the CO and XO directly and is not considered a member of the Weapons Department.

Radio reported we had an immediate message on the 1800Z broadcast. It turned out to be a contact report. The XO directed the Quartermaster to plot it on a chart of the Bering Sea and called the Captain. The chart showed a long, narrow, ellipse about 200 nm by 20 nm, oriented Southwest to Northeast and well west of our current position.

I moved off when the CO came in. He looked at the chart and discussed it with the XO before making a decision.

"We'll continue as planned. The contact is classified only as a possible submarine and the message didn't say why they think so. So it's possibly not a submarine too. The contact ellipse is obviously a line of bearing from a T-AGOS ship and half of the ellipse is west of our area. It would also take 22 hours at full speed to get there and we'd have to go much slower when we approached the area. The P-3s from Adak are probably already on their way. We'll see if more information develops."

He came over to me. "How's your first watch?"

"I'm learning but I'm not busy. There is plenty of time to talk."

"The watch is built around what we'd need to track a submarine for hours or days. If we get contact you'll be plenty busy."

"What is T-AGOS? That's new to me."

"I'm sure you've seen them in your book research, but they're not very glamorous. They are small ships carrying a very long towed array, much better than ours though not as good as the fixed SOSUS arrays. Their advantage is mobility. If there is something of interest in the Bering Sea, they can be positioned to cover it. They have Military Sealift Command civilian crews and are often out in huge storms because the areas of interest, like the Bering Sea, are tough environments. It's not an easy assignment.

"They do a good job but I've seen plenty of initial reports that don't hold up. Their data is satellite linked back to SOSUS though they have a limited onboard analysis capability. I don't know where this report was handled. It's Sunday too and even SOSUS doesn't have its full talent in on weekends. It's a reason for a bit of caution."

I'd forgotten it was Sunday. "I guess I should write a log entry on your decision."

"A good idea. The XO can help you. Good hunting." He left and turned into Sonar.

"The ship will be shooting water slugs," passed over the 1MC. A few seconds later, the torpedo tube rumbled.

A few minutes later I saw Boyle was at the fire control console, pushing some buttons. He was in the weapon control mode.

"What are you working on, Petty Officer Boyle?"

"I'm testing the torpedo we just reloaded in tube #1. We check that it is accepting all presets and that we can control it over the wire. I'll repeat that for the other torpedoes when they are reloaded after we exercise their tube."

"What can you change besides search depth, pitch angle and ping interval?"

"Well, first would be floor and ceiling; that's the deepest or shallowest the torpedo can go. We could use that to protect friendly surface ships from our torpedo or to create a haven for ourselves. It's used in exercises but not so much in reality because it creates a zone for your target to hide too, and we can't change these settings over the wire."

"How are we protected if our torpedo acquires us?"

"If we have the wire we can shut it down or turn it around. Without the wire, we're protected by the anti-circular-run feature. When it runs out it counts propeller revolutions. If it turns around too much, it counts down twice as fast and shuts down at zero. We can override shutdown over the wire. That requires us to hold down the override button. If we let go or lose the wire, the torpedo shuts down."

"The wire sounds important."

"It is. We can steer the torpedo after launch if the target tries to evade. The torpedo can tell us over the wire when it detects and acquires a target, display the target on the fire control system and the Doppler presented by the target. We can set Doppler in or out over the wire as well as before launch. With Doppler in, the torpedo ignores returns from objects that are stationary or moving slowly. That eliminates false returns from the surface or bottom but we can't use it if our target is also moving slowly."

"What if we lose the wire?"

"Then there is no chance of changing anything after launch. There's a wire canister in the torpedo tube that pays out wire as we move and one inside the torpedo. We generally keep the wire if we're under 10 knots and it generally fails as we approach 20 knots, in between that, maybe, maybe not.

"Back to settings. We can set trajectory to 'shallow' or 'direct.' In direct the torpedo runs at the search depth to the enable point; that's the point it turns on its active sonar. In shallow, it goes to 150 feet during the run, diving to search depth just before enable. Running shallow saves fuel and increases its range but it runs

164

noisier. We can't change trajectory over the wire. Finally we set course and the enable run. Both of those can be changed over the wire."

"The fire control system is very important. What if we have a problem?"

"We're not completely helpless. Above the attack console we have the emergency preset panel."

He indicated a panel above and right. Just below it, the status light for tube four's outer door changed to open.

"It's just switches and dials that let us set the presets into the torpedo without any computer interface. We'd need to use plots to solve the target's course, speed and range and compute the torpedo intercept course manually. At this panel we can just set the torpedo gyro angle, how many degrees it turns, left or right, once it exits the tube. The tubes are offset 10 degrees left or right of our heading and we need to take that into account. It's not easy but we have practiced it."

"The ship will be shooting water slugs," came, again, over the 1MC. A few seconds later, the torpedo tube rumbled.

Chapter 21 – News

Bering Sea – 55° 46.1' N 172° 25.0' W
Monday, August 19, 1991
0100

There was a knock on the door. Seaman Hamm entered with a wake-up-call for my 0200 watch. The early morning watches weren't mentioned when I volunteered. I washed up and grabbed a quick shower before going to the Wardroom. The CO was there, reading from some yellow sheets that were used for radio printouts. Rinaldi and Gonzales were there making sandwiches from fixings on the table.

I started making a turkey and cheese for myself. The fresh baked bread was delicious. There was no lettuce or tomato.

"Good morning Tom. We got this four hours ago. It's the news dump that is used to fill out the broadcast. There's news of a coup in the Soviet Union. We don't have anything from official channels and most of this appears to be speculation, not fact."

"What is known?"

"Gorbachev was on a vacation in the Crimea. His status is unknown. Somebody named Yanayev heads the junta or, at least, is its public face. The Defense Minister may be a member and probably KGB too. They say Gorbachev is sick and claim to control the Soviet Union's nuclear arsenal. We haven't seen any developments on the last broadcast or this one. It should be around noon in Moscow."

"Do you think the recent deploying subs have anything to do with the coup?"

"Your guess is as good as mine. I know that if I were plotting a coup in Moscow, deploying a few submarines in the Pacific would not be on the top of my to-do-list."

"It doesn't really affect our current mission," ENG said.

"It could," I said. "It's the first coup in a nuclear power. How will the U.S. react to that?"

"I think ENG is right," stated the Captain. "We don't know what's happening and we've nothing on our operational traffic. We are just adding our guesses to those of the press. ENG, let me know if we get anything new, but we'll continue as planned."

"Yes, sir," said Gonzales. "If you'll excuse us, we need to relieve the watch."

I finished the last bite of my sandwich and, grabbing my coffee, followed the others to Control. They paired up with their counterparts. I was relieving the COB. I sat next to him on the benches in front of fire control. He handed me the lined pad with the narrative. The last entry was, '0659 Sunset.' There was nothing else except a 0230 entry of a CO's Comment acknowledging the news report of the Soviet coup.

"It's been quiet except for the news reports. The news dump was replaced by sports in the last two cycles, baseball scores and preseason football. The fathometer watch gets stationed at 0500. The plan is to get a 0552 satellite fix. It will still be dark then. That's about the time we turn to 328°. We should reach shallow water an hour or so later. We'll shoot trash before then."

"Was there anything more on that possible sub contact to the West?"

"No. You had a second message on your last watch but nothing since. Adak did fly on it but nothing was reported. We have gotten reports of other P-3 missions. They appear to be keeping a barrier along the 180 meridian."

"What does the crew think about the change in plans?"

"Most are excited. A few are concerned that our deployment schedule could change. The break from drills means more sleep for most and that's always appreciated."

"Well, I relieve you as JOOW."

"I stand relieved." He handed me the lined pad after removing the page with the entries for his watch. "Good luck."

The other watches relieved as well. ENG announced that we would speed up to 12 knots at 240 feet until we went to periscope depth to compensate for the time we'd lose there. As a consequence we'd station the fathometer watch at 0400 instead of 0500. LT Gonzales ordered the changes. We lost the broadcast because with the added depth and speed we no longer had enough wire on the surface.

I went to check the chart. Flores was replotting our projected positions based on the speed change. It was clear that, even at 240 feet we could go many miles beyond the 100 fathom curve before reaching dangerous water.

"We think we'll be about a day ahead of them when we reach the 100 fathom curve." Rinaldi had come beside me. "If they did what we projected, that is."

"And if they didn't?"

"Then they could be anywhere. With no cueing to indicate where to search it was always a long shot to find them. For all we know they could be heading into Pet-er right now, planning on enjoying a few vodkas this evening."

"It's hard waiting for something to happen. The drill schedule made a busy day, even for an observer."

"Enjoy the break."

There was plenty of time to talk and that's mostly what we did. There was, of course, speculation on the coup. Petty Officer Sheldon was first to tire of that and successfully ended that line by saying that he didn't see how changing one communist dictator for another would have much impact on anything in the U.S. We shifted to sports, baseball pennant races, NFL and which were the best college teams for the upcoming season.

FTG2(SS) Boyle was working on a project in the overhead of Control. He told me he was stringing microphones for a cassette recorder. One would be over the periscope stand and one toward the forward end of fire control. The Captain asked LT Gonzales to set it up in case we had success. The audio record could help us reconstruct what happened.

We gained contact on a trawler to the Northeast. ENG had the section track it for an hour. LT Gordon took the forward fire control console with Boyle working independently on the second. Smith worked the geographic plot while Frye and Mitchell took shifts on the time-bearing plot. PNSN Miller recorded bearings every 15 seconds while announcing them to the others. We made a few small course changes to refine the solution. It appeared to be about 35,000 yards on a southeast course.

After that exercise I asked Gonzales if I could visit Sonar. That was not a problem as long as I kept him, as OOD, informed of my location. Sonar was bathed in subdued blue lights and the orange glow from the computer screens.

"Tom, welcome to Sonar," STS1(SS) Johnson greeted me.

"Good morning everyone. I stopped by to see how the towed array changes your operations."

"Sure. We have Petty Officer Darnell monitoring the array here." He indicated a large rectangular box with a big display screen mounted aft of the regular sonar consoles. The BQR-20 can display every beam of the TB-16 towed array. This is Sierra-7, the trawler you were tracking. We can also analyze the signature." Darnell adjusted the display. "These are lines from the screw, 384 RPM on a single four bladed prop. The high RPM is a clue it's a trawler. We have 60 Hz from the electrical system and some harmonics. These are from a diesel engine."

"What's the other contact here?"

"It's not a contact. That's most likely Akutan volcano in the Aleutians. The bearing checks out."

"Have you seen any sign of our targets?"

"Not really. Sierra-5 on the last watch was a 50 Hz tonal to the west. Half the world uses 50 Hz electrical systems, including the Soviet Union. Without any other indication the XO and Captain decided to monitor it and keep going. It faded after an hour. We'd really want some other indication it might be a submarine."

"Do you think we'll find them?"

"I don't know that, but if we get close enough, we'll detect and classify them."

0607

We were at periscope depth and ventilating. Control was rigged for black. The satellite pass was underway and Radio had just announced we had an immediate message on the broadcast that was printing out after the satellite downlink. Sanitary tank #2 was blown and venting. We had a couple loads left on the trash evolution including shooting the expended oxygen candles. We were on our new 328° course, but were still in over 100 fathoms of water.

The fix completed first. Flores plotted it, showing us about a mile north of our expected position. ENG called the Navigator on the phone and directed Flores to reset to the satellite fix.

Radio then reported being clear on the 1200Z broadcast. We received a new news dump too. A few minutes later the trash was gone and we went down to 180 feet, speed two-thirds, 7.5 knots, and rigged for white. The floating wire antenna kept us copying the broadcast. We resumed burning oxygen candles. We had suspended that in anticipation of ventilating while at periscope depth.

RM2(SS) Warner came to Control with the new message and several copies of the news. Rinaldi and Gonzales initialed the message and kept a copy of the news. ENG told Warner to take the board to the Captain and he left.

"The message was just a confirmation of the news we've seen. There's been a coup, Gorbachev's status is unknown, the Emergency Committee claims control over the Soviet nuclear arsenal. It did confirm that the Defense Minister is part of the Emergency Committee but it is not known which of the military commanders, like the head of the Strategic Rocket Forces, are backing the coup. The message says continue operations as directed."

"What's in the news?" LT Gordon asked.

"I just skimmed it," ENG said. "Let's see. It seems there's opposition to the coup. Boris Yeltsin addressed a crowd of tens of thousands from on top of a tank in front of the Russian parliament building."

"I didn't know Russia had a parliament," said Gonzales, "and who's this Yeltsin?"

"He's the president of the Russian Soviet Socialist Republic," said the Captain, who had just entered Control carrying the message board. "He actually won a fair election to that post. Before that he was the Soviet equivalent of mayor of Moscow, so it's a good guess that he has many contacts with the people that make a city, like Moscow, work."

"If he really stood on a tank," I observed, "that would imply some parts of the military are in the opposition."

"Yes, that's possible," the Captain agreed. "I would guess most of the senior commanders, if they didn't sign on beforehand, are being noncommittal until they see who will win out. Promise aid, but delay sending it, citing logistical problems. If the coup fails, you spin the delay as support for Gorbachev, and if it appears to be succeeding, you solve the problems with a Herculean effort and proclaim your loyalty to the new powers-that-be."

170

"Do you think the coup could fail?" ENG asked.

"It could," said the Captain. "They will have to break up the opposition. They might have generals to order the military into action but do they have captains, majors and colonels willing to fire on civilians? That was the Chinese problem in 1989 in Tiananmen Square. The local troops wouldn't fire on the citizens of Beijing. They needed to bring troops from outside. They were an established government. It could be impossible for the junta get such support. The very act of asking communicates weakness."

"So, Captain, what do these developments mean to us?" Gordon asked.

"As our bosses said, continue operations. We're just following the news from Moscow like everybody else."

0830

We were in the Wardroom, grabbing a bite of breakfast after watch relief. I'd turned over JOOW to LTJG Banner. He had seen the news before coming on watch. NAV came up to review the chart and discuss shallow water navigation with the XO. We had over 40 fathoms beneath us. The Yellow Sounding was 25 fathoms and Red Sounding 20 fathoms. The best option if in doubt was to turn left toward the 100 fathoms curve.

PNSN Miller knocked and entered. He wanted to get my narrative to type it for the patrol report. ENG looked it over, added a CO Comment about the CINCPACFLT message and the news on the coup and handed it over.

ENG asked Gonzales and Gordon to draw a small-scale representation of our track to the shallow water search area. They got positions from the Quartermaster and plotted them onto a chart. By 0900 everyone was heading to bed except for ENG. He headed aft.

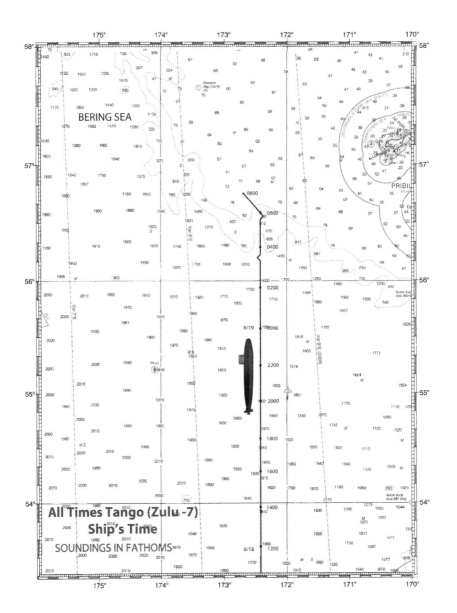

Chapter 22 – Flash Traffic

Bering Sea – 57° 50.2' N 173° 45.2' W
Monday, August 19, 1991
1900

We had just sat down to dinner. The phone screeched for attention and the Captain picked it up.

"We're getting flash traffic. They interrupted the ZBO to send it."

MS2(SS) Glenn entered carrying a tray with sliced meatloaf. I took a piece. I'd skipped lunch. It was a common event for those on an overnight watch. After dinner it was back to Control. We were passing around mashed potatoes and green beans when there was a knock on the door and RM2(SS) Leonard entered with the message board. He gave it to the Captain.

"Damn. We're authorized to sink any Soviet SSBN we believe is preparing to launch its missiles. They must have some scary intel to authorize something like this. I don't think it has ever been done before."

"Did they give any explanation?" XO asked.

"Yes, but not much. They say it is not clear who is in control of the Soviet nuclear weapons. I'd have hoped they had something more solid to take such a step. Perhaps they do but can't share it without compromising sources or methods."

"Captain, you seem troubled by this message," observed Banner from his normal seat opposite the CO.

"Well, besides the fact that Washington thinks the situation is bad enough that someone might start flinging nuclear missiles, it presents a real problem to me, us. Every week or two our boomers are given a missile readiness exercise. They go through the entire launch sequence except for actually launching missiles. If the Soviets do the same thing, and I expect they do, there would be no way of telling the difference between exercise or real unless we waited to hear the sound of a missile launch. But we can't wait. The warheads on a single missile could kill millions and they could empty all their tubes before our torpedoes could stop them. For now, that's a theoretical problem because we don't have contact."

"I don't think it's likely that someone in the Soviet Union is going to decide to hold a missile exercise in the middle of a coup," I said.

"Put that way, no. That's not how it works however. Somewhere there's a 'Quarterly Drill Schedule' signed by some general or admiral. In a remote communications center a junior officer is starting his watch and sees that he is supposed to transmit the implementing message in two hours. What does he do? More than half won't give it a thought and transmit it as planned. A few smart ones will try to contact their boss or even the general. How many would hold the message on their own responsibility? Less than one in ten is my guess."

"How much time do we have to figure out what's happening?" Gonzales asked.

"That's another problem. On our exercises the standard is to simulate the first launch within fifteen minutes of the receipt of the implementing message. If we assume the Soviets have similar capability, it defines our time limit. The issue is that we don't know when the clock started. By the time Sonar picks up indications of launch preps, the clock has been ticking for some minutes. I also figure 3 to 4 minutes for our torpedo to reach them. Would they have the nerve to complete a launch sequence with a Mk-48 homing on them?"

"Surely they were aware of these issues before they gave the order," I added.

"COMSUBPAC certainly is and they would have briefed CINCPACFLT, but this must have come from the Joint Staff and White House. Operational issues are not their concern. That's our problem."

"Have there been more news reports from Moscow?" asked McCarthy, the oncoming EOOW.

"The crowds around the Russian Parliament building grew to over 100,000 and some other local leaders have come out against the Emergency Committee," XO replied.

"The longer there is defiance, the weaker the junta appears and the more desperate they might become," the CO stated. "It's night in Moscow now. We'll see what tomorrow brings."

2000

We were up in Control relieving the watch. The last watches had been uneventful. I took a look at the COB's narrative. The only entry was a course change to 348° a couple hours ago.

"Do you have anything for me, COB?"

"Sunset will be 0712 Z, just after midnight, ship's time. We passed over the 100 fathom curve twice and NAV got a fair bottom contour fix. We're in about 70 fathoms of water now. We passed east of a suspected pinnacle but never saw it. There are some others plotted near the track just after your watch ends. The plan is to be East of those, then turn to the Northwest. The depth will change to 150 feet as it gets shallower in parts of the track."

"I think the Captain expected to see them by now if they were doing what he expected."

"He was up last watch looking at the chart. We'll keep on this search for another day. By then we'll be near the 180 meridian boundary."

"What do you think of the message we just got?"

"I've never seen anything like it. In 26 years as a torpedoman, I never fired a warshot. Some of the younger guys are excited, but I'm thinking they're going to shoot back."

"Well, we haven't found the Delta yet. COB, I relieve you as JOOW."

"I stand relieved. Good luck."

The others relieved their counterparts. The XO called everyone together on the periscope stand to review the plan for the next watch. First up was to shoot a BT buoy to update the environment. Beyond that, it was just keep searching.

Chapter 23 – Flyby

Bering Sea – 58° 29.0' N 174° 06.3' W
Tuesday, August 20, 1991
0045

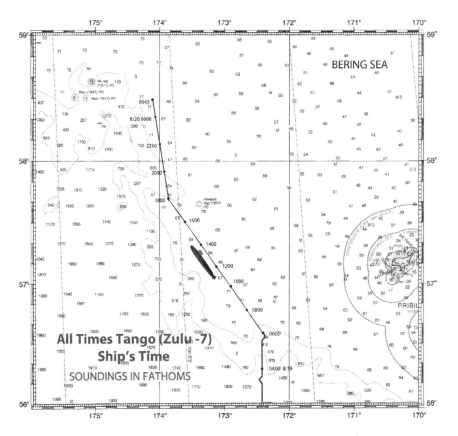

The watch was uneventful, slow, boring. My only entry was '0712 Sunset,' The official messages and the news reports had nothing new. Sports scores would have been welcome. That changed with one announcement.

"Conn, Sonar, have a new contact, a noise level, bearing 061°, sending it to fire control as Sierra-11."

"Let's track it," XO directed. "Sonar, do you have any classification on the contact?"

"We're working on it. It's sounds like a rainsquall but we haven't seen any other rain this watch. It has a good right bearing rate too."

The XO went to the phone, probably calling the Captain.

"Can I go to Sonar for a few minutes?" I asked Gonzales. He assented.

Sonar was busy. Johnson was leaning over Darnell on the center console as he adjusted the display.

"I have it on the array," said STS2(SS) Stanley. "I think it's a five blade."

Johnson shifted to the towed array display and studied the image.

"I think that's two fives."

"You're right."

"Send the array contact to Control as Sierra-12. Conn, Sonar, sending you the same contact on the towed array as Sierra-12. We see two, five bladed, screws on Sierra-11/12. Classify contact as possible Delta Class SSBN."

I didn't want to disrupt their routine, so I returned to Control. The Captain was on the periscope stand talking to the XO.

"Designate Sierra-11/12, Master-1," announced Gonzales. I noted the time in my log, 0750 Z.

"Chief of the Watch, station the Fire Control Tracking Party."

"Station the Fire Control Tracking Party aye." He passed it on the 1MC.

"Mr. Ryan, you can keep your narrative log as your assignment."

"Who is in this party?"

"The Fire Control Tracking Party is fire control and Sonar as manned on battle stations."

"Conn, Sonar, Master-1 bears 102°. It's approaching the baffles."

"Captain has the conn. Helm, right full rudder, steady one-eight-zero."

"Right full rudder, steady one-eight-zero, Helm aye. My rudder is right full."

"Just before the turn we had crossed bearings at 2,100 yards," announced ET1(SS) Smith on the geographic plot. "Believe it is a minimum range."

"Conn, Radio, dropped synch on the broadcast."

Personnel were starting to file in to man stations. XO donned his headset. ENG came in looking like he jumped into his coveralls straight from bed.

"What do we have?" ENG asked Gordon who was manning the first console.

"A possible Delta. My solution is rough. A course to the South or a bit East of that, speed 3 to 6 and range 2,500 to 4,500. We're in a turn now."

"OK. I'll take over." Gordon shifted to the aft console and called up Master-1.

"Just before the turn, time 51, we had crossed bearings between the sphere and towed array of 3,100 yards," Smith reported.

The Navigator and LTJG Banner were next to arrive. Banner went to analyze the geographic plot, freeing Smith to just plot, but it was more like collaboration.

"Navigator has the deck. Captain retains the conn."

Gonzales shifted to his normal spot on the attack console, letting FTG2(SS) Boyle work the target solution on the console normally dedicated to weapon control.

"XO, get Sonar to start a broadband recording."

"Passing one-seven-zero to one-eight zero."

LTJG McCarthy arrived but LT Gordon stayed on the aft console as the ship was not manning damage control parties.

"Steady one-eight-zero."

"Get a curve," XO said.

"Fire Control Tracking Party is manned," reported COW.

"Very well. Attention in Control. Intend to assume trail of the Delta. We will try to work out to a position 5,000 to 7,000 yards just abaft his starboard beam. XO, remind Sonar to search around in case our Delta has his buddies in the neighborhood."

"Sonar reports starting the recording," XO reported. "They request we pass a solution every minute."

"I'll pass the solutions," Boyle announced.

"Mr. Ryan, write down everything you can," the CO urged. "You'll be reconstructing this after watch and you can't have too much."

"Have a curve," reported Jackson from plots.

"Sonar reports the array is stable, passing bearings as Sierra-12."

"Ekelund range, 3,600 yards, time 54."

"I have a good solution," ENG announced, "course 175°, speed 5, range 3,400."

"We need to move out a little. Helm, right full rudder, steady two-two-zero. Maneuvering, make turns for 5 knots."

"Right full rudder, steady two-two-zero, Helm aye. My rudder is right full."

"Maneuvering acknowledges turns for 5 knots."

"We had crossed bearings before the turn of 6,200 yards, believed to be a maximum. The cross from the sphere and towed was about 3,000 yards. Our solution looks good for 170°, speed 5, range 3,000."

"Passing two-one-zero to steady on two-two-zero."

"Chief of the Watch, can you have your messenger fetch my patrol orders book? It is on my desk. Our theoretical problem has become real."

"Yes, sir."

"Steady two-two-zero."

"Get a curve."

"The Ekelund won't be much good, XO. There's not enough change in bearing rate. I need to work further out on the beam and we'll have to accept less than optimal courses."

"I have an excellent solution," ENG said. "Course 170°, speed 5, range 3,800."

"Yes, ENG. It looks good. I plan on keeping the Fire Control Tracking Party for about half an hour more, then shift to section tracking."

"Sonar reports array stable."

"Captain, your book."

SN McArthur handed him a green book. He opened it and signed an entry. Then handed the book to the Navigator.

"NAV you're oncoming OOD, you can be first. Mr. Ryan, after XO, ENG and Sonar get their chances, copy it verbatim as a CO Comment in the narrative."

"The solution looks good," said Jackson. "The bearings are falling right on the expected position."

"The solution range is 4,200 yards," ENG said. "That looks good, plus or minus 200 yards. Range is opening slowly."

"The range from sphere and towed array is now 4,400 yards," Banner said from the geo plot.

"Conn, Radio, copying the broadcast," came over the speaker. "We missed the 0800 Z ZBO."

"NAV, ask Radio to suspend reports on the broadcast unless we get flash traffic. Every time we turn we'll drop synch. I don't need the extra chatter now."

"Yes, sir."

"Helm, left full rudder, steady one-six-zero."

"Left full rudder, steady one-six-zero, Helm aye. My rudder is left full."

"Mr. Ryan, you're next with the book," said McArthur handing me the book.

I wrote: CO's Comment. Received CINCPACFLT message authorizing an attack on any Soviet SSBN preparing to launch missiles. This order is unprecedented. With the coup, conditions in the Soviet Union are also unprecedented. I must assume that the authorities authorizing this action have good information justifying it. If we fail to take action when we should, millions of lives are at risk. If we take action when we shouldn't, only hundreds, the crews of the Delta and Haddock, are at risk. I intend to take action if needed.

If we act it needs to prevent the missile launch. Our standard is to launch with 15 minutes of the receipt of the directive. I assume the Soviets have similar capability. However, when we detect launch preps, the clock has already been running some minutes. I want to shoot our torpedoes within 10 minutes of detecting launch preps and 7 to 8 minutes is better. To achieve that I direct the following:

Sonar – If you see any change in the SSBN that might indicate launch preps; slowing, going shallower, use of air, call Conn about possible launch indications. Start a broadband recording. I will ask you again before we shoot if indications are still consistent with missile launch. I know you cannot be certain. The responsibility for any action is mine solely.

Conn – When Sonar reports indications of possible missile launch, man battle stations and make tubes 3 & 4 ready in all respects. FTOW begin the voice recording in Control. Load countermeasures, fore and aft, settings, swept, shallow.

Remember that a false alarm is better than being slow if an actual launch is in progress.

That was it. I initialed it in one of the JOOW spots. While I was writing we steadied on our new course and continued tracking Master-1.

"Chief of the Watch, secure the Fire Control Tracking Party. Which section is oncoming?"

"Section 1, Captain."

"Secure the Fire Control Tracking Party, section 1 eat and relieve the watch," passed on 1MC.

"Captain, do you want me to take the conn?" XO asked.

"It's OK, XO. I'll hold the conn while we sort out the watches."

LT Cohen entered from Sonar. "NAV, I'm ready to relieve you as OOD. We're still running the broadband recording in Sonar. Keep up the solutions every minute."

"I'm ready to be relieved. We're on one-six-zero, speed 5, 180 feet. The Captain has the conn. Burning candles continuously forward with #2 Burner and #1 scrubber. We're clear on the 0600 Z broadcast and have been getting pieces of the 0800 when we're steady. We're on the starboard quarter of the Delta."

"I have the contact picture from Sonar. What about the pinnacle we passed a few hours ago? We're headed back in its direction."

"Yes, I need to look at that and project the Delta's track. We have at least 6 hours. I think we can get a Loran-C fix over the wire."

"Helm, right full rudder, steady one-eight-five. Maneuvering make normal two-thirds turns."

"Right full rudder, steady one-eight five, Helm aye. My rudder is right full."

"Maneuvering acknowledges normal two-thirds turns."

"I relieve you, sir."

"I stand relieved. Quartermaster, LT Cohen has the deck, Captain retains the conn."

While they were relieving ENG took over from the XO, but stayed at the forward console. As CDO there was nothing to do while the CO had control. Jackson shifted from plot coordinator to relieve Gordon on the aft console. Banner remained on the geo plot where ET2(SS) Zhou had replaced Smith. He motioned me to come over. I showed him the narrative.

"I've got the picture. I can do the plots and the log. I relieve you as JOOW."

"I stand relieved."

I went down to the Wardroom, leaving the action behind. In the Wardroom the faux leather cover had been removed. The bare table beneath was covered in a long strip of grid paper that was used on the geo plot. Over it was taped a strip of plain white tracing paper. Gonzales and Gordon were laying down Haddock's track. It took over an hour but they reconstructed our initial encounter with the Delta.

Here it is:

ENCOUNTERING MASTER-1 DELTA I SSBN

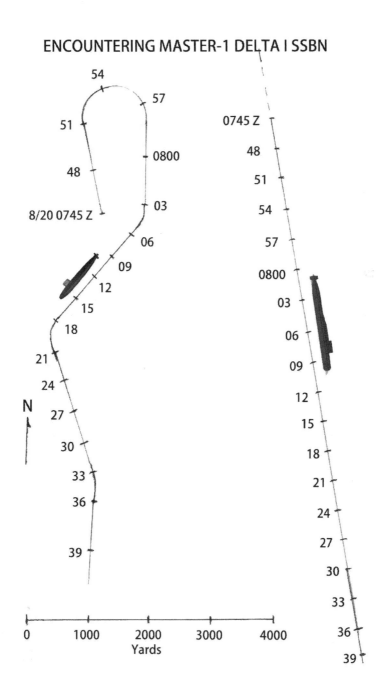

Chapter 24 – Master-2

Bering Sea – 58° 21.7' N 174° 06.3' W
Tuesday, August 20, 1991
0230

I returned to Control after smoothing my narrative with the XO. It was quiet. I looked at the plot. Haddock was about 6,000 yards and a little aft of the Delta's starboard side. A couple extra engineers were helping Petty Office Zhou on the plots. ET2(SS) Lynn was the off-going RO and EM3 Lamar was this section's AEA. The CO authorized securing the AEA watch to free extra personnel for tracking. The other watches would record his logs.

ENG, as CDO, had taken the conn. The CO was still in Control, but just observing.

"Conn, Sonar, we're picking up a 300 Hz line on the towed array. We had Maneuvering shift bus frequency and it's not us. Bearing is 126°. Classified as possible submarine."

"Sonar, Conn aye. Can you send it in ATF to fire control?"

"It's too weak for ATF. We'll buzz bearings as Sierra-13."

"The bearing indicates the new contact is ahead of Master-1 by about 4,000 yards if it's on the same track," Zhou reported from his plot.

"Designate Sierra-13, Master-2," announced Cohen. He was tracking the Delta. "Mr. Jackson, start a track on Master-2."

Jackson called it up on the aft console. FTG1(SS) Quinn started working it too on the second console.

"Do you want the conn, Captain?" ENG asked.

"No, you're doing fine. Just continue to shadow the Delta. It's our primary concern. If Master-2 is leading this parade, I'm perfectly happy to just get an occasional bearing on him. If he does anything interesting, call me right away."

"Conn, Sonar, we're getting some hits of a five-blade doing 50 turns. Master-2 is a possible Victor III class SSN, doing about 5 knots, same as Master-1."

"Thanks Sonar. That's two down. Can you find the Akula?"

"Conn, we're looking."

"Course 170°, speed 5 works with a range of 7 to 10 thousand yards," said Jackson.

"The range would be 8,200 yards if he is on the same track as Master-1," Banner said looking at the plot. "It is tracking well but Master-2 could still be offset a little from Master-1."

"Captain, if Master-2 is on the same track as Master-1, we must have passed right by him before we detected the Delta," I observed.

"Yes, Mr. Ryan, it certainly seems that way. A Victor III is quieter than a Delta I. At least they don't appear to be aware of us."

"Helm, right full rudder, steady one-eight-five. All ahead two-thirds. Maneuvering make turns for 6 knots."

"Right full rudder, steady one-eight-five, all ahead two-thirds, Helm aye. My rudder is right full, Maneuvering answers ahead two-thirds."

"Maneuvering acknowledges turns for 6 knots."

"Passing one-seven-five to steady on one-eight-five."

"It looks like your plan worked," I said.

"Yes, I look like a genius. You have to realize that luck played a big part. A few thousand yards east or west and we pass by both submarines without detecting them."

"Didn't Napoleon prefer lucky generals? I think you made some of your luck."

"Steady one-eight-five."

"If my luck holds we won't need to attack the Delta. We had a news update. There are still huge crowds by the Russian Parliament building. If the junta can't disperse them, they're in trouble. Can they find soldiers willing to murder for them?"

"What do you think?"

"I think they're in trouble, but why speculate. We'll know in a few days. ENG, I'll be in my stateroom. Find a time to blow #2 sanitary this watch. Drop back to about 135° relative from the Delta. You can ease up to 150 feet to minimize air."

"Aye, Captain."

"On a different matter, how are you coming on the Engineering tests?"

"Everybody has taken them and we're grading."

"Good. We'll make some time as we head off station to review them with the department. OK. Have a boring watch."
He left. I followed.

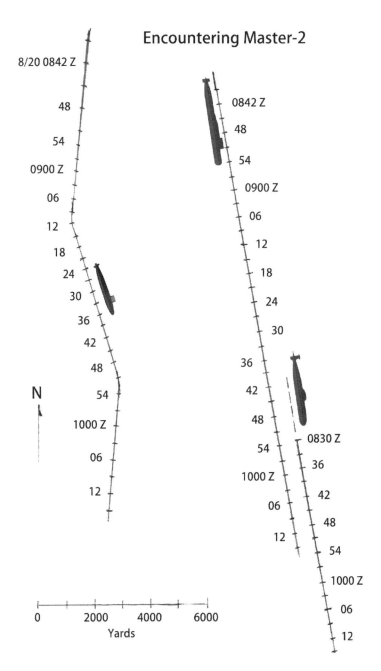

Encountering Master-2

Chapter 25 – In Trail
Bering Sea – 57° 26.5' N 173° 45.5' W
Tuesday, August 20, 1991
1400

We were back on watch. Haddock had been following the Delta I and Victor III for over thirteen hours. There was no sign of the Akula. The Soviet submarines were almost retracing the track we'd taken.

We had a couple extra engineers assisting on plots. ET1(SS) Seabright was assisting ET1(SS) Smith on the geo plot. EM3 Owen was this section's AEA. With that watch secured, he was doing the time-bearing plot. Most of the electricians and nuclear ETs had been to school on the plots. LTJG Reed, off-going EOOW, was assisting as plot coordinator.

"My stack is falling apart," LT Gordon announced from the forward fire control console. "Possible maneuver by Master-1."

"The last two bearings didn't track," agreed Reed.

"It's a possible turn to the left," said Seabright.

"Sonar, Conn, do you see signs of a maneuver by Master-1?" ENG asked over the open mike that lets Sonar monitor events in Control.

"Conn, Sonar, we've seen a drop in the strength of the signal. Master-2 has faded as well. Master-1 is still at 5 knots."

"Confirm maneuver by Master-1 and likely Master-2. Anchor range about 5,500 yards."

I noted the maneuver in my log while ENG got on the phone.

"Helm, left full rudder, steady one-four-zero. All ahead two-thirds, Maneuvering make turns for six knots."

"Left full rudder, steady one-four-zero, all ahead two-thirds, Helm aye. My rudder is left full. Maneuvering answers ahead two-thirds."

"Maneuvering acknowledges turns for six knots," added Petty Officer Sheldon, COW.

"Passing one-five-zero to one-four-zero."

"ENG, what do you have?" The CO entered Control.

"We have a maneuver by Master-1. Master-2 faded. We think they turned left as the signal is weaker. I'm turning to one-four-zero and 6 knots."

"Steady one-four-zero."

"Sounds good. This is about where we turned onto three-four-eight on the way up. They might be turning to follow the shallow shelf." He went over to the navigation station. "It looks like one-two-zero to one-three-zero are his best options, if that's the plan."

They went about working the problem. Gordon and FTG2(SS) Boyle fiddled with fire control while LT Gonzales shifted between them and the plots. ENG and the Captain watched from the periscope stand.

"We have crossed bearing at 13,500 yards," said Reed, "believe to be a maximum."

"ENG, you need to generate more bearing rate to lock down the solution. Plot, what's the last bearing to Master-1?"

"092°, sir," replied Owen.

"Try zero-nine-zero and slow so we don't close his track too much."

"Yes, Captain. Helm, left full rudder, steady zero-nine-zero, all ahead one-third."

"Left full rudder, steady zero-nine-zero, all ahead one-third, Helm aye. My rudder is left full. Maneuvering answers ahead one-third."

"Mr. Ryan, you can add a comment that we think Master-1 and Master-2 changed course to remain on the shallow shelf. That's pure speculation on Master-2. We'll see if we get him back when we regain position on the Delta."

"How are they maintaining their positions as they sail together?"

"A good question, Mr. Ryan. They could have preplanned the track, but perhaps, they have a super high frequency, narrow, beam, low power device, like our fathometer, that lets them determine range or more."

"Passing one-zero-zero to zero-nine zero."

"There's a definite right bearing rate on this leg," said Reed.

"We always want to see some bearing rate," said the CO. "Zero bearing rate means a danger of collision. I'd normally like to shadow a submarine from a very deep depth so we can have some vertical separation. In this op in shallow water there is no room. We probably have depth overlap with the Delta or Victor. My estimate is that the Delta is about at our depth so they can be ready to launch and copy their communications. The Victor is probably at 70 to 80 meters to get depth separation from the Delta."

"Steady zero-nine-zero."

"Get a curve,' ENG directed. "We should get a decent Ekelund."

"Conn, ATF on Master-1 is not holding, buzzing bearings."

"I think we're lucky to still have the Delta on the sphere," said Gonzales.

"I'm liking a course of 125°," Gordon said. "Range is about 7,500 yards."

"We have crossed bearings on plot, about 2,200 yards, believed to be a minimum range," added Reed.

"Ekelund range, 6,500 yards," said Owen.

"We're about 155° relative. We need to move more to the beam," said ENG. "Helm, right full rudder, steady one-six-zero, all ahead two-thirds. Maneuvering make turns for 6 knots."

"Right full rudder, steady one-six-zero, all ahead two-thirds, Helm aye. My rudder is right full. Maneuvering answers ahead two-thirds."

"Maneuvering acknowledges turns for six knots."

"The longer we stay in contact the easier it gets. We did a twelve-hour tracking exercise at the training center, involving three watch sections, to prepare for deployment. We had a target maneuver on each watch. We've doubled our experience in the last day."

"Passing one-five-zero to steady on one-six-zero."

"My solution is looking good," Gordon asserted. "Course 125°, speed 5, range 6,800 yards."

"Steady one-six-zero."

"Get a curve."

"Conn, Sonar, back in ATF on Master-1."

"Your solution looks good on the plot," Reed said. "The range may be longer though."

"Ekelund range, 7,200 yards," Owen announced.

"Conn, Sonar, we have Master-2 on the towed array on a 300 Hz line, bearing 104°. We'll buzz bearings."

"That would put Master-2 about 4,000 yards ahead of Master-1," Smith said after laying down the bearing line on his plot. "That's what we had before the maneuver."

"ENG, it looks like you have a good handle on things. I'm going to stop into Sonar and head to my stateroom."

That was our excitement for the watch. We worked back to about 120° relative from the Delta and about 5 to 6 thousand yards. We had more news from Moscow on the 2200 Z broadcast. The Emergency Committee declared a curfew. It was ignored. There were reports of military forces deploying and clashes resulting in some deaths. However, there was no military action at the Parliament and the large crowds remained. Our orders remained unchanged.

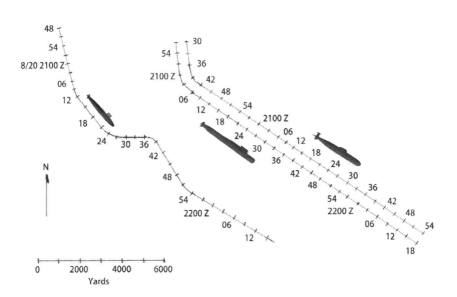

Chapter 26 – Delousing

Bering Sea – 56° 22.6' N 170° 50.9' W
Wednesday, August 21, 1991
1135

We were back on watch and Haddock was still tracking the Delta I and Victor III submarines. There was still no sign of the Akula though, if it were ahead of the Victor, it would be outside of our detection range. The Captain had no intention of exploring that possibility. He was content to continue shadowing the contacts we held.

We were originally directed to pull off and transmit a contact report after being in trail for 24 hours. The CO decided to ignore that requirement because it would leave us unable to intervene in event of a missile launch.

We had additional news from wire service reports but nothing more on official traffic. The military clashes in Moscow yesterday appear to be confirmed but they backed off. There was no report of action today and large crowds continue to gather at the Russian Parliament. There were claims that members of the Emergency Committee were fleeing Moscow. The consensus on Haddock was that things were coming to a conclusion.

It had been uneventful. We marked sunrise at 1605 Z, 0905 ship's time. The normal cycle of day and night had no impact on us, or the vessels we were tracking. Haddock was about 130° relative to the Delta I at a range of 5,500 yards, an ideal position on its aft, starboard quarter.

"The last bearing to Master-2 didn't track," Ohanian reported from the plots. He was helping out as plot coordinator before taking the 14-20 EOOW watch.

"The last dots here are tracking off too," agreed Boyle from the second console of fire control. He was on Master-2 while LT Gordon worked Master-1 on the first console.

"Master-1 shows no change," said Gordon.

"Sonar, Conn, any sign of a change in Master-2?" Gonzales asked over the MC.

"Conn, Sonar, wait one…Master-2 is getting stronger. We're starting to pick it up on the sphere. It's still at 50 turns. We're seeing more of a left bearing rate, possible maneuver."

"Confirm maneuver on Master-2," XO announced. He had the conn as CDO while we were in contact. He got on the phone to the CO.

"Helm, right full rudder, steady one-five-zero, all ahead one-third."

"Right full rudder, steady one-five-zero, all ahead one-third, Helm aye. My rudder is right full, Maneuvering answers ahead one-third."

TM3(SS) Wheeler had the helm with PNSN Miller on the sail planes.

"What do you have, XO?" The CO had arrived.

"We have a confirmed maneuver by Master-2. So far Master-1 seems to be steady. I've slowed to one-third and I'm coming right to one-five-zero."

"Passing one-four-zero to steady on one-five-zero."

"I'd been expecting this. I'm surprised we hadn't seen it sooner. Our Victor is going to see if anyone is trailing his buddy. They were on 125°, try 305° as his new course."

"Steady one-five-zero."

"What should we do?"

"You've already done it, XO. We've slowed to be quiet and turned to avoid closing the range. Now we'll see how good his sonarmen are. But if they're doing what I think they're doing, we have an advantage. They're looking astern of the Delta and we're not there."

"He looks steady on plot," Ohanian said.

"We have crossed bearings on Master-2 at 3,000 yards, believed to be a minimum range," said ET1(SS) Smith.

"Master-1 is still tracking," reported EM1(SS) Lipinski, the oncoming EO who was assisting Smith on the geo plot.

"Based on the geometry and relative speeds, try 150-200% of that for his actual range," CO suggested.

"That could put him close enough to detect us," Gonzales said.

"It's possible," the Captain agreed. "We'll see. There's nothing more we can do about it now."

"I'm looking at a solution on Master-2 of 305°, 5 knots and a range of 5,500 yards," said Boyle.

"That looks good on plot," Ohanian said. "We should be close to CPA."

"Helm, left full rudder, steady one-two-zero, all ahead two-thirds. Maneuvering make turns for 6 knots. I don't want him to track into our baffles," XO explained.

"Left full rudder, steady one-two-zero, all ahead two-thirds, Helm aye. My rudder is left full. Maneuvering answers ahead two-thirds."

"Maneuvering acknowledges turns for six knots."

"Ideally they should have turned right or left for 15 minutes, or so, as a setup maneuver before doing the delousing maneuver. The setup gets us out of position and the second maneuver has a good chance of detecting us as we try to regain our trail position. That might be hard to coordinate between two submarines though."

"Passing one-three-zero to steady on one-two zero."

"We're east of where we started our shallow water search," XO observed. "They can only continue this track for another day or so before running into Alaskan waters. What will they do then?"

"Steady one-two-zero."

"If we stay with them we'll find out. Maybe they just turn around.

"If we didn't need to be ready to take out the Delta, I'd prefer to be a couple thousand yards further out. We showed we can still hold the Delta at that range, but torpedo run is too long; he might evade our shot."

"Master-2 is maneuvering again, bearing rate is dropping," Ohanian said. "I think he turned away to his right."

"Conn, Sonar, Master-2 increased speed to 80 turns."

"Confirm maneuver on Master-2," XO announced. "Do you think he's returning to his base course of 125°?"

"That would be my guess," said the Captain. "I suppose he didn't see any intruders."

"We won't get crossed bearings on his new course and speed," Gonzales said, checking the geo plot.

"I think we have a handle on his course and speed," XO said. "We can get a maximum range for 8 knots. I think you can probably guess his track and see how it works."

"He's still in his turn," Boyle observed.

"Conn, Sonar, lost Master-2 on the sphere, still hold on the towed array."

"We have about 6,500 yards if he's doing what we expect," said Ohanian. "He should be about steady on his new course. We're forward of his beam."

"If he didn't detect us on his last leg, he won't spot us now," CO insisted. "I'm thinking he's concentrating on his partner to get back in formation."

We worked the problem for 10 minutes, trying variations. We settled on course 125°, speed 8, range 6,800 yards at 1924 Z for Master-2. Master-1 was tracking very well on course 125°, speed 5, range 5,500 yards. That put Master-2 about 5,800 yards astern of Master-1.

"It looks like the excitement is over for now," the CO said. "Keep up the good work. I'll be in my stateroom." He left.

At 1930 Z, XO ordered ahead one-third, explaining he wanted to let Master-2 get ahead of us faster. At 2000 Z we turned to one-three-five. Master-2 was almost abeam.

We lost LTJG Ohanian and Petty Officer Lipinski just before 1300. They were going to eat before their watches. It was Wednesday; lunch would be burgers and fries.

At 2018, "Conn, Sonar, underwater telephone from Master-2. Master-1 responds. Master-1 again. Master-2 now."

We had them around 500 yards apart almost abeam of each other.

"Can we tell what they said?" I asked.

"The system is scrambled. It would be in Russian anyway," said Gonzales.

"They might be able to do something with it ashore," the XO said. "Sonar, Conn, do you have the communications on your work tape?"

"Conn, yes we do."

"Sonar, save that tape and mark it with date, time and subject. Have there been more comms?"

"Conn, no. Four transmissions only."

When we turned over to ENG and section 1, Master-2 was almost back on station. We went to the Wardroom to grab our lunch second seating before reconstructing the delousing maneuver and smoothing the narrative. We saw the news that followed the 2000 Z broadcast. There were more reports that the junta members were fleeing Moscow.

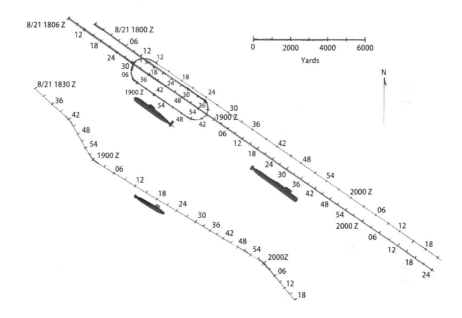

Chapter 27 – Battle Stations

Bering Sea – 56° 14.9' N 170° 20.2' W
Wednesday, August 21, 1991
1615

"Man battle stations." The general alarm sounded over the speakers. "Man battle stations."

Gonzales, Gordon and I were in the Wardroom finishing up the analysis of our last watch. We left everything on the table and headed out. The Captain was ahead of us, moving toward Control.

"What do you have, ENG?" asked the CO on arrival.

"Master-1 one slowed to 3 knots from the 5 knots they've been transiting at. Sonar started picking up new equipment running, so I called battle stations. We're on one-three-zero, speed 6, at 180 feet. We have him bearing 070° at about 6,000 yards. Making tubes 3 & 4 ready.

"I have the conn. Good work, ENG. Helm, left full rudder, steady zero-nine-zero. Maneuvering make normal two-thirds turns."

"Left full rudder, steady zero-nine-zero, Helm aye. My rudder is left full."

"Maneuvering acknowledges normal two-thirds turns."

"Navigator has the deck, Captain retains the conn."

"When we steady we'll check if Master-1 still looks like he's in launch preps. If so, intend to shoot a two torpedo spread from tube #3 first and #4 second."

"Conn, Radio, dropped synch on the broadcast."

"WEPS, use the 300 foot, plus 6 settings on the torpedoes. Set the floor at 400 feet. We'll risk a bottom impact. Doppler out on tube #3 and Doppler in on #4."

"Yes, Captain." Gonzales had taken his spot and was checking the settings Boyle was entering. "Tubes 3 and 4 are ready in all respects."

"Battle stations are manned throughout the ship," reported Lloyd, the COW.

"Captain we have a 34 fathom sounding. There is just over 380 feet of water in this area," NAV reported.

"Thanks, NAV. Are we voice recording in Control and broadband recording in Sonar?"

"Yes, Captain," answered ENG from the first console from where he was solving the Master-1 problem."

"Passing one-zero-zero to steady on zero-nine-zero."

"Captain, do you want plus 5 degrees on tube 3 and minus 15 on tube 4?" Gonzales asked.

"Yes."

"Steady zero-nine-zero."

"Solution looks good at course 125°, speed 3 knots, range 5,400 yards," XO reported.

"That's about an 1,800 yard enable run, high to medium," Gonzales added.

"Both signal ejectors are loaded with countermeasures, swept, shallow," NAV reported.

"Firing point procedures, tubes 3 and 4, tube 3 is first," Captain announced.

"Ship ready," reported COB from Dive.

"NAV, take the conn for a minute. Just hold steady. I'm going to Sonar. We have to be sure."

"I relieve you of the conn. Navigator has the deck and the conn."

The Captain hurried aft and entered Sonar. It was hushed in Control for a couple minutes. The Captain emerged from Sonar and made haste back to the periscope stand.

"Captain has the conn. Reports."

"Solution ready," XO said.

"Weapons ready. We'll insert the offset just before launch. Mr. McCarthy, you take weapon control on the first unit, tube 3, after launch."

"Take weapon control, tube 3, after launch, aye."

"Master-1 just started using lots of air. That's good enough for me," the Captain stated. "Match sonar bearings and shoot tube 3."

"Bearing matched." ENG reported.

"Plus 5 offset inserted," Boyle said.

"Offset verified," Gonzales said. "Shooting tube #3. Standby. Fire."

There was a rumble as the tube cycled.

"Torpedo course 077°, enable run 1,500 yards, said Boyle. He passed a paper that went to the plot. "Shifting to tube #4."

"Sonar reports our unit running in high speed," announced the XO.

"Shoot tube #4 on generated bearings."

"Minus 15 offset inserted."

"Offset verified. Shooting tube #4. Standby. Fire."

There was another rumble.

"Torpedo course 057°, enable run 1,500 yards.

"Good wire on the first unit," reported McCarthy.

"Sonar reports second unit running in high speed."

"Good wire on second unit."

"Sonar reports underwater comms from Master-2. Master-2 is cavitating. Countermeasure on bearing of Master-2, 093°. Master-1 is cavitating heavily, increasing speed. Countermeasure from Master-1, bearing 069°. First unit is slowing, starting search."

"Mr. McCarthy, set Doppler in on first unit."

"Set Doppler in, aye. Command sent…accepted."

"Second unit slowing."

"At least we got him out of launch mode."

"Shot looks good from plot," reported Jackson. "He's still in the cone."

"Master-2 could counter fire," said XO.

"I don't think so. He holds our unit but can't fling his weapons without endangering his partner."

"Detect," shouted McCarthy, obviously excited. "Acquired. Doppler, minus 18 knots. It's Master-1."

"Sonar reports first unit increasing speed."

"Here he is," said Boyle pointing at his screen.

"Show me a right 20° steer on the second unit," Captain requested.

Boyle turned a knob and the screen projected the new course a bit to the left of the displayed symbol of Master-1.

"Send it."

"Right 20 steer inserted at time 29.5. Accepted."

"We can't afford to just wound him."

"Detect. Acquired. Unit 2."

"Sonar reports second unit speeding up."

"First unit is 400 yards to go. Doppler, minus 22," McCarthy reported.

"1,500 yards on second unit," Boyle added.

"Lost the wire on first unit."

"Sonar reports an explosion on bearing of Master-1."

"WEPS, secure tube #3 and reload with Mk-48."

"Secure tube #3 and reload a 48, aye."

"Second unit is still locked on. Doppler has dropped to minus 10 knots. It's 600 yards to go."

"Mr. McCarthy, get back to Master-2. We need to know what he's doing."

"Lost wire on second unit."

"Sonar reports explosion on bearing of Master-1."

"WEPS, reload tube #4 too. Make tubes #1 and #2 ready in all respects assigned to Master-2. NAV get the position of Master-1 at the second explosion on the chart. We'll need latitude and longitude."

"Sonar reports many transients from Master-1. They no longer hold propulsion noises. Master-2 is at 280 turns and drawing right, bearing 136°. ENG, shift to Master-2," XO added. "Captain, what are your intentions for Master-2?"

"Master-2 is not an authorized target, but he has plenty of reason to attack us. If he does, we'll counterattack. I'm going to try to disengage if I can."

"Reloading tubes #3 and #4 with 48s. Making tubes #1 and #2 ready, assigned to Master-2," WEPS acknowledged. "Wires ejected and outer doors secured on tubes #3 and #4."

"Sonar reports Master-2 is slowing," XO said.

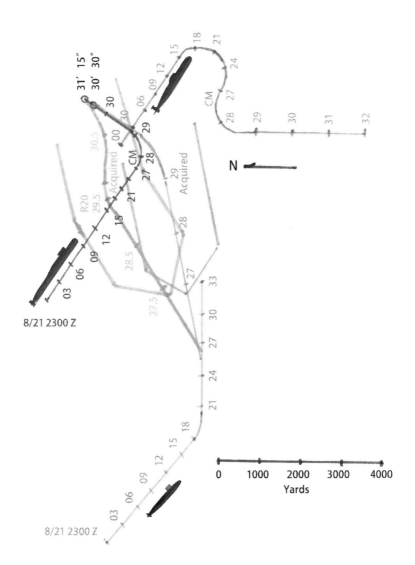

N

31' 15"
30' 30"

8/21 2300 Z

8/21 2300 Z

0   1000   2000   3000   4000
Yards

Chapter 28 – Evasion

Bering Sea – 56° 13.6' N 170° 14.5' W
Wednesday, August 21, 1991
1632

"Helm, right full rudder, steady two-three-five."

"Right full rudder, steady two-three-five, Helm aye. My rudder is right full."

"We have Master-2 at about 6,000 yards," XO reported. "That's rough. We're just restarting our track."

"We're shifting paper on the geo plot," said Jackson.

"Tubes #1 and #2 are ready in all respects," WEPS reported.

The Captain grabbed the announcing system mike.

"This is the Captain. I'll update everyone on what has been going on. We detected the Soviet missile submarine making launch preparations. As we were directed in such a situation we attacked it with two torpedoes, both hit." You could hear a cheer from below. "He had a buddy, a Victor III class attack sub. We are not authorized to attack it but he has plenty of reason to attack us. If so, we will defend ourselves. We'll stay at battle stations until we resolve the situation with the Victor III."

"Captain, Sonar believes Master-2 is changing course. His speed is down to 8 knots."

"He heard two explosions and knows he doesn't need to evade our torpedoes. I should have sent one in his direction just to keep him running."

"Mr. Cooper, the Air Regen watch asks if we can may resume burning candles? The last one went out about fifteen minutes ago," COW relayed.

"Captain?"

"OK, NAV, resume burning candles. We might be a while."

"Chief, resume burning candles forward."

"Resume burning candles forward, aye." He relayed the order via the phone talker.

"Passing two-two-five to steady on two-three five."

"Plot has crossed bearings at 1,800 yards, believe minimum range. He may have turned around and be heading north."

The whole room reverberated in sound for several seconds.

"What was that?" someone asked.

"Conn, Sonar, Master-2 is active on his Shark Gill, 2.4 kHz, high power, bearing 142°."

"Helm, steady two-three-two, all ahead one-third."

"Steady two-three-two, all ahead one-third, Helm aye. Steering two-three-two. Maneuvering answers ahead one-third."

"Dive, plane down to 220 feet."

"Plane down to 220 feet, Dive aye. Full dive on the sail planes."

"NAV how does the array look?"

The sound came again.

"Sounding is 32 fathoms. We should be clear even at one-third."

"Helm, steer two-two-eight."

"Steer two-two-eight, Helm aye."

"Sonar will be buzzing bearings," XO said. "The active is screwing up ATF. Captain, your intentions?"

"Do you hear his pulse? The pitch ramps down and back up. I've heard it before from a modern Soviet destroyer. The transmitted sound is compensated for the Doppler produced by the ship's speed. There's only one reason to do that. They have a low Doppler filter to exclude all the bottom and surface returns.

"Helm, steer two-two-four.

"They're probably getting a beautiful return off us and their computer is not displaying it because I'm giving them zero Doppler."

"Steering two-two-four."

"We need to get closer to the bottom. XO, tell Sonar to retrieve the towed array. Let me know when it starts coming in."

"Retrieve the towed array, aye."

"Helm steer two-two-zero."

"Steer two-two-zero, Helm aye."

"Sonar reports the active is a twelve-second pulse, sweeping in bearings from beam to beam, every forty seconds."

"I have a fair solution, course 010°, speed 8, range 3,200," reported ENG.

"I'm in short range tactics on the torpedoes in tubes #1 and #2," WEPS said.

"Helm, steer two-one six." Periodically the CO would adjust course a few degrees as the bearing to Master-2 changed. We were always close to ninety degrees from the bearing.

"We're getting crossed bearings around 1,200 yards, a minimum range," Jackson reported. "The maximum range for 8 knots is about 3,500 yards. We're looking at course north, about 2,800 yards."

"At 220 feet."

"Sonar is…" XO paused as a new pulse echoed in the hull. "retrieving the array now."

"Dive, plane down to 280 feet. New Yellow sounding 15 fathoms, Red 10."

"Plane down to 280 feet, Dive aye."

"Sounding 28 fathoms," NAV reported. "Captain how close to the bottom do you intend to go?"

"Probably closer. Maybe really close. Suspend Red and Yellow soundings. Let me know if you see 10 fathoms or less."

"Tube #3 is reloaded. I need to shift weapon control to check out the weapon."

"Wait until we pass into Master-2's baffles, then just the minimum we need to have confidence in the weapon."

"Master-2 bears 084°," XO said. "He's past CPA and opening. CPA was 2,500 yards."

"Maybe his damn sonar will get quieter when we're out of the beam. It's starting to give me a headache," COB complained.

It did get quieter. You could still hear the sound inside Haddock, but not the crescendo of noise we had as the beam passed by our bearing. Even the residual sound diminished as Master-2 moved away.

"Sonar reports the array is stowed."

"Tube #4 is reloaded. Both tubes took longer because we needed to move the bunks to clear the loading line."

"I understand, WEPS. You can do your checks on the tubes. We're in his baffles and we should know if things change. NAV, I'm going to stay at 280 feet and see what Master-2 intends."

"At 280 feet," COB reported.

"Helm, come left, steady one-zero-four."

"Come left to one-zero-four, Helm aye. Passing one-one four to steady on one-zero-four."

"If he keeps heading north, we'll be able to slip away."

"Why not just run away at high speed?" I asked.

"One reason is he's faster than us by 4 to 5 knots. I also don't want to put him in my baffles where I won't hear if he's launched a weapon. If we were a 688 class, it might be a good option."

"We have an excellent solution on Master-2, course north, speed 8, range, 4,500 yards," XO reported.

"We have crossed bearings at 4,000 yards," Jackson said. "That's a minimum, but should be close to his real range. The fire control solution tracks well on plot."

"Welcome to the new Zulu day, August 22nd," NAV announced.

"Sonar reports Master-2 is late for his next active pulse."

We had still been able to hear the pulses directly, but by now, they weren't loud enough to intrude on normal activities.

"It appears he has secured active," the XO added.

"Helm, all ahead two-thirds. We'll start moving off."

"All ahead two-thirds, Helm aye. Maneuvering answers ahead two-thirds."

"Sonar reports underwater comms from Master-2, bearing 004°. They're back in ATF."

"NAV, where is Master-2 relative to where we think Master-1 went down. Master-2 is about 6,000 yards north of us."

"I'll check Captain. That puts him about 2,000 yards from Master-1."

"Possible maneuver from Master-2," ENG reported. "To his right."

"Helm, all ahead one-third."

"All ahead one-third, Helm, aye. Maneuvering answers ahead one-third."

"More underwater comms," XO reported.

"Is there any reply or any noise from where we think Master-1 is?"

"No, it's all Master-2. We haven't heard Master-1 since a couple minutes after the second explosion."

"Underwater comms continue."

"If Master-2 continues to turn right he'll pass about 500 yards from Master-1," NAV said.

"And be heading back toward us," the Captain added.

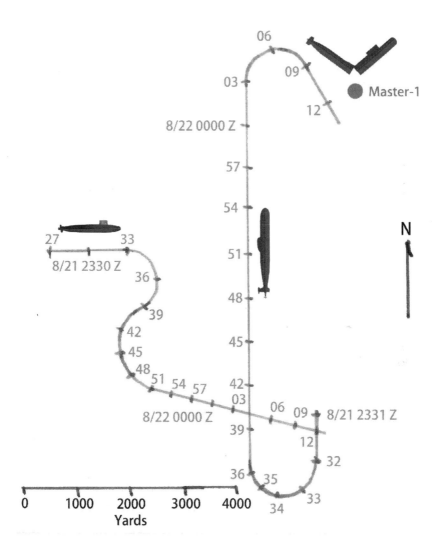

Chapter 29 – Attack

Bering Sea – 56° 12.0' N 170° 12.8' W
Wednesday, August 21, 1991
1712

"Helm, all-stop, left full rudder, belay your headings. Dive, 350 feet."

"All stop, Left full rudder, belay my headings, Helm aye. Maneuvering answers all stop."

"350 feet, Dive aye. Full dive on the sail planes."

"Dive, be ready to hover on the trim pump. I'm using the turn to bleed off our speed. It also points our quietest aspect at Master-2."

"Be ready to hover on the trim pump, aye. Chief of the Watch, line up to pump and flood auxiliary trim."

"Captain, sounding is 17 fathoms. We're only 34 feet above the bottom at 350," NAV reported.

"I know. We might get closer than that. Call out every two feet inside the final twenty."

"We have a decent solution on Master-2 after his turn," XO reported. "We have course, 145°, speed 8, range 5,500 yards. Sonar reports they're changing the broadband tape."

"Thanks, XO. WEPS, weapon status?"

"Tubes #1 and #2 are fully ready and assigned to Master-2. Normal tactics set with Doppler set in. Enable run is 1,900 yards and dropping as he closes."

"Doppler in is good. Tube #2 will be the primary tube."

"Zero bubble," COB ordered. "Full rise on the sail planes. Pump 3,000 from auxiliaries to sea. Captain, 340 going to 350, preparing to hover. We're a little below one knot indicated."

"Maneuvering requests permission to spin the shaft," reported a phone talker.

"Spin the shaft as needed, astern only." It was relayed to Maneuvering.

"Sounding is 32 feet. SINS has our speed at 0.7 knots," NAV reported.

"Helm, rudder amidships."

"Rudder amidships, Helm aye. Passing zero-five-two to the left."

"Sonar is back recording."

"Range is 4,500 yards and dropping. We'll need to shift to short range tactics soon."

"Shift to short range tactics now, WEPS."

"At 350 feet, still sinking slowly. Zero your stern planes. Chief of the Watch, pump auxiliaries to sea another 3,000."

"Pump another 3,000, aye."

"Possible maneuver from Master-2."

"ENG, don't touch your range or speed, just adjust your course to the right to match his bearing rate," Captain directed.

"Dive, your negative depth rate is fine. Let us sink to the bottom at about five feet per minute. Trim us about a half degree up bubble."

"Yes, sir. Chief of the Watch, pump forward trim to auxiliaries 500 pounds."

"I'm still pumping to sea. I'll shift suction to forward trim to sea for 500 pounds."

"JA talker, signal ejectors standby to launch countermeasures."

"Signal ejectors stand by to launch countermeasures, aye. They acknowledge."

"If I tell you to launch, don't repeat it back, just relay it."

"Yes, sir."

"ENG, your solution looks good. He's steady. What's his course?"

"170°."

"I hope he doesn't do what I think he's going to do. If he does, there will be no firing point procedures. I'll just tell you to shoot tube #2. Be ready WEPS."

"We're ready."

"Sounding 14 feet. We're at 0.3 knots," NAV said.

"Maneuvering, stop the shaft." He passed that by 7MC and they acknowledged. "We're bottoming in just over 380 feet of water. You may feel a bump." This went on the 1MC.

"8 feet."

"Torpedo in the water," came over the speaker. "Second torpedo in the water."

"Launch countermeasures. Shoot tube 2."

"Shooting tube #2. Standby. Fire." The now familiar rumble of a torpedo launch echoed in the Operations Compartment.

"Torpedo course 015°, enable run 1200 yards," Boyle said.

"Rig for depth charge."

"Rig for depth charge," sounded over the 1MC, followed by the collision alarm. "Rig for depth charge."

There was a thunk from below. The Bow Compartment door was slammed shut.

"Shot looks good from plot," Jackson said. "So do theirs."

"Sonar reports our unit running in high speed. Both the incoming torpedoes are active. One bears 060°, the other 010°. Master-2 is cavitating and increasing speed."

"Countermeasures are away."

There was a bump and the deck tilted a bit to starboard. Everyone lurched forward as our remaining speed was dragged off by the bottom contact.

"We're on the bottom, 382 feet, 1.5° starboard list," COB reported.

"Good wire on the unit," Boyle said.

"WEPS, shut the outer door on tube #1. Chief of the Watch, open the main ballast tank vents."

"Open the vents, Chief of the Watch aye. All vents indicate open."

"Our unit is slowing."

"Detect," Boyle shouted. "Acquired. Doppler plus 12 and increasing. It's Master-2."

"Sonar holds our unit speeding up."

"WEPS, eject the wire and secure outer door on tube #2."

"Yes, sir. Tube #1 outer door is shut."

"Sonar reports the starboard torpedo has maneuvered. Its bearing rate is now zero."

"Chief of the Watch, normal blow all main ballast tanks with the vents open."

"Normal blow, aye. Blowing all main ballast tanks. Vents are open."

"I hope this works," the Captain muttered to himself. I wrote it down.

"Explosion on bearing to Master-2. Transients. Turns dropping."

"Forget him. Tell me about our incoming torpedo."

"Bearing 056°, steady."

A loud boom reverberated through the hull, but there was no motion.

"What was that?" XO asked.

"A second explosion from Master-2. A big one, like a dozen torpedoes," Sonar reported over the 21MC.

"Mark his best position on the chart, NAV"

"Sonar reports incoming unit increasing in D/E, now plus 3. Plus 7. It's on a 400-yard range scale. Plus 11. Plus 15. Plus 19."

"Chief of the Watch, secure the blow."

"Secure the blow, aye. Blow secured."

"Plus 25. Plus 45. It's close."

A second boom sounded. This one shook the ship. The deck was tilted a little more when the shaking stopped in a few seconds.

"All stations report damage," NAV directed. It went out on the JA phones.

"Chief of the Watch, shut the vents."

"Shut the vents, Chief of the Watch aye. All vents indicate shut."

"Bow Compartment reports no damage. Operations Middle Level, no damage, Operations Lower Level, no damage. Engineering reports no damage."

"IC1(SS) Keller, the battle stations AEF, stopped aft of fire control. "No damage in upper level."

"XO, anything on the second torpedo?"

"It passed into our baffles with a high left bearing rate. It should run out of gas in about 3 minutes. They hold nothing on Master-2 now."

"Air Regen asks if you want to continue burning candles," COW reported.

"No, no more candles, we should get a chance to ventilate. Also secure rig for depth charge."

"Secure burning candles and secure rig for depth charge,

aye."

"Secure from depth charge," passed on the 1MC.

" I screwed up. I should have not resumed candle burning for battle stations. That's peacetime thinking. It's a fire and explosion risk I should have neutralized."

"Don't be too hard on yourself," I offered. "You're reviewing your mistakes and the other CO isn't."

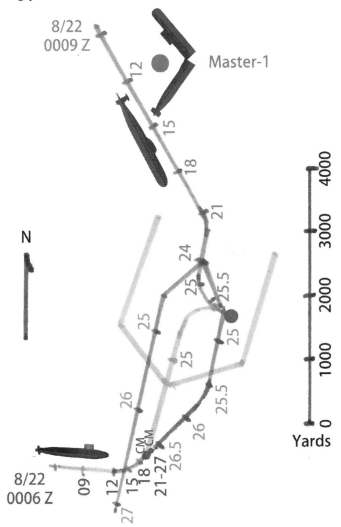

Chapter 30 – Aftermath

Bering Sea – 56° 12.2' N 170° 12.0' W
Wednesday, August 21, 1991
1730

"Quiet in Control," said the Captain in the loudest voice he'd used since I'd been onboard. "I know we're excited, but we're still at battle stations," in a softer voice.

"First order of business is getting off the bottom. COB, pump us light until we lift off. We'll float up fifty feet before we put on speed."

"Pump to sea until we lift off, Dive aye. Chief of the Watch, pump auxiliaries to sea."

"Pumping to sea. We need to put a reserve air bank on service. The normal blow took bank #5 down to 2800 psi."

"Shift to bank #4, Chief of the Watch," NAV directed.

"Shift to bank #4, aye. Shifting now."

"WEPS, reload tube #2 with a Mk-48."

"Reload tube #2 with a 48, aye." He passed it out over his phones.

"This is the Captain." He was on the 1MC. "A quick update. The Soviet Victor III SSN fired two torpedoes at us. We fired one back. He missed. We didn't." There was another cheer from below. "We bottomed to help evade his fire. We're lifting off the bottom soon. I think we are out of opponents but we'll do a search to make sure. Then we'll see if there are survivors we can rescue."

"Do you think there are survivors?" I asked.

"No, but we have to check. The water isn't very deep. A sealed compartment might have somebody alive. Some Soviet subs have an escape capsule. I don't know if that includes the Delta I or Victor III. We'll look. NAV, when is sunset?"

"0644 Z, Captain. We have about 6 hours of light."

Haddock rolled upright as the list came off.

"381 feet. We're rising," reported COB. "Secure pumping."

"Pumping secured."

"380 feet."

"WEPS, when we secure battle stations, assemble a rescue party in the Crew's Mess. Get everything you can think of to haul people on to the deck. Have the ship's divers standing by with their warmest wetsuits. We won't put anyone in the water unless they have a jacket and a harness tied to the ship."

"When will we surface?"

"We won't unless we see someone. I want to be ready. Anyone in the cold water won't last long."

"370 feet."

"Maneuvering, spin the shaft as necessary ahead and astern."

"Sonar reports they hold no contacts."

"We haven't located the Akula. If he's anywhere within a hundred miles he could have heard the explosions."

"330 feet."

"Helm, all ahead two-thirds, steady as you go."

"All ahead two-thirds, steady as you go, Helm, aye. Maneuvering answers ahead two-thirds. Steering zero-four-six."

"Dive, make your depth 200 feet."

"200 feet, Dive aye. Five up."

"Helm, left full rudder, steady two-seven-zero."

"Left full rudder, steady two-seven-zero, Helm aye. My rudder is left full."

"Captain, if we used the authority to attack the Delta, we were tasked to pull away 100 nm and report ASAP," NAV said.

"Yes, I saw that. Well, after we search for survivors is as soon as possible. And if we need help, I intend to ignore that 100 nm requirement."

"At 200 feet."

"Captain," Boyle said, "we're almost done the audio recording from Control. Do you want me to start another cassette?"

"No, that should be fine. Have another blank one ready in case we need it."

"Passing two-eight-zero to steady on two-seven-zero."

"XO does Sonar hold anything?"

"I'll check." He spoke into his headset. "No contacts."

"Dive 150 feet."

"150 feet, Dive aye."

"Steady two-seven-zero."

"Tube #2 is reloaded with a Mk-48." WEPS reported. "I'd like to drain and secure tube #1 and check the weapon in #2."

"That's fine, WEPS."

"At 150 feet."

"Helm, right full rudder, steady zero-five-zero."

"Right full rudder, steady zero-five-zero, Helm aye. My rudder is right full."

"XO, do we have anybody onboard who speaks Russian, even at high school level?"

"I don't know. We'll ask around on the phones."

"NAV, how does our track on zero-five-zero look relative to where we think Master-1 and 2 are resting?"

"We'll pass about 1,000 yards north of Master-2 and 3,000 from Master-1."

"Helm, continue right to zero-six-five."

"Continue right to zero-six-five, Helm aye."

"That will put CPA to Master-2 at under 500 yards."

"The Crew's Mess is sending ET3 Wong up. He speaks Russian."

Petty Officer Wong, an average looking young Chinese-American, entered by the starboard passage. He was the ETOW in my section 3, the fathometer watch in our shallow water operations. He stopped by where the Captain was seated on the periscope stand.

"Petty Officer Wong, you speak Russian?"

"Yes, Да. I took it in high school."

"Good. Why didn't you take Chinese?"

"I already spoke Chinese. I wanted something different."

"Russian is difficult."

"Not compared to Chinese."

"Good point. I want you to say, 'we will help, make noise,' on our underwater comms transmitter. What is that in Russian?"

"Мы поможем. Сделайте шум. I think."

"Passing zero-five-five to steady on zero-six-five."

"You can start now. Send it once a minute. XO, tell Sonar what we're doing and to listen for any noise."

"Yes, sir. What about the Akula?"

"It's a risk. We had no indication that he's here. We'll take the chance to try to save some lives."

"Can they hear and understand it?"

"I've no idea. We'll try some high power active pings too. They'll hear those for sure."

"Steady-zero-six-five."

"XO, does Sonar have any contacts?"

"No, sir, and no reaction to our first transmission."

"OK, secure from battle stations."

"Secure from battle stations, Chief of the Watch aye. Secure from battle stations, section 1 relieve the watch."

"Captain, dinner might be delayed," said Banner who was wrapping up his plot. "The galley is secured for battle stations."

"You'll do your best. What's for dinner tonight?"

"Mexican."

"Talk about bad timing. I'll pass. XO, you can start without me. I'll retain CDO until 0200. You and ENG get some sleep."

"We're good," ENG insisted. "You don't need to take the watch."

"I'd want to stay here anyway while we search for survivors. You'll have a lot to do tomorrow in reconstructing this. I'm particularly interested in how close that incoming torpedo was."

"Yes, Captain. I'll be up at 0200," XO said.

The watches turned over. LT Cohen came from Sonar, his battle station and relieved NAV. The CO gave him the conn. Jackson, from plot coordinator, assumed JOOD. There was no JOOD on the battle stations bill. I turned the narrative log over to Banner. Section 1 would do the reconstruction of the last hours.

"Petty Officer Wong, take a break," suggested the Captain. He had shifted to sit on the fire control benches, leaning back on the console. He looked tired. I sat down on the next bench aft. "Mr. Cohen, ask Sonar to transmit three, omni, pings at max power."

It was done and repeated. There was no response.

"Conn, Radio, we're not getting a signal off the wire. We should have plenty on the surface at this depth and speed."

"Mr. Cohen, we'll retrieve it once we're at periscope depth." He passed that to Radio.

We cleared baffles, taking a course to pass over Master-1, no contacts. Slowing to one-third we went to periscope depth. It was a calm, clear day with just a few white clouds in the sky.

Wong resumed his Russian on the underwater telephone. We went to 52 feet to expose more scope and see further. The Captain ordered #1 scope raised too. Jackson took that. There was nothing on

214

the water. We tried active sonar again when we neared Master-1. Nothing.

We had one message on the broadcast. It was flash precedence. Gorbachev had returned to Moscow and was in control. The plotters were under arrest. Our authorization to attack a Soviet missile submarine was rescinded. The date-time group of the message was 212322Z AUG 91, seven minutes after we'd gone to battle stations and four minutes before we'd fired our first weapon. We had dropped the broadcast when we turned to get in firing position. The message would have been transmitted within a few minutes of its date-time group. It must have been released almost immediately after Gorbachev's return. The change is not effective until we receive it and that could have taken 12 hours.

We pulled in the floating wire. We got back 127 feet. The rest was gone.

Section 2 was coming on. NAV and LT Nguyen took over on watch and on the periscope search. The COB came in with Petty Officer Glen, who was carrying a tray with a cheeseburger, fries, a glass of ice and a can of Pepsi. The Captain protested about special treatment, but not very hard. It was put on the plotting table and he stood behind it to eat.

We thanked Petty Officer Wong and secured his transmissions. The active sonar was repeated several more times with no success. We changed course to crisscross the area where the action took place. Jackson spotted a couple chunks of black material in the water. It might have been some pieces of the hull coating the Victor III used, or, it might not. There was nothing else.

Periodically we'd raise the snorkel mast to pressurize the ship. We were running an air charge to replace the air we'd used in evading the torpedo. The Captain didn't want to ventilate.

After finishing his meal, the Captain started writing on a pad of paper. I took the opportunity to talk to him.

"What are you doing?"

"I'm drafting the message reporting what we've done. I need to tell what happened, explain why, anticipate and answer their questions and not leave any loose ends. Simple. But you've been hanging around and that's not what you really want to ask. Go for it."

"What are you feeling now? Almost everybody is excited but you look…down."

"Churchill said, 'There is nothing more exhilarating than to be shot at with no result.' I guess most are feeling that now. I can't help going over my mistakes. It's just my nature. If I'd been better at disengaging, the crew of the Victor would still be alive. Perhaps if I'd gone to high speed when our units were homing and the Victor was evading, we could have pulled away. But I needed to be able to reattack if our units missed.

"I also didn't think the Victor's torpedoes could detect us on the bottom. The bubble screen from the blow with the vents open was my last ditch backup. If that didn't work we were dead.

"I don't think perfection is achievable in combat. Survival is good enough."

"How about you? This trip is more than you bargained for. You have more combat experience than anyone in the Submarine Force that's not here. What do you think?"

"It's amazing what you do with so little information. Submarine combat is like a gunfight between blind men."

We searched two more hours with no result before moving off toward deep water.

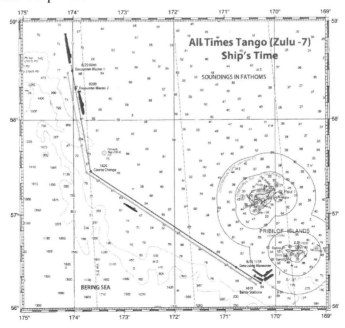

Chapter 31 – Transmit

Bering Sea – 55° 12.4' N 174° 13.8' W
Thursday, August 22, 1991
0900

We had the 02-08 watch. It was quiet. Section 2 had run four hours on course one-eight-five at ten knots. On clearing the 100-fathom curve they streamed the towed array to its full scope. When we came on we searched, both on sphere and array, on two different courses before turning to course two-five-five and going to periscope depth for a broadcast. At 0300 we went deep at 15 knots. We turned over in transit. The plan was to be at periscope depth at 0900 to transmit the report of our action and we were. We had just started ventilating. We would shoot all the trash and expended candles before we finished.

In the Wardroom after watch the forward end of the table had plots spread out, reconstruction of the events of yesterday. It looked so clear on paper. Section 1 had done these last evening while Haddock searched for survivors. They hadn't done detail on the Victor's torpedo shot yet. The estimate was that it passed directly over the sonar sphere about 100 to 150 feet above our hull.

We'd had some breakfast and were discussing what was next. My narrative was done, less than a page for the first time in days. The Captain came in and took his seat. Breakfast for him was coffee and a pastry. The XO entered with a number of papers.

"These are the typed drafts of yesterday's watches. They'll be ready for your review soon. Mr. Cohen will convert the reconstructed plots to standard size so we can Xerox them for the report. We'll be caught up by this evening."

"That's good. We could be dropping everything off in Adak in a couple of days."

"We'll be ready."

"Yesterday I had a chance to talk with Petty Officer Wong, the guy who knew Russian. He had a year at Berkeley before signing up. His parents had him on track to be an M.D. but he rebelled. From his cultural background, that took guts. See if he's interested in being an officer. We can nominate him as a fleet input for a NROTC scholarship. He's getting his sub qual board today after less than 5 months on Haddock."

"Captain," said MS3(SS) Glenn, who had just entered from the Pantry. "The Supply Officer asks your approval on a menu change. He's on watch now and asked me to bring it to you." He handed him a sheet of paper. "We have the money, he said to tell you."

"Surf and turf, steak and lobster tails tonight. OK." He signed.

"Thank you." Glenn left.

"Since everyone will be up for dinner tonight. I'll do an operations brief after dinner for the crew and we can execute the security statements. Have our reconstructed plots available. I'll do a second session for the off-going watch at 0200."

"That's a good idea. I'll put out a revised POD."

He left to take care of it. The CO, WEPS and I were the only ones left in the Wardroom.

"Captain, these are the Torpedo Record Books for the weapons we used. The entry to close them out is straightforward. I was thinking about the classification. Expending three warshot torpedoes might lead to questions."

"Yes, I see. Just hold them here. I'll check with Sub Group SEVEN when we reach Japan."

He left with the books leaving me alone with the Captain.

"What do you think happens now?"

"The most likely thing is we drop our data package off in Adak and continue to Japan. Tom, if you want off in Adak, it can be arranged. You'd probably fly on a P-3 to Barbers Point or Whidbey Island. It has already been a longer trip than you imagined."

"No thanks. I'll stay to the end if you'll put up with my questions."

"OK, fair enough. In more detail, our message is hitting D.C. and Pearl now. It's top secret, so it will be hand routed to the people who need to see it. Our operational order was issued by CINCPACFLT but clearly higher authorities were in on the attack authorization.

"I imagine that the attack authorization was controversial. That argument might be refought now that the coup is over and folks start thinking about how they explain two missing Soviet submarines if anything gets out."

"Will that be a problem for you personally? I thought you'd be a hero."

"Perhaps a secret hero. The citation on the medal reads for doing something unspecified of great value to the United States. But if I did something wrong, it's easier for both sides of the argument to blame me than to scream at each other. Anyway that's why they pay me the big bucks; to make those decisions and accept responsibility for them. I get $100 a month Command Responsibility Pay. Fact."

"How will they know if you acted properly or not?"

"I have broadband sonar recordings of the Delta. They'll go to NAVSTIC. They can analyze them, and if anyone can, tell us what was going on. I have audio recording of our battle stations procedures, plus our logs and narrative and my orders on how I intended to execute the attack order they gave me. I think I have everything well documented."

"So, you expected to be second guessed?"

"It was a possibility."

"Why collect all that if it might be used against you?"

"I'd like to know. I won't feel any better about killing over a hundred Russian sailors, but knowing that I did so on proper justification helps. The math is unforgiving, possibly saving millions by killing hundreds."

"Yes, the needs of the many outweigh the needs of the few."

"Or the one. Don't quote Spock to me. Anyway, I expect COMSUBPAC will have my back if I acted reasonably based on the information available and the time constraints. RADM McKinney would go to the mat for one of his captains if he thought he were right."

"I hope it works out. When should we hear something?"

"Possibly early evening our time, more likely tomorrow. They'll certainly cancel the search mission. Only the Akula is left and there's no point in doing a massive search effort for one submarine in the entire Pacific Ocean. We'll see. Patience is a good submarine virtue."

Chapter 32 – Briefing

Bering Sea – 54° 11.7' N 173° 28.7' W
Thursday, August 22, 1991
1900

The Captain came in and took his seat. Every officer not on watch was at dinner. A line had formed in the passageway leading to the Crew's Mess too. Surf and turf was popular at anytime. Tonight, it was a victory dinner.

The table had its usual white tablecloth. The new addition was small cups of melted butter by each place setting. There were a couple baskets of the very tasty bread Haddock baked each night and some sticks of butter. None were reaching for it, a change from normal. They wanted to save room for the main course.

The first tray Glenn brought out was filled with fairly large lobster tails. As the guest, it was offered to me first. I used the serving tongs to select a good looking tail.

"You can take more than one," the Chop reminded me. "There is no change in our charge to you whether it's tacos or tails."

I took a second. Glen offered the tray next to the CO who took one. XO was on watch so Rinaldi had the seat opposite me. He was handed the tray that was then passed down the table and up my side. By the time it came back we were selecting steaks. These were T-bone steaks in a variety of doneness from rare to well. I selected one I thought was medium. It was good but you would not compare it to those of a quality steakhouse. I used some A-1 sauce on mine. Baked potatoes and green beans completed the service.

Haddock was steaming inside a self-selected 40 nm square in the middle of the deep Bering basin. We were still on patrol and searching but it was just going through the motions while we awaited a response to our message. There was nothing so far. We were copying the broadcast every four hours. There was plenty of time to ventilate and get rid of the trash we'd stored while in shallow water. The Akula was still unaccounted for but we didn't think it was anywhere near us.

"Your guys did a good job, Chop."

"Thanks, Captain."

"We listened to our broadband recording," said Cohen, "to verify it was properly recorded. It was. Senior Chief and Johnson both still think the Delta was in launch mode. You didn't shoot until he started using lots of air. You can hear the initial rush of air and it drops off, then there's another rush. There were four cycles before our units masked the target. It certainly looks like he was pressurizing something, probably his missile tubes."

"That's good to hear. Our tapes will go through the most sophisticated analysis. We had to make a judgment based on what we have here. I'm on in under two hours. How are you doing on the incoming torpedo?"

"We have a problem," admitted Gonzales. "We have the time when the torpedo shifted to the 400 meter range scale but it was somewhere inside of that range when that happened. We have the elevation angles recorded by sonar, but without knowing the range, we can't convert that to depth."

"An interesting problem. Does anyone have a suggestion?"

"Work it backward," ENG said. "Assume it went off right above our hull, then run the range back using the 40 knot speed of the ET-80A. It covers 4,000 yards in three minutes so, thirty seconds before it exploded, it was 665 yards out."

"That will work. We already have the timeline from the tapes but our starting point was the active range-scale shift."

"Looks like problem solved," Captain said. "Don't forget to allow for our half degree up bubble and 1.5 degree starboard list."

"We're factoring that in by subtracting a degree from the called elevation angle."

Glenn came in with a new tray of lobster tails. Everyone took another. Chocolate ice cream was dessert. Then it was time to relieve the watch.

2100

The Crew's Mess was packed. Every seat was taken and the passageway was filled with standees all the way back to the ladder to lower level. Officers were intermixed with crew. XO and COB had taken spots on the first tables next to the aisle leading to the Galley. The reconstructed plots were taped to the forward bulkhead.

"The Captain doesn't want anyone to call 'attention on deck' or get up," XO said. "We're too crowded for that."

The Captain entered from the Pantry door. Though the aisles were packed, room was created almost instantly that let him reach the front of the space easily.

"The first thing for today is to recognize four of our sailors that completed their submarine qualification. Petty Officers Michaels, Tanner and Wong and Seaman Miller come forward."

They were seated next to the COB who got up to let them out. The Captain pinned silver dolphins on their coveralls above the left chest pocket and shook each sailor's hand. He remarked that Wong completed his qual in just five months. Tanner, Wong and Miller were on watch, temporarily relieved for the ceremony. They headed back to their stations after getting their dolphins. I was, technically, on watch too but there wasn't any need for a narrative keeper so ENG secured me for the briefing.

"Next we'll pass out security statements for everyone to sign, including me. We'll check off the returned ones against the sailing list. The operation we are on is classified top secret. Because of what happened it's really higher than that. Knowledge of what we did will have a very limited distribution. For obvious reasons we don't want the Soviet Union to find out we had anything to do with the loss of their submarines. They might not even know they're missing yet.

"Most of you are cleared to the secret level. You've been exposed to material of a higher classification, and in a few minutes, I'm going to go over everything that we've done in the last few days. You have a great story but you can't tell anyone, not wives, girlfriends or buddies on other submarines. Even if they say they know, you can't confirm it. If anyone does ask about our operations, report that to us. If it's some time in the future, tell your chain of command you need to speak to the Special Security Officer and report the contact to him. If you think that's tough, think of our guest, Tom Ryan. Many of you are fans of his books. I am. He has his next bestseller but can't write it."

The form had a place to print name and identification number; Social Security numbers for me and the crew. It discussed the penalties if information were divulged. They were severe enough. There was a place to sign and date it. I did. Everyone passed the forms back to the front where they were stacked on the table by the XO.

"Any questions on the forms? No. Good. As I brief the ops, if you have a question, raise your hand.

"We were tasked to locate and track three submarines that were missing from Petropavlovsk on the Kamchatka Peninsula. They were a Delta I class SSBN and a Victor III and Akula SSN. We were given a search area that included the entire Bering Sea east of the 180 meridian. We decided to search the shallow water because that's the hardest place to find a submarine."

"Why search where it's hard?"

"Because that's where a sub trying to hide would go. The Soviets have used shallow water before, but I can't tell you how we know that." There was a soft laugh from the group. They had an idea on how.

"While we were searching we received news of a coup in the Soviet Union. The junta claimed to be in control of the nuclear arsenal. That must have alarmed Washington. They authorized us and other submarines to attack any Soviet missile submarine believed to be preparing to launch its missiles. That order was unprecedented. No submarine had ever gotten such authority. We didn't have contact when we received it.

"The first chart shows our initial detection of the Delta. We were heading northwest and it southeast and we passed right by. We turned around and got in trail. Once we were shadowing the Delta we picked up on the Victor III that was leading the Delta by about 4,000 yards. We must have passed right by the Victor without detecting it. That shows you how tough making the initial contact was."

"We tracked both submarines for almost two days. I haven't heard of an open-ocean trail of two submarines before. It might be a first. This plot shows where they changed course, and this one, where the Victor searched for anybody trailing them.

"At 1615 yesterday we went to battle stations because Sonar detected possible launch preparations from the Delta. At 1626 we fired a two Mk-48 spread at the Delta. That's shown on this plot. It appears the Victor alerted the Delta to our attack. The Delta tried to evade but we scored two hits."

"Why didn't the Victor shoot at us?"

"It probably didn't hold us, only our torpedoes. They would also worry that they might hit the Delta. The Victor rang up flank speed to escape our torpedoes, slowing when he heard the two explosions.

"The Victor started searching for us with active sonar. We all heard his pings echo through our hull. We were essentially invisible to his active sonar. If he had stuck to passive he probably would have detected us. The active put so much noise in the water that passive, for him, was impossible. He secured active and tried contacting the Delta. He got no response.

The Victor's next leg was passive and he did detect us. He fired two torpedoes at us and we shot one back. I was not authorized to attack the Victor until he fired on us. The problem with two SSNs attacking at short range is that neither one can evade the other's attack. They could sink each other. He tried to evade. We tried to hide from his torpedoes on the bottom. He chose…poorly." Another laugh.

"We searched for survivors and found none. Then we pulled away to transmit a report of what we'd done. That went out about 12 hours ago. We haven't heard anything back. By tomorrow I expect we'll know where we go from here. Any questions?"

"Why did you use tubes #3 and #4 to attack the Delta?" I asked.

"They are the lower tubes. The Mk-48 will sink a few feet while the propulsion system comes up to speed. The upper tubes give a better margin if you're near the bottom."

"So you were planning to be near the bottom to attack the Victor before we attacked the Delta?"

"The plan was to disengage after the Delta attack but I had to allow for the case where I couldn't disengage. I thought being near the bottom offered the best chance to survive an encounter with the Victor III. I planned accordingly. Combat is like chess in that you need to think several moves ahead."

"What happened to the torpedoes fired at us?" Chief Allen asked.

"The plot all the way on the right shows that action. Hold on, I need my laser pointer." He fished it from his right hip pocket. "The orange lines are his torpedoes, a two torpedo spread running down the same course about 1,000 yards apart. He might have an automatic setting in his fire control for that tactic; it's common. The torpedo on the left is actually aimed closer to us but never detected us. The one on the right detected us and turned toward us. It tracked right over the sonar sphere and exploded about 150 feet above the bow compartment. LT Cohen just finished a diagram of that."

He came forward and he and the CO removed the initial detection plot and put the new one in its place. There was silence as the assembled crew took it in.

"I'm proud of every one of you. It was a whole ship effort to do what we've done. We had so many volunteers from Engineering to help out on plots that Senior Chief Jay had to use a signup sheet that he filled up in an hour. That's besides those on the regular watch.

"You're all combat veterans now. This was a little more intense than lobbing cruise missiles at Iraq. When a friend boasts of what his ship did in the Gulf War, just smile.

"That's all for now. We'll put out the word as soon as we find out what's next."

Personnel stayed in place as the Captain left. Then the crowd dispersed.

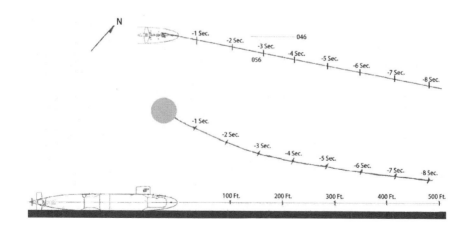

Chapter 33 – New Orders

Bering Sea – 54° 16.1' N 173° 14.3' W
Friday, August 23, 1991
0100

I was back on my watch. My only entry this watch was sunset at 0648 Z, just before midnight, ship's time. We were at periscope depth to get the 0800 Z broadcast, ventilate, grab a satellite fix and blow #2 sanitary tank. We were already ventilating and the tank was venting off after being blown to the ocean. Since it was after sunset, Control was rigged for black and the curtain was drawn about the periscope stand to make that area even darker. However, tonight we had an almost full moon shining in the clear sky. You could see the waves reflecting the moonlight. The sea was pretty, but empty, except for us.

I was taking a turn on the periscope. I could see the craters on the moon clearly.

"Conn, Radio, copied the 0800 Z ZBO. We have three op-immediate messages on the broadcast."

"Conn aye," said Gonzales. "These are probably what we've been waiting for. I'll call NAV and the CO."

There was really nothing for us to do but wait for the messages to print and continue with our periscope depth evolutions. We had twenty minutes left until the Transit pass. We'd secure ventilating and go down once it was onboard.

0130

We were on our way to 400 feet, ahead two-thirds. Control just rigged for white. I was still blinking from the sudden change in illumination. The Captain and NAV came to Control and went to the navigation station. ENG joined them.

"I don't need the chart to know that our track takes us to San Diego," said NAV "We exit the Bering Sea by Amukta Pass. We're close to there now."

"Let me update everyone," said the Captain in a voice that included all the watches in Control and Sonar through the open mike. "We just got three messages. The first suspends the current

226

search operations for all three subs. We know why but the message gave no details. The second switches us back to our normal broadcast. Our traffic will be duplicated on both broadcasts for the next 24 hours. The final one gives us a track to return to San Diego. The PIM starts at the southern end of Amukta Pass at 0000 Z on the 24th. We still have the Bering until 2359 Z on that day. We get into San Diego on the morning of September 2nd, Monday, Labor Day."

"Why San Diego?" I asked.

"They didn't say. I can think of a few reasons but such speculation is pointless. Everyone will still do it though. I have your final narrative entry, Mr. Ryan. 0810Z received CINCPACFLT 230643Z AUG 91. Suspended patrol operations."

I wrote it down. As an ending for a book, it wouldn't do.

"We will suspend the CDO watch. Make your reports to me. We'll only need an OOD for now. You can decide who gets it for the remainder of the watch. We'll go back to our regular underway bill on the 14-20 watch and shift to the five-watch schedule the next day, just in time for field day."

"What about drills?" ENG asked.

"We'll use Friday to wrap up the patrol report. It would be a good time to review the tests with the Engineering Department. Weekend will be the normal underway schedule and we'll resume our drills on Monday. I think we can skip the Tuesday and Thursday battle stations next week."

"We had plenty last week," stated Gonzales.

"I'll make that happen," ENG said.

0200

The Crew's Mess was not as packed as the first session but several who had been at the first briefing were at the second. There were just a few standing. Everyone knew we were headed back to San Diego. The grapevine isn't as fast as the 1MC but it's not behind by much.

The Captain started by recognizing Tanner, Wong and Miller who were in attendance at this brief, having just gotten off watch. Then came the security statements for those that hadn't executed them earlier. The briefing on our operations went exactly as before except the graphic with the final 8 seconds of the incoming torpedo was already posted on the forward bulkhead. I saw many that were realizing, as I was, that it could have been our final 8 seconds too.

"Almost everyone already knows that we're headed back to San Diego. We'll be there Monday, September 2nd, Labor Day. I don't know why we were directed to San Diego and it wasn't explained. Nor, do we know how long we'll remain there. Obviously, there will be a major revision in our schedule."

"Captain, are you in trouble?" blurted out Petty Officer Wong. There was a murmur from the group. Lots were thinking that but only a relative newcomer would say it.

"I don't think so. I had a rational reason for every action I took. If I made mistakes I'm ready to be accountable for them. That's part of my job. But any errors were my errors, not yours. I think I had the best crew any skipper could ask for."

"What do we do if questioned?" Petty Officer Boyle asked.

"Easy, tell the truth. Don't worry about how it affects anything. Facts and truth are always the best way. We have nothing to fear from the truth."

"That's why you had me taping in Control…and Sonar," Boyle stated.

"Of course. But look, there's no reason to speculate. We'll know what's up soon enough. Meanwhile we have plenty to do. We'll be back to a normal routine tomorrow. Get some rest."

Chapter 34 – Homeward Bound

Northern Pacific – 50° 35.2' N 163° 19.3' W
Saturday, August 24, 1991
1900

"Tonight's pizza is brought to you by Sonar Division," explained the Chop. "We allow divisions to volunteer to finish the pizza and serve on occasion." That last was for me.

Petty Officer Johnson came in carrying a pepperoni pizza on the large rectangular trays the ship used. I used the spatula to remove a piece then the Captain took one before the tray was passed around the table. Petty Officer Reinhardt entered with another pizza.

"This is our special for today," said Johnson. "We call it our multi-meat pizza."

The new pizza had pepperoni, ground beef, ham, Canadian bacon, and some chunks of spicy chicken. The Captain and I took pieces. The XO tried a piece.

"It's good. You've done a good job tonight. Well done, Sonar."

It was way too much meat for my taste but I finished it. The next pizza was Hawaiian style and was very popular.

Haddock had just finished a southerly transit of Amukta Pass and was on the track that would return us to San Diego. When NAV finished plotting the track it raised many questions. The speed of advance was a leisurely 12.5 knots. We could easily return by September 1st or even earlier, if they wanted us to.

It's like there was some special reason they wanted us arriving on September 2nd. They certainly didn't seem in eager to see us. Perhaps they wanted to see if there is any reaction from the Soviets about their missing submarines. There was nothing so far as we could see from the news stories used to fill the broadcast. Things in the Soviet Union seemed confused in the wake of the coup. Gorbachev was back but Yeltsin might be the one calling the shots.

I'd talked to the CO in his stateroom during the field day earlier today. He had been reading "Wonderful Life" by Stephen Jay Gould. He browses the UCSD bookstore, looking for titles that strike his interest to read on deployment. He's read some other books by

Gould. His own view was that life is common in the universe, but mostly, single cell. His believes that if we could drill down 100 meters on Mars, we'd find it there.

I was really there to get some insight about what he was thinking, without the need to act in control in front of other officers and crew.

"Has some time given you new thoughts on the battle?"

"I still believe my actions were reasonable. The review of our tape by Sonar should clinch it. Anybody can make a mistake in the heat of battle. I encouraged them to call an event early. The analysis after was under no such pressure. That still leaves the problem in distinguishing a drill from the real thing. The chain of command should have, at least, acknowledged the problem and provided guidance. I can't do anything about that but I'll at least fight like hell if they try to blame me.

"Even if I was right, I don't feel any better about killing the crews of the two Soviet submarines. We'll never really know what the Delta was up to. I wish I weren't the one responsible for their deaths."

"At least you know that you can handle combat," I observed.

"If that was handling it, I don't much care for it. My stomach hurt the whole time. My mind was racing through half a dozen courses of action. I had to struggle to remain calm or everyone might panic."

"A successful struggle, I'd say."

"When the Victor's torpedo was homing, all I could think was that I'd killed everyone. Myself, I could accept, but I regretted not saving my crew."

"But you did. You did better than I, for what that's worth. When the Victor fired I was writing everything down in my narrative. After, I could only make out half of what I'd written.

"What do you think happens when we reach San Diego?"

"An investigation, most likely. I'll deal with it when we get there. There's no point in worrying about it."

I talked to others to get a sense of the range of reactions. Most of the crew was excited they had kicked some Russian butts. That's not much different from the "we're number 1" displays after sports matches. There were a few more restrained. They recognized how close we came to joining the Russians on the bottom of the Bering Sea.

Back in our stateroom I had a chance to draw out the XO.

"What are your thoughts?"

"I'm happy we'll be back in San Diego soon. I should be able to turn over to my relief before Emily starts her next course of chemotherapy."

"The change in plans works out for you. That's good. What were your thoughts about our battle?"

"We train at battle stations frequently but this was different. I guess nothing is really at stake in training. The attack on the Delta was almost like we trained. After that things got complicated. When we turned attention to the Victor we were almost starting from scratch."

"What were you feeling?"

"I was nervous. I knew he wanted to get revenge for sinking his partner. I can still hear in my mind his active pulses echoing inside our hull. You think, how can he not be detecting us? The Captain seemed to know what to do and that helped a lot. I was concentrated on solving the fire control problem, and also trying to find tactical alternatives to recommend. I didn't come up with anything. At least we did get a solution on the Victor."

"From my vantage it looked like everyone in Control worked like a finely coached team. The CO told me he likes to think of himself as your coach."

"I hope I'm able to do as well when I'm a CO."

I'd bet he would.

LT Nguyen was EOOW during battle stations. They followed the action along with other compartments by a running commentary from the Control JA talker, using a low voice like a TV golf announcer. He was disappointed not to be where the action was.

LT Gordon was still determined to leave the Navy after his obligation was up. Combat only increased that desire.

LT Cohen was in Sonar. His job was to report information to Control, normally through the XO on the phone circuit. There was so much info, he had to decide what was essential and only report that. When the Victor shot, he grabbed the MC to save time. Sonar never reported that the Victor launched a torpedo countermeasure in its attempt to evade. It wasn't logged either. It's on the tape though.

ENG was so focused on solving the fire control problem that he lost track of what else was going on.

The COB was a Master Chief Torpedoman. I spoke to him during this afternoon's field day. He'd been training his entire career to do what we'd done. We should be heroes, he thought. The lack of any messages from our chain of command disturbed him. He was proud of the way his crew performed.

I spoke to LTJG Banner between seatings of our pizza dinner. He is the only officer not trained through the nuclear program. As Supply Officer, he is a member of the Supply Corps. During battle stations he analyzes the data from the geographic plot and gives maximum and minimum ranges and independent estimates of course, sped and range. When we shoot, they plot our torpedo, called a unit to avoid confusion with incoming fire, to confirm it is properly directed.

"Chop, what are your impressions of your first combat experience?"

"I'm excited, more so now than at the time. I was more focused on my part of the job during battle stations to feel much at the time. It's one of the things I like about being a submarine supply officer. I'm part of everything and not shut out of our operations as I would be on a large warship. These billets are highly prized."

"Why, besides what you just said?"

"This is independent duty. I'm just out of training, a LTJG, and a department head. At a Naval Supply Center, on a carrier or big amphibious ship, I'd be the junior man in a large department. Here I'm in charge. Our CO and most submarine skippers don't get too involved in supply issues as long as you keep everything running smoothly and don't run out of toilet paper."

Going by our food service, I had to think he was doing well. I'll need to diet when we get back,

I spoke to NAV during second seating. He was working on paperwork concerning the patrol report at the forward end of the table while the just relieved watches, LT Gonzales and LTJG McCarthy had pizza on the aft end.

"NAV, as OOD you had a good chance to see the big picture during the battle. What did you think?"

"Yes, the Navigator is typically the OOD for battle stations. I concentrate on the navigation picture, a real concern in shallow water, and the routine running of the ship so the Captain can concentrate on the tactical picture. I think I learned a lot."

"For instance?"

"I think the Captain had a plan. You brought it out when you asked why he fired the lower tubes at the Delta. He had the second attack in mind from the start."

"Our orders didn't allow that," Gonzales objected.

"Until he attacked us. The orders never considered that the missile submarine might be in company with another. They should have considered it since there were three submarines deployed. Had the Victor withdrawn, the Soviets would know we'd sunk their missile sub. Now it's a mystery what happened. That also helps us. There's no need to offer up a sacrifice to appease the Soviet Union and every incentive for everybody to keep things quiet."

"That's cynical. We searched for survivors. Were we planning to kill them?" McCarthy asked.

"No, of course not, but the odds for survivors were nearly zero. In World War II all survivors were from submarines that managed to reach the surface. No one got out if they were sunk while submerged."

"Do you think we could have avoided the Victor?"

"If we had gone to standard or full speed when we pulled astern of the Victor on his active search we could have opened another 7,000 yards, minimum. He wouldn't have detected us when he did turn around."

"Why didn't you recommend it to the Captain?"

"I thought about it. I guess it sounded a lot like running away."

"What was going through your head when the Victor fired at us?"

"By then I knew the CO intended to avoid it by bottoming. I'd never considered that as an option. As Navigator I'm trained to avoid hitting the bottom. I'm sure there will be no objections to our tactic since it worked. I guess we lost paint off our hull when we slid to a stop."

"But one of them homed in on us."

"I don't mind admitting I was scared as it closed in," McCarthy said.

"I would say a quick prayer each time I shot," Gonzales added. "I hoped the torpedo would run true. When theirs was homing I said a few for us."

"I was surprised. I thought being on the bottom would work. I could see the CO did too. He had a plan in case it didn't and that one worked. As I said, I learned a lot. I think, with combat experience, there's no need for an Engineer tour."

The CO's point was that he'd be a better CO with more engineering experience, but I didn't bring that up. No doubt the experience of the last few days would be important too.

Tomorrow was Sunday, a day of rest. I wondered if the lay leader services would be better attended. The officers showed a videotape in the Wardroom, 'The Godfather III.' The CO attended. Before the start, Glenn brought in a big bowl of popcorn. The Crew's Mess was showing 'Pretty Woman.' It was packed.

Chapter 35 – Back to Routine

Northern Pacific – 47° 17.3' N 151° 01.2' W
Monday, August 26, 1991
1200

Yesterday we received a message directing us to copy our previous broadcast at some point within a 24 hour window while remaining on our current broadcast for normal traffic. It had a single message directing us to mark all our patrol materials, 'TOP SECRET – ACCORDION.' Accordion was a code word to limit distribution of the information. The name itself had a top secret classification.

There are many different compartments used to limit distribution of sensitive information. Officers and key crew have access to compartments relating to Haddock's operations. The CO has access to several others. He said he knows the names of a few more compartments but doesn't know what they involve.

The Ship's Office made up a stamp and spent a couple hours marking all materials and every page of the patrol report. The final step before we packaged everything up was for Petty Officer Boyle to prepare slides from our reconstructed plots. He set the ship's Nikon up on a stand on the Wardroom table with extra lighting on the sides. The camera could also mount to take photos through the periscope, its official purpose.

The materials were placed in two boxes that originally held reams of copy paper. The large reels of broadband sonar tape made a third box. A packing list of all materials went in the first box. The boxes were double wrapped with the classification on the inner wrapping. The outer wrapping was marked 'Open by Special Security Officer Only'. They would be hand delivered to Submarine Group FIVE when we arrived.

The CO retained a copy of the patrol report and the completed slides in his safe.

All drafts and rough notes were collected and shredded. NAV and LT Cohen searched the officer staterooms, Ship's Office, Control, Sonar and Radio looking for anything related to our operations we might have missed. They found a couple pieces that they shredded. The shreds were then put in burn bags and stored in Radio for the final step when we reach port.

On Sunday we removed the Mk-48 from tube #1. The empty tube was fired and the weapon reloaded. The other tubes had been fired for real.

Sunday was also the day LTJG Reed completed his OOD qualification. His gold dolphins, symbol of an officer qualified in submarines, would have to await approval by Haddock's squadron commander. He was assigned the 08-12 OOD watch and would be a drill team member for the following two watches.

Now I was in the Wardroom for the first drill briefing. The first drill would be high chlorides in condensate, leading to high steam generator chlorides. The levels in the port steam generator would be high enough to require single loop operation after an initial blowdown of both steam generators. As explained to me, a blowdown drops the chloride concentration to 70% of the original value, but if levels are high, blowdowns might use more water than the ship has in reserve. Then it is more efficient to completely drain and refill the steam generator and that requires taking the affected loop out of service. There would be actions needed all over the propulsion plant and there was a big team of monitors assembled.

The next watch section would recover the isolated loop. The drill would impose a problem on the fast recovery startup that would require troubleshooting and snorkeling. That drill would be briefed in four hours. Many of the monitors on this drill would be on watch for the recovery. They know there's always some problem on the recovery.

Looking over the group as ENG explained the drill. I could see that the excitement present in the first days after our battle had faded. Going back to a normal underway routine probably caused most of the change. The crew still seemed to have much extra energy and they were visibly quite happy. Perhaps it was quiet confidence from their success.

1100 Wednesday, August 28, 1991

We were seated in the Wardroom for the weekly Wednesday lunch of burgers and fries. An added treat today was fried onion rings. We were less than five days to home. The married officers and crewmen were looking forward to seeing their families. Families will be informed of our arrival about a day before by the wives phone-

236

tree. There was disappointment among the younger single crew about not going to Japan.

I'd talked to ENG. He was quite happy with the drills so far. Today we'd do a small primary coolant leak that would put us, again, in single primary loop operation. The leak would require the exercise of radiological procedures and personnel decontamination. While they practice leaks and decontamination, they'd never had such an incident for real. The lack of actual radiological problems is quite typical among the Submarine Force units. The second afternoon watch would do the loop recovery. There would be a problem, resulting in Haddock snorkeling.

I stopped into Sonar as we were transiting at 20 knots. STS1(SS) Johnson was the Sonar Supervisor. Sonarmen Stanley, Darnell and Cross and Yeoman Ellis filled out the watch. The watches rotated on the consoles with the extra taking a break. The rotation keeps them alert. That and frequent coffee runs. STS3 Cross just completed one and was passing out cups. There were cup holders convenient to all the men.

The space had its usual subdued blue lighting. Everyone was relaxed. They had had no breaks when searching for and shadowing Master-1 & 2 and appreciated a slower pace. There was a single contact, a large merchant opening to the East, probably headed to San Francisco or Los Angeles. We discussed what they saw tracking the Soviet submarines and they explained how they track our torpedoes and the ones fired at us.

I worked on my notes. They were only about people and procedures. Any mention of our operations was off-limits. I'd agreed to have the XO review my notes. I'd been careful and there were no problems. I would write a fictionalized version when I got home to preserve my memory of the action. With my other writings in progress there would be nothing to suggest it were anything but my imagination.

There was plenty of time to talk to individuals. Petty Officer Wong agreed to apply for an ROTC scholarship. He liked the idea that his college education would not depend on his family. The XO thought he had an excellent chance of selection given his aptitude scores and excellent record for his year at Berkeley. All of those credits would transfer and meet his math and science requirements.

Chapter 36 – Surprise

Eastern Pacific – 39° 56.8' N 132° 41.6' W
Thursday, August 29, 1991
1700

We were at periscope depth preparing to emergency ventilate the Engine Room with the blower to recover from the simulated fire. I had watched from the Engine Room Upper Level. Haddock used lots of monitors to run a major fire drill. There were safety monitors at hatches to make sure no one fell through since they had restricted vision with clear shower caps over their facemasks. Monitors were assigned to attach the shower caps and remove them once smoke cleared. There was someone with each of the three fire hoses, two in upper level and one in lower, monitors at the scene of the fire on both levels and a couple in Maneuvering.

Haddock used red flashing strobe lights to indicate a fire. A green strobe indicates flooding. White was a steam rupture and yellow, an oil or hydraulic leak. For flooding or steam leaks an air hose blasting simulated the high noise environment of those casualties so the crew could experience the difficulty they'd find communicating. A heat gun, really an industrial blow dryer, was used to provide a realistic display for the thermal imager.

A bad battery on the thermal imager and a stuck-shut fire hose nozzle were simulated to complicate the damage control efforts. The crew was familiar with these anomalies and spare batteries and replacement nozzles were staged in case of need.

Still, it requires good coordination to replace a bad nozzle. The business end of the hose needs to communicate with the valve, perhaps almost 50 feet away, to pressurize and depressurize the hose. The hoses are actually pressurized on the drill but they don't open the nozzle.

The head of the hose has three men, a nozzle-man, a backup to feed the hose and a phone talker. The nozzle-man is preferably in an OBA, oxygen breathing apparatus, a self contained system that uses a chemical process to generate oxygen and frees him from the need to plug in an air hose. The ship carries six of those, staged throughout the hull. Five were used in this drill.

Normally only one person is chosen to startup the OBA and expend a canister of the chemical. Today was the quarterly drill where everyone lights off. Start times are recorded in DC (Damage Control) Central, the Crew's Mess. We have to evacuate the OBA wearer before the canister gives out as he can't change to a fresh one in a smoke filled space.

As you might imagine, there is a lot going on. The crew performed superbly, like a carefully choreographed production number. ENG said they try to throw in new complications and variations to keep the drill from becoming stale.

With the fire simulated out and re-flash watches stationed, I headed forward to observe in Control. The CO was there, sitting on a fire control bench, his usual spot for drills.

"Commence emergency ventilating," was passed on the 1MC as I arrived. MM1(SS) O'Leary, the COW, opened the outboard induction and ventilation exhaust valves. The indicators shifted from bar to circle, opened the head valve and started the low-pressure blower. Aft the Engine Room door and the ventilation damper were opened to complete the lineup. We were emergency ventilating.

After a minute of ventilating the ship secured from the drill but continued ventilating while we copied the broadcast.

"Conn, Radio, copied the 0000 Z ZBO. We have three messages, one of them is immediate."

"It could be our local op-area assignments," Nguyen, the OOD, speculated. It was but there was something else.

A half hour later in the Wardroom the drill critique had finished. The Captain asked ENG and Senior Chief Jay to stay behind and the XO to invite the COB.

"The message was to inform us we have a surprise ORSE, starting on September 2nd. The personnel transfer is 0900 off Ballast Point and we return the next day, after the exam."

Then the XO and COB arrived and he repeated the announcement.

"We're ready," Jay asserted.

"There was also a 'Personal For' from Squadron THREE. Commodore Summers gives a bit of background. Apparently, Haddock was COMSUBPAC's nominee for this quarter's surprise exam. It was supposed to be on arrival Japan. We'd pick up the Board and take the exam en route to Guam. Our operations changed our schedule and destination, but not the exam. A conflict with a scheduled exam made the 2nd our date. I guess that explains the slow transit.

"The Commodore said that, in view of our operations, if we, materially or mentally, are not ready for the exam, he would try to get it postponed. He has some indication from COMSUBPAC that it might be possible. I want your views on that."

"The crew is ready. We're pumped full of energy," COB stated.

"Engineers are ready to go," Jay reiterated.

"Yes, sir. We can do it," ENG agreed.

"I hear you. COB, Senior Chief, talk to the crew to confirm your impression and get back to me in an hour."

"We will," COB said and he and Jay left.

"I think they're right," XO said.

"Probably. I want to be sure. XO, let's put out our ORSE preparation checklist, just the 72 hours and under parts. LT Cohen can do the discharge audit for the current quarter."

"Yes, sir. We have it on the computer."

"I heard we're having an ORSE Monday," Banner said, entering the Wardroom.

"Yes, Chop," XO confirmed.

"Draft a message requesting what you want to pick up on the personnel transfer, just the minimum you need for 24 hours."

"That's just some lettuce, tomatoes, fruit, milk and fresh eggs. I'll work out the quantities."

"We'll do a standard ORSE menu. A working lunch and a dinner you can get on the table quickly in spite of power interruptions."

"Italian is the best bet. It's quick and everybody likes it."

"That's good. Have your message ready in a couple hours."
Banner left.

"XO, you and ENG check with the other officers."
They left to do that.

"You're not as eager as your crew," I observed.

"Yes, I don't like the exam. I've had bad experience and good too. I remember the bad more. I think I'm more tired than my crew from our operations."

"It seems most of your training is oriented to engineering."

"You noticed that. Yes, my goal is to always be ready, which helps when they spring an exam on you. I've also seen the strategy of intensively working up to an exam fail spectacularly. Our last ORSE was graded above average. That really means top third and it's a good grade for an older boat, the best grade in the squadron."

"How will you decide?"

"I expect we'll do it. The hardest part of the preparation is to get the crew up for the exam. It's like a football team getting up for a big game. If my crew is ready, willing and eager, I'd be a fool not to seize the opportunity."

The XO, ENG, COB and Jay then returned to the Wardroom.

"You're early. That wasn't even 15 minutes."

"It was unanimous," COB stated. "Everyone wants to do it. We know we'll have an exam before inactivation so, let's get it over with."

"The officers agree. Personally, I'm happy I can do it before my transfer. You won't need to bring a new XO up to speed."

"It's decided then, though we'll still be doing our normal drill schedule even when we're not facing an exam. ENG, what do you want on drills?"

"I'd like the normal schedule tomorrow. I want Mr. Ohanian to take the morning session tomorrow. They always insist on the newest EOOW taking the evolutions on the second morning. We'll give him some of the simple drills they like so he has some experience with them. For Saturday, I'd like no morning drills, but right after lunch, run all three sections through a practice ORSE, using a full drill package from a recent exam. We'll do a field day on Sunday and assemble the records."

"That's a good plan. I want to start right now cleaning out the extra gear from the spaces. We can't have stuff like the exercise bike, weight set, extra rags and paper towels, spare copier and paper, cluttering the space. Fortunately, we have extra space in the Torpedo Room. Coordinate with WEPS. Put most gear in the outboard lower stows."

"We'll get on it," said Jay.

"We need to clear out to let Petty Officer Glen set up for dinner. COB, let me know whom we can leave ashore on the personnel transfer. We'll need to clear some berthing for the ORSE Board and Mr. Ryan. I'm afraid the Commodore gets your spot in the XO's stateroom. We could drop you off if you prefer."

"I'm good. No way will I miss this."

"Fine. We can talk more at dinner. I've a message to draft to my boss."

Chapter 37 – Preparations

Eastern Pacific – 37° 17.5' N 129° 37.2' W
Friday, August 30, 1991
0830

There were just a few drill monitors assembled in the Wardroom for the briefing. The drills planned for Ohanian were basic. It would start with a condensate salinity alarm with negative chemical samples for chlorides and normal steam generator samples. That should lead to a recommendation to clean the salinity cell.

Next would be performance of the check on the reactor protection and alarm system. An error during the test will result in a reactor cutback. The cutback will clear once the EOOW orders cutback override and they will recover the control rods. An improper value will also be entered on the test form to see if Ohanian spots the error in the EOOW review of the completed test. The final drill will be high temperature on the ion exchanger inlet, requiring securing flow from the RPCP and restoring temperatures by using the bypass at the primary sample sink. Cause of this problem will be an insufficient seawater flow to the reactor plant fresh water system due to improper adjustment by the Machinery Upper Level watch.

The drill team headed aft and I went with the CO to Control. Rules during the examination state that only watches, drill monitors and the Board can be in the spaces prior to the start of any drill. Others are staged in the Crew's Mess.

LTJG Reed was OOD. The CO and I sat on the benches by fire control. There was a call on the phone. Reed passed it to the Captain who gave permission to begin.

"You don't like the ORSE." I stated.

"Right, I've had bad experiences with them. I've had good too, but you get scars from the bad. My training plan on Haddock is to make sure I never have a problem here. I feel confident. We're ready. You never can be sure what might happen in the exam though."

"You said you're always training for an exam."

"Yes, I believe in a level effort training program. I've seen the alternative, working up to the exam, fail spectacularly on my first submarine."

"That wouldn't work on a surprise exam. What happened?"

"High salinity starboard condensate. Request minimum depth and speed."

Reed acknowledged the 7MC report and ordered one-third and 150 feet.

"They didn't do surprise exams back then. The exam was simpler too. As crews have gotten better the standards have become higher. An average crew today would be excellent by the criteria of 20 years ago.

"Anyway, my first CO was the classic one-man-show. He ran everything and no one made a move without checking first. We had an exam scheduled in a few weeks and a couple weeks at sea to train. He decided to put his most experienced officers in as the exam EOOWs. The Navigator, Sonar Officer and Damage Control Assistant were all excellent officers but they'd been standing OOD watches. I think I was his best EOOW but I was standing DOOW. It was quite unusual, then and now, for a nuclear trained officer to stand the DOOW beyond what was needed for qualification."

"Why?"

"OK. When a submarine is at periscope depth it is subject to visual or radar detection. The probability depends on the amount of mast exposed, the sea state and the ship's speed. When you have about a sea state 3, there are waves and white caps and blowing foam. It's tough to pick up a periscope. If seas are flat, sea state 0, even a couple feet may be too much. The periscope mast itself is very tiny, but moving through the water, it kicks up a tail of spray. The rule of thumb for acceptable speed is sea state plus two knots.

"So in calm seas you are going to periscope depth at 2 knots and planes have very little effect. You also, at low speed, have a risk of stalling out between 150 feet and periscope depth. You get stuck in the mid zone, shallow enough to collide with a surface ship and too deep to see and avoid it.

"When we absolutely had to be right on the mark, I could do it and nobody else could, reliably. It's a matter of pumping yourself light at 150, getting a good upward rate initially and bringing the

244

water back in so you're perfect when you reach assigned depth. Too light and you float up and expose the top of the sail. Too heavy and you sink back to 150 feet. It's a matter of feel and anticipation."

"You didn't volunteer to be EOOW."

"No one volunteers to be in the crosshairs of a one-man-show. Anyway our first drill was loss of high-speed main coolant pump running indication. That's not a full drill today. You've seen us run it. In this case they didn't spot that the pump was, in fact, running. There ensued a rapid series of pump shifts that invoked the loop low-flow interlocks and ended up with five main coolant pumps running in fast speed. They hadn't turned off the pump with the bad indicator light.

"Next we had a reactor scram drill. A mistake on the EPCP caused a loss of all AC power throughout the ship. That also caused a full reactor scram as we lost power to the control rod drive mechanisms."

"How does that happen?"

"To shift the electric plant into a half power lineup, you first open the MG-TG breaker on the side where you are securing the turbine generator. Then you parallel the two turbine generators together and secure one of them. Here the Electrical Operator omitted the first step. When he paralleled the turbine generators we had a closed loop of all electrical buses. It was unstable. There were big power surges and both turbine generator breakers and MG-AC breakers tripped; lights out.

"I was on DOOW at periscope depth when the lights went out. It also meant we lost all hydraulics, though we still had what was left in the hydraulic accumulators. I kept my planesmen calm, not cycling their planes, until we got busses reenergized, about 30 seconds later.

"We compounded the error by starting a fast recovery startup. The loss of all AC power casualty procedure did not allow for a fast recovery because the nuclear instruments had been de-energized. It is allowed today if the instruments look normal upon restoration, but we have better instrumentation technology. I told our CO that they couldn't do the startup. He got the reactor plant manuals from the Wardroom, looked it up and stopped the startup. We then followed proper procedure but the mistake could not be undone. Even the Board hadn't realized that the fast recovery startup was prohibited but that was no help.

"Now you know why I have the overnight watches practicing electric plant shifts each night and why we have an EPCP monitor for major drills."

The first drill was over and we headed deeper and increased speed.

"Good officers are not enough. They need experience. The more I can give them in training the better they'll be able to handle the surprises the real world throws at them."

"Maneuvering rings up all stop," Helm reported.

"All stop," Reed ordered. "Dive, 350 feet."

"Answering all stop."

"340 feet coming to 350 feet.

"Conn, Maneuvering, power-flow cutback. Recovering now."

"Conn, aye."

"Mr. Ohanian is doing fine. There's no excitement in his voice making the reports. That's a good sign. He'll still be nervous during the exam but not as much with some drills under his belt."

"Cause of cutback was operator error. Ready to answer all bells."

"Conn aye. Helm, all ahead standard. Dive, 400 feet."

They answered and we resumed transit. Since the next drill won't involve Control the CO left to look at the Torpedo Room stowage. I headed back to the Wardroom.

XO was in our stateroom working on papers.

"These are forms we are asked to give to the Board on arrival." XO said without me asking. "There is information about personnel and qualification. They ask some questions like, 'When was the last time the CO and XO entered the reactor compartment?' Just by asking it encourages us to inspect it. We go every time we open it. The Engineer is, except on rare occasions, the last man to leave the compartment before we lock it up."

"What is he looking for?"

"Number one is that there is nobody in the compartment before we lock the door. That, of course, should never happen since we have a radiological control point set up in the Tunnel and log

246

everyone going in or out. It's similar to what you've seen us use on radioactive spill or leak drills. He also looks for any abnormal conditions, like a leak from a valve. We inspect for problems right after we open the compartment but you have to make sure some issue hasn't popped up at the last minute."

"What if we had a problem while we're underway?"

"Then we might need to do an emergency Reactor Compartment entry. We set up the control point in the Tunnel and stage everything we think we'll need. Personnel wear anti-contamination suits, the yellow outfits, and EABs. We can ditch the masks once we ventilate the compartment, verify the atmosphere is breathable and there's no airborne radioactivity. We full scram, inserting all the rods, and open the door immediately. By the time the door is open it should have radiation levels low enough to enter, though we stick a Geiger counter through the door first to verify that. That's brought in with the first person. Then we do what is needed, close out the compartment and restart the reactor as soon as the door is shut. I had to do one on my last submarine because we had a couple RC bilge alarms and needed to verify we didn't have a leak."

"Are leaks into the Reactor Compartment common?"

"Common, no, but they have occurred. A few years ago there was an issue on S5W plants, like ours, with cracking in pressurizer heater wells. The issue was fixed throughout the fleet by reinforcing the wells."

"I see. What are some of the other items?"

"We need to tell them of any incident reports we are filing. We report any material issues, like a leaking heater well, or a human error that caused damage or reactor protection system activation. We have one for the RCDC ground. Since the electrical tape is a temporary fix, it is a preliminary report. We'll close it out when we replace the damaged wire. They look to see if there are issues with the extent of corrective action for personnel problems and if repairs were properly retested. Mistakes there can be very significant, even leading to failure of the exam, or worse."

"What's worse?"

"Relief of personnel, starting with the CO. The standards are high."

"I know. It seems like the examination drives much of your training."

"That's true. When the ORSE Board starts looking closely at an area, everyone with sense looks at that area on their own ship. When they see a problem in one ship they check if others have it too.

"The discharge audit started out that way. They found discrepancies between the ship's deck log, the engineering log and the discharge log on times and amounts and inconsistencies in how calculations were made. They were small but called into question the reliability of data the Navy was providing on the impact of nuclear ships on the environment. Everyone took a beating in the beginning and corrections were issued, but now, we have standardized procedures. Everything is double checked before being reported and the Board just spot-checks our work."

"I've seen your procedures. Everyone is very professional."

"Thanks. The standards throughout the force are high. They need to be high to maintain a perfect nuclear safety record."

"What about Thresher and Scorpion?"

"The wreck sites are monitored periodically. I've heard there is some contamination, at very low levels, in the immediate vicinity. With the hull, reactor vessel and fuel rods, any escape of radioactivity would be very slow and with the tremendous dilution in the ocean there would be no impact on the environment."

"We gave the Navy a couple more places to monitor."

In the afternoon we ran a steam rupture leading to single loop with the next section doing the recovery. Everyone seemed happy with the results. The CO was not happy with the Torpedo Room stowage of gear removed from Engineering. He wanted it stacked neatly and secured with strapping and cargo nets. It was done.

Chapter 38 – Dress Rehearsal
Eastern Pacific – 33° 31.3' N 123° 37.4' W
Saturday, August 31, 1991
1200

"This is the Captain. We will be conducting a dress rehearsal for ORSE. We'll do three sections of drills starting with section 3 that is on now. Only the watches and drill monitors may be in the propulsion plant when the drill is initiated. The off-going watch, now section 2, will muster in the Crew's Mess and wait for a ship's alarm or the Casualty Assistance Team to be called away before laying aft. Section 1 personnel not tapped as monitors, will muster in the Crew's Mess too."

I was in the Wardroom when the Captain made the announcement over the 1MC. The XO, NAV, ENG, LT Cohen representing WEPS who was on watch, SUPPLY, COB and EMCS(SS) Jay were assembled. Everyone had shifted to working khaki. That and dungarees for enlisted sailors was the uniform for ORSE. Official shoes were required too, not the comfortable shoe policy that was fine for normal operations. I had on black Dockers and a knit shirt to get in the spirit: though I kept my Topsiders. The Captain entered. He had changed to the standard, plain-toe, black shoes.

"Before we do the brief I want to go over whom we will leave ashore for ORSE. Obviously, we're taking all the engineers. We need to free five bunks for the ORSE Board and Mr. Ryan. XO?"

"Chief Moore will take the patrol report to Group FIVE. The Chop can spare Chief Aquino and he can arrange crew berthing for our arrival and carry our work package to Dixon. We'd like to send Senior Chief Harvey too. He can explain what we saw and how we analyzed the acoustic information."

"I can't send him. I need to send Petty Officer Johnson instead. I'll explain it later. XO have Johnson stop by my stateroom after the ORSE brief tomorrow."

"Yes, sir. Johnson still gives us a berth free. We were thinking FTG1(SS) Quinn and MM1(SS) Garcia, as an auxiliaryman he's an engineer but he doesn't have responsibility for the diesel and isn't our ORSE diesel operator. We were also thinking of TM3(SS) Stokes and Seamen Rogers and McArthur. Chief Aquino can use them to clean up around our berthing area."

"I'll shift some assignments for berthing to free a stack of three racks in the nine-man bunk room. The Board senior member and Mr. Ryan can bunk in the Chief's Quarters. Tom, we'll make you an honorary Haddock CPO, a certificate and all. The others ease the hot bunking situation."

"Are we port and starboard anywhere?"

"Two of the four sonar operators because we're keeping planes three section. We can handle it in Sonar for a day," said Cohen.

"OK, ENG bring in your drill team."

We changed people. The XO left as he is on-scene in-charge for ship's emergencies and doesn't get told what the drills will be. LTJG Reed and LTJG Ohanian led a big group. This would be a big drill.

"The first drill is a series of bells, including flank. Captain, here is the sequence." ENG handed him a card. "ORSE normally asks to hold flank so they can observe parameters. We'll hold it five minutes. On the shift to flank, main coolant pump #4 will fail to start in fast speed, not just an indication problem. They should start #6 in fast once they recognize the problem. Cause will be a bad fuse on the fast-speed breaker. Petty Officer Nichols has the bad fuse to install when we get aft.

"The finale will be loss of main lube oil from flank. Once the shaft is locked a fire will start in the Main Lube Oil Bay in Lower Level. A minute later it will spread to Upper Level on both sides of the reduction gear. It will require two hoses in Upper Level and one in Lower Level to extinguish the fire.

"The second person to enter the Engine Room in an OBA will light it off. Also the first nozzle used on the starboard side hose will be stuck shut. Once we have three working hoses for one minute we will simulate the fire out. When emergency ventilating commences we will secure.

250

"Mr. Reed and Chief Jay briefed you on your assignments down in the Torpedo Room. Are there any questions?"

"How do I simulate the readings on the atmosphere analyzer? Petty Officer Dixon asked.

"You should have a group of 3x5 cards. Red are for during the fire and yellow for Engine Room and AMS when emergency ventilating. Just hold the card over the readout with the actual reading when he's drawing a suction on an affected space."

Dixon nodded and relooked at the cards.

"Get in position."

Everyone filed out. I went with the Captain to Control. Section 3 did well. They spotted the pump failure right away and started another. The shaft was stopped and locked in 25 seconds and the fire, while complex, was handled smoothly.

By 1400 section 1 was relieving the watch and a new drill brief was beginning. This section would get high salinity in port condensate, leading to high steam generator chlorides, blowdowns and single loop operation.

I was back in Control. Haddock had dropped to one-third and was going to 150 feet in response to the initial port condensate salinity alarm. The first indication that something was wrong was when Maneuvering reported shutting down the starboard side. A couple minutes later they found port condensate contaminated and starboard was not. Then they needed to restore the starboard side before they could secure port.

That was enough for the Captain. He went to the 1MC.

"This is the Captain. Secure from the drill and restore the propulsion plant to a normal lineup. We're going to recycle and try this again."

He got on the phone to Maneuvering and had ENG put on the line.

"What went wrong? Debrief on the 2MC and setup to start again. I didn't want a busted drill to be their final memory before the exam."

"What happened?"

"A contaminated sample on starboard condensate. The watch didn't check the backup before taking action. They sorted it out when they saw the port side sample and backup were positive, but by then, they'd already secured the starboard side. Mr. Gordon, or somebody, should have questioned the disconnect between the port salinity alarm and positive chlorides on starboard."

A half-hour later with everyone back in position we ran it again. This time it went smoothly. There were no issues with the single loop transition or the steam generator blowdowns.

With section 2 taking the watch and the loop warming up, the final drill was briefed, a loop recovery with a delay in the fast recovery startup leading to snorkeling. It went smoothly. I thought it should, since they practice it enough. Even with the glitch on the second set we had completed the drills in just over 5 hours. For the exam there would be a dinner break between the second and third sets.

Section 1 took the watch. It was their normal watch time until 2000. The other sections assembled in the Crew's Mess for a critique. ENG reviewed each drill and the problem that led to a repeat of the second set. Then the Captain took the floor and emphasized that he didn't want anybody to act any differently during ORSE. They didn't need to act faster, just do everything like you do in our training. He said they'd do fine.

After dinner we did a critique for section 1. There was a bit more discussion about what went wrong and why. Here the CO expressed confidence in their ability and said they'd do fine on Monday. After the critique the Captain spoke privately with LT Gordon.

I asked him what he said to Gordon. He said he reassured Gordon that he would do fine. Mistakes are part of learning. As Captain he feels he needs to support his officers so they know he'll back them when they do their jobs.

Chapter 39 – Getting Ready

Off San Diego – 31° 38.7' N 118° 57.8' W
Sunday, September 1, 1991
1200

Haddock had entered the local operating areas around San Diego where we would hang out until we entered port for the personnel transfer tomorrow morning. Since it was Labor Day weekend, we were the only submarine, indeed, the only Navy ship, not in port. Submarine Group FIVE had assigned us the entire area south of the harbor entrance.

On tap for today was an ORSE briefing by the CO in the Crew's Mess, a short field day and a second brief for those on-watch earlier. It would also be a day of final preparations. Damage control equipment gets rechecked, the expiration dates of chemicals examined, the battery charged and steam generator chemistry adjusted. There were piles of books stacked on the deck in the Wardroom as records were assembled. The ship would normally read and reissue TLDs today but that will be deferred to September 3rd.

The crew, both nuclear and not, officers, chiefs and enlisted, were assembled. The CO entered.

"Before we start the brief, Mr. Reed step forward. Commodore Summers has approved your qualification. Well done."

He pinned the gold dolphins above Reed's left pocket.

"We have a lot to cover today. We'll start with the schedule. I expect to surface at about 0500. Maneuvering watch will go down at about 0730. We will remain rigged for dive except for the Bridge and the torpedo-loading hatch. We will have a reduced topside contingent because we only need to tie up the torpedo retriever. We should have a tug in standby but we shouldn't need to tie it up. Personnel going ashore wait in the Crew's Mess until we call you up. We will be taking on about a dozen boxes of fresh vegetables, fruit and milk. We secure maneuvering watch right after we clear the harbor outbound and we'll be in position to dive as soon as Bridge is rigged.

"The ORSE exam starts when the Board arrives. Doc will issue them TLDs and they'll start in the Wardroom on record reviews. The first event for most will be written exams. LT Gonzales and LT Cohen are coordinating the administration and grading. When you've taken your exam relieve someone on watch so he can take his. If you're on record reviews, take your exam when they move on to somebody else.

"A word on the exams. We generally use 2.8 for passing, 3.0 for EOOW and EWS. Each question is graded on a 4.0 scale. Partial credit is awarded, so don't leave a question blank, then we have to give you a zero. If you can write a few correct things about the subject of the question or even where you'd look for the answer we can give you part credit. A 2.0 is a lot better than a zero when we compute your final score.

"Don't discuss the test questions with anyone, even with someone who has already taken it. We don't want anyone who hasn't taken it to overhear. I don't want the Board to be able to question the integrity of the process. That would be a bad mark against us. On the other hand, I do want you to look up the right answers for anything you struggled with. You might see that question again when you take a knowledge interview the next morning. It's a good plus if you can answer it then.

"Lunch will be 1300. Fix it yourself sandwiches, French fries and fried onion rings. The Board will work through lunch.

"A Board member may ask you a question. For example, 'Why did you do, or didn't do, this or that?' If you know the answer tell him. If not, tell him you'll check and get back to him. Report all questions you get to ENG or Senior Chief Jay. We need to know so we can be sure we close them out before the morning. They might have suggestions on how we could do things better. Write those down and we'll decide later when and how to implement them. Do not volunteer information about things they haven't asked.

"One more thing about talking to Board members. We received clearances for our riders during the exam. As expected, Commodore Summers will be with us. He is cleared for our operations. If he asks you about something, you can answer. The Board's senior member is Captain Welch, formerly CO of Tunny.

He's also cleared for our operations but the other members are not. Don't discuss our past operation when they are present.

"When they finish record review, about 1500, they will brief ENG, XO and me on the ground rules for the exam. We already know them but it's a formality. After that they head aft to inspect the engineering spaces, including Diesel, for cleanliness and material condition. A junior officer is assigned to accompany each member and note his comments. Ask for explanation if you are not clear of his meaning. We have four kits of flashlight, rag, clipboard, pen and paper made up. The inspection ends when we're ready to run the first drill set, so sooner is better.

"We get to decide which section has first drills. The others follow in sequence. You'll know who is going first by lunch. Mr. Reed will inform the personnel who will be drill monitors. The first group assembles in the Torpedo Room while the Board is briefing me in the Wardroom. You'll get your assignments and a preliminary brief on the drill. When they head aft we will finish up in the Wardroom and start the first set.

"Only the people on watch, our drill team and the Board are allowed in Engineering before the start of the drill. I want you to do drills during ORSE exactly like we train every week. If you do that we will do fine during the exam. Don't be nervous. Our training has prepared you for anything the Board will throw at us. We've probably already run the drills we'll get tomorrow, several times.

"We will have dinner between the second drill set and the third. We're having Italian tomorrow. The time will be shorter than normal. We want to wrap up the third session.

"When the third set is over we have a break for rest until morning. At about 0600 we start plant evolutions and knowledge interviews. Mr. Ohanian is EOOW for evolutions. We will let you know which section will have the watch. However there will be frequent changes as people are relieved to be ready for interviews.

"How should you handle interviews? They will interview you two at a time using the officer staterooms. Both should participate. They'll ask you something directly if you don't speak up. If you get a question you know the answer to, talk and talk and talk about the answer. They have only 15 to 20 minutes. The more you talk about something you know the less time they have to ask about something

255

else. If you find you made a mistake, admit it. Often their follow-up questions are used to see if you recognize you answered incorrectly. If you're in a hole, stop digging.

"They often ask us to hold an EOOW, EWS, ELT seminar based on a topic we used recently. They might ask to see us hold divisional training on a topic they select. If you are in a seminar, participate. Good participation and lively discussion are the marks of a good session.

"Keep the spaces clean and remove trash from the spaces throughout the exam. The Board will give us the grade Tuesday morning and we will put it out right away.

"Any questions?"

"Could you tell us when everyone has taken their tests so we can discuss them without problem?" Seabright asked.

"Yes, we can do that. We'll pass it on the 1MC."

"What's the most important part of the examination?" Shafter, the ELT, asked.

"We get graded in six areas, and if we fail one area, we fail overall. The first is operations. This is mostly based on our drill performance and counts 40%. Level of knowledge counts 30% and is based on the tests and interviews but the drills also factor in. Chemistry and radiological controls and administration both count 10%. These are mostly from the record reviews. Cleanliness and material condition each count 5%.

"The Board is looking to see that we are operating the plant safely, that we can train ourselves effectively and that the plant can support the ship's mission as a nuclear attack submarine. We demonstrated that last point very effectively and I know we can do the rest. You'll do fine.

"Next up is field day. Then, try to get plenty of rest tonight." He left and the crowd scattered.

"**Commence field day,**" passed on the 1MC.

2130

The field day secured 90 minutes before dinner, allowing for a second briefing for those on watch earlier.

There were many last minute preparations going on. Books were stacked everywhere around the Wardroom. I had stepped out to the Crew's Mess and saw Sonarman Johnson sitting alone at an aft table with a cup of coffee that didn't look touched. He was staring at it. There was no movie tonight and the mess was empty.

"What's the problem, Earl? I heard you get to go ashore a day early. I figured you'd be happy."

"Tom, do you know why I'm going ashore? The Captain told me I'm HIV+."

"How?" I was stunned.

"The usual way when you didn't have a transfusion or use IV drugs. The Captain said he wasn't interested in how it happened. I was going to say something but he made it quite clear, without directly telling me, that I shouldn't."

"I can't serve on submarines anymore. I start with an evaluation at Balboa and see what that shows. I feel fine, normal, though. I would like to finish this trip. I don't want to leave early."

"Did you ask him about that? It can't hurt. All he would do is say, no."

"I will," he said with determination and his features brightened. "Come with me for support."

"Yes," I agreed.

He got up, leaving his coffee. We walked forward to the passage to Officer Country. The door to the Engineer's stateroom was open. Rinaldi, still in his khakis, was fast asleep in the middle bunk. A cigarette with an inch of ash was in his right hand that was draped over his chest. I stepped in and took it, putting it out in the ashtray on his desk. I shut the door behind me and caught up with Earl outside the CO's door. He knocked.

"Come in."

He opened the door.

"Petty Officer Johnson and Mr. Ryan," he said shifting to sit on his bunk and leaving the chair for Johnson. "Sit down. I assume you've told Mr. Ryan your situation. What can I do for you?"

"I'd like to stay for the ORSE so I can finish this trip."

"I thought you might want to see where you are medically, but if you want to stay, I don't think an extra day would hurt anything. I will need to tell the XO, COB and Doc your situation. They would know anyway in a couple days."

"Thanks, that's great." He was visibly happy.

"Is there anything else? As you leave ask the XO to stop in. Tom, you look like you have questions."

"How does what you did square with Navy policy?"

"Captain, you wanted to see me."

"Yes, XO. Johnson will be staying and we can send Senior Chief Harvey ashore. Johnson is HIV+. I just told him but he wants to finish the trip with us and I agreed."

"We're supposed to put him ashore."

"Yes, but at this point, a day can't hurt. If the letter with his results had come a day earlier, I wouldn't have been able to take him and, I think, we're all glad we had him with us. Tell the COB and Doc his status. Just keep an eye on him to check his mood."

"I'll take care of it." He left.

"Now Tom, I'm Captain. I support all Navy policies. What do you imagine Navy policy to be?"

"Aren't you supposed to discharge homosexuals?"

"Absolutely. Anyone I know to be homosexual will be discharged. I don't know that about Johnson and I'm way too busy to make finding out a priority."

"Isn't that just ignoring the policy?"

"Let me tell you a story, a true story. Johnson is the second sailor I've had to inform about their HIV status. It was in 1986 and I was an XO. The Navy had instituted testing for all personnel. We had one positive. There was no treatment back then so you were giving a possible death sentence. The procedures called for the CO to personally inform the man with the squadron chaplain there for support. I made the arrangements, but when the time came, everyone was there except the Captain. He was in our squadron's office, meeting with the Commodore. It wasn't known how long he'd be so I decided to do the meeting.

"Our sailor had spent 8 years in the Navy and was planning on getting out in 3 months. We discussed his situation and what was known about it, which was not very much. We didn't even know if HIV+ status would lead to AIDS. I said he might want to consider reenlisting. He would need his medical benefits. The next day he agreed. There was a problem though. To reenlist a sailor must be evaluated as medically qualified. That's routine but no guidance had been provided on what HIV+ status meant on that evaluation.

"I drafted a message to the Bureau of Naval Personnel, BUPERS, and the CO agreed to send it. We recommended our sailor be able to reenlist. COMSUBPAC sent their message, endorsing our position. About two weeks later BUPERS sent out guidance to everyone, referencing our message and a few others. HIV+ sailors would be allowed to reenlist if otherwise healthy. If HIV+ status progresses to AIDS, the person would be medically retired and still get full health benefits plus retired pay or disability from the VA.

"Now, do you think BUPERS didn't know how these men got to be HIV+?"

"What happened to your sailor?"

"He's healthy, still in the Navy, attached to Dixon."

"Why was the CO away?"

"I didn't ask, just told him I took care of it. I don't know how doctors handle giving bad news every day. At least the outlook on HIV is more promising today. I could give Johnson some hope."

"Still, gay sailors must have problems with their straight crewmates."

"Maybe on bigger ships. On a sub everyone knows you. If you're good at your job you get quite a bit of slack. I was on a boomer that had a storekeeper who acted quite gay and probably was. For the mid-patrol party he'd make up as a girl. It was popular. He looked prettier than some of the girls I dated, but perhaps five weeks at sea altered my perceptions. He was an excellent storekeeper and helped everyone. He had no problems. Johnson won't either."

Chapter 40 – Surface, Surface, Surface

Off San Diego – 32° 24.6' N 117° 42.3' W
Monday, September 2, 1991
0445

Haddock was at periscope depth. I was up in Control for my first surfacing. Since it was night Control was rigged for black. NAV had the deck and conn. The CO was up, looking out the scope. I'd had a chance to look. The sky was overcast with a crescent moon peeking through some gaps.

"Dive, prepare to surface without air."

"Prepare to surface without air, aye."

"**Prepare to surface without air,**" went out on the 1MC passed by the COW.

The Captain went off the periscope stand, standing forward by the DOOW.

"Captain, the updated torpedo settings are entered," reported FTOW Lopez.

"Thank you, Petty Officer Lopez. Mr. Ryan, you should be getting sleep. Why are you up?"

"I only have a day to go. I figured I could handle it. Why didn't you let the XO handle the surfacing?"

"He needs his rest. For today he's more important than I. He starts with medical and personnel exposure record reviews and is involved in all the major drills. I just watch."

"The ship is ready to surface without air," reported ET1(SS) Field, COW.

"Very well. Captain, request permission to surface the ship."

"Surface the ship, NAV."

"Surface the ship, aye. Dive, surface without air. Helm, all ahead two-thirds."

"Surface without air, Dive aye. Chief of the Watch on the 1MC, surface."

"All ahead two-thirds, Helm aye. Answers ahead two-thirds."

"**Surface, surface, surface,**" went out on the 1MC. Then there was the diving alarm, sounding three times then again, "**surface, surface, surface.**"

"Full rise both planes," COB, the DOOW, ordered. "Fifty feet, forty five, forty, thirty five." Haddock was slowly getting shallower. Finally, "thirty two feet and holding. Chief of the Watch start the blower on all main ballast tanks."

"Start the blower, Chief of the Watch aye." He opened the induction, head and low pressure blow valves and started the blower. "Blower running on all main ballast tanks, 6 psi back pressure."

"Request to open the lower bridge access hatch," COB said.

"Open the lower hatch but hold off on the upper," NAV ordered. "I want to get some air in the ballast tanks first. There's no rush."

"Yes, sir."

The Auxiliaryman of the Watch rotated the locking mechanism counterclockwise, unlatched the lever and pushed the hatch upward into the bridge access trunk.

"Energize the running lights," NAV ordered.

"Energize the running lights," COW acknowledged.

The Auxiliary Electrician Forward opened a panel and flipped a switch. He had the Bridge Box with him. LTJG Reed entered from aft.

"I'll take the watch when the Bridge is manned," he announced.

"Back pressure is 13 psi." COW said.

"After deck is dry," NAV said, looking aft with #2 scope in low power. "Crack the upper hatch and rig the Bridge."

The Auxiliaryman went up the ladder. The AEF stayed below.

"Hatch is cracked, air flow is in," AEF relayed. "Equalized, hatch is open."

The Auxiliaryman came down and the AEF and Reed went up, carrying the Bridge Box and bag.

I looked up through the access trunk. The clamshell over the cockpit was opened and the circle of the upper hatch opening became a lighter shade of black.

"Energize the Bridge Box," I relayed from above. A large rotary switch near the hatch was turned.

The AEF came down and SN Hamm went up with a pair of binoculars as lookout.

"This is Mr. Reed. I'm ready to relieve you."

"I'm ready to be relieved. We're on course north, ahead two-thirds, on the surface with the low-pressure blower running and an air charge in progress. We will hang out about four miles south of 1SD until we station maneuvering watch at 0730."

"I relieve you sir."

"I stand relieved."

"Quartermaster, this is Mr. Reed, I have the deck and the conn." Came over the MC. "Chief of the Watch, tanks are full, secure the low pressure blow, surface ventilate."

"Secure the blow, surface ventilate, Chief of the Watch aye. Blow secured."

"Surface ventilate," came from the 1MC.

"Captain, I've been relieved by Mr. Reed," NAV reported. We will station the piloting party at 0700. Sunrise is 0626."

"Thanks NAV. I'll be in my stateroom. There's still time for some sleep."

Chapter 41 – Personnel Transfer
Off San Diego – 32° 36.2' N 117° 15.6' W
Monday, September 2, 1991
0800

I was standing on the top of the sail, looking at Point Loma, a couple miles north, as Haddock prepared to enter San Diego. The maneuvering watch was stationed. LT Nguyen and LTJG McCarthy were in the cockpit and the CO was standing beside me. Lookouts were on both sail planes.

COB had lent me one of the ship's blue working jackets. It was cool this morning, not yet even 70° F, unusual for a Southern California summer. Everyone was wearing a jacket. The officers and chiefs wore khaki and enlisted wore blue. The sky was cloudy with a steady breeze that made it feel cooler. At least it didn't appear to be threatening rain.

McCarthy had the conn. It was his first time on maneuvering watch on the Bridge so Nguyen was talking him through it. The Captain was just observing and chatting with me about the weather and the continuing puzzle of what was happening in the Soviet Union in the wake of the failed coup.

We turned onto the channel course, three-five-three, heading inbound. I could see many pleasure boats headed out to enjoy the holiday on the water. The subpar weather was no deterrent to many. It was easy to pick up the range markers in this direction as you weren't looking over your shoulder. McCarthy adjusted course a bit to the left to center Haddock in the channel.

"Bridge, NAV, we hold you on track. We hold the torpedo retriever on the scope headed past Ballast Point, outbound."

"NAV, we see it," replied Nguyen. "Control, open the torpedo-loading hatch and send the small boat handling party on deck."

They acknowledged and the hatch opened immediately and 6 men went on deck in orange lifejackets. The COB was leading them. They rigged a cleat aft of the sail on the port side and established phone communications.

"Do you have the squadron flag, Mr. Nguyen?"

"Yes, sir. It's in the bag. Slow to one-third for the transfer, Mr. McCarthy."

He ordered it. The retriever was a few hundred yards away headed opposite our course.

"Mr. Nguyen, we'll render honors to port as she passes."

"Yes, sir. On deck, attention to port."

Everyone on the Bridge turned to face the port side. On deck, personnel were in a single line, also facing port.

As the bows of Haddock and the retriever passed, Nguyen called, "Hand salute."

The personnel on the retriever were at attention, facing Haddock. They raised their hands in salute and a couple seconds later dropped them.

"Two," Nguyen called and we dropped our salute. I didn't salute, just stood straight facing port. "Carry on," Nguyen ordered.

The retriever passed astern of us and reversed course to come along our port side. As it came close a line was tossed from its bow and secured to our cleat. It was pulled tight and the retriever settled in along our side. It lowered a ramp from its aft deck to our deck. Several khaki clad officers came across.

"Submarine Squadron Three arriving," Nguyen said on the 1MC.

He raised a blue and white flag on the pole below the U.S. flag. A similar flag was hauled down from the retriever.

"Control, send personnel going ashore topside," Nguyen said once the oncoming group went below.

Our men came topside, most had small duffle bags with stuff. The three boxes with our patrol data were passed topside and transferred to the retriever by our departing personnel. They then passed the boxes with our fresh provisions, stacked on the aft deck of the retriever over to us. The topside crew passed them below. Finally, the retriever raised the ramp and we cast off its line. It backed quickly clear, then drove ahead of us back to port.

We were just passing Ballast Point inbound. A tug was idling just off the submarine piers and started to move in our direction.

"Bridge, NAV, we're inside Ballast Point. You have good water to starboard up to the North Island dock."

"We'll head that way," Nguyen said. "Mr. McCarthy, let's go to two-thirds and aim for the North end of the dock."

"Yes, sir." He sighted over the gyro repeater. "Helm. All ahead two-thirds, right full rudder, steady zero-two-zero."

It was acknowledged and Haddock swung right heading for the dock. We passed the Submarine Base. The piers were full of submarines enjoying a holiday weekend in port. Nguyen was scanning the parade of outgoing pleasure craft nervously.

"There's no gap for us to turn around in," he stated.

"After the next one goes by, start your turn and sound the danger signal. They'll get out of the way."

"Yes, Captain." Thirty seconds later. "Now, Mr. McCarthy."

"Helm, left full rudder, steady one-seven-three."

Nguyen bent down to the whistle lever. It sounded five times, a second or two each with a second between. The effect was like magic as the smaller vessels moved to stay well clear of us.

Haddock swung around smoothly as the tug followed off our starboard side. We finished a little on the Submarine Base side of the channel and McCarthy ordered one-seven-zero to bring us back to the center. Nguyen thanked the tug for its services on the bridge-to-bridge radio and ordered on deck personnel below.

Just before Ballast Point we were passed to starboard by a large cabin cruiser with two, beautiful, bikini-clad ladies lounging on towels spread over the front deck. Everyone enjoyed the view.

Binoculars were well used. They waved at us. The cool, cloudy, weather obviously was not interfering with their fun, or ours.

The deck was reported rigged and the Captain suggested standard. We sped up to standard, passing the cruiser for a second time. There were no wives on Ballast Point as Haddock left this time. The base receded as we sailed away.

McCarthy turned over the conn to Nguyen when we turned past buoy 5. He needed to be ready for the chemistry and radiological controls record reviews. We sped up to full speed and turned south after passing 1SD. The maneuvering watch was secured at that point and the Captain lay below, followed by the extra watches. Section 3 had the watch post maneuvering watch.

I was in the cockpit as the Bridge was prepared for dive. About twenty minutes after maneuvering watch we were ready. LT Gonzales down in Control relieved Nguyen. I climbed down the ladder as Nguyen was completing the final steps to secure the Bridge. The circle of daylight above diminished as I descended, winking out as the opening was covered.

Chapter 42 – ORSE Begins

Off San Diego – 32° 31.6' N 117° 18.3' W
Monday, September 2, 1991
1000

I headed to the Wardroom to see what was happening. The CO was in his stateroom talking with the ENG.

"We have the drill package," Rinaldi said to me. "It's virtually identical to what we ran for our rehearsal. The bell sequence is different. The main coolant pump problem is a failed indicator. On the main lube oil fire the issue is a ruptured fire hose. The second set is condensate chlorides leading to blowdowns and single loop. After dinner, the third set is a loop recovery with an issue on the startup."

"We get to propose causes for the problems and decide which section takes the first drill set," CO added.

"The chloride drill didn't go well last time," I noted.

"Yes," ENG agreed. "That was section 1. I think we should start with section 1. The fire is straightforward. Sections 2 and 3 should have no problems with single loop and recovery."

"OK, ENG. Get to work on the drill guides. Propose the simplest cause that we can find easily. We get no bonus points for making it hard. They should be ready to review your training records around noon."

"Yes, sir." He left.

"The record review is in full swing," the Captain said to me. "The senior member, Captain Welch, starts with the XO and Doc on exposure and medical records. This gives the ENG a chance to organize the drills. Then he shifts to training records. The other members do chemistry and radiological controls, reactor controls records and the last looks at diesel, electrical and mechanical records."

"I was headed to the Wardroom to check out what was happening."

"Let me introduce you to Commodore Summers first."

He got up, grabbing a book off his desk, and knocked on the XO's door. There was a yes from inside. He opened the door.

Summers was seated at the outboard desk I had used. He was in dress khaki, wearing the eagles of his captain rank, a bar of three ribbons and gold dolphins over the left pocket and the command at sea insignia over his right.

"Commodore, this is Tom Ryan, the author, who was supposed to be riding with us to Japan. Tom, Commodore Summers, Commander, Submarine Squadron THREE."

"I've read your books, Mr. Ryan. I guess you got more than you expected on this trip."

"Tom, is fine, Commodore. I wouldn't have missed it for the world."

"Commodore, you might want to read this." He handed him the book, his copy of our patrol report emblazoned with the 'TOP SECRET – ACCORDION' stamps.

"Thanks, I do. The COMSUBPAC Chief of Staff is flying in tonight. I'm told he'll be doing an informal one-officer investigation of the circumstances on your patrol. You'll be told to keep all hands aboard until he's done."

"I won't do that. My crew has been through a lot. I'm going to let them have a night with their families. He can investigate all he wants Wednesday. Read the report."

"That won't go down well."

"They can't fire me twice."

"I'll get back to you after I read this. NAVSTIC has two analysts waiting to take your sonar tapes back east. They have a jet standing by at Miramar. We should have some preliminary results by the time we get in tomorrow."

"That's good. I want to hear what they say more than anyone. I'll leave you to your reading."

He shut the door. He went into the Wardroom. I followed. He took his usual seat. Along the inboard side of the table, XO and Doc were seated on each side of Welch, who was wearing working khaki and the eagles of his rank. He had gold dolphins over his left pocket with the command pin just below. Another officer was seated with Mr. McCarthy and Petty Officer Davis, the Leading ELT, on the outboard side. The forward end held another board member with Mr. Jackson and Chief Allen. The table had some pastries on a plate and a bowl of fruit; bananas, peaches and white seedless grapes from our new stores. A few pieces had been eaten.

"Captain Welch, this is Tom Ryan, the author, who has been riding us since we left San Diego back on August 10th. We've provided you a copy of his clearance. He has propulsion plant access."

"Pleased to meet you. I guess all us have read some of your stuff. We have LCDR David Porter, opposite me, reviewing chemistry records and LCDR Ross Harkins, doing Reactor Controls records. LCDR Lindsay is in Crew's Mess, doing the remaining records. I'm afraid, even with your access, we won't be able to have you in Engineering during drills."

"I understand."

I sat on a chair at the forward end and watched and listened. The Board was looking through the stacks of documents that had been assembled. They asked some questions and sometimes dug out other books or documents. Once, Chief Allen left and returned with a technical manual. He showed Harkins a page from it. It appeared to resolve whatever the question was.

The CO got a call and spoke on the phone. A minute later, the diving alarm sounded and we submerged.

I went through the Pantry to the Crew's Mess. The forward inboard table was taken over for record review. LT Gordon and Chief Lloyd were there with LCDR Lindsay so they must have been doing diesel records. The other tables were filled with engineers taking written exams. LT Cohen was monitoring and working on a paper at an aft table.

"How are the tests going?"

"We have a few on-watch personnel to go and those that are tied up in record reviews. NAV, Reed and I are working on the answer keys. Once the Captain approves those we'll start grading."

"You don't need to take it yourself?"

"Anyone who passed the Engineer Exam is exempt. We also can't be assigned as EOOW for drills."

"I see."

I left and walked back to the propulsion plant. The tile decks had been recently scrubbed. Trashcans around the spaces were empty. Everyone seemed very alert.

I stopped into Sonar on the way forward. Petty Officer Renner was the Sonar Supervisor.

"I thought Petty Officer Johnson had section 3."

"Yes, he does normally. He wants to be on for the drill sets so Petty Officer Gardner and I are splitting the other watches."

"Are you tracking anything?"

"No. The normal ORSE area is usually very quiet."

I went to the Chief's Quarters where I'd shifted some of my stuff before maneuvering watch. My bunk had fresh sheets. There were no chiefs asleep at this hour. I took my laptop and sat at the small table in the lounge area with a cup of their excellent coffee and typed some notes.

On the way back to the Wardroom I saw the Commodore standing outside the CO's stateroom. He was holding the patrol report.

"There's a lot in here that was not in your message."

"I just stuck to the bare facts in the message. There's not much space for context and I didn't want to leave loose ends."

"I know but 'He missed' doesn't give the feeling you get when you see he missed by 150 feet. I hadn't seen the orders you were given before and I don't know if COMSUBPAC commented on them. I hope they did. Your actions seem reasonable to me."

"Thank you, sir."

"I'll support you on liberty call tomorrow. I think I'll keep the Chief of Staff busy reading this report. Tom, are you going to write about this?"

"When they'll let me. I think that will be a long time from now."

"Probably. I think I'll grab some lunch."

He handed the patrol report back to the Captain and went into the Wardroom. The CO returned it to his safe.

"That's a good idea."

We went to the Wardroom. The ENG was seated with CAPT Welch. There were fixings for sandwiches out on the table. These included fresh-baked bread, lettuce, tomato, cheese slices, turkey and roast beef, mustard, mayonnaise and ketchup. I took a plate and made a sandwich. There were pitchers of lemonade, iced tea and a sweet red drink called bug juice. There was always coffee.

The chemistry and RC records wrapped up about 1400. That would allow some time for McCarthy and Jackson to take their tests. Lindsay in the Crew's Mess was working through electrical records and Welch continued with the Engineer. At 1500 they were ready for the formal briefing for CO, XO and Engineer. They agreed to let me observe.

The ENG left to call the XO and arrange for section 1 to take the watch to be ready for the first drill set. He quickly returned with the XO. The ORSE Board sat along the bench outboard with CAPT Welch aft. The CO had his usual spot with Commodore Summers to his right. The XO and ENG took the next chairs. I sat on the forward bench.

CAPT Welch began. "CINCPACFLT has tasked us to examine ships to assure safe operation of their nuclear propulsion plants. At no time during the examination should you take any action that, in your opinion, would compromise safety. You may suspend or halt the examination at any time if you consider that it is unsafe to continue. Are there any material conditions that would impact the examination?"

"No," the Captain answered.

"We noticed a preliminary incident report on a RCDC ground," said Harkins. "What is its status?"

"The ground was caused by a break in the insulation of one wire," ENG said. "It was repaired temporarily by covering the break with electrical tape. That fix completely resolved the ground issue. We intend to replace the damaged wire in port. It will not impact the examination."

Harkins nodded and Welch continued.

"Which section will lead off the drills?"

"Section 1," ENG replied.

"To provide a sense of urgency to the drills we will assume a tactical situation that you are transiting with a PIM speed of 15 knots and are behind your PIM. Will the XO be a participant in the drills?"

"Yes," the CO said.

"Then we'll excuse the XO before we continue."

He left.

"Do you have any questions about the maneuvering bells?"

The Captain shook his head.

'No," Welch continued. "On the flank bell, request you hold flank until I inform the Engineer we are ready to continue. What will be the cause of the bad fast speed main coolant pump indication?"

"A blown fuse on the #4 main coolant pump fast speed breaker," ENG said.

"Where will the rupture be in main lube oil?"

"On the first fitting on the discharge of #1 MLO pump."

"On the chloride casualty, what will be the source of the chlorides?"

"A tiny tube leak in the port condenser."

"On the loop recovery, what will be cause of the failure of rod I-3 to move outward?"

"A blown fuse leading to the mechanism."

"Are there any other questions? Then we'll begin our inspection. ENG, inform me when you are ready to initiate the first drill set."

"Our officers are standing by outside to accompany you," CO stated.

The Board got up and left, meeting up with the designated junior officers who were equipped with clipboard, paper, rag and flashlight.

"ENG, bring in your drill team and get started."

Chapter 43 – Drill Sections 1 and 2
Off San Diego – 32° 06.8' N 117° 41.3' W
Monday, September 2, 1991
1545

With a major fire drill on the first set, it was a large group that filed into the Wardroom. LTJG Reed and Senior Chief Jay had briefed the drills and given assignments to everyone down in the Torpedo Room while we were getting the briefing.

The Captain started by admonishing everyone to run the drill for ORSE just like we do in our own training. The ENG took over and went over who was responsible for various indications and anomalies. The fire was to be presumed out once two hoses are pressurized and working on the fire. He asked for questions. There were none and everyone headed aft.

I followed the Captain. He went by way of the Pantry to check on the Crew's Mess where section 3 and non-drill personnel from section 2 were assembled. They'd pre-staged OBAs from the forward spaces, broken out breathing masks and had radiation monitoring equipment in standby.

In Control the NAV was on watch. COB and Chief Lloyd had DOOW and COW. Gonzales and Cohen were in their rooms grading the exams. Everyone had taken them. The CO asked the NAV to go to 500 feet, standard speed, starting point of the next drill. Then he went on the 1MC and announced that the written exams were completed and we were starting the ORSE drill period. Only personnel on watch and running drills were allowed in engineering spaces.

LTJG Ohanian came to Control to say that the assistants on the inspection had been sent forward. He had numerous items written on the paper on his clipboard. I don't think he had only one page either.

We leveled off at 500 feet. The Captain checked the chart and returned to the periscope stand as the phone called for attention. He picked it up, spoke a bit and returned it to its cradle. We were ready to begin.

The first bell was all ahead full. He just told the NAV what to order. When speed approached 20 knots, back full was ordered. You could feel the ship shudder as the prop tried to drag our speed away. Sonar called, reporting we were cavitating. When we got to one knot by SINS, all stop was ordered. After 30 seconds, we went to full speed again. When speed neared 20 knots, flank was ordered.

There were no reports from Maneuvering. This was considered a good sign. Speed built to just over 25 knots. A couple minutes after, Maneuvering reported the pump indication issue and said it was fixed. We held flank for 5 minutes before the CO got a call. We dropped to a full bell. Next was back emergency. We cavitated again. This was again held until we were below one knot. All stop and ahead full were the last bells before the loss of main lube oil and fire.

The ENG waited for speed to build before beginning. Our first indication was Maneuvering ringing up all stop on the engine order telegraph. A 7MC report followed immediately. The NAV ordered 150 feet with 10 degrees up bubble. Haddock took the up angle as we used the residual speed to achieve a shallower depth. About 30 seconds from the initial report Maneuvering reported the shaft locked and propulsion shifted to the EPM. The NAV immediately ordered all ahead two-thirds on the EPM, equal to our normal one-third. Even without prior knowledge of the drill, the NAV knew we were seconds from the fire.

It was about 5 seconds.

"Fire in the Engine Room." The general alarm sounded for several seconds. "Fire in the Engine Room."

By the second announcement there was a line of people headed aft along the passageway to the Tunnel.

We reached 150 feet and started a turn to enable Sonar to check our previously baffled area. We still had 9 knots indicated but that bled off quickly in the turn. When we had the report of no contacts the CO directed NAV to go to periscope depth. We headed up at 3 knots. On the way we got the report that the fire was out and re-flash watches stationed. 'Prepare to emergency ventilate the Engine Room with the blower' was passed immediately. The ship was ready by the time Engineering was rigged and we commenced emergency ventilating. Two minutes later came word to secure from the drill. That was passed to all by the 1MC.

Engineering section 2 was directed to take the watch. While that was happening the Board came forward to work in the Wardroom compiling their notes. The next drill brief would be in the Torpedo Room. Meanwhile the crew re-stowed the damage control gear. We restored main engine propulsion, secured ventilating and went deep.

Ten minutes after the drill the CO, ENG and the new drill team were in the forward end of the Torpedo Room briefing the next drill. It took about 15 minutes and everyone was sent to his station. When Senior Chief Jay verified the watch was relieved and we were cleaned up from the first set, the ENG would tell Welch we were ready.

I went with the Captain to Control. This drill would start at full speed with main coolant pumps in fast speed. They were in fast from the last drill. The ENG already had permission to start when he was ready. We were just waiting on the report.

It came with a request for minimum depth and speed. One-third was ordered and we started up to 150 feet again as the Casualty Assistance Team was called away. We listened to the drill by monitoring the 2MC. Jackson was doing well. He'd downshifted main coolant pumps right away and his section had no problem identifying and securing the affected side. That was the problem during our ORSE rehearsal.

The Captain checked his watch. I checked mine. It was 1745.

"COB, have your messenger inform Mr. Banner that he should be ready for dinner at 1830, give or take 10 minutes."

"Yes, Captain. You have that, Seaman Miller?"

"Yes, COB. Dinner at 1830, give or take 10. I'll tell the XO too."

He left.

We got the report of high chlorides in the steam generators and started the initial blowdowns. By the time both generators were done we had the levels; too high to correct by blowdown alone. The most contaminated steam generator, port, would be drained and refilled and the other handled with blowdowns. The shift to single loop operation went smoothly and shortly we were ready to add chemicals and blowdown the starboard steam generator. While this was going on, they determined the source of the contamination was the port condenser by checking everything else and ruling it out.

Banner, the Supply Officer, came up.

"We'll be ready. It's really too easy when you don't kill my power. How is it going?"

"Good, in my opinion. We're ahead of schedule. In my experience poor exams tend to run late and good ones finish early. We might even get some sleep tonight."

The next set of blowdowns started. We would do three in rapid succession on the starboard steam generator. In a real casualty there would be five. The ship practiced doing the full five once each year.

When the third blowdown finished we got word to secure from the drill. That still left us to restore the port condenser, turbine generator and main engine and set up for loop recovery for the next watch.

Dinner would go down at 1825. Engineering section 3 would eat and relieve. Forward personnel would be from section 2 after the meal. We headed down to the Wardroom.

Chapter 44 – Dinner
Off San Diego – 32° 12.2' N 117° 38.7' W
Monday, September 2, 1991
1825

The Wardroom was set for the meal with the usual white tablecloth and napkins. The manuals that crowded the space during record reviews were now in their normal places. The Board members were standing outboard. My place would be the chair next to Commodore Summers with the XO and ENG on the next two. SUPPLY had his normal spot. There were two spots for the oncoming OOD and EOOW, Cohen and McCarthy. Others would eat in the Crew's Mess or at their desks.

The Captain and Commodore entered together and took their spots. Everyone took seats.

Two trays of warm garlic bread were in place. Everybody tried a piece. It was tasty. I took a second, as many did. First out was a big bowl of spaghetti, followed by meatballs and a tomato sauce. There was meat lasagna too. I tried a small piece.

The conversation was awkward. How the ORSE was going was off limits. We couldn't talk about our operations because the junior members weren't cleared. The Commodore brought up the unusually cool summer San Diego was having. It didn't go far. We talked some about events in the Soviet Union. Nobody had any good idea of what might develop and the Commodore probably had read some intelligence assessments. Baseball and the upcoming football season weren't much better as topics. We were three weeks behind on the news; except for the scores we'd gotten on the broadcast.

Cohen and McCarthy ate quickly and were excused to take their watches. The ENG clearly wanted to leave to prepare for the upcoming drill set. The Captain saw his discomfort and excused him.

Dessert was a scoop of chocolate ice cream.

Banner asked to be excused. He was oncoming DOOW. He got compliments for the meal from Welch.

I was asked if I had a new book coming out soon. I admitted one was planned for next summer. I've not finished it yet. I was asked if it would include anything from this trip. My answer was 'not anything specific, but I've learned a lot about how a submarine runs.'

The CO excused himself, telling Welch that we'd inform him when we were ready for the loop recovery. I left too.

Gonzales was outside the CO's stateroom.

"These are the exam results. We had three failures. They were all junior personnel, not fully qualified. There were four questions with an overall failing grade."

"That sounds good. Turn everything over to them right after the drills finish."

"Captain, we're ready to brief in the Torpedo Room," ENG reported.

We left.

Chapter 45 – Drill Section 3
Off San Diego – 32° 14.2' N 117° 36.7' W
Monday, September 2, 1991
1930

The recovery of the isolated loop starts out as a controlled evolution. Since the battery was fully charged, the CO decided we would go to 150 feet and not go to periscope depth or prepare to snorkel unless we encounter problems in the fast recovery startup. That's how it would normally be handled with the scenario used for ORSE and how we've trained. Because it does start as a planned evolution, Casualty Assistance Team personnel will be on station from the start.

The monitors were briefed and headed aft. The ENG would inform the Board. The CO and I headed to Control.

LT Cohen had rigged Control for red as we were just past sunset and we might need to go to periscope depth. He had us at 150 feet, ahead one-third and had cleared baffles and held no contacts. The red lights cast an ominous glow over the space.

"You can get set up, Mr. Cohen."

"Yes, sir." He grabbed the 1MC mike. "Casualty Assistance Team lay aft to assist in single loop recovery. Rig ship for reduced electrical power." On the 7MC, "Maneuvering, Conn, prepare to shift propulsion to the EPM."

"Prepare to shift propulsion to the EPM, Maneuvering aye."

"Mr. Cohen, let's turn back to north while we set up. I want to keep our baffles clear."

"Yes, sir. Helm, left 15 degrees rudder, steady course north."

"Left 15 degrees rudder, steady course north, Helm aye. My rudder is left 15 degrees."

"The ship is rigged for reduced electrical power," reported Petty Officer Field, the COW.

"Conn, Maneuvering, ready to shift propulsion to the EPM."

"Helm, all stop. Maneuvering, shift propulsion to the EPM."

"Answers all stop."

"Shift propulsion to the EPM, Maneuvering aye."

"Passing zero-one-zero to steady on north."

"Answering bells on the EPM."

"Conn aye. Helm, all ahead two-thirds."

"All ahead two-thirds, Helm aye. Answers ahead two-thirds. Steady course north."

"Conn, Maneuvering, we are ready to recover the port loop. Request to scram the reactor for loop recovery."

"Yes, Mr. Cohen."

"Maneuvering, scram the reactor and recover the loop."

"Scram the reactor and recover the loop, Maneuvering aye...Reactor scram."

Cohen passed on the 1MC, "Reactor scram for loop recovery."

A minute later, they had reopened the port loop cutout valves.

"Conn, Sonar, hold new contact, Sierra-46, bearing 345°. Classified as a possible submerged submarine."

"Mr. Cohen, I'm going to Sonar."

I followed. We entered the blue gloom of Sonar. Johnson was the Sonar Supervisor.

"How sure are you it's a submarine?"

"It's close. It has a good right bearing drift. It's quiet."

"I think it has a seven blade," Petty Officer Gardner said from the center console. Johnson and the Captain leaned over his shoulder to look at the screen.

"I concur," Johnson said. "That means it's a U.S. submarine..."

"Or the Akula," the CO finished. "All of ours are in port enjoying the holiday. Send it to fire control."

"We are," Johnson answered as we hurried out the door to get back to Control.

"Where are we?"

"They just opened the steam stop," Cohen said.

He pulled down the 1MC mike.

"This is the Captain. We have detected an unidentified submarine in our operating area. Due to the changed tactical situation, I am suspending the ORSE. Remove all simulations and

280

recover the propulsion plant." He continued. "Man battle stations. Do not relieve the watch in Engineering until the plant is self sustaining."

The COW sounded the general alarm.

"Man battle stations."

"I have the conn. Helm, all ahead one-third."

"Captain has the conn," Cohen stated.

"All ahead one-third, Helm aye. Answers ahead one-third."

"Conn, Maneuvering, commencing a fast recovery startup."

"Conn aye. You have permission to discharge purified coolant overboard."

"Permission to discharge, Maneuvering aye."

People were arriving for battle stations. The XO, NAV, WEPS and COB were first.

Commodore Summers arrived.

"What's going on?"

"As I put out on the 1MC, we have an intruder in our area. I think it's the Akula missing from Petropavlovsk. That's the classification from Sonar. He certainly knows we are here. They couldn't miss the noise from the blowdowns we did in the last drill set."

"How certain are you? Your senior chief went ashore when I came on. How good is his backup?"

"That's Petty Officer Johnson, the leading first. He's good. I'd trust him with my life."

"How about with your career? With questions about your judgment off Alaska, an error here could be fatal. I can't help you if you're wrong."

"Fatal is what I'm worried about, literally, not figuratively. As they said in the ORSE brief, I can suspend or halt the examination at any time I consider it unsafe to continue. With an unknown submarine in our area, I consider it unsafe. That's my call."

"You had better be right. What are your intentions?"

"These are international waters. He has as much right to be here as we do. When I get the plant back, I'll pull off and send a contact report. For now we'll stay quiet and hope he doesn't notice us."

"Why battle stations?"

"I want to be ready for anything. If he shoots, I'll shoot back. WEPS, make tubes 1 and 2 ready in all respects."

"Make tubes 1 and 2 ready in all respect, aye."

"Navigator has the deck."

"Mr. Cohen, take the ENG's spot on fire control until he arrives," XO ordered.

"**Reactor is critical,**" came over the MC. NAV relayed it on the 1MC.

"Commodore, would you call CAPT Welch and explain the situation."

"Yes." He went to the phone box.

"I'm loading countermeasures in both signal ejectors," NAV reported.

"I think Sierra-46 maneuvered a few minutes ago," Cohen said.

"Designate Sierra-46, Master-3," Captain directed.

"**Reactor is self sustaining.**"

"Secure from reduced electrical. Rig for patrol quiet," CO passed on 1MC. "Rig Control for white."

The bright white lights replaced the red.

"**Commenced discharging. Ready to shift propulsion to the main engines.**"

It was a new voice on the 7MC. Nguyen must have relieved as EOOW.

"Helm, all stop. Maneuvering, shift propulsion to the main engines."

"All stop, Helm aye. Answers all stop."

"**Shift propulsion to the main engines aye.**"

"Captain, tubes 1 and 2 are ready in all respects. I've set short range tactics as we don't have a good handle on range."

"That's good, WEPS."

The ENG, Jackson, McCarthy and Seabright were the last to arrive and take stations.

"Answering bells on the main engines. Can give you about 60%. Five minutes to full capability, shorter if you direct emergency heat-up rates."

"Helm, all ahead two-thirds. Dive 500 feet, fifteen down bubble." Over the MC, "Conn aye. Normal heat-up is satisfactory."

"Ahead two-thirds, Helm aye. Answers two-thirds."

"500 feet, fifteen down, Dive aye."

"Battle stations are manned," COW, now Chief Lloyd, reported.

"Welch understands the situation. His folks will stay aft for now. We'll see where we go after we resolve our contact."

"Helm, right fifteen degrees rudder, steady zero-nine-zero. Helm, all ahead standard."

"Right fifteen degrees rudder, steady zero-nine-zero, all ahead standard, Helm aye. My rudder is right fifteen to come to zero-nine-zero. Answers standard."

"Maneuvering make turns for 12 knots."

"Turns for twelve, Maneuvering aye"

"Petty Officer Boyle, can you start the voice recording? XO, have Sonar start a broadband tape."

"We've been recording since just after battle stations," Boyle said.

"Attention in Control. Master-3 is a possible Akula class SSN. We don't know what he intends. He probably knows we are here, somewhere, because he couldn't have missed our steam generator blowdowns on the last drill set. I intend to pull away from him and report the contact. The future actions will depend on what our bosses direct. We're at battle stations in case he gets frisky. I want to be able to shoot back if he shoots at us. Carry on."

"At 500 feet," COB announced.

"Conn, Maneuvering, ready to answer all bells. Secured discharging."

Chapter 46 – Boom

Off San Diego – 32° 18.5' N 117° 32.4' W
Monday, September 2, 1991
2013

"Steady zero-nine-zero."

"Let's get a solution on him now," the Captain urged. "The course change should help."

"We're looking at 310° to 320°, speed 10 and 3,000 to 5,000 yards," ENG said. "We're in his baffles."

"WEPS, set Doppler in. Tube #2 is primary."

"Doppler is set in. Tube #2 primary aye."

"Sonar believes Master-3 is maneuvering," XO reported.

"Concur," ENG agreed. "He turned away."

"Plot is getting crossed bearings about 4,500 yards," Jackson said. "They could be near his range."

"He's searching for us," the Captain said. "Why is he searching for us?"

"Master-3 has turned to an easterly course," Jackson said. "We're not getting any crossed bearings on plots."

"Get a curve here and we'll change course."

"This is damned odd," commented Commodore Summers. "They've never come to the Pacific Coast before…that we know of."

"I'd like to know if the Akula has anything to do with the subs we encountered off Alaska. I doubt we'll ever find out."

"Shifted to normal tactics, 1,500 yard enable run," WEPS said.

"We have a curve," Jackson reported.

"Helm, left fifteen degrees rudder, steady three-zero-zero."

"Left fifteen degrees rudder, steady three-zero-zero, Helm aye. My rudder is left fifteen."

"We have a fair solution. Course 120°, speed 10, range 5,000 yards," XO said.

"Torpedo in the water, bearing 344°, from Master-3."

"Helm, ahead flank, cavitate. Dive 1300 feet. Launch countermeasures."

"Torpedo bears 346°. Master-3 is speeding up and cavitating."

"WEPS, shoot tube #2."

"Shoot tube #2. Standby. Fire."

Control rumbled with the sound of the tube firing.

"Sonar, is there a second torpedo?"

"Only hold one torpedo from Master-3," came over the MC.

"Is it active?"

"Not yet. Hold our unit in high speed."

"Shit. It's a nuke. Dive, 150 feet, 25 up." The CO looked at the gyrocompass. "Helm, steady three-two-two. Chief of the Watch, rig for depth charge."

"Rig for depth charge." The collision alarm sounded for a couple seconds. "Rig for depth charge."

"150 feet, aye. 700 feet starting up."

The down angle became an up angle, then steeply up.

"Steady on three two-two."

"We lost the wire," Boyle reported.

"WEPS, secure tube #2 and shut the outer door on tube #1." He got on the 1MC. "This is the Captain. I believe a nuclear torpedo has been fired at us. I think we'll be far enough away to survive. Buckle in and hang on. You'll feel two strong shocks then it should be safe to move."

"Torpedo bears 358°, drawing right quickly. It's still not active."

"Maneuvering, this is the Captain. Due to the extreme tactical situation, place the battleshort switch in the battleshort position."

"Battleshort to battleshort, Maneuvering aye. We are in battleshort."

"Maneuvering, if I can, I'll order a lower bell. Slam the throttles shut and downshift main coolant pumps as quickly as you can. Then open back up to answer the bell."

"Yes, sir. I understand."

"Be ready for anything. Try to restore the plant as much as possible."

"Yes, sir."

"Doors are shut on tubes 1 and 2."

"145 feet coming back to 150."

"COB, ease us up to 120."

"120 feet aye."

"The torpedo is in our baffles. We're cavitating."

"How long has the torpedo been running?" the Captain asked.

"Two minutes, thirty seconds," I answered. I'd been writing everything on a pad of paper.

"It won't be long now. Everyone grab onto something." He hugged the #2 scope barrel.

"Master-3 is slowing."

"Helm, all ahead standard."

"All ahead standard, Helm aye. Answers standard."

Time seemed to slow as seconds ticked off.

"We only need a few more..."

The hull rang and I was thrown against the periscope stand rail that I'd been holding.

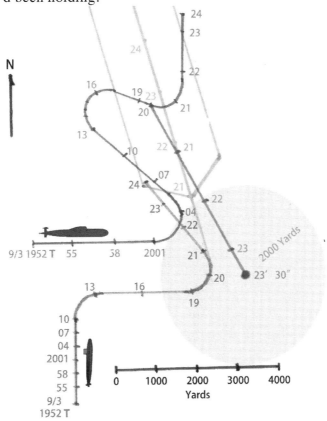

Chapter 47 – Damage Control

Off San Diego – 32° 21.1' N 117° 31.4' W
Monday, September 2, 1991
2024

"Maneuvering rings up all stop." Helm practically shouted.

"Answer all stop," the CO said, forcefully but calmly.

"Starboard buses are down," COW reported.

"Flooding in the Engine Room," the MC speaker announced.

"Maneuvering rings up standard," Helm announced in a more normal tone.

"Answer standard. Chief of the Watch, stand down. We're only at 120 feet. I'll give them 30 seconds. Announce the flooding."

Chief Lloyd had stood and was reaching toward the emergency blow valve levers. He backed away and picked up the 1MC mike.

"Flooding in the Engine Room." The collision alarm sounded. "Flooding in the Engine Room."

"The flooding has stopped. Flooding is not main seawater."

"No effect on trim," COB reported.

"We've lost sonar and fire control," XO reported.

"Starboard buses are reenergized," COW said.

"Captain, you're bleeding," I said. "Your right temple."

"Pass me a paper towel."

The Quartermaster handed him one. He folded it twice and pressed it to his forehead. The boat rocked to port.

"What was that?" the COB asked.

"The surface wave kicked up by the explosion. Base surge," the CO stated. "Not dangerous to us."

"Conn, Maneuvering, the flooding is isolated. Main seawater is restored. We lost the starboard AC buses. They are restored. Able to answer all bells."

"Why did you ring all stop initially?"

"We had a power-flow cutback. We were one-slow, one-slow with the bus loss and the starboard main coolant cutout valves became unlatched. Going to 'open' on the valves fixed the cutback. We would have scrammed without battleshort."

"Return battleshort to normal."

"Return battleshort to normal, Maneuvering aye. The battleshort switch is in normal."

"Helm, all ahead two-thirds."

"All ahead two-thirds, Helm aye. Answers ahead two-thirds."

"Where do we stand on sonar and fire control?"

"Sonar is coming up now in casualty mode." XO reported.

"They are requesting the corpsman in Machinery Lower Level," reported the JA phone talker.

"Chief of the Watch, get damage and casualty reports from all compartments." NAV directed.

"Sonar is up. We have broadband," XO said.

"Do we have Master-3 or our unit?"

"My congratulations," Summers said. "How did you know we'd be far enough away?"

"I didn't, but it's the only possibility worth planning for."

"Sonar holds Master-3; nothing on our unit. Mster-3 has developed a rattle. They're buzzing bearings to Master-3. Reverbs from the explosion are raising havoc with ATF."

"Dive, make your depth 500 feet."

"500 feet, Dive aye. Fifteen down."

"WEPS, reload tube #2 with a Mk-48. Make tubes #1 and #4 ready in all respects."

"Reload tube #2 and make tubes #1 and #4 ready in all respects, aye. We'll need to use the emergency preset panel if we don't get fire control back."

"I know. NAV, reload countermeasures in the signal ejectors."

"NAV aye. I've already ordered it."

"Captain, we have the damage report." Lloyd said.

"Proceed."

"We have a couple dozen with bumps, bruises and minor cuts, including yourself. MS3 Stout sustained a deep cut on his right thigh from an improperly secured knife in the Galley. MM2 Porter, the AMS Lower Level watch broke his left leg. Doc is stabilizing it and we have a team from the forward DC party that will evacuate him to the Wardroom. #1 R-114 plant is isolated due to the flooding. #2 and the LiBr plant are working. The evaporator control panel was sprayed with salt water. It's down and electricians are working to clean it up. We have a steady stream of water leaking from #2 main seawater pump mechanical seal, about a quart a minute. Engineering requests permission to pump bilges as needed. That's it."

"It could be worse. Engineering, pump bilges as necessary." He picked up the 1MC. "Captain again. We took a nuke and are still here. We're still at battle stations. We have some unfinished business to take care of with an Akula. Secure from flooding, secure from depth charge. Remain rigged for patrol quiet."

"At 500 feet"

"Doc wants to know if he can come up and treat you, Captain," the JA talker reported.

"Tell Doc I'm fine. He should treat me last."

"Yes, sir."

"Captain," Summers began. "I know you want to get the Akula. I support that. But we've no fire control and other damage. We're also required to send a NUCFLASH report."

"If we report, we lose our chance to sink him. We can do it without fire control. We've practiced it."

"We have Master-3 on a northwesterly course at about 5 knots," Jackson reported. "Range 3,000 to 5,000 yards."

"Sonar, could Master-3 hold us?"

"Conn, Sonar, not a chance in a hundred. He's looking back toward the explosion. That whole semicircle is a mass of noise. We only hold him, most of the time, because of his rattle. Conn, he's speeding up. I think he's going to flank."

"Helm, all ahead flank."

Chapter 48 – Pencil and Paper

Off San Diego – 32° 22.3' N 117° 32.5' W
Monday, September 2, 1991
2034

"Answers flank."

"At 500 feet."

"Helm, right 10 degrees rudder, steady zero-four-zero."

"Right 10 degrees rudder, steady zero-four-zero, Helm aye. My rudder is right 10."

"Attention in Control. He's faster than us so we don't have much time. Plots need to give us as much as possible. Intend to shoot Master-3 with one Mk-48 torpedo using the emergency preset panel."

"Tubes #1 and #4 are ready in all respects. What presets do you want?"

"Set minimum ceiling and maximum floor, Doppler in, short ping interval, shallow trajectory. What's a good search depth and pitch angle in the mid depth band? We need to give our unit the best legs in a stern chase."

"400 feet at +4 pitch angle is good if we're not concerned he'll go very shallow."

"Use that. We'll set enable run and gyro angle just before launch."

"Passing zero-three-zero to steady on zero-four-zero."

"Petty Officer Boyle, where do we stand on fire control?"

"We've tried the normal things and no luck. There are other things we can try but they take down sonar while we reboot. We figured that was out."

"You figured right. Just backup WEPS on the presets."

"Sonar has Master-3 at 28 knots if his turns per knot is similar to our prop. They are in ATF. He's noisy at flank."

"I hope whatever is loose doesn't rip off. I keep picturing a flapping access panel on his pod in my mind."

"He's about 20 miles from Point Loma," said NAV.

"We have crossed bearings at 4,600 yards," Jackson said. "Evaluated as a maximum range. We have a curve."

"Sonar has a bottom bounce range of 3,000 yards," XO said.

"Firing point procedures, Master-3, tube #1." CO stated. "Commodore, as SOPA, I need you to declare Master-3 a hostile force to make everything legal."

"You already shot at him."

"Self defense, but he's running away now, maybe headed to nuke San Diego."

"Master-3 is designated a hostile force."

"Log that Quartermaster," NAV directed. "Time 2040 Tango."

"Ship ready," COB stated.

"Helm, left 10 degrees rudder, steady three-four-five."

"Left 10 degrees rudder, steady three-four-five, Helm aye. My rudder is left 10."

"Solution is ready but rough. Course 020°, speed 28 knots, range 3,500 yards," XO said. He was standing over the geo plot.

"Weapon is ready except for enable run and gyro angle."

"WEPS use 3,800 yard enable run and right 25 degrees gyro angle. I'll shoot when he bears 020°"

"Passing three-five-five to steady on three-four-five."

"Call out the bearings, every degree."

"Yes, sir," said Seaman Miller, the bearing recorder.

"Steady three-four-five."

"010°"

"Bottom bounce range, 3,800 yards."

"011°"

"WEPS, set enable at 4,000 yards."

"012°"

"4,000 yards set, right 25 set."

"013°"

"He'll run 1,500 yards while our unit is pre-enable. We can't afford a long stern chase at his speed."

"014°"

"Plot likes course 020°, the shot should be good. Minimum range, 2,500 yards."

"015°"

"Ekelund range, 4,000 yards."

"016°"

It became very quiet in Control. The CO looked closely at the preset panel, verifying the settings.

"017°…018°…019°"

"Shoot tube #1."

"Shooting tube #1. Standby. Fire."

There was the rumble of the firing tube.

"020°"

"You can belay calling the bearings, Seaman Miller."

"Sonar reports our unit running in high speed."

"Secure tube #1 and reload with a Mk-48."

"Tube #2 is reloaded but we can't check the weapon out without fire control. Reload tube #1 with a 48, aye."

"Shot looks good on plot."

"Range is the big issue," the CO commented to the Commodore. "If I overcalled the range and had too long an enable run it could blow right by him."

"Buzzing bearings to Master-3. They can hold the rattle over our unit's sound.

"No change in Master-3," Jackson reported from plot.

"Our unit is slowing. It's searching."

"Come on," Gonzales muttered.

"Our unit is speeding up. Sonar holds our unit in high speed."

"Well done," Commodore Summers said. "I've never seen anyone get a hit with the emergency preset panel on exercise shots."

"Thanks. We did it once a couple years ago. We still have to close the last few hundred yards to make it official."

"Explosion on the bearing to Master-3. Turns are dropping…transients…He's trying to blow.

"Helm, all ahead two-thirds, right ten degrees rudder, steady zero-four-zero. Chief of the Watch, secure from battle stations, secure from patrol quiet."

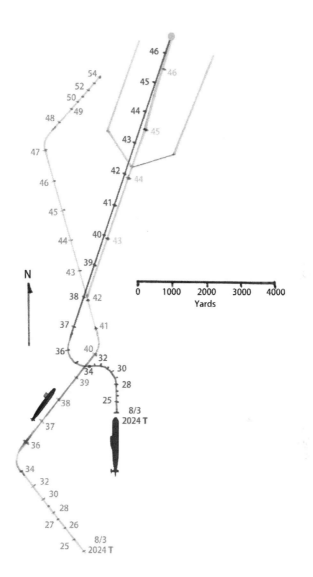

Chapter 49 – Aftermath
Off San Diego – 32° 27.1' N 117° 32.1' W
Monday, September 2, 1991
2054

We had secured from battle stations but nobody was leaving Control. The XO was still on the sound-powered phone headset with Sonar. The ENG was seated in front of his blank console. Jackson and Banner were working on the plots, marking bearings to Master-3.

"He's trying to blow ballast but it isn't working. There are no propulsion sounds. He's sinking," XO reported. There were scattered comments and cheers of approval.

"Quiet in Control. They're dying. Quartermaster, what's the sounding?"

"543 fathoms beneath the keel."

"Over 3,000 feet, certainly too much with the pressure hull ruptured."

"Bulkhead failure," XO said. "Another and another."

"Attention in Control. We will surface and look for survivors. I'm very sure the Akula Class has one of their escape capsules. We'll see if they were able to use it. We also have to report what happened. Dive, 150 feet. Rig Control for red."

"150 feet, Dive aye."

The red lights replaced the white.

"ENG give me a full report on plant status. I'll also need an ELT to draw an air sample on the Bridge right after we surface. I want to know what's outside before we draw it into the ship."

"What about ORSE?"

"The Commodore and I will handle that."

ENG wrapped up his headset and left.

"XO, what time is it? Which section has watch?"

"Almost 2100 and section 3 is relieving after battle stations. Sonar reports Master-3 is on the bottom." He removed his phones.

"Let's split the time between now and 0600 into three watches and let everyone get some sleep. Check on our injured.

We'll plan for maneuvering watch at 0800 and Ballast Point at 0930. If Doc thinks we need to, we'll come in at night."

"WEPS, you take charge of reconstruction. Collect all the materials and classify everything like our patrol report. We'll submit this data as an addendum."

"Yes, sir. What about fire control? When we surface can we drop sonar to see if we can restore it?"

"We'll do that. Have a team standing by to man the deck if we find somebody. I don't think we can transfer people from an escape capsule to our deck. I'd prefer to get a torpedo retriever out for that. We have to be ready for what might develop."

"Captain," began Nguyen who had just come in from aft. "I've been relieved as EOOW by Mr. Ohanian. I'm here to relieve the NAV as OOD."

"Well done during battle stations, Mr. Nguyen. Give me a quick update on the propulsion plant."

"Yes, sir. Thank you. When I said I wished to be where the action was, I was thinking of being in Control not wishing to have the action come to me as EOOW.

"We have full propulsion capability. The valve operating system has been restored and we're starting our post primary discharge checks. The flooding was on the inlet of #1 R-114 air conditioning plant. It's isolated and we've wired the isolation valves shut. We lost #1 air conditioning seawater pump to isolate the area. #2 R-114 and the LiBr plants are carrying the load. The electricians have flushed the evaporator control panel with fresh water. They are drying is out. They're using heat guns to help. We were starting a primary sample as I headed forward."

"Good. How bad is the leak from #2 MSW pump?"

"We can manage it. We're pumping bilges several times an hour."

"At 150 feet."

"Thanks, Mr. Nguyen. Conn, Sonar, any contacts."

"No contacts."

"Helm, left full rudder, steady two-nine-zero."

"Left full rudder, steady two-nine-zero, Helm aye. My rudder is left full."

"Captain, one more thing. The ORSE Board was in the plant for the whole time. They were taking notes."

"Don't worry. You did fine. It's why we had you, an experienced EOOW, there."

"Captain, we'll run midrats all night. Breakfast at 0700 will be steak and eggs."

"That sounds good, Chop. Start breakfast at 0500 for the last oncoming watch and keep it running until maneuvering watch. 0700 will be for the Wardroom."

"Senior Chief Spillman has relieved me of the Dive," COB reported. "The evaporator is down. Do we need water hours?"

"Where are we on potable water?"

"About 70%."

"That should last until we're in port if everyone takes Navy showers. I don't want to close the showers. Even with the evaporator I wouldn't make potable water until we were sure there's no radioactive contamination in the water from the nuke."

"Passing three-zero-zero to two-nine-zero."

"Mr. Nguyen has relieved me as OOD," NAV reported.

"Very well, NAV. You can work on the hard copy NUCFLASH. Have Radio ready to come up on the secure voice net to Group FIVE. We'll get them to patch us in to CINCPACFLT on a secure landline."

"Why not just go direct on satellite secure voice?" Summers asked.

"Too many commands monitor it. We're the only one out so we'll be alone on the local net."

"Steady two-nine-zero."

"Sonar, any contacts?"

"Hold no contacts."

"Rig for black."

The lights went out. Nguyen drew the curtains around the periscope stand. Nguyen, the CO, Commodore and I were in the cocoon of more total blackness.

"I'll take it up, Mr. Nguyen. Dive, 58 feet. Helm, all ahead one-third. Raising #2 scope."

"58 feet, Dive aye. Five up."

"All ahead one-third, Helm aye. Answers one-third."

"#2 scope and fairing indicate up."

The CO lowered the handles and began to sweep around in low power.

"Passing 100 feet. 80. 70."

"Breaking."

The CO turned rapidly around, once, twice, three times.

"64 coming to 58."

"No close contacts."

He made a slow sweep in low power and shifted to high power.

"No contacts. Dive, surface the ship. Give me a good long normal blow. I'll tell you when to stop. We won't be using the blower. Stay at one-third."

"Surface the ship, Dive aye. Chief of the Watch."

"Surface, surface, surface," COW passed on the 1MC. The diving alarm sounded three blasts. "Surface, surface, surface. Normal blowing all main ballast tanks."

"50 feet, 40, 35, 30, 29, 28, 27. 27 feet and holding."

"Aft deck looks clear. Give me 10 more seconds and secure the blow."

"Blow secured. 27 feet."

"Mr. Nguyen, take the scope. Chief of the Watch, raise the BRA-34. Dive, open the bridge hatch and take air samples."

Nguyen took the scope and swept around, standing on the narrow step fitted around the scope's well.

"Captain, give me the conn. You have plenty to do already."

"You're right. Two-nine-zero, one-third, on the surface."

"I relieve you of the conn. Quartermaster, Mr. Nguyen has the deck and the conn."

"Captain, Mr. McCarthy here. I have Petty Officer Davis with me. We'll take charge of the surveys."

"BRA-34 is raised."

"Captain, take a break," I whispered to him. "You're not yourself. It's like you're in a manic state and you're bleeding again. You stopped pressing your wound when you went to periscope depth."

He looked at his right hand that still held the folded paper, barely visible in the darkness where the only light was provided by the dim glow of displays. He pressed it back to his forehead.

"You're right. I can think of so many things I need to do."

"They don't all need to be done right now."

"Commodore, you're SOPA. Would you like to make the official report of our action?"

"Yes, do you have the format and data that I'll need?"

"I have it out here," NAV said. "Radio is on the Group FIVE net and the Control mike is ready. Rig for red in Control and you'll be able to read it. Run the mike over to fire control."

"Rig Control for red," Nguyen ordered. "Energize the running lights."

It was only slightly brighter on the periscope stand because of the opaque curtains. The Captain, Commodore and I moved to fire control, still down, where NAV had a sheet of paper. The Captain sat on the forward bench. He had some blood on the right side of his face down to his cheek but the pressure on the towel was stopping fresh flow.

Senior Chief Spillman came over. On the surface, planes in emergency, he was Control Room Coordinator. He didn't like what he saw and had COW make a phone call. I asked for a fresh paper towel and one that was wet. The Messenger went for them.

The mike was activated. There were a couple seconds of tones as crypto locked before it was ready to transmit.

"Submarine Group FIVE, this is Submarine Squadron THREE actual, embarked on Haddock, over."

"Squadron THREE this is Group FIVE, over."

"Group FIVE, I have top secret, flash traffic for CINCPACFLT Can you patch us through on a secure landline? Over."

"I can patch you to COMSUBPAC Command Center quickly. Over."

"That will do. Over."

"Standby. Over."

"Squadron THREE, this is COMSUBPAC, over."

"This is Squadron THREE actual embarked on Haddock. I have OPREP-3, Pinnacle, NUCFLASH report for CINCPACFLT Over."

"Say again. Cancel that. Standby. Over."

There was a minute delay. I'd gotten the fresh paper towels and folded the dry one for the Captain to apply pressure while I used the moist one to wipe off the dripped blood on his face. He seemed calmer.

We had the upper hatch and bridge clamshell open. The ELT was monitoring the auxiliaryman for contamination below the lower hatch.

"This is CINCPACFLT standing by. CINCPAC and NMCC are on the line. Over."

"This is Submarine Squadron THREE actual embarked on Haddock off San Diego, California. I have an OPREP-3, Pinnacle, NUCFLASH report. Over."

"This is NMCC. We have a satellite report of an anomaly in your area. Go right to the narrative. Pause frequently to see if we want clarification. Do not transmit any hard copy. Over."

"This is Squadron THREE, WILCO. Beginning narrative. Haddock was conducting ORSE operations in San Diego local operating areas. ORSE Board and Squadron THREE actual were embarked. While conducting engineering drills, about 0300 Zulu, September 3rd, contact on an Akula Class SSN was obtained. The propulsion plant was restored and battle stations manned. Intentions were to pull away and report the contact. At 0320 Z the Akula fired one torpedo. Haddock returned fire with one Mk-48. CO Haddock correctly evaluated the Akula's torpedo as a nuke and evaded. The torpedo detonated at about 0323 and thirty seconds Z. Haddock sustained some personnel casualties, none life threatening, and material damage but was still mission capable. Over."

"This is NMCC, where is the Akula now. Over."

"This is Squadron THREE, I was getting to that. Sunk. After immediate damage control efforts, Haddock pursued the Akula that was traveling at flank speed toward San Diego. As SOPA, I declared the Akula a hostile force due to its use of nuclear weapons and proximity to populated areas of Southern California. At 0342 Z Haddock fired one Mk-48 that impacted about 0346 Z. Sonar

299

confirmed hull implosion on the Akula. Haddock is on the surface, searching for survivors from the Akula. Over."

"This is CINCPACFLT Well done to you and Haddock. Details on Haddock's casualties. Over."

"This is Squadron THREE. All credit goes to the crew of Haddock. You don't know even half the story."

The CO stood and asked for the mike.

"This is Haddock actual. We have a crewmember with a broken leg, one with a serious laceration and a couple dozen with minor cuts and bruises, including me. Fire control is inoperative, sonar is in casualty mode, #1 R-114 air conditioning plant is isolated to stop flooding in the Engine Room, the evaporator is down due to grounds from the flooding and we have a significant leak from the mechanical seal of #2 main seawater pump. Over."

"This is COMSUBPAC actual. Haddock is directed to remain on the surface. When do you desire to return to San Diego? Over.

"WILCO, Admiral. We are planning on 0930 at Ballast Point. Injuries do not need immediate evacuation. Out initial air and contamination surveys from the Bridge are clean. Recommend airborne monitoring for possible fallout. South County and Tijuana might be at risk. We could also use an air search for survivors. Over."

"This is COMSUBPAC. 0930 Ballast Point, approved. We'll arrange the rest. Over."

"This is CINCPACFLT Use the same classification for this action as your last patrol report. Package your data for transfer on return to port. Continue to monitor this net. Over."

"Roger. Over."

"CINCPACFLT, out."

While on the radio, Mr. Reed had relieved as OOD on the Bridge.

The CO handed the mike to NAV and sat down. He looked tired. Doc had been standing by, aft in Control, and came next to the CO when he sat.

"Let me fix you up."

"Am I last?"

"You're the most seriously hurt that's not already cared for. Is that good enough?"

It was. Doc started with a local anesthetic and went to work. CAPT Welch of the ORSE Board came over.

"What can I do for you?"

"You've already done plenty. The first principle of reactor safety is, don't get sunk. When I heard your initial report, I figured you'd be embarrassed when the contact proved false. We stayed in Engineering during battle stations. It was instructive. We want to finish the exam. We won't need any evolutions or interviews tomorrow morning. ENG arranged for Mr. Harkins to monitor the primary sample you are drawing right now. The only other thing we need is for your people to read the calibrated TLDs we brought. We'd like the Corpsman, if possible."

"Doc is busy. Why not have the ELT do it after he does the sample?"

"That's acceptable. The Wardroom is medical central right now. COB gave us the Chief's Mess area to meet. If the Wardroom is free we can debrief at 0600. We can do Crew's Mess if needed."

He left.

"Control, Bridge. We have the searchlight set up. We lost most of the nonskid paint over AMS and believe the stern running light is out."

"Control, aye," said Spillman. "We'll make the reports."

"I've got it Senior Chief," the CO said. "Doc, how are our other casualties?"

"I put a splint on Porter's leg. I got morphine from the XO and gave him a shot. He's resting comfortably in a bunk in the Bow Compartment. We'll get him to Balboa in the morning to have it set. Stout took fifteen stitches. He's fine. I have two others with more stitches than you. Most were just a Band-Aid. You're done, two stitches and a bandage."

"Remind me not to hug the periscope next time someone fires a nuke at us."

"We are done in the Wardroom. The Board can have it back."

"Thanks. I'll leave them where they are. Take me to Porter and Stout. I want to look in on them. Senior Chief, I'm heading below. I'll be in the Wardroom in a few minutes.

I went directly to the Wardroom. It was already clear and Cohen, Jackson and Banner were working on reconstructing the encounter. They had each made a sandwich and had cups of coffee. I made a turkey sandwich for myself with lettuce and tomato.

A few minutes later there was a commotion from Crew's Mess. I stood and passed through the Pantry to see what was happening. The space was packed. Everyone was standing and applauding. The CO was trying to get them to stop by gesturing with his arms for them to sit. It took a couple minutes.

"I should be applauding you. I'm proud of everyone. Thank you."

He went back through the Pantry and took his normal seat at the table. I followed. Petty Officer Glenn came in after us.

"Can I get you anything, Captain?"

"Do you have any soup?"

"We have tomato soup. Can I get you a bowl?"

"Yes, thanks."

"Captain, you look better," I said.

"I feel better. I was a little hyper earlier, I guess. I decided I don't much like combat."

"Not liking it, that's probably a good thing."

The ENG came in and Glenn returned with the hot soup. He placed it in front of the CO and put down a spoon.

"Thank you, Petty Officer Glenn. ENG, what do you have?"

"Some good news to start. The evaporator is coming up. We'll make water to reserve feed until we can test for radioactivity in the seawater and output. We've started entering port checks on the discharge system. They'll be done and tags hung by 2300."

"Good."

"The seawater valves isolating #1 R-114 plant are tagged and wired shut. We also lost #1 air conditioning seawater pump in that arrangement. The flooding was from a sound isolation fitting in the piping. It's an easy fix for Dixon. The #2 main seawater pump could be a big problem. The leak is about a pint a minute in slow speed on the surface. It's about a gallon per minute at fast speed at 500 feet."

"It's worse in fast speed?"

"Yes, about four times worse at equal depths. There's not much room to pull the pump. It could be hard to fix."

"We'll have to see what they say. COMSUBPAC directed us not to submerge. We have the ORSE debrief at 0600 tomorrow."

"I'm worried about that."

"Don't be. We did well. We saved their lives, and ours."

"Speaking of that," LT Cohen interrupted, "we have the reconstruction of the nuke. It looks to be 3,000 to 3,500 yards away at detonation."

The CO, ENG and I stood up and took a look at the plot on the forward end of the table.

"Almost half of that was because he led his target and hadn't picked up our turn," he added.

"We were lucky," CO said.

"How did you know it was a nuke?" ENG asked. "I never considered that."

"They normally shoot two torpedoes, like the Victor. Those go active almost immediately. A dumb torpedo has to have a really big bang."

The XO came in.

"The Commodore is trying to sleep. I hope he can. I can't. He said we should look at whom we want to recognize with awards. You earned your Purple Heart today, Captain."

"For two stitches, I'd be embarrassed to wear it. We can award it to anyone with more than two stitches or for a broken bone. Get some recommendations for other awards, including for the patrol. We'll be told what we can submit in a few days."

"Yes, sir. If you'll consider a counter argument, you did get your wound from a nuclear weapon."

"A good point but it's decided. Where do we stand on a patrol report addendum?"

"I wrote the draft of our narrative," XO said. "Look it over and we can go smooth when you're done. We've got the other stuff packed except for the material here being used for reconstruction. Mr. Cohen, we'll need you to reduce the plot to 8 by 10 for the report."

"Give us another two hours."

"OK XO, I'll get started on this, right after I have a sandwich."

We found no escape capsule or other sign of the Akula. A helicopter was seen searching the area but did not contact us. Later there was a low-flying airplane, possibly a P-3, seen overhead. It moved away toward the Mexican coast. The crescent moon rose just before 0100 and helped the search.

Fire control and full sonar capability were restored about 0300. They needed to reseat several circuit cards and use a backup disk pack on the computer.

Uniform for entering port was to be whites for personnel topside.

Chapter 50 – Debrief
Off San Diego – 32° 32.2' N 117° 21.3' W
Tuesday, September 3, 1991
0545

The ORSE Board was in the Wardroom with Commodore Summers. We had a copy of their notes. It didn't contain any grades. All six sections made a thick stack of paper. The CO was sitting in his stateroom with the door open. All the Engineering Department Officers and Chiefs, plus the COB, were assembled in the passageway outside the officers' staterooms. The ENG was outside the CO's door reading the comments.

"They list the #1 R-114, the evaporator and #2 main seawater pump."

"Don't worry about it, ENG."

"They have comments on the plant casualty from the nuke."

"ENG, have a cigarette. The smoking lamp is lighted for you from now until we dock, any space, any time."

He didn't waste time. He lit up. It helped.

LCDR Harkins opened the door.

"We're ready for you, Captain."

The CO was in for five minutes before opening the door.

"Everyone come in."

We filed in. The Board was along the outboard bench with CAPT Welch aft near the CO's seat. Commodore Summers had the chair to the Captain's right. Everyone was smiling, a good sign. The XO and ENG took the next chairs. Nguyen got the last chair while Gordon, Jackson, Reed and McCarthy squeezed into the forward bench. The COB, the other Chiefs, Jay, Allen and Dawson, and I stood along the aisle.

"ENG, put out the cigarette," directed Summers.

"I gave him permission, Commodore. We survived a nuke. We can handle a few minutes of secondhand smoke." He turned to Welch. "I know you like suspense, but we're short on time. Could we do the bottom line first?"

"Yes, we can. We evaluated Haddock's operation of the propulsion plant excellent overall. Congratulations, Mr. Rinaldi. You passed. Operations was rated excellent, Level of Knowledge, excellent, Administration, above average, Chemistry and Radiological Controls, above average, Cleanliness, average, Material Condition, below average. By our normal measure the material problems would be a failure, but given the unusual circumstances under which they occurred, we adjusted that grade.

"Captain, you would normally write Admiral DeMars a personal letter on your ship's ORSE. I'm certain he would also like your views on plant performance during your recent operations. Try to keep it to the secret level so it can be shared with senior personnel that aren't cleared for operational details. You may assume Admiral DeMars is fully aware of the operational background."

"Certainly, I shall."

"Good. I'll tell them to expect it when I check in with the exam results. Mr. Porter will go over the drills."

"We ran a series of maneuvering bells with a main coolant pump indication failure. We evaluated that drill as average. Do you wish me to cover our comments?"

"We have them on our copy. Assume we don't want the details unless I ask."

"We ran a loss of main lube oil and Engine Room fire. We evaluated that drill as average. Next section was high chlorides in condensate leading to steam generator blowdowns and single loop operation. We evaluated that drill as above average.

"It gets trickier here. You suspended drills in the middle of recovery from the isolated loop. That was obviously the proper call. We continued to observe plant operations.

"We evaluate you on reactor safety," Welch interrupted, "but also on whether level of training and knowledge enables you to operate in support of ship's mission requirements. Normally we extrapolate from what we see in drills and interviews. Here we got to observe first hand. Continue, Mr. Porter."

"Yes, sir. The recovery from single loop was evaluated as excellent. The heat-up rate was slightly over four degrees per minute. Propulsion restoration was prompt and watch reliefs did not delay events. The turnover between Mr. McCarthy and Mr. Nguyen was seamless.

"Circumstances required the CO to order use of battleshort. The Board endorses this decision."

"We were initially split," explained Welch, "between outright approval and asking D.C. for guidance. You only had seconds to decide. It was the right decision. Our endorsement should insulate you from anyone trying to second-guess you.

"The tactical threshold for using an emergency heat-up rate during the recovery is considerably lower than that for battleshort. We all agreed that you would have been justified in using it during the recovery." There were nods from other board members. "You decided against it. What was your thinking?"

"Heating the plant faster would have required discharging coolant faster to maintain operational levels in the pressurizer. That's superheated water into a sea pressure of about five atmospheres, I didn't know how noisy that might get and didn't want to raise our risk of detection by the Akula. I don't think anyone has monitored that for noise, at least, I'm unaware of such a test."

"I don't know of one either," admitted Welch as Summers shook his head to indicate no also. "That might be a good point to raise in your letter to NR."

"I'll do that. Anyway, I saw it as a tradeoff between noise and time and chose to minimize noise. Another consideration was that we were relieving watches to man battle stations in the propulsion plant and I thought it was best not to vary from the routine we were trained for during the process."

"I see. Mr. Porter, please continue."

"A loss of both starboard AC buses, power-flow cutback and flooding in the Engine Room were experienced as a simultaneous casualty. Actions in this casualty were evaluated as excellent."

"I'd love to be able to run that for future exams," Welch said. "I think it exceeds the safety parameters for a training drill though. I want to commend Mr. Nguyen on his actions. He immediately ordered cutback override. When flooding was reported he leapt up on his chair to operate the emergency closures, holding onto pipes in the overhead with one hand. He needed to do that to reach them. He directed the electric plant and cutback casualties while fighting the flooding. It was very impressive. Your RO and EO on battle stations were also excellent."

"Well done, Mr. Nguyen." Nguyen did a seated bow toward the table in acknowledgement, sporting a big smile. "Did you see any problems?' CO asked.

Porter responded. "On recovery from flooding, the steam supply to the starboard air ejector was not reset. This caused a lowering vacuum. The problem was recognized and corrected without impacting propulsion. We consider that a positive.

"When you went to flank after the explosion, lowering steam generator water levels were experienced in both steam generators. This was because #1 feed pump tripped off when the starboard buses were lost so only one feed pump was running. This was also recognized and corrected without delaying the answering of the flank bell. The regular Lower Level watch was put out of commission with a broken leg and a member of the aft DC party assumed the watch with no turnover."

"Under combat condition, perfection isn't required," Welch explained. "Your plant operations supported the ship's mission. We can stop here unless you have questions."

"That's good. Let's let Petty Officer Glenn set up for breakfast."

"Captain," said Summers, "with your permission I'd like to address the crew on the 1MC."

It was, of course, granted and he left to make the announcement.

Chapter 51 – Last Breakfast

Off San Diego – 32° 33.7' N 117° 19.4' W
Tuesday, September 3, 1991
0700

The Captain came in and took his seat. He had changed into a white uniform. The shoulder boards had a star and three stripes. He had three rows of colorful ribbons over the left shirt pocket, topped by gold dolphins. A name tag and the command pin were over his right pocket. He had standard, blue and white sneakers instead of the brown deck shoes he prefers.

Others were arranged like the debrief. ORSE was along the bench with McCarthy, Banner and Nguyen filling the remaining bench space. McCarthy and Nguyen were also in white. I sat to the right of Commodore Summers with the XO and ENG taking the other chairs. There would be time for second seating before maneuvering watch.

The table was set with a white tablecloth, unusual for breakfast where the brown Naugahyde cover was normally used. There was a plate of sticky buns set out with the bread and a pitcher of fresh milk.

Petty Officer Glenn entered with a tray of steaks, arranged from medium rare to well done. Fried eggs, scrambled eggs, bacon, and hash brown potatoes followed. Everybody was hungry.

Banner passed out mess bills to the Commodore, ORSE Board and myself. Checks were to be made out to the U.S. Treasury. Mine was over one hundred dollars, a ridiculously small charge, considering how well I'd eaten.

Everyone was in a good mood, the excitement from having survived a very close brush with death. The ENG enjoyed a cigarette with the meal, making the most of a privilege that would soon end. Board members were getting details of the encounter with the Akula that they were, now, obviously cleared for. We still couldn't discuss the earlier action with them. They and Commodore Summers had signed security statements that would be included with the data package. The previous statement the crew and I had signed would apply to the latest events.

The discussion soon turned to the question of how the Akula was able to employ a nuclear weapon. The Soviet Union employs Permissive Action Links, similar to what we use, to prevent unauthorized use of nukes. It should be similar; we freely gave them the technology. Since there's no reason to suspect Gorbachev of wanting to start a nuclear war, the codes needed to unlock the weapons were probably passed during the recent coup.

That thought had implications about what the Delta I SSBN we met earlier was up to. From his expression I could see that the CO had made that connection, and certainly, those in D.C. would as well.

Chapter 52 – Return
Off San Diego – 32° 34.8' N 117° 15.7' W
Tuesday, September 3, 1991
0800

Maneuvering watch was stationed. I was in Control, below the hatch, dressed in my harness. It was somewhat cool, about 68°, with a small breeze but I didn't think I'd need a jacket.

"Request permission for Mr. Ryan to lay to the Bridge," I told the phone talker.

He relayed the request. "Go on up."

I went up the ladder toward the bright circle of light. The access trunk had been wiped down overnight to remove moisture and oil.

"Request to enter the Bridge."

"Come on up," replied Nguyen.

I handed up the lanyard from my harness and he attached me. I climbed into the cockpit, a tight fit for three. The flying bridge was rigged. I climbed on top of the sail and looked around. The sun came out from behind a cloud, giving welcome warmth and brightening the ocean's surface.

"Captain to the Bridge," the phone talker announced.

We had both periscopes and the IFF/UHF mast raised. I looked aft and saw where we'd lost the nonskid paint over the AMS. The base coat, also black, was still in place. On the starboard side of AMS you could faintly make out the ribs of the frames supporting the outer steel skin of the ballast tanks, dished in slightly by the force of the shock wave.

The Captain came up beside me.

"We have a nice day, even if a bit cool, to return home."

"Any day is a good day for returning home," he said.

He had his orange harness fastened over the white uniform. The gold band on his white hat was in use as a chinstrap, its nominal purpose.

"Petty Officer Johnson, you're not supposed to be on the Bridge for maneuvering watch."

Johnson, in his enlisted whites and harness was on the port plane as lookout.

"I asked the COB if I could take it and he approved."

"I'll have to talk to him about unauthorized changes to my watch bill."

"Bridge, NAV, three minutes to the turn, right to zero-three-five. We have been assigned north side, middle pier, inner berth."

"Bridge aye."

"Bridge, NAV. We hold the torpedo retriever outbound. It's flying a one star flag. Believe Submarine Group FIVE is embarked. It looks like they intend a transfer before we reach buoy five."

"It's calm enough, Mr. Nguyen, send the small boat handling party topside after we turn and slow to two-thirds."

"Yes, sir."

"This is NAV, mark the turn, right to zero-three-five."

"Helm, right fifteen degrees rudder, steady zero-three-five," McCarthy ordered on the 7MC and the JA talker relayed.

"Right fifteen degrees rudder, steady zero-three-five, Helm aye. My rudder is right fifteen."

"Helm, all ahead two-thirds."

"All ahead two-thirds, Helm aye. Answers two-thirds."

"Seaman Porter to the Bridge with a one star flag," reported the talker.

Porter didn't come up. He handed the flag to Nguyen who stuffed most of it in his pants pocket. It was blue with a single five-pointed white star in the middle.

"Passing zero-two-five to zero-three-five."

"Control, Bridge, have the small boat handling party lay topside."

"Small boat handling party lay topside, Control aye."

"Hatch is open," Johnson said.

Half a dozen men came topside in their white uniform, sneakers and orange life jackets. COB was in charge. They manned a phone headset and started rigging all the cleats, both sides, aft of the sail.

The retriever was headed out and would pass along our port side as it did before ORSE.

"Mr. Nguyen, we will render honors to port. It looks like it is Admiral Everett."

"Deck, we will render honors to port, standby," Nguyen relayed by phone.

The sailors on deck formed a single line facing port.

"Attention to port," "hand salute," "two" and "carry on" were ordered as the retriever passed. It turned around to approach. McCarthy slowed us to one-third. The retriever tossed us a line that went on the cleat just aft the sail. It settled alongside and the brow was lowered. Admiral Everett was first aboard followed by a lieutenant. Senior Chief Harvey and Chief Aquino, carrying a traditional broom, completed the transfer.

When the Admiral came on Nguyen announced, "Submarine Group FIVE arriving," and replaced the Squadron THREE pennant with the one star flag.

The retriever backed clear and sped up to return to port. We increased speed to two-thirds.

"Bridge, Control, Chief Aquino requests to come up with a broom and duct tape. The broom is a gift from the Admiral."

"Send him up," Nguyen replied.

"Bridge, NAV, hold you on course following the turn. Five minutes to the next turn, left to three-five-three."

Aquino passed the broom and tape to Nguyen

"Cut me off a couple long pieces of tape and pass up the broom."

The Captain set the broom next to the aft, port post of the flying bridge and had me hold it while he secured it with the tape.

"What's the broom about?"

"In World War II it symbolized that you were returning to port after expending all your torpedoes, a good war patrol. We still have torpedoes left."

"But you're out of targets."

"Right. In modern usage it means the submarine displaying it has done something very good they want to brag about. Our excellent ORSE grade would definitely qualify so nobody will look for anything else.

"The traditional spot is taped to the periscope but this will do."

"Admiral to the Bridge," Control announced.

He came up, dressed in a khaki uniform with a harness, and joined us on top of the sail. He congratulated the Captain to start. The CO introduced me. Everett was another of my readers.

"Bridge, NAV, hold you on track. One minute to the turn, left to three-five-three."

"I have much good news and some bad news. I'll begin with the good. The COMSUBPAC Chief of Staff caught the morning flight to Honolulu. His investigation is cancelled. If the Akula used nuclear weapons, the others might have too."

"We figured that as well. Even if it was what needed to be done, it doesn't make me feel better about killing them. Has there been any reaction from the Soviets on the loss of their submarines?"

"Not yet. The estimate is that, if they were involved in the coup, they'll keep it quiet. On that point, a submarine communication site in Siberia dropped off the air three days after the coup failed and hasn't come back on. A satellite image shows two tanks and six armored personnel carriers stationed on the grounds that weren't there when last imaged before the coup. Some think it could have been used to bypass normal naval and strategic command and control channels."

"Mark the turn, left to three-five-three."

"Helm, left fifteen degrees rudder, steady three-five-three."

"Left fifteen degrees rudder, steady three-five-three, Helm aye. My rudder is left fifteen."

"The analysts from NAVSTIC took your tapes over to SUBTRAFAC yesterday. They have equipment there from the latest 688s, much better than what you have onboard. Both thought the tapes showed the Delta preparing for a missile launch. The preliminary results from back east confirm that.

"You may have saved millions. There is speculation that the target was Moscow. The time matches when Gorbachev landed there very closely. Heaven only knows what the Soviets might have done, detecting a missile launch on Moscow from near Alaska."

"Passing zero-zero-three to steady on three-five-three."

"Helm, steady three-five-zero."

314

We were turning late and McCarthy was adjusting to get onto the entry range.

"Steady three-five-zero, Helm aye. Steady three-five-zero."

"The bad news is Haddock isn't going anywhere until you go to the shipyard for decommissioning. We can't get you in early either so you'll be spending lots of time tied up to the pier. NAVSEA thinks you took between 0.8 and 1.3 times your design shock. Looking at your hull when I came on, I think they have a point. You can't be certified for submerged operations. They want to look at everything. Haddock just became a NAVSEA research project.

"The official reason is that it is uneconomical to fix your #2 main seawater pump. That story has the added virtue of being true."

"At least the taxpayers got their money's worth from Haddock."

"Helm, all ahead one-third, steer three-five-three. Control, send line-handlers on deck."

"All ahead one-third, steer three-five-three, Helm aye. Answers one-third. Steering three-five-three."

"Send line-handlers on deck, Control, aye. They are laying topside."

"I've cancelled the XO's orders. Since you'll be in port, he can assist his wife's treatment. You'll need someone you trust in charge of Haddock when you're traveling. You're going to D.C. next Monday."

"Mr. McCarthy, we will take the tug on the starboard bow with a split head line," said Nguyen. "The tug will push our bow in and we'll use the outboard for the stern."

"I should lower it then. Maneuvering, lower the outboard, test and shift to remote."

The deck was rigged. The lines were taken out of stowage lockers set into the deck and faked out on the hull ready for use. The tug came around and tied up, two lines to two different cleats from its bow to ours and a line from its stern to a cleat aft of the sail. Pulling the stern line aligned the tug along the hull. The outboard was made ready and pointed to 270°, ready to push our stern toward the pier. We were approaching Ballast Point. There were only a few pleasure boats out on the weekday.

"One final item. COMSUBPAC is flying in with CINCPACFLT on the fleet commander's plane. They'll be landing late afternoon. I've arranged a reception for your officers at my quarters for this evening. My den is secure. We'll break away to discuss your operations at some point. I expect quite a bit of alcohol will be flowing. I've arranged transportation for everybody and their wives. My aide is giving your XO the details.

"Mr. Ryan, we've arranged a room at the hotel you booked before your trip. You are, of course, invited for tonight. We have transportation for you too. I know Rear Admiral McKinney is a fan of your work. He'll be interested in your perspective."

"Thanks, I'll be there."

"Good. We start at 1900. There will be heavy hors d'oeuvres with the liquid refreshments. Admiral McKinney also requested to have lunch with your crew in Crew's Mess tomorrow. He'll have some remarks after lunch."

"We'll get it set."

"When we are abeam of Dixon's bow you can turn left with full rudder to turn into our berth," Nguyen prompted.

"Helm, left full rudder, belay your headings."

"Left full rudder, belay my heading, Helm aye. My rudder is left full."

As we started our turn Dixon sounded its horn. The McKee and the submarines in port picked it up. The sound echoed across the water.

Epilog
Submarine Base San Diego
Saturday, November 16, 1991
1315

I met Earl Johnson walking from the parking area to the Submarine Training Facility. He was wearing a navy blue chief petty officer uniform with large medals instead of the normal ribbons.

"Congratulation on your promotion. How are you doing?"

"I'm fine, Tom. The doctors have me on two different meds. One is experimental. They seem to be doing the job. I'm not cured, but my immune system is working, at least for now."

"That's good news. I've read about some of the new advances. Where are you working?"

"I'm at NAVSTIC in Suitland, Maryland. I don't get to ride the boats. I'm working on training materials for submarines. I'm using much of the stuff from our operations."

"I have a home near Annapolis. Give me your number. My wife and I will have you over for dinner."

He handed me a business card from his pocket.

"Are you going to be able to write about us?"

"I was told I could publish it as fiction, but only after Haddock has been decommissioned for twenty years. The clock on that won't start ticking for a year or more."

We were at the main entrance. There were a couple Marines outside by the door. Inside was a Marine sergeant seated at a desk. Two men in dark suits were behind him in front of the door to the rest of the building.

"Identification please," said the sergeant.

I handed over my Maryland driver's license. Johnson used his military ID. The sergeant checked his list. Haddock's crew was already assembled inside in the auditorium for the 1400 ceremony and there were check marks by their names and for family members. We were a couple pages down. He added two checks.

"They're on the list."

One of the men spoke softly into a microphone.

"Are you Secret Service?" I asked. "Is the President here?"

"The President is at Camp David all weekend. Please go in."

We did.

USS Haddock (SSN 621)
Commissioned December 22, 1967
Decommissioned April 7, 1993

Cast of Characters

Narrator
Thomas Ryan - military novelist

Commander, Submarine Group FIVE
RADM Michael Everett

Commander, Submarine Squadron THREE
CAPT Harry Summers

ORSE Board
Senior Member - CAPT Peter Welch
LCDR David Porter
LCDR Ross Harkins
LCDR David Lindsay

USS Haddock (SSN 621)
CO - CDR William (Bill) White
XO - LCDR George Johnson
ENG - LCDR Ronald (Ron) Rinaldi
NAV - LCDR Henry Cooper
CSO - LT José Gonzales
Sonar - LT David (Dave) Cohen
MPA - LT Tony Nguyen
DCA - LT Anthony (Big Tony) Gordon
RCA - LTJG Thomas (Tom) Jackson
EO - LTJG Nicholas (Nick) Reed
CRA - LTJG Kevin McCarthy
Comm - LTJG Jeffery (Jeff) Ohanian
Supply - LTJG Bruce Banner

COB - TMCM(SS) Joseph (Joe) McHenry, DOOW

Engineering Department
M & RL Divisions
MMC(SS) Richard Dawson - LPO, EWS
MMI(SS) Jack Davis - LELT, EWS
MM1(SS) Jefferson (Jeff) Harper, Leading 1st, EWS

MM1(SS) Edward Alan, Jr., ERS
MM2(SS) Michael Howard, ERS
MM2(SS) Dennis Porter, ERS, ELT
MM2(SS) Charles Roberts, ERS
MM2(SS) Edward Patrick, ERS, ELT
MM2(SS) Jeffery Dean, ERS
MM2 William Michaels, ERUL, ERLL
MM2(SS) Paul Franklin, ERUL, AMSLL, ERLL
MM2(SS) Keith Johnson, AMSLL, ERLL, ELT
MM3 Mark Powers, ERUL, ERLL
MM3 Paul Shafter, AMSLL, ERLL, ELT
MM3 Andrew Rove, ERUL, ERLL
MM3 Frank James, ERLL
MM3 Daniel Lee, ERLL

E/IC Divisions
EMCS(SS) Walter Jay - Eng LPO, EWS
EM1(SS) David Ray, EWS, EO
EM1(SS) Edward Lipinski, EO
EM2(SS) Craig Allen, EO
EM2(SS) Greg McKinney, EO
EM2(SS) William Nichols, EO, Log Room
EM2(SS) Keith Hammond, EO
EM2 Charles Tanner, SPCP
EM3 Gary Sheldon, AEA
EM3 Scott Owen, AEA
EM3 Edward Lamar, AEA
IC1(SS) James Keller, COW
IC2(SS) Dean Baker, AEF
IC3(SS) Alex Frye, AEF
ICFN Edward Marks, AEF
FN Jason Reams, mess cook

RC Division
ETC(SS) Dennis Allen, EWS
ET1(SS) Michael Smith, EWS, RO
ET1(SS) Kevin Seabright, RO
ET2(SS) J. R. Zhou, RO
ET2(SS) Richard Lynn, RO

ET2 Eric Dixon, AMS UL
ET2 James Craig, AMS UL
ET3 Jeffery Hughes AMS UL

A Division
MMC(SS) David Lloyd, LPO, DOOW, COW
MM1(SS) Sean O'Leary, Air Regen, COW
MM1(SS) Jorge Garcia, Air Regen
MM2(SS) Andrew Shanks, Air Regen
MM2(SS) William Gary, Air Regen
MM3(SS) Billy Ray Christensen, AMR1, Aux Fwd
MM3(SS) Thomas Bradley, Aux Fwd
MM3 John Mitchell, Aux Fwd
MMFN Tony Vincent, mess cook

Combat Systems Department
Sonar Division
STSC(SS) Richard Harvey, LPO, Sonar Sup, DOOW, COW
STS1(SS) Earl Johnson, Sonar Sup, COW
STS2(SS) David Gardner, Sonar Sup
STS2(SS) Lincoln Renner, Sonar Sup
STS2(SS) Edward Miller, Sonar Sup
STS2 Forrest Stanley, Sonar Operator
STS3(SS) Craig Johnson, Sonar Operator
STS3(SS) Joseph Speer, Sonar Operator
STS3(SS) Kevin Reinhardt, Sonar Operator
STS3(SS) John Howard, Sonar Operator
STS3 Roger Smith, Sonar Operator
STS3 Paul Cross, Sonar Operator
STS3 Jeffery Beam, mess cook
STS3 Daniel Schroeder, mess cook

Torpedo Division
TM1(SS) Gary Sheldon, LPO, COW
TM2(SS) Mark Carmichael, Torpedo Watch
TM2(SS) Randy Paul, Torpedo Watch
TM3(SS) Brad Stokes, Torpedo Watch
TM3 Scott Smith, mess cook

FT Division
FTG1(SS) Edward Quinn, LPO, COW, FTOW
FTG2(SS) Jerome Boyle, FTOW
FTG2(SS) Anthony Lopez, FTOW
FTG3 Kenneth Lane, FTOW

Deck Division
TM3(SS) Glenn Wheeler, LPO, Torpedo Watch
SN(SS) John McKay, planes
SN Stephen James, planes
SN Doug Ham, planes
SA Fred McArthur, planes
SA Edward Rogers

Operations Department
Quartermaster Division
QMCS(SS) Andrew Spillman, LPO, DOOW
QM1(SS) George Lamar, COW
QM2(SS) Keith Holt, QMOW
QM3(SS) Ramon Flores, QMOW
QMSN Harry Porter, planes, mess cook

Radio Division
RMC(SS) Jefferson Moore, LPO, DOOW, COW, RMOW
RM2(SS) Charles Warner, RMOW
RM2(SS) Paul Leonard, RMOW
RM3 Alan James, RMOW

ET Division
ET1(SS) John Field, COW, ETOW
ET2(SS) Samuel Scott, ETOW
ET2(SS) Mark Law, ETOW
ET3 Gordon Wong, ETOW, planes

Supply Department
Storekeeper Division
SKC(SS) Romeo Aquino, LPO, COW
SK3(SS) Phillip McGarett, planes

Mess Management Division

MS1(SS) William Randolph
MS2(SS) Patrick Broccoli
MS2(SS) John Michael
MS3(SS) Andrew Glenn (Wardroom MS)
MS3 Stanley Stout
MSSN(SS) George Allen

Executive Department
Medical
HM1(SS) Danny James, COW

Yeoman
YN1(SS) Thomas Mason, LPO
YN3(SS) Christopher Ellis, Sonar Operator
PNSN Edward Miller, planes

Addendum

Organizations
NMCC – National Military Command Center (In Pentagon, Arlington, VA)
CINCPAC – Commander in Chief Pacific (Camp Smith, HI)
CINCPACFLT – Commander in Chief Pacific Fleet (Pearl Harbor, HI)
COMSUBPAC – Commander, Submarine Force Pacific (Pearl Harbor, HI)
COMSUBGRU FIVE – Commander, Submarine Group FIVE (Submarine Base, San Diego, CA.)
COMSUBROM THREE – Commander, Submarine Squadron THREE (Submarine Base, San Diego, CA, normally onboard USS Dixon (AS-37))
BUPERS – Bureau of Naval Personnel (Millington, TN)
NAVSEA – Naval Sea Systems Command (Arlington, VA)
NAVSTIC – Navy Scientific & Technical Intelligence Center (Suitland, MD)
NIS – Naval Investigative Service, now NCIS, Naval Criminal Investigative Service (Quantico, VA)
SUBTRAFAC – Submarine Training Facility (Submarine Base, San Diego, CA)

Naval Ranks
Ensign (ENS) (Marines – 2nd Lieutenant)
Lieutenant (junior grade) (LTJG) (Marines – 1st Lieutenant)
Lieutenant (LT) (Marines – Captain)
Lieutenant Commander (LCDR) (Marines – Major)
Commander (CDR) (Marines – Lieutenant Colonel)
Captain (CAPT) (Marines – Colonel)
Rear Admiral (lower half) (RADM) (Marines – Brigadier General)
Rear Admiral (upper half) (RADM) (Marines – Major General)
Vice Admiral (VADM) (Marines – Lieutenant General)
Admiral (ADM) (Marines – General)

Naval Ratings
ET – Electronics Technician

EM – Electrician's Mate
FTG – Fire Control Technician
FN – Fireman, equivalent to SN for engineering ratings
HM – Hospital Corpsman
IC – Interior Communications
MM – Machinist's Mate
MS – Mess Management Specialist
PN – Personnelman
QM - Quartermaster
RM – Radioman
SA – Seaman Apprentice
SN – Seaman (if accepted into a rating will have rating designation first, e.g. QMSN)
STS – Sonar Technician Submarines
TM – Torpedoman
YN - Yeoman

Abbreviations
AEA(AEF) – Auxiliary Electrician Aft (Auxiliary Electrician Forward)
AMS – Auxiliary Machinery Space
ASW – Anti-Submarine Warfare or Auxiliary Seawater (depends on context)
ATF – Automatic Tracking Feature (Sonar)
BCP – Ballast Control Panel
BT - Bathythermograph
CO – Commanding Officer (CDR White)
COW – Chief of the Watch
CP – Coolant Purification
CPA – Closest Point of Approach
CPO – Chief Petty Officer
DOOW – Diving Officer of the Watch
ELT – Engineering Laboratory Technician
EOOW – Engineering Officer of the Watch
EPCP – Electric Plant Control Panel
EPM – Emergency Propulsion Motor
ERLL – Engine Room Lower Level
ERUL – Engine Room Upper Level
ERS – Engine Room Supervisor

ESM – Electronic Support Measures (detect and analyze intercepted radar signals)

ETOW – Electronics Technician of the Watch (SINS & ESM)

EWS – Engineering Watch Supervisor

FTOW – Fire Control Technician of the Watch

DCA – Damage Control Assistant (LT Gordon)

DOOW – Diving Officer of the Watch

DR – Dead Reckoning

IFF – Identification Friend or Foe (Subs generally only receive and don't transmit)

JOOD(W) – Junior Officer of the Deck (Watch) (Normally an instructional watch)

MCCOV – Main Coolant Cutout Valve

MCP – Main Coolant Pump

MFP – Main Feed Pump

MG – Motor Generator (also SSMG for Ship's Service Motor Generator)

MLO – Main Lube Oil

MPA – Main Propulsion Assistant (LT Nguyen)

MS – Main Steam

MSW – Main Seawater

OOD – Officer of the Deck

P-3 – Antisubmarine Aircraft, Long Range with 4 Turboprop Engines

POD – Plan of the Day

QMOW – Quartermaster of the Watch

RC – Reactor Compartment or Reactor Controls (depending on context)

RCA – Reactor Controls Assistant (LTJG Jackson)

RMOW – Radioman of the Watch

RPCP – Reactor Plant Control Panel

RPFW – Reactor Plant Fresh Water

SCP – Ship Control Panel

SINS – Ship's Inertial Navigation System

SLO – Shaft Lube Oil

SOPA – Senior Officer Present Afloat

SOSUS – Sound Surveillance System

SPCP – Steam Plant Control Panel

SPM – Secondary Propulsion Motor (Outboard)

T – Tango Time (Pacific Daylight Savings Time)

T-AGOS – Small Vessels Mounting a Surveillance Towed Sonar Array System

TG – Turbine Generator (also SSTG for Ship's Service Turbine Generator)

torr – A unit of pressure equal to 1 millimeter of mercury in a barometer.

UHF – Ultra High Frequency

XO – Executive Officer (LCDR Johnson)

Z – Zulu Time, Universal Time, Greenwich Mean Time

ZBO – List of messages on a broadcast (sent at the start and the end)

Rules of Ukkers

Rule #1- The CAPTAIN is always right.
Note: Rule #1 will probably be usurped by a senior operational commander if not waived by the Captain.

Setup

Rule #2 - There shall be four players, forming two teams of two. Teams sit at opposite corners of the board. Two dice are used and are rolled in turn by each player, rotating to the left. Unless teams have already been determined, the two highest rollers on the first round form one team, the highest roller taking the red pieces.
Note: In rolling for teams, the general dice rule, "one tie; all tie" applies, unless the tie does not affect the team alignment. A special application of Rule #1 allows the Captain the choice of dice.

General Play

Rule #3 - Play starts with all four pieces of each player in its Home Harbor. Play starts with the player having the red pieces. A SIX on one or both dice entitles a player to move one piece out to start around the board and to another role of the dice. When more than one piece is on the board, the move may be split between two pieces, but each piece must move the full amount shown on one die. All moves must be made, if possible, and the move must maximize the forward motion of all pieces of the player's color.
Note: A double that entitles a player to Up Tit does not entitle him to another roll of the dice. It is considered appropriate to go to Harbor Stations to enhance the probability of rolling a SIX. It is not necessary to move the six spaces to be entitled to another roll, however, the requirement to make the maximum forward motion remains.

Tits

Rule #4 - A Tit may not be passed by an opponent. A Tit may be killed by an opposing Tit with the roll of a proper double. An Impregger may not be killed. A mixed Tit is no Tit at all, even under Special Circumstances.

Kills

Rule #5 - A kill may be executed by contriving to land on a space occupied by an opponent. Killed pieces are returned to its Home Harbor. No player may kill from a mixed Tit. A Killer may kill a Tit with the roll of the proper double as if it were a Tit.

End of Voyage

Rule #6 - To complete its journey safely, a piece must reach the center of the board through its own color entrance by an exact count of one or both dice. Failure to roll the exact count required may force a piece to Back Uk if another piece cannot make the move indicated. It is required to make the maximum forward moves. A Back Uk is accomplished by counting forward to the center of the board, then moving backwards around the board to the end of the turn, including extra rolls obtained by rolling a SIX. All rules concerning Tits and Kills are applicable to the backing piece.

Note: Should the Back Uk continue until the Home Harbor of the piece is reached, the piece enters Home Harbor, counts four and then leaves. No roll of SIX is required unless the move ends with the piece still in its Home Harbor.

Victory Laps

Rule #7 - A player may elect to continue around the board rather than moving up its color spaces to the center of the board. This option may only be used twice by each team.

Partners

Rule #8 - A player whose pieces are all in the center of the board may assist his partner by rolling the dice in his turn and moving his partner's pieces. A player must qualify for this important role by first rolling a SIX. This roll must be at least one turn after the last piece has reached the center of the board. The first move of the partner's pieces may not occur until the next turn after the SIX is rolled.

Special Rules

Rule #9 - The use of Voodoo, black magics, special incantations or any other acts not obscene or disruptive, for the express purpose of causing the dice to roll a predetermined number or numbers, is allowed. If there is a question about whether the behavior is appropriate, see Rule #1.

Rule #10 - This is a gentleman's game, cheating is expressly forbidden.

Note: A simple, inadvertent violation of the rules is not considered as cheating, unless the violator is caught.

Glossary of Terms

Breafs - Closing up behind an exposed opponent piece.

Breakers - A roll which forces the breakup of a Tit.

Back Uk - The reverse movement of a piece caused by failure to enter the center of the board and inability of other pieces to make forward moves.

Glom - A mixed Impregger or Ridiculous that is, of course, totally vulnerable.

Harbor Stations - Pieces closed up, ready to get underway.

Home Harbor - The large square with the same color as the pieces. Arrows mark the harbor exit channel.

Hot Briefs - Occupying the space immediately behind an opponent's vulnerable piece.

Impregger - Three pieces of the same color on a board space.

Killer - The last piece of a color not yet in the center of the board.

Missers - Missing the opportunity to kill by rolling the wrong numbers.

Mixed Tit - Pieces of different color occupying the same space.

Mixed Tit, Special Circumstances - The only case where opposing pieces may occupy the same space without a kill occurs when a kill, otherwise legal, is invalidated by being started from a Mixed Tit.

Race On - Rolling a ONE-ONE or a ONE-TWO.

Ridiculous - All four pieces of the same color on the same space.

Standby - Poised on the brink of getting the last piece to the center of the board.

Tit - Two pieces of the same color on the same space.

Up Tit - Moving a Tit forward by rolling doubles.

Made in the USA
Middletown, DE
14 March 2015